2024 Literary Titan Silver Award
2024 PenCraft Award for Literary Excellence - Best Book
Winner/Suspense
2024 Firebird Book Award - Fiction
2024 TAZ Award - Mystery
2024 Hawthorne Prize - American Writing Awards (Finalist)
2024 Best New Fiction - American Bookfest Best Book
Awards (Finalist)
2024 Best New Fiction - American Best Book Awards
(Finalist)
2025 International Impact Book Awards - Realistic Fiction

Early Praise for
What Lies We Keep

"What Lies We Keep will captivate fans of writers like Jennifer Weiner, that best-selling expert at writing about family secrets and the ties that bind, but it's Janet Roberts' brilliant and fresh prose, and her big-hearted, messy, real characters that set this work apart. Roberts honors the complexity of what it means to be human and flawed, grounded and lost, while giving readers a page-turning tale of love and deception and, ultimately, hope. There is no easy ending here, and I'm so grateful for that."

    - Lori Jakiela, author of *They Write Your Name on a Grain of Rice*

"In her compelling novel about the devastating impact of lies and the search for a fulfilling life, Janet Roberts balances a thrilling plot of corporate greed and corruption with credible, richly-drawn characters. Through sharp dialogue, cinematic descriptions, and even a covert FBI operation, this novel explores the relationship between a husband and wife in the aftermath of one well-intentioned but misguided decision. *What Lies We Keep* raises powerful questions: Are lies justified if they are made to protect the ones we love? Can success be defined by more than social status and salary? I devoured this creative, twisty story with its flawed by sympathetic characters."

- Jill Caugherty, author of *The View from Half Dome* and *Waltz in Swing Time*.

"Janet Roberts' *What Lies We Keep* examines what happens when we keep things from those we love and how that can lead to a tangled knot that can be difficult to unravel. Instead of protecting his loved ones, Ted's lies lead to hurt and heartbreak—and possible criminal charges. Charlotte and Ted must work through both his mistakes and the fractures in their marriage. A wonderful book with in-depth and flawed characters as well as a how-will-they-get-out-of-that plot."

—Pamela Stockwell, author of *A Boundless Place* and *The Tender Silver Stars*

"A thought-provoking dissection of a once-stable marriage and the fault lines that erupt when one member crosses an ethical line, resulting in repercussions that threaten the very essence of the family unit. Moving between the gritty streets of Pittsburgh and the wide-open ranches of Montana, *What Lies We Keep* is a realistic, moving novel of complex relationships, the corrosive power of secrets, and the challenges a couple must face when the things they hold dear are the very things that may tear them apart."

—Maggie Smith, award-winning author of *Truth and Other Lies* and *Blindspot*

"Readers will enjoy this evocative exploration of a marriage in crisis as well as behind-the-scenes insights into cyber-crime. *What Lies We Keep* is a novel about betrayal and loyalty, truth and lies, regrets and the possibility of redemption. Don't miss it!"

—Deb Atwood, author of *Moonlight Dancer*

"In *What Lies We Keep*, author Janet Roberts illustrates a gripping story that dives into the complexities of modern life, where lies, marriage, cybersecurity, and the clash between corporate and country living collide. Each character is rich with their own moral dilemmas. With its compelling narrative and relevant themes, this book is sure to captivate readers and leave them pondering the complexities of truth and trust long after they turn that final page. It left me asking, 'What is next for the McCords?'"

—Andrea Kittelson, Cybersecurity Awareness Expert at Rockwell International

"*What Lies We Keep* is such a wonderful read! And the characters are so accurately and beautifully portrayed that even when/if not agreeing with their choices, one can't help but want them to succeed and overcome their challenges. The plot is outstanding. Makes one truly reflect on how much lies can affect our lives no matter how much the person telling them believes that in doing so they are protecting their loved ones. A few lines don't really give this book justice: I loved reading it and loved 'witnessing' Ted's and Charlotte's journey (especially hers!)."

—Mora Durante Astrada, Global Head of Security Education and Awareness for Zurich Insurance

"*What Lies We Keep* is a gripping and emotionally charged novel that explores the complexities of relationships and the power of secrets. The author does a fantastic job of creating authentic and relatable characters, each with their own flaws and struggles. The writing is beautifully crafted, with vivid descriptions and emotional depth that will keep readers turning the pages until the very end. I highly recommend *What Lies We Keep* to anyone looking for a gripping and emotional read that will stay with them long after they finish the last page."

—Claire Hughes, cybersecurity awareness expert

"This is my favorite style of suspense novel: well-developed characters without too much 'fluff.' I'm here for the story! Every paragraph is packed full of clues and new developments, and the dialogue gives just enough insight into the characters' motivations. Both of the main characters are multidimensional and flawed, and there are no easy answers for either of them. No spoilers, but I wonder if I would have made the same choices they did. I also liked the authentic little descriptions of everyday Pittsburgh places contrasted with the beautiful scenery of Montana. Don't judge me too much for this comment in a book review, readers, but this one would also make a great movie. I didn't want to put it down, and I'll be looking for more from Janet Roberts."

—April Kline, Pittsburgh resident and avid reader

To: Danielle
Happy Reading!
Janet M. Roberts
7-30-2025

WHAT LIES WE KEEP

JANET ROBERTS

What Lies We Keep

Cover designer: Ashton Smith

Author photo: Mariah Treiber Photography

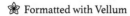 Formatted with Vellum

To all the women who, like me,
found their superpower later in life.

some people hit rock bottom before
they change themselves drastically
because at that distance they can
best see who they really want to be

Yung Pueblo, Inward

CHAPTER 1

The digital screens on the kitchen appliances screamed 5:00 a.m. He knew he should crawl back into bed. It had been like this for six months now, ever since the promotion at work. Waking up with sweat across his brow and his back just before the reoccurring dream headed toward a disastrous end, as if his mind were a savvy film editor cutting out an ending he hadn't the fortitude to handle. Each time, he carefully felt the area around his body, without waking Charlotte, to make sure it wasn't so bad that the sheets were damp, and then walked as quietly as possible to the open area of their apartment housing the kitchen and small living room. No amount of effort to return to sleep worked these days. Nagging concerns that it was more premonition than dream rolled up in him with all the discomfort of a chronic stomachache. Logging into his work laptop settled his fears. Focusing on a stack of emails—a pile of problems to be solved and tasks to be completed—reassured him that he was necessary, valuable, not someone they would discard like an old rag no matter what he'd done. In his mind, there had been no way but the path he'd chosen. But words didn't seem to alleviate the mild trembling in his hands.

Lies were like that. They felt justified as a route to sparing others hurt, a path to keeping things balanced, a necessary evil. Lies spawned subsequent lies until the entangled mess required putting one's ethics on the shelf now and then to simply manage life. This was the well-worn mantra Ted told himself in the wee hours of the morning to justify how he'd moved up and into a manager role. They needed the money. Jesse needed the money. He'd put everything he held sacred on the line. He couldn't allow the twin detractors of guilt and regret to weaken his resolve. He'd done what he needed to do for the people he loved most.

It was quiet at this hour, streetlights reflecting against windshields sprinkled with soft, multicolored leaves and a touch of dew that wasn't quite frost. Late September always hinted at colder weather just around the corner. A few more hours and the neighborhood would awaken. People brushing off the comfort of blankets and sleep would appear below to warm up vehicles parked bumper to bumper in urban uniformity along both sides of East End Avenue. Others would hurry to the bus stop to catch the 61A. The world around him stepping into the day. Ted's itch to join their ranks felt as natural as breathing. It was all he'd left his life in Montana to pursue.

Similar to the residences of most of their neighbors, the roomy but older apartment harkened back to another time. A solid brick building whose faded glory showed in the slight dip and sag of the front steps, old woodwork in need of refinishing, plumbing with ancient cast-iron pipes, and registers emitting solid boiler-powered heat. A faded, elderly lady in need of a facelift with all the architectural character Charlotte loved. Ted wished they could buy a home in the neighborhood, but he'd told Charlotte he lusted after the big, refurbished homes near Frick Park or the luxury condos on Mt. Washington. Another lie placed carefully to postpone a little bit longer her aching desire to own a home, just until he could restore the funds missing from his account at the company's credit union, which he'd drained. Thankfully, the account was in his name only. A few more months and he'd have replaced at least three quarters of what he'd felt forced to remove. His promotion to manager was making that possible.

"Tell her the truth about the ranch," Jesse had advised.

"She'll want to move back to Montana," Ted had said. "You know she has this fantasy about living there."

"Would that be so bad?" Jesse replied.

Just thinking about the endless hours in the saddle herding cattle, sore muscles from the physical labor, then falling into bed exhausted, worn out, only to do it again the next day made the muscles tighten in Ted's neck and shoulders. He felt a slight pain and, looking down, realized he'd clenched his hands at the thought of returning, to the point where tension ran all the way up his arm and into his shoulders. Jesse viewed ranch life as freedom from the chains of a rigid, corporate structure. Freedom to work for himself and to answer to himself only, to own his own destiny. Ted saw it as a beautiful trap, the land and mountains casting stunning views on a life where progress, as Ted defined it, was limited. He saw freedom in a place where his computer skills and cyber knowledge prepared an even path upward to clearly definable roles that would fund a nicer, easier life for his family. He and Jesse had had discussions about this, a few of which were heated, so they'd agreed to disagree and move on. Charlotte alternated between agreeing with him and then with Jesse, her chronic indecision making Ted feel he was required to make the tough decisions.

"It's not what I want. And it's not really what she would want once she got a good taste of it," he told Jesse, hoping to shut down the topic.

"You never know. It could turn out to be really great for both of you, and I'd love for you to live closer. You could work in Bozeman, and I'd run the ranch."

"Yeah, we miss you too, but no, Jesse, I'm not leaving the opportunities here for some smaller place with no career path."

"It's your call, brother." Jesse sounded more resigned than disapproving, tired of what was a conversation they'd had before.

"Dad should have left the ranch to you. We both know that," Ted said. "And even if he had, I'd still be helping you when times got tough."

"He loved you more," Jesse answered. "We both know that too."

Jesse, his younger brother who loved their family ranch, who lived a straight and honest life, who loved but rarely understood Ted. He wished he could be fully honest with Jesse. All this hiding secrets from people he loved, covering up old lies, creating new ones. Only a few more years and he could sign that ranch over to Jesse, shake the albatross from his shoulders along with the memories of the last words between him and his father, and move on. Another six months and he could pretend he'd settle for a house in their neighborhood and hire a realtor.

"Hey, there . . . couldn't sleep again?" He didn't realize Charlotte was in the living room until she slid down next to him on the couch, resting her head on his shoulder as his fingers tapped the laptop keys. "How long have you been out here?"

"About an hour, I guess."

"You work too much."

She looked beautiful—hair tousled, eyes drowsy as they fought the need for a little more sleep. He knew she was weary of him working long hours.

"I tried to go back to sleep and I couldn't, so I figured I'd get some work done," Ted said as he carefully minimized the screen and slid his hand over the USB flash drive he'd inserted earlier.

"It's not healthy, Ted," she replied. "We need to get you a sleeping pill or some solution to this insomnia. I'm going to ask Dr. Collins tonight."

"The therapist can write prescriptions?" Ted fought the urge to roll his eyes, as he did, privately, about most things related to Dr. Collins. It was his first experience with a marriage counselor and, he hoped, his last. He'd agreed to go because he loved Charlotte and she thought this was the key to some sort of marital happiness. He thought otherwise but kept his comments to himself.

"She's a licensed psychiatrist. She can prescribe medication."

"I'd love to sleep a good eight hours," Ted said. Dr. Collins might prove to be good for something after all, even if it came in the form of a little white pill.

Seven years of marriage and several months of marriage counseling had taught him a few things, such as when to keep his mouth shut and when to agree.

"Did you work on your list . . . for tonight?" Charlotte tapped the cover of Ted's iPad, closed and lying on the coffee table.

"Done. Insomnia was good for something, I guess." The marriage counselor had asked them to create a list of what they loved about each other and what drove them to the problems they'd been facing. He'd thought about objecting to what seemed a silly request that solved very little, but Charlotte had leaned forward, excited, attaching herself to the counselor's words. "I had zero problems listing what I love about you."

Ted smiled at her as, in a flash of memory, he could see her auburn hair lifting on the breeze while they rode horses across the land and into the mountains near his family's ranch. His sole thought had been to wonder if she would agree to marry him as he nervously fingered the ring box in his jacket pocket. He'd envisioned a life for them with a steady income they could count on, medical benefits, a modest home of their own, children. The opposite, in his mind, of the insecurities of ranch life. They'd been halfway to that dream when his parents died in an automobile accident, and he discovered his father actually could reach back from the grave to maintain a level of control over him. Their deaths had created the uphill battle he found himself trudging along now.

"Can I see it? Your list?" Charlotte asked, reaching for his iPad.

"No, we'll do this together, later . . . with the counselor." Ted grabbed the iPad and popped it into his backpack, removing the USB from his work laptop at the same time. He'd need to actually create a list, quickly, during his lunch hour. "How about your list? Done?" He was a little nervous about what she might say about him tonight.

"Hmmm . . . sort of." Charlotte stood, heading for the kitchen. He could hear her opening cupboards, pulling items to make coffee.

"I'd say you don't trust me, which makes list-making

hard, but I know where that will take the conversation." He purposefully kept his tone light, something practice had made perfect where this topic was concerned, but he still felt an anger that never quite grew a scab and healed.

"I let that whole San Francisco trip go. You know that." Ted watched her move around the kitchen, her back to him, alert for body language that said otherwise. Maybe arms crossing her body, biceps tightening, chewing on her nails. And then, there it was as she yanked the cabinet door so hard it banged and pulled out one, not two, coffee mugs.

Ted knew she was lying. It ate at her insecurities that he'd gotten drunk on a business trip, woke up fully clothed, his coworker Missy asleep next to him, his mind a blank as to how she'd ended up in his room. The story had trickled out, with various twists, until it reached Charlotte. He'd been explaining ever since that nothing had happened. But who was he to call anyone out on lying these days?

"We were happier in Montana," Charlotte said. "We were more . . . more . . . I don't know, centered? Before you took this job, we were different."

Here we go again. Ted clutched the arm of the couch and closed his eyes, willing himself to keep the inward groan rolling up his chest from escaping through his mouth.

"We were kids then, Charlotte. Everything was easier. We'll both be thirty years old this year, and I want to move forward, not go back," Ted answered, hoping his voice sounded steady, calm, the opposite of the turmoil flushing his cheeks. He turned sideways on the couch, watching Charlotte move gracefully around the kitchen. "A ranch is nothing but hard work and very little money. We have a nice life here."

This was the kind of crap he thought they should hash out in counseling and that, if Dr. Collins was as good as she claimed, their sessions would be less one-sided in favor of Charlotte. But he wasn't about to drop a bomb in their marriage therapy sessions and start a fight. He'd decided after the first round with the good doctor that her goal was to agree with Charlotte about what key topics they should be covering and he was just along for the ride. Not that the topic of Charlotte's ideas about living in Montana didn't come up with the counselor, but it never moved from what Ted viewed as a fantasy lens of "living a simple life" to reality. There he sat with two women who had grown up in the city's suburbs, their biggest childhood chore involving keeping their bedrooms clean, as the only expert on actual ranch life in the room but deferring to Charlotte's view to keep things amenable. To Ted, simpler meant poorer. Neither Charlotte nor Dr. Collins had ever had to live that kind of life. What he'd gleaned so far in their five months of therapy was that meeting in college, dating exclusively, marrying quickly following graduation, and having a child two years later had left them unprepared for the hard work of marriage in a way that didn't appear to affect other couples they knew.

Charlotte ignored him, pulling down cereal for breakfast, bread and peanut butter to make and pack a sandwich for Kelsey's lunch, and refusing to answer. He supposed she knew it could end up in an argument and she'd rather drop it now, hash it out later. But Ted thought they could save a lot of money on therapy if they could simply talk things through without a mediator and without anger and tears. The last time he suggested this, Charlotte said they would revert to the habits they needed to break rather than chart a new course. He assumed she thought therapy would accomplish some sort of new life for them. He was relatively cynical regarding the outcome she envisioned, but he'd keep showing up and giving it a try. Somewhere within himself he knew it was a half-hearted try, and this, alone, doomed the therapy journey to a less-than-successful outcome. If he could keep his current plan on track, he'd buy a house for his family in less than a year, and that, he believed, would be a much more effective game changer than Dr. Collins.

"You have a full day today?" Ted asked.

"What?" Charlotte paused, brows pulled inward in confusion. The brewing coffee was beginning to smell good.

"You're making Kelsey a sandwich, so I thought she must be going to the kindergarten after-school program rather than home with you."

"Oh, right, right . . ." Charlotte nodded, turning back to the kitchen counter. "I'm at the museum until noon, then lunch with Leah, and I'm on a deadline for an art gallery review for the newspaper . . . plus we have counseling later. I'll pick Kelsey up a little later than usual, and then Shay said he'd babysit."

Shay, Ted's colleague at work and best friend since their move to Pittsburgh. Other than Jesse, he'd never had as close a friendship with another man. He valued Shay like a brother. Shay had run interference after the San Francisco debacle, but he'd warned Ted that one more mistake that big and Charlotte would leave.

Ted walked into the kitchen and poured cream into the bottom of a mug, then added the coffee, one of the few habits he'd picked up from his father.

"Can you grab a coffee and sit with me before we go our separate ways?" Ted asked.

Charlotte's face softened, and she brought her mug—black, no sugar, he knew—with her, sitting down slowly, careful not to spill the hot liquid. He took her hand and squeezed, feeling the current between them he'd felt on their first date, a connection that all the ups and downs in their lives had not yet diminished, even when they chose to ignore it out of anger or disappointment in one another.

"Before my job, we were poor," Ted said. "We agreed Pittsburgh had better opportunities. You wanted to be near family, but now you rarely make any effort to see them beyond asking if they will babysit Kelsey."

"You know how difficult my mother can be, Ted," Charlotte responded. "And be honest . . . you don't really like my family all that much."

"I like some of them . . . maybe not your mother," Ted answered jokingly, hoping to lighten the mood with what was usually their mutual annoyance with Charlotte's mother. "The ranch should belong to Jesse. He loves Montana. He loves his life. And we can always visit."

"Should belong?" Charlotte was staring at him now, that questioning look she got when she was working on a new story for the newspaper crossing her face. "Art left the ranch to Jesse because you didn't want it."

"Right," Ted said, quickly covering the slip. "I meant the ranch should always belong to Jesse."

"Yeah, of course," Charlotte said.

It saddened Ted to see the wistful expression on his wife's face. If he kept pushing this conversation, he would open the door to something unpleasant.

"Let's talk about Montana vs. Pittsburgh with Dr. Collins, okay?" Ted hoped he could find a way to convey that moving to Montana wasn't necessary. Charlotte and Kelsey did not take a back seat to his work life, as she often claimed. Nothing could be further from the truth. Everything he'd done, everything he was doing, was for the wife and daughter he could not imagine life without and the younger brother he loved deeply. Jesse deserved that ranch, and Charlotte deserved to own rather than rent a home.

Charlotte nodded and gave him a tired half smile.

"Finish up that coffee. I'm going to take a shower," Ted said, standing and heading toward the hallway leading to the bedrooms and bathroom. He wanted to wash it all away, the sleepless nights, the lies he'd just told, yet again, woven into the fabric of the ancient lies his father had dumped on his shoulders.

"Don't be late tonight, Ted," Charlotte called out behind him.

She'd laid down the rules months ago. Go to marriage counseling, or she was taking Kelsey and moving out. He hadn't missed a session, and he wouldn't, no matter what the day would bring.

CHAPTER 2

Charlotte walked quickly, purposefully, through the lobby of the natural history museum, pushing wisps of hair out of her eyes, trying to tuck them into the messy, hastily done ponytail she'd created at a red light on the drive to work. She'd been slow getting ready this morning, her mind in a million places, and had put together mismatched clothes, then tugged on a blouse that still had strawberry juice spots and should have been in the laundry basket. Finally, on her third try, she'd managed to quiet her thoughts, which bounced between getting the list in her head on paper before marriage counseling and facing her work projects, long enough to put on a favorite, comfortable dress and sweater. She hadn't wanted to admit to Ted that she not only hadn't written up her list, but that she wasn't sure Dr. Collins was worth the money they were paying her.

Right hand holding the strap on the messenger bag slung across her body, she plowed forward rather than going right to skirt the majestic marble pillars and ran into a young docent, almost knocking the girl—who was leading a group of visitors to the diorama of the camel and the

Bedouin rider under attack from a fierce lion—over. Normally Charlotte went the other way, as she appreciated the history of the piece but hated its violence.

"Oh, I'm so sorry!" Charlotte could see the frowns on the visitors' faces. "I didn't see you."

"It's okay," the guide answered, adjusting a red, wool beret knocked askew and now dipping precariously over her right ear. She smiled reassuringly at her tour group. "This is Charlotte McCord. She handles development and marketing writing for the museum and is an arts and entertainment reviewer for the local newspaper."

Charlotte felt her cheeks grow warm as she blushed, embarrassed, and managed a small smile. She probably should thank the docent for making her string of part-time and freelance jobs seem impressive.

"I'm facing a deadline for a few things, and my mind was in a million places. I need to slow down and be a little more careful," she said. The truth behind her misstep into the docent was she'd been lost in thought about her husband.

The visitors smiled, and a few laughed in agreeable understanding. Charlotte backed away, waving to the group, then yanked open a polished wooden door, "Development" in gold lettering carefully displayed across the center, "Only Employees" stenciled beneath. Her footsteps created a quiet echo as she entered the small, empty office area she shared with three other staff members. She wished she wasn't so conflicted about what a career meant to her; she should be able to decide, like Ted, what she truly wanted and go after it. She'd started, deleted, and restarted, then revised, her list for their counseling session tonight. She hated her lack of confidence, her inability to state her feelings without worry. Making tough decisions and sticking to them was not her specialty.

Dropping her bag on a desk, Charlotte sat down and paused, taking a moment to try to breathe in the good of her marriage and exhale the fears and doubts. This morning's looming deadline for a marketing brochure about the new exhibit coming to Bird Hall needed to take priority. Yet, a niggling feeling that something more than the stress of their marital issues, more than Ted's tendency to be a workaholic, was at work here. She felt the existence of a tension-filled secret that was keeping her husband up at night. It moved around in her head like the old worn and scratched vinyl records her mother had liked to play when she was a child. It hit the damaged groove and replayed again and again as she dissected what he might be keeping from her, what the source of his anxiety could be. Charlotte had been with Ted long enough to know that he could be secretive, that he struggled to open up, and some topics he simply put up a wall that there was no getting around. But they were things they'd argued about, and she'd learned to simply accept or work around. Her gut feeling said there was something new and troubling going on with Ted.

She'd seen just a tiny bit of his computer screen, and it wasn't a list for Dr. Collins. There was a box in the middle that showed the progression of a download, the progress line looking close to the far right end of the box. Then he'd shut the laptop lid quickly, and, as she rose to go and make coffee, she saw him pull out the USB and pocket it, turning slightly as if it were somehow a covert move. He'd said all the right words this morning, and who was she to fault him for lying about doing his therapy homework when she had done the same? Still, she looked for what lay beneath the words, the thing that felt like an insidious threat to their carefully constructed life but somehow eluded her. If her marriage didn't get back on track soon, this cobbling together of various little jobs would not be enough if she had to go it alone with Kelsey.

Charlotte switched on the older desktop computer just as her phone jingled a Beyoncé tune. It was Leah, lover of Queen Bey. She felt the usual mix of desire to lay her troubles at the feet of her best friend and resistance to stacking what felt like career and marital failure up against Leah's successful career and free, single lifestyle. She pulled the phone out of her bag and swiped right.

"Hi, Leah."

"Hey, Charlie. Are we still on for lunch today?"

"Yes. Where do you want to go?" Charlotte was less interested in eating lunch than in picking Leah's brain for a little life and career advice.

"Hmmm . . . let me call a few places, then I'll make a reservation and text you."

"Leah, nothing fancy. I'm not really dressed for it today."

"Charlie, I've never known you to be particularly 'dressed for it,' as you put it, but you always look great."

Charlotte's face flushed with anger at the condescension and judgment in the words, despite the humorous tone of their delivery. "'Dressed for it' is what I do when I'm required to have lunch with my mother," she shot back. Quietly, she reminded herself that fancy clothes and perfect makeup had always been available to her, whereas Leah had grown up longing for exactly what she now had the means to provide herself with. Still, Charlotte knew she was Leah's only close female friend and the one person who could check Leah's insecurity-fueled arrogance. Women, generally, did not like Leah. Charlotte usually chose to dress a little more bohemian because tailored suits and haute couture reminded her too much of her mother. It irritated her that Leah's hang-up on the importance of clothes and appearance could get to her in a way that felt as if her confidence were being undermined.

"Okay, sounds like you need a friend, a nice healthy salad, and a little prosecco. Let me work it out."

Charlotte picked at a hangnail, eyeing her hands as she imagined Leah tapping perfectly manicured nails across the phone keypad, searching her OpenTable app for a place she liked.

"Sounds like your usual idea of slumming, something four-star or less," Charlotte said with a laugh in spite of the small flash of irritation. It was an old misbegotten twinge of insecurity that, like any bad habit, she should discard. It didn't even make sense. She smoothed down the floral boho dress she'd snagged at a secondhand, vintage store and rolled up the sleeves of her not-yet-ancient cardigan. Depending on the location, she might ditch the sweater. She'd always had the means to dress like Leah. Even now, Ted's income was such that she could forego her love of vintage clothes for something new and smart-looking, but she felt at home rummaging in secondhand shops, imagining the story behind each piece of clothing. Back in her closet at home, zipped in a nice airtight garment bag, were the classic clothes she pulled out when necessary for Ted's very few corporate events, for funerals, and at times to please her mother. "If I decide to drink prosecco in the middle of the day, then it's on you."

"I think it's exactly what you need. Text you the details in a bit."

With a quick "bye," Charlotte tapped the red button on her phone and hung up. Leah Hanson had been her best friend since the first grade, and, although they might have grown in different directions, she was still the first place Charlotte went to unload a problem. But the last few times she'd run to Leah, she'd left irritated, making her wonder if what had been a friendship was now more a habit she needed to break. Charlotte scrolled through her contact list, then hit a name.

"Charlotte?" The man's voice on the other end was a soft baritone. She smiled, imagining him, evenly matched dreadlocks tied back, hazel eyes going from tired to alert as he worked his way through a morning coffee.

"Hey, Shay. Still available to babysit tonight?" Charlotte knew at times his friendship with both her and Ted could be difficult for him, especially, like now, when they weren't getting along very well.

"Yep, can't wait to see my favorite little five-year-old!"

"You know you miss watching *Frozen* repeatedly until your eyes start crossing." Charlotte smiled, amused, thinking of little Kelsey standing up on the couch, a small, freckled arm around Shay's shoulder as she instructed him to turn on her favorite Disney movie.

"Sadly, I know all the songs!" Shay chuckled, and she imagined the smile on his face.

Charlotte opened her mouth to let him know her schedule for the day and when she'd pick up Kelsey and be home, then realized not only did he not need that information, but because Shay, like Ted and most of their friends, was not a fan of Leah, he probably didn't need to hear she was hanging out with Leah for lunch. Although she usually rolled her eyes when they made remarks, even defended her friend at times, deep down she was aware that Leah was somewhat of a predator where men were concerned.

As if on cue, Charlotte's phone dinged with a text from Leah.

Floor 2 @ Fairmont, 1:00ish.

"Okay, Shay! See you later, and thanks again for watching Kelsey!"

Charlotte looked up to see Grace, her colleague and friend, watching her with a look of concern. She picked at a few pieces of lint on her sweater, dropping them in the trash can next to her desk, and wondered if she looked as tired, stressed, and disheveled as she felt.

"You doing all right today, Charlotte?" Grace reminded her of everything she loved about the museum—a polish and prestige from another time, a work of art in and of herself.

"I didn't sleep well last night, and then I almost knocked the docent over in front of her tour group out there." Charlotte waved her hand toward the door. "I'm a little off my game this morning."

"Have you considered Margaret's offer to come on full-time here?" Grace asked, gently tucking a strand of hair behind her ears. Her thick, white mane was like a carefully layered snowfall, hitting just below her ears but not quite to her collar. "Kelsey's in kindergarten at least part of the time now, and all this running here and there has to be hard for you."

"I'm considering it. Margaret and I just need to be in the office at the same time to discuss her offer, I guess."

"Well, I'm ready to go part-time. You'd be doing me a favor."

Charlotte walked to Grace's desk and gave her a quick hug.

"If I work anywhere full-time, it will be here. This is, by far, my favorite job and work environment."

"You and I need to find some time, too, Charlotte. I know something is bothering you," Grace said.

Charlotte turned her head to hide the tears that threatened to spill over and onto her face. Grace was more motherly to her at times than her own mother. If there was one thing Charlotte had observed, it was that Grace had a good sixth sense about people and genuinely cared about Charlotte.

"I'm having lunch with Leah today, and then . . ." Charlotte stopped, considering whether to tell Grace she and Ted were in marital counseling. She'd opened up a lot to Grace, but in this she felt embarrassed, as if she was the sole owner of their crumbling marriage. "Let's meet on Saturday morning and take a walk. Ted will have Kelsey. Frick Park or Schenley?"

"Frick Park. I'll meet you at the tennis courts near Braddock Trail at, say, nine?"

"Putting it in my calendar now," Charlotte said, returning to her desk to pick up her phone, her fingers punching it into the Google calendar. Even as she hit "save," she felt lighter. Lunch with Leah today. Tomorrow was Friday, her slow day. She would catch up on housework and her freelance assignments, then have a nice hike with Grace on Saturday as well.

"I'd better get to work. I need to finish the new brochure." Charlotte decided she'd email the final document to her boss with a note requesting both approval and to set up a meeting to discuss moving her to a full-time position. She smiled at Grace, then, hands on the keyboard and eyes on the screen, she got to work. For the first time today, she felt stronger, as if she was stepping forward on a path of her own, something that didn't involve Ted and would give her a bigger sense of independence.

CHAPTER 3

Ted swiped his security badge across the electronic eye embedded in the chrome-plated turnstile, the remains of a still-warm latte in his left hand. The barriers automatically swung open, and he walked to the rows of sleek, metallic elevators heading ever upward. He felt a sense of accomplishment mixed with insatiable longing when he breathed in the beauty of the skyscraper. It represented all he had achieved and all he'd hungered for since he left the McCord ranch.

He was tired this morning from lack of sleep and running late because he stopped at Starbucks for more coffee and a breakfast sandwich, so it was a light crowd waiting for a ride to the twentieth floor. The lack of sleep would catch up with him later in the day, and over-caffeinating probably wasn't the best idea, but for now it was moving him forward. As he stepped into the elevator, a young man with a maroon University of Montana sweatshirt, worn jeans, and a courier package jumped in behind him.

"Go Griz," Ted said with a grin.

"Hey, man . . . a Grizzlies fan in the 'Burgh?" The courier looked surprised.

"Yeah, born and raised."

"Ahh, cool! I can't wait to get back. Love it out West."

"My wife says the same thing," Ted said as the doors opened to his floor.

He swiped his badge again outside a set of heavy glass doors with River City Trust etched just above eye level in gold, grabbing the handle as the light turned green and pulling hard to swing them open. He'd loved information security since the day he discovered it in a digital forensics class. He'd grabbed as many classes on the subject as the school offered. In his senior year, he scraped together enough extra money to add cybersecurity certifications to his resume.

The gray landscape of repetitive low-walled cubicles mixed with pockets of long, rectangular open seating rolled out before him like the outdated wooden carrels he'd seen in older libraries as a child. There was a similar semi-hushed quality perforated by the clicking of keyboards and the random beeps and tunes coming from the many smart-phones, tablets, and computer monitors. The music of his world.

Cybersecurity let him in on all the company secrets, and, as a McCord, he'd learned early in life to keep a secret. Like Pandora's box, secrets released could hurt others, especially those he loved. He'd perfected the ability to lock them away. It was the ideal profession for him. Unlike ranch life, here he could carefully map his success by his job title and hold on to each step as he worked toward the next. He'd built a path in his mind that would lead to the head of cybersecurity and then chief information security officer one day, a climb he'd gladly started the day he was hired. It was all a fierce game with success heavily dependent on a yearly performance evaluation, commonly known as "the PE." Ted had latched on to the PE and the ensuing corporate game board like a child to his mother's milk. Its results became the measure he used to validate himself each year. No Nielsen rating was ever more closely watched, no strategy more calculated, no goal more obsessed about than his determination to score as high as was possible on the PE.

He headed out into the sea of cubicles, looking for Shay as he walked. Ted saw the workplace as an elevation to a strata where he could garner respect. But his recent promotion had been something altogether different, outside the normal climb. It had been a result of desperation rather than an earned reward.

"You don't seem as excited as I thought you'd be," Shay said to Ted a few days after he'd received his promotion.

"It's a lot of extra work and responsibility. I'm just a little stressed is all," Ted answered. He could feel his stomach churn, coupled with a sharp level of fear that the constant, grinding guilt might end up causing an ulcer. His promotion wasn't earned in an acceptable way. A fervent belief that it was deserved after years of hard work mingled with the fear that his life could come down like a house of cards. Uncertainty ran amok in his digestive tract as though he'd eaten rotten fruit, its effects slow and lingering. He eyed, through the conference room window, the bottle of antacid tablets on his desk that he now routinely popped like a child devouring Skittles. Worse was facing Shay knowing he'd lied, and it was a living, breathing, daily lie that, if exposed, could cost him a friendship.

"It can be a soulless, driving environment, my friend," Shay said, his long legs and lean runner's physique stretched outward from the conference room chair where they were taking a break. "It's all an illusion. It can disappear in a moment. You have to take from it without letting it take you."

"I like feeling there is a path upward for me and that it's me who controls my destiny."

Shay shook his head in disagreement. "Just one corporate reorganization, and poof, your big climb is sidelined, all personal control gone. I'm simply saying don't let it suck you in. Don't lose sight of what really matters."

"What matters is buying a home for Charlotte . . . a nice car and maybe a private school education for Kelsey."

"Your wife feel the same way? Because every time I've talked to her, she sounds like she wouldn't mind going back out West."

"She grew up with a lot of money. She doesn't get being poor." Ted tried not to feel a level of annoyance that his best friend and his wife were having private conversations about what was best for his family. Although the three of them were good friends, this topic was not, in his opinion, up for decision, and yet it kept chasing him around like a sheep-herding dog.

"Well, dude, I grew up poor too," Shay answered with a laugh and a smile. "You know my story—single mother, not the best and not the worst neighborhood, and on my own ever since she died. I want to do well enough to have security, but I won't get obsessed with this place. I can like myself just fine without it."

"I get where you're coming from. But I'm sick of hearing about the damn fantasy life she imagines we'd have in Montana. It's a non-discussion no matter how hard Charlotte wants to nag me about it." Ted took a deep breath and put up his hand as if to say "enough," then stood. He must have seemed inordinately angry to Shay over something so insignificant. He had to curb his worries and calm down, act normal.

Shay stood and patted Ted on the shoulder, the light, friendly touch of athletes on a field showing support for one another. The silent language of men that said he got it and he'd back off, that he wasn't taking sides against Ted. Ted simply wanted, at least while he was at work, to focus his energies on both hiding his stress and on monitoring the very present pressures he'd put himself under.

Pittsburgh had moved beyond its stereotype as an industrial, blue-collar town to a high technology corridor. Opportunities abounded everywhere. Each morning, Ted looked out of the office windows onto the sun-dappled Monongahela River and felt pride mixed with stubborn determination. Much of what drew him to Shay was his friend's solid belief in himself, a quality Ted craved but found elusive in the face of his own ongoing need for affirmation from his employer. Shay encompassed quiet confidence as easily as sliding into a comfortable old jacket and could just as easily shrug off internalizing the pressures from work. He was his own man and, privately, Ted's hero, but Ted was under no illusions that he could evolve in the same direction. He wasn't wired that way.

"My mother always believed I'd return to my roots," Ted said, shaking his head as if in dispute with the specter of her as they walked out of the conference room. "To an understanding of the land and the people I'd been born into."

"Maybe you should think about that, Ted," Shay answered. "Not actually moving but tapping into that concept. Put the job in perspective."

Now, six months later, as he walked back to his cubicle, Ted wished he could tell Shay how much he had been forced to change his perspective after Pearl Ann and Art

McCord died two years ago in a car accident. Most of his responses to Shay were reflexive, based on the person he was before Art saddled him with ownership of the ranch when he should have given it to Jesse. His final move, like a hand reaching out from the grave, to attempt to force Ted back to Montana. Art's last will and testament, adding yet another layer to the secrecy he had once demanded of Ted, and which Ted now kept tucked deep inside himself to protect his brother. He'd seen less and less of his father in the years before his death. His promises to Charlotte and to his mother to visit more often rarely occurred, and, when they did, he and Art invariably argued, the trip soured, and the time between visits lengthened. Charlotte had given up and gone to Montana several times without him, taking Kelsey.

He'd decided not to tell her his father left ownership of the ranch to him, not Jesse. A secret he knew had the potential to cause yet another marital rift if she found out. Nor would he tell Jesse the truth as to why their father had made such a decision. Jesse, who loved that ranch with all his heart, deserved ownership. That was one secret his parents had taken to their graves and, he hoped, so would he. Art's will stipulated that Ted couldn't sell the ranch for four years after his death. Two more years and he could sign it over to Jesse, free and clear, lifting the albatross off his neck and his credit rating.

"You're late." The raspy voice behind Ted spoke of a thousand cigarettes smoked to the butt. It was the voice of Ted's nightmares, shaking him out of his own random thoughts and into the present.

"I don't work for you anymore, Geri," Ted replied, turning around.

After two miserable years on the Vulnerability Management team where, although he liked the work, he'd suffered under Gerilyn Leslie's brutal style of micromanagement, he gave up trying to advance his career and made a lateral move to a role as a penetration tester. There Ted spent his days in peace, pretending to hack his own company to find its vulnerabilities. He'd moved up a little, to senior member of the team, still pen testing but also scanning specific employee actions online at the request of human resources if they showed suspicious behavior. He'd lobbied hard to make the change and move away from Geri. When she'd tried to stop him, he went to human resources and filed a complaint. He had a big target on his back now where Geri was concerned, but once he'd shaken himself of her, he'd liked coming to work each day. He liked testing the company's network. He liked the elevated access to the system and feeling valuable. He liked knowing secrets and keeping them. He liked managing the people doing the work he loved, now that he'd been promoted to a level equal to Geri's.

"News flash, Geri. I'm a manager now. And it's not a factory where we punch a time clock."

"I don't know how you got a manager-level position, but I'm still watching you." In contrast to the casual dress of most of Ted's coworkers, short, stout Geri wore a suit to work nearly every day. Her dark hair, lightly flecked with gray, was cut like a helmet. All of which made Ted smile as he thought about the nickname the staff had privately given her: Ms. Voldemort.

"Now, now, getting nasty makes me feel like you're creating a hostile work environment," Ted said with a wink as she turned an angry shade of red. "I'll bet Dora in HR would love to hear about that!"

Ted's complaints about Geri opened the door for his

coworkers, who had been suffering in silence, to go to Dora and complain too. He'd heard that Geri was on human resources' watch list and had been warned to grow a new persona. The conflict between them ran so deep that now they were barely civil to one another, which wasn't healthy for the rest of the office, but they seemed unable to stop themselves. The better Ted did out from under Geri's thumb, the nastier it became.

Ted stepped into his cubicle, a two-by-four-foot box tucked in the corner against the wall. Being a manager did not come with an office, unfortunately. He'd need to move up another level to garner that privilege.

"Poking the bear again?" Simon stood up and sipped his coffee, tattooed arms resting on the wall between their cubicles as he watched Ted unpack his backpack and set up his laptop, iPad, and iPhone.

"She started it."

"She always does. But walking away isn't a bad idea."

Ted shrugged. "Don't you have some threats to research?"

Simon smiled. As a fellow threat intelligence analyst, Ted knew Simon liked having a little sporting fun with him but had decided he did not like Ted enough to work for him. In the six months since Ted had been promoted, only Simon had jumped ship to another team, although Ted expected Connor to leave any day now.

"She's a bully. I'm a manager now, not her subordinate."

"You know they interviewed one of her friends to be manager instead of you. You got the job. I'll bet she's super pissed off."

"She doesn't have any friends."

"Evidently, my fellow cube mate, she does. Inside the company and outside."

Ted had enough on his mind without Geri still sniffing around, ready to pounce the minute he made an error.

Ben Keene, a vice president in the information security division and, since Ted's promotion, his boss, greeted them as he walked by, heading toward his office. "Morning, Ted . . . Simon."

Ben often cut through the cubicle aisles and past the rows of open seating to say hello, talk to employees a bit. Most people liked him for his common touch. Ted had seen a cruel side to the guy that he didn't want aimed his way.

"Hey, Ben," Ted answered with a smile.

"Ben," Simon said, giving a mock salute and a grin.

"Ted, sent you an invite. I want to see you later," Ben said, throwing the words over his shoulder.

Ted and Simon both stood, silent, as Ben waved his hand and kept moving.

"Wonder what you did now," Simon said as soon as Ben was out of earshot.

"Mind your own business, Simon," Ted answered. The same nervous tic that made his mouth twitch when he'd first met with Ben to ask for a promotion was kicking in again.

"You appear to love being a boss man in corporate purgatory," Simon said, giving Ted a grin and the same mock salute he'd offered to Ben minutes before.

"Hey, have a little respect." Ted expected his morning snark from Simon like he expected a long line at Starbucks. Just part of the daily routine.

Ted snapped his laptop onto the docking station, wishing he could reach over and wipe that smirk off Simon's face. After Simon moved to a different team, Ted was left with Shay and Missy, which could be uncomfortable at times for different reasons, and Connor, who also did direct work for Ben that made Ted wary, knowing what he knew about Ben. Connor was even quieter and more covert than Ted believed himself to be.

Simon sat down and turned toward his monitor. "With Geri working against you, you don't have much chance of getting somewhere here, Ted. Just my two cents." He plugged in his headphones, tapped his favorite music app icon, and focused on the screen.

"You might be surprised," Ted whispered to himself. "Sometimes we make our own chances."

CHAPTER 4

I t was sunny with a fall chill to the air, the light sliding
gently through the tall windows to play on the empty
wine glasses at each neatly set table. Looking across the
expanse of upscale Floor 2 restaurant, Charlotte saw Leah
even before her friend, bent over her phone, raised her head
and waved. Set in the Fairmont Hotel, an eco-friendly high-
rise looking down over Fifth Avenue, it was a favorite of
Leah's. It was the type of place Charlotte had grown up
thinking was normal and affordable to everyone. She
wondered if Ted ever came here for lunch. He'd love it,
expensive or not, and see it as yet one more aspirational
item to achieve. Charlotte saw it as fitting more within her
mother's world than her own.

"Prosecco?" Leah raised her glass with a smile.

Charlotte nodded her affirmation as Leah ordered,
adding another for herself. "Just one. I'm on deadline for a
project at the museum today." Even her mother didn't
drink midday, that she knew of, which made her wonder
about what might be going on with her career-driven
friend. But considering she was facing counseling with Ted

later, she decided a little fortification might not be a bad thing.

"You won't even feel a drink or two in a few hours. I've got a meeting right after lunch and I'm sure I'll be fine," Leah said with a shrug.

"Is the meeting with your new guy, Leah?" Charlotte asked with a smile after their drinks arrived and they'd both ordered the same salad with salmon. Watching her friend sip wine at noon made Charlotte wonder about the validity of any upcoming meeting being work-related, but who could tell with Leah.

"Who says I have a new guy?" Leah reached for a bread-stick, avoiding eye contact.

Charlotte paused for a second to enjoy the view. She was so rarely in this part of downtown. Outside, a sea of people moved in every direction along the street—backpacks, purses, or messenger bags slung cross-body, looking down at cell phone screens or crossing the street, heads slightly nodding and lips traveling in time with whatever beat moved through their headsets and earbuds. Most appeared to be heading for Market Square or PPG Place, a building Kelsey insisted was a glass palace complete with a princess.

"You did . . . about a month ago, and that's the last I heard of it." Charlotte turned back to face Leah. As she said it, she realized she'd been so caught up in her own life she hadn't poked Leah about the guy during their texts and calls. Her friend hadn't offered any new information either. A covert side to Leah where her love life was concerned was unusual. Usually, at least with Charlotte, she enjoyed sharing details about her conquests, brief as many of them often were.

"Oh, you know how fast they come and go with me, Charlie." Leah leaned back in her chair, laughing at her own self-deprecating humor. This was something Charlotte loved about Leah, the way she could take her most maddening qualities and not only acknowledge them but mention them with humor and in jest at herself.

"Then you seriously never tried to pick up Ted's friend Shay?" Charlotte felt the smile stretch across her face, her shoulders softening as she relaxed and fell into a bit of fun.

"Is that what he said?" Leah's face broke into a broad smile. "I think that's wishful thinking on his part. He's not my type."

"Hmm . . . so now you have a type?" Charlotte winked, amused. "Okay, you don't have to tell me. But it's not like you to avoid giving me all the details, even if he'll be gone soon."

"Can we talk about something else?" Leah's face looked flushed from more than the wine, and she shifted from joking to seeming somewhat uncomfortable. Charlotte saw a flash of irritation that disappeared quickly, making her even more intrigued.

"Sure, no problem." Charlotte curbed her curiosity for now. "You know I just want you to be happy."

Leah began a rather fierce attack on the lettuce, cutting it into manageable pieces. When she looked up, her face had softened into an easy smile. "I know, Charlie. I'm seeing someone, but it's a little complicated, so another time, all right?"

"I care about you, Leah. You know that. I've been there when it was bad, and I want you to find someone who really loves you."

Leah looked at Charlotte and nodded, decades of shared memories passing between them. Charlotte would bet a hundred bucks he was married. It wouldn't be the first time, or probably the last. Her elegantly dressed, successful friend regularly picked unavailable men and ran at the first hint of actual feelings. She felt a twinge of empathy. She carried within herself the reason Leah was commitment-phobic, the traumatic event that had driven her to this outwardly controlled person in such a perfect shell. There was so much history between them that it softened their differences now.

Charlotte glanced around the restaurant—the rise and fall of soft voices, the clink of silverware and glasses, a gentle ambiance that could be jarred in an embarrassing way if she continued to pester Leah about something she wasn't ready to talk about. "We're here to have lunch, catch up. I need your advice, but not about Ted."

Leah laid her fork down carefully and took a sip of water, then waved to the waitress and ordered a third glass of prosecco. This was not a good sign, even surprising considering Leah's mother's history, and Charlotte wondered what was truly going on. She shook her head with her hand over her wine glass to let the waitress know she was not going to follow Leah's lead. What type of meeting did Leah have after lunch that she could show up half in the bag? The restaurant was part of a hotel, which begged the question of where Leah was actually going after Charlotte left.

"If I were you . . ." Leah smiled, her face relaxed, her hands managing her salad slowly rather than fiercely now.

"You're not." Charlotte laughed.

"I would find a gorgeous guy, get laid, get my confidence going, and maybe spice up my marriage."

"I think you're getting drunk." Charlotte offered a smile despite the twitch of annoyance she felt inside. This was classic Leah, making her feel boring, as if she were a woman in need of a fix which, for Leah, always meant sex.

"Remember that little fling you had behind Ted's back in college?" Leah whispered, grinding the words out slowly.

"Fling seems a big word for a drunken one-night stand," Charlotte answered. "And remember, I said I'm not here to talk about Ted."

Charlotte wasn't going to escape Leah taunting her a bit, mainly because many of their strongest connections lay in their past. In the present, they tried a little harder to come to a central point from the divergent directions they had been gradually sliding toward these past few years. When Leah came to Montana to visit her while they were in college, Charlotte had been dating Ted for two years and sleeping with him for almost as long. They'd argued because Leah liked to party hard and Ted wanted Charlotte to refuse. And then there was Leah, making mocking good-girl remarks to her, challenging her to go a little wild for a change. A group of them, all girls, piled into someone's beat-up Ford Festiva and headed to a bar in a small town nearby. The legal drinking age was nineteen in Montana back then.

"Wasn't his name Randy?" Leah smiled a smirky little grin again. She was enjoying this; it was an amusing joke to her. "He was hot, Charlie."

Charlotte tried to shake off the uncomfortable feeling of being at a fork in the road between the Leah she had grown up with and this Leah, whose snarky remarks had a mean undercurrent that radiated across the table toward her. She forced a laugh.

"He was hot. Now, can we talk about something else? I need your advice on my career."

Leah's eyebrows rose with interest. This was not something Charlotte tended to bring up, professing contentment with her gamut of small jobs and usually talking about Ted or Kelsey or some article she was writing.

"Running to the ladies' room," Leah said. "All that wine, you know! Be right back."

Charlotte watched her walk a straight and sober line, stopping to tap the shoulder of a guy at the bar and say a few words, then on past the hostess and out to the hallway where the bathrooms were located. She closed her eyes and thought about Randy, her long-ago hookup. There had been a few times, in the months afterward, when she'd thought her sex life with Ted was better for having screwed Randy. But all of that was so long ago. She never really thought about old history the way Leah did. She was firmly a here-and-now kind of person. It made her wonder if Leah thought they had nothing else in common anymore, or if it was a shield Leah used to keep things she didn't want to share private. Taking these little trips down memory lane, catching up about things Charlotte would rather forget, avoided what was currently happening in her life and Leah's.

"How's our little Kelsey?" Leah asked when she returned, her face pink from the alcohol but more relaxed.

"She's great," Charlotte said, relieved to be on safer ground as she fished around in her oversized tote and pulled out a small crayon drawing. "She asked me to give this to you . . . for your refrigerator, she said."

Kelsey's drawing depicted Charlotte and Leah each holding one of the little girl's hands. Her rendering of the sunshine and trees surrounding the three of them was a little larger than life. In the early days, when Kelsey was a baby, Charlotte would catch a sad, wistful look on Leah's face as she held her or as Charlotte chatted about her. Only she knew the source of that sorrow, the soft spot under Leah's hard carapace where she locked certain things away.

It was good to see Leah relax and enjoy this bit of an offering from the child.

"Who's the dog owner?" Leah asked, pointing to what appeared to be a small brown dog in the picture.

"Guess who's asking for a dog?" Charlotte rolled her eyes. "I have my hands full as it is. She'll have to make do with visiting my mother's new puppy for the time being."

"Your mother got a puppy?" Leah smiled as she folded the drawing and set it down on the table. "I'm trying to imagine her managing that."

"Poor little thing is already in obedience training. His carefree days as a puppy will be short-lived, I imagine," Charlotte said with a laugh. "I think my mother hopes having a puppy means I'll bring Kelsey out to Sewickley more often." She paused for a moment. "You should get a dog, Leah. You love them, and you wouldn't be alone."

"I do love them, but it's too much work. You know I don't like to be tied down. How about you get a dog, and I'll dog-sit now and then?" Leah smirked as she unfolded the drawing and pointed to Kelsey's depiction of the dog. "So how are things between you and your mother? The same? I like your mother, but that's in comparison to mine, so the bar isn't set too high," she said. "Your mother has never liked me, though."

"In the old days, she thought you were a little wild, maybe a bad influence. She apparently likes you now," Charlotte said. "She's very impressed with your job . . . 'career,' to quote her . . . and asks about you just before she asks me when I'm going to do something 'more' with my education."

"You don't mind leaving Kelsey with her?" Leah asked. "Not afraid she'll come home sure she's destined to marry well or run the world somehow as long as she lives near her grandma?"

"Actually, she's careful with Kelsey," Charlotte admitted. "I think she's afraid I'll stop taking her out there."

Charlotte waved the waiter over and ordered a coffee, trying to shift her thoughts, but the image of her mother cast a shadow now. No matter what Ted achieved in his career, no matter how well he provided for her and Kelsey, Charlotte could still feel her mother's disapproval that she'd married someone from a ranching family rather than a local boy from her family's social set.

"I love a bit of reminiscing, Leah, but I'm thinking of some career—or job—changes and want your opinion."

"Charlie, you know I've been hoping for a long time you'd drive your own ambitions forward rather than have everything be about Ted's career," Leah said, her brows arched and upper body leaning forward. "I'd love to help you."

"I need to sort out, from my many little jobs, how to create a career or career path," Charlotte said. "Talking about my mother makes deciding even more stressful. You know I try not to bring my Rosalyn baggage with me when I'm out and about with friends."

"Remember when she threatened to refuse to pay your tuition at the University of Montana after you secretly applied and were accepted?" Leah asked with a grin.

"Instead of the more acceptable Carnegie Mellon, Yale, or NYU. So, I said 'fine' and that I would take out student loans. She was terrified word would get out and people would think she was cheap," Charlotte replied with a little chuckle, deciding to roll with Leah and reminisce.

"And, oh my God, when you brought Ted home!" Leah laughed so loudly people at other tables turned to look.

"Shhh . . . keep it down," Charlotte chided her friend with amusement. "She thought he was 'nothing serious' when she'd visit me at college. When we got engaged my senior year, I thought she was going to have a coronary."

"Charlotte, come home right now! We need to discuss this," Leah said, imitating Charlotte's mother in hushed tones but with such alarming accuracy it caused Charlotte to burst into loud laughter herself.

"Thanks." Charlotte wiped her eyes with the edge of her napkin. "I needed that." She was going to have trouble keeping Leah focused on the present and not taking little walks down memory lane. But, as long as they were on this topic, was it safe to ask about Leah's mother? In grade school, they had both been part of a pack of boys and girls living near one another. By junior high, they'd bonded and become best friends over their different, but difficult, relationships with their mothers. It was the year Leah's father left the family, the divorce forcing her mother to find a low-paying job and move to a smaller, less expensive home, propped up by alimony, child support, and a modest income, when she could curb the drinking and hold a job.

"Now that we covered my mother, Leah, how's yours?" Charlotte hoped her mercurial friend wasn't going to, once again, shift back inside a hard shell.

"She's been sober a year now, but she's had some health issues lately. She might have to give up her little gardening business," Leah answered. She'd finally stopped drinking and ordered a cappuccino, which she stirred slowly with a tiny spoon. For a moment, Charlotte saw in Leah's face the sad, young teenager she had known so well. As so often happened, Charlotte felt a twinge of resentment that lunch would be over soon and the whole hour would have been about Leah. Leah driving the conversation, ignoring her requests, and now Leah dropping this bomb about her mother that left Charlotte feeling she'd be selfish and lacking empathy to switch things to her own needs. Ted had the ability to do this to her too, and a large percentage of her frustration and resentment was aimed at herself as much as at Leah.

"What kind of health issues?" Charlotte asked.

She liked Leah's mother, a former artist who battled her demons through creating beauty, whether it be gardening or painting. She often wondered with amusement whether she and Leah might have been switched at birth.

"She's in the early stages of cirrhosis of the liver, and they discovered a small, malignant tumor on her breast," Leah said, the sunlight playing softly on her features, showing the beginning of crow's feet around her eyes under the careful application of makeup; a beautiful mask that matched the choice of a lightweight, tan Michael Kors suit.

"Why didn't you call me?" Charlotte asked.

"And tell you what, Charlie? That my mother got sober a bit too late and her lifelong battle with the bottle has now caught up with her?" Leah's face and tone hardened, banishing the softer glimpse Charlotte had seen just a few moments ago. She was back to the hard-driving investment banker whose "take no prisoners" attitude allowed fewer and fewer behind the wall and into her private thoughts and feelings.

"Let me help, Leah. Maybe I can stop by to see her or just be a sounding board for you as I'm sure you have to manage caring for her around your job."

"My brother and his wife check in on her regularly, and she's managing treatment well. I hired a lawyer to make sure she has Medicaid and Social Security disability, and I send money, but it's my brother's turn to manage our mother."

A shadow had dropped over Leah, the energy emanating from her arctic-like, making the air conditioning feel warm in comparison, belying the bright sun outside.

"I want to understand, Leah, I do," Charlotte said, her eyes filling with tears she struggled to hold back. "But that's so harsh."

"Seriously, Charlie? I know all about your own relationship with your mother. Would you drop your life and run out there to wait on her if she fell ill?" Leah's hand shook ever so slightly before she tucked it in her lap, out of sight.

"I'd like to think I would help her, unpleasant as it might turn out to be, but I guess you don't know until you're in that position, right?" Charlotte refrained from saying that she wanted a better relationship with her mother and she was sure she would put their differences aside and be there if her own mother was facing a devastating diagnosis.

The lunch had rolled in a disappointing direction, and she didn't know how to salvage things. She'd come for advice but ended up with wisps of an old childhood friend interspersed with a stranger she didn't much like. Leah seemed erratic, hopping from nostalgic and fun to sharp-tongued, to a harsh and unkind person. Charlotte wasn't sure she wanted any advice from the woman sitting across from her.

"I'm dealing with it," Leah said. "I'm making sure she's financially set up, but I'm not getting emotionally sucked in. You wait, this will have her drinking again in no time." She sighed, then gave Charlotte a look that clearly indicated she wanted to drop the subject. "So, what did you want to ask me? About your job or career?"

Charlotte was past the point where she cared to hear what Leah thought about her career options, but talking about work and careers would move them away from things that appeared to stir up Leah's unpredictable temperament. She held her breath, unsure what to expect after the roller coaster of mood swings she'd seen so far.

"A full-time position is opening at the museum. I hate thinking I might have to give up my freelance writing, but I'm not sure I can juggle that, Kelsey, and a full time job. You've made an amazing career for yourself. What do you suggest?" Charlotte asked.

"I'd take the full-time job at the museum," Leah said. "Don't look at it like a ladder the way Ted does. Think about what will make you independent, and then just move forward and let it take you where you land."

"Independent of Ted?" Charlotte asked. "I'm not looking to go it alone."

She was irritated now, the desire to stand up and simply leave pushing strongly from within. But in the end, she was her mother's daughter and she would not make a scene in public.

"Look, Leah, I don't think working for a nonprofit will ever result in my being the sole provider. I'm not trying to do that." Charlotte caught herself twisting the ends of her hair, an old habit signaling frustration, and clasped her hands in her lap. Why would Leah even think her goal was to leave her husband? "Ted's salary is what not only pays our bills, but moves us forward. This is about me, developing myself, finding a new way."

A strange look passed over Leah's face. She seemed uneasy, troubled. She turned her head to look out the window, answering without making eye contact. "I just had an odd feeling when I saw Ted in line at Starbucks the other day. About that promotion he got." Leah tapped her manicured nails on the side of the cappuccino mug. "He says he's doing well, but he seemed nervous about it. Dark circles under his eyes, and he gave me a sense that he was hiding something or that he didn't feel confident the job would pan out well over time."

Charlotte knew Ted and Leah picked up morning coffee at the same Starbucks and often ran into one another. Still, it was frightening to hear someone else noticed the same things she was seeing and worrying about at home. She shifted in her seat and sighed.

"He's been weird ever since he got that job. He can't sleep at night; he's working all hours. At first, I wrote it off to the fact that we're in marital counseling." Charlotte was done talking about her career. She wanted a graceful exit before Leah took the conversation in a, yet again, disturbing, frustrating direction.

"On a couple occasions, Ted asked me questions about how international money transfers work," Leah said. "Asked out of nowhere, but then backed up and said he was just curious."

Charlotte could hear warm concern in Leah's voice, but her eyes were sharp, her look a bit feral. The dichotomy of it put Charlotte off-balance. Her words felt fake when linked to such powerful, probing intensity.

"I suppose he figures you work at a bank and that's your area of expertise. Maybe it had to do with an investigation at work." Charlotte looked at her watch, hoping to send Leah a hint. She glanced around for the waitress, wondering if she could leave since Leah was picking up the bill, or whether it was better to flag their server down, get the check in front of Leah, and get going as quickly as possible.

"Does he talk to you about work?" Leah leaned forward, her focus tight, intense. "I mean that cyber stuff he does must be interesting."

"He's really tight-lipped when it comes to specifics about his work. It's all confidential."

Charlotte hesitated. Ted did tell her things from time to time, but she knew she shouldn't share. "I can tell you a little bit, but, Leah, it stays between us, got it?"

"Got it. Of course. Like I said, he was asking me odd questions."

"Well, HR sometimes asks him to check on employees they think might be doing something they shouldn't."

"Hmmm, like what?"

"Sending confidential information to their home email, or accessing databases or accounts that they don't have the right to look at—you know, like celebrities who bank there. You probably have top-end clients too."

"I know what kind of clients you mean," Leah said with a laugh. "So how, exactly, does he check?"

"Tracking the person's name to the asset tag number on the front of their laptop, he drops a software package onto the laptop behind the scenes, then monitors what they do without their knowledge. No alarms go off. They have no idea what is happening. It's all captured in a log, and Ted gives HR a report of his findings."

"Seriously, Charlie? That's creepy!" Leah whispered, leaning in to make sure no one heard her. "I wonder if my bank can do that to me."

"Probably," Charlotte said. "All companies have cyber teams and can do this. But the request has to come from HR."

"Has he found anything really interesting?"

"I think so, but that's the part he won't share." The look of disappointment crossing Leah's face left Charlotte feeling uncomfortable, as if she'd somehow betrayed Ted even though she hadn't spilled anything confidential. "I think he's been working on something really intense, really confidential, since just before his promotion. Whatever it is, he won't share with me at all, but I feel like it's eating at him. I've tried to write it off to the new job pressure, but I'm not entirely sure."

Leah abruptly waved the waitress over and asked for the check, then handed over a credit card. Even though she was relieved to finally be able to close this strange lunch down, Charlotte felt dismissed.

"To be honest, I'm tired of everything being about Ted's career, Ted's job stress, and I was trying to talk about me today, Leah." Charlotte could hear the irritation in her voice. "Do you want me to be independent because you think something more serious is wrong . . . with Ted and his job, I mean? Is that where these questions are coming from?"

"I don't know," Leah said. Charlotte saw the mask go up again, felt the intensity subside and the less-than-authentic version of Leah take over. "Something just feels off with him. I'm looking out for you and Kelsey, Charlie. You have to be able to take care of her, with or without him."

"With or without my parents too," Charlotte added.

"Exactly. If anything goes wrong, do you want to live with your mother full-time and have her raising Kelsey while you work? I mean, you're already in marital counseling."

Charlotte gave a soft, slight shake of her head and shifted her gaze to the window. Her mother, Rosalyn Coleman Porter, a self-proclaimed distant relative of the famed Andrew Carnegie clan through the wife of the steel magnate and philanthropist's brother Thomas, rested in her conscious mind like a fixture she was unwilling or unable to remove. The "Carnegie connection," as Charlotte and her brother liked to call it, was a fact Rosalyn had reminded

Charlotte of on occasion when she wasn't thrilled with her choice of boyfriends.

"Remember when I did that genealogy research online and burst her bubble around all that Carnegie stuff?" Charlotte smiled, trying to ease the tension and change the subject, almost a sixth-sense reaction to Leah's pushy questions about Ted.

"Oh, yes. What was it you said to Rosalyn and she didn't speak to you for a week?" Leah let out a chuckle, and Charlotte could feel the mood between them easing into a familiar groove.

"I said, 'We are as close to the man himself as Jim Beam or Wild Turkey is to Glenlivet.'"

"One of your better comebacks, I'd say, Charlie."

The image of Rosalyn—her back straight, a cream silk Giorgio Armani blouse falling softly across a body toned and honed to perfection through hours of yoga, tennis, and swimming, and tucked neatly into black Marc Jacobs trousers, manicured nails resting upon folded hands—was so clear to her, in this moment, that Charlotte wondered if her mother would suddenly move from apparition to reality and sit down next to her at the restaurant table.

"Ready to go?" Leah signed off on the bill, then slid her credit card into a slim Gucci wallet, which she transferred to a soft leather bag Charlotte estimated cost more than two months of her part-time salary. She tucked the picture from Kelsey inside and stood to leave.

"Yes. I need to get back to the office," Charlotte said, her car keys out, slinging a plain, black tote over her shoulder. "Thanks for lunch."

They stood a moment, hesitant, then Charlotte stepped forward and gave Leah a quick hug before walking through the restaurant door. The escalator to the lobby was immediately to her right, but she turned back, thinking Leah was not far behind her and wondering if she should put space between them until Leah moved out of this strange phase, or invite her over to spend some time with Kelsey. She wished she had gone to Grace with her career questions and concerns rather than Leah. It would have been much more focused on Charlotte's needs and probably more productive. Leah had simply left her queasy and a little insecure about her marital stability, amplifying her already heightened concerns about Ted.

Leah wasn't there, nor was she in the restaurant foyer. Charlotte glanced into the restaurant, and there, midway into the left side of the elegant, oval-shaped bar, sat Leah, a drink in front of her, a mildly familiar-looking man in a business suit to her right with his hand on her back, his head leaning into hers, face intent, listening. Charlotte hesitated, struggling to place the man in her memories, but she was unable to remember, and if she didn't get moving, she'd soon be running late. Charlotte watched Leah pick up a martini glass and take a sip. She was drinking as if she hadn't just had three glasses of wine and survived a childhood with an alcoholic mother she was so ready to emotionally abandon.

Headed down the escalator, Charlotte clutched the railing to keep herself steady. A jumble of feelings were rolling through her, and, in her head, she clearly heard the commentary both Ted and Shay had made once, a while back, when the subject of Leah arose. Comments that caused her to fiercely defend her friend.

"She's borderline psycho."

"She's two steps from going over the edge."

Stepping out onto the sidewalk, Charlotte shook her head and took a deep breath to clear her thoughts. Leah was not psycho. She would not, could not, think this about the friend who had always been there for her. Leah was smart, successful, and mildly emotionally damaged, but wasn't everyone on some level, in some way, that only those closest to them knew? Yet, even as she silently argued with the negative thoughts poking at her mind, her gut told her something was going on with Leah that wasn't good. Whatever it was, she should try to get to the heart of the changes in her friend and help Leah before she upended all she had worked so hard to become.

Charlotte started the car and headed toward the museum, making a mental note to visit Leah's mother the next time she dropped Kelsey off at her parents' home for a weekend visit.

CHAPTER 5

It was late afternoon when Ted tapped the side of Missy's cubicle to get her attention, causing her to jump. She pulled the small white earbud out of her right ear and looked up at him. He had thirty minutes before his meeting with Ben, and then he was heading home.

"I need you to run a pen test in the Mortgage and Loan division." He had to admit, it felt good to be a manager, good to delegate to others the often tedious work he'd once done and just focus on analysis of the results they brought in.

He'd learned Missy was fine if he just gave her an assignment and left her to manage on her own. An introvert, she preferred to plug in earbuds, plug herself in as well, and just do the job with as little fuss as possible.

Missy nodded. "When do you need the results?"

"End of next week."

"Okay, that works."

Missy reinserted her earbud, jotted Ted's request on a Post-it note, and returned to her computer screen, a quiet dismissal emanating from her body language and actions. He could delegate work to his team, but he couldn't make at least half of them like him. He'd heard rumors floating around about his promotion, none accurate, delivered by people who felt he wasn't the most qualified person for the role. He wondered what Missy had heard, then shrugged it off. He was their manager, not their friend, and as long as they did good work, he could ignore how they might feel about him. In need of the one friendly face he could always count on, Ted stopped at Shay's desk on his way back to his own just to say hello. Shay rolled his chair back and pointed silently toward Connor's cubicle, which sat on the other side of the wall from his.

"What's up?" Ted whispered as he leaned over the side of Shay's cube wall. "Want to grab a small conference room and talk?"

Shay stood up and followed Ted, closing the door behind him as they entered a small room rarely used. They sat at the end of the conference room table closest to the door.

"Connor hasn't been in for three days." Shay's face was serious, concern laced with a bit of anger.

"I told him he could work from home. He said his parents are in town."

"His parents died in a plane crash when he was eighteen," Shay said, tapping his fingers on the table, then shifting in his chair. "Something's off, I'm telling you, Ted."

"Seriously? Let me see if he's online and ask about the project I gave him," Ted said. He could hear the irritation in his own voice at realizing he'd been lied to, not that that surprised him when it came to Connor, but it added to his inability to have much, if any, control of this employee in the way he did over the rest of his team. Connor, for all intents and purposes, belonged to Ben. His reporting to Ted was pretty much a technicality. The people-management side of the job, he was learning, could be exhausting. "You're sure he doesn't have family in town?"

"I'm sure. I went by his place after work last night because the whole team wondered what was up with him. It was dark, no lights, windows closed and blinds drawn. I tried the buzzer a couple times, but no one answered." Shay slouched back, stretching out his legs, and waited.

"I'll check when he last logged in to the system. He's probably just blowing off work a little bit." Ted saw Shay's gaze drop and realized his foot was nervously tapping the floor, his knee bobbing up and down. He put his hand down to still the movement of his leg, wishing he could do the same to the apprehensive tingle running up the back of his neck.

Shay looked as if he were about to make a comment, then shrugged, his lips in a tight line, and stood to go.

"You know Ben owns the guy, Shay. Not much I can do."

"I'm not his biggest fan, Ted, but what if something is wrong . . . he's hurt or in trouble?" Shay stood silently by the door, waiting.

"Ben's meeting with me soon. I'll ask him if he knows what's up with Connor," Ted answered. "In the meantime, I'll try to call him."

"Well, you know what I think. Connor is always working on something for Ben the rest of us don't know about."

"I know, I know. I've probably cut Connor too much slack. He reports to me, and he can't just disappear or always be working on projects without me knowing what he's doing." Ted stood to leave, hoping he'd managed to close the conversation. Shay could be as relentless as an investigator.

"Are you saying you don't know what Ben's got him working on?" Shay asked. "I mean, Ted, you're his manager."

Ted was tempted to tell Shay that he had a pretty good idea of what Connor might be working on, but that opened a Pandora's box between him and Shay that might damage their friendship. Was an omission between friends equivalent to a lie? Ted didn't know. What he believed was the less the people he cared about sat inside his current circle of truth, where Ben and Connor were concerned, the better. But Shay might not see it the same way.

"Connor missing work could simply mean he'd been out drinking and went off the grid for a while, not totally uncommon where he's concerned. I'd like to write him up, maybe fire him, but you know he's under Ben's protection."

"Office politics. The reason I don't want to be a manager." Disgust rolled through Shay's voice.

"I'll look into it. I promise." Ted moved toward the door, forcing Shay to open it and leave with him.

Twenty minutes later, he picked up his laptop and headed for Ben's office.

"Hey, Ben!" Ted said, pasting a smile on his face that he hoped looked genuine as he stood in the office doorway. He was surprised to see Dora from Human Resources seated in one of the two chairs across from Ben's desk.

"Ted. Close the door and have a seat." Ben looked serious. There must be a pretty high-profile investigative request from Human Resources in the works for Dora to speak with him in person rather than file an online request form or send a confidential email. He hoped this didn't have anything to do with Connor.

"Hi, Dora." Ted sat down, eyeing what looked like a printout of system logs on Ben's desk. He hadn't met with Dora in person since he'd complained about Geri targeting him and her overall management style a few years ago. "I haven't had a request for an HR investigation in a while."

Dora and Ben exchanged a look that Ted couldn't quite decipher. She was silent, serious, and made no direct eye contact with Ted. He felt a light sheen of sweat on his forehead and neck. Something was wrong, but he couldn't put his finger on it.

"Ted, I'm going to get right to the point. We know what you've been up to. I've got the logs here in front of me," Ben said, his voice low, smooth, but with a hard edge that escalated the tension that was always lying between him and Ted.

Ted could feel Dora watching him. He put his hand forward as if to reach for the sheets of paper in front of Ben, but Ben shifted the pile toward himself, leaving it just out of Ted's reach. "I should be allowed to take a look at the logs if I'm being accused of something here."

He looked at Dora for support, watching her seeming hesitance. Ben kept his hand resting lightly on the logs. A deep-seated nausea was churning in his belly, but Ted tried again, pushing forward.

"Could you explain? I have no idea what you're talking about." He clutched his laptop where it rested across his thighs, trying to stop his hands from shaking. A glance down showed his white knuckles.

"We know you set up rules to move money from several lower-profile customer accounts into a savings account in your daughter's name at Western PA Bank." Ben leaned back in his chair, hands resting on its arms, the fluorescent lighting overhead reflecting off his monogrammed cuff links. Ted thought he saw the flicker of a smirk on Ben's face. "Fortunately, it set off a few alarms, and we caught the money transfer shortly after it occurred."

"I did no such thing! I don't have any account at Western PA for myself or my daughter, and if I did, I wouldn't steal to put money into it." His chest tightened. He wiped a hand across his forehead where drops of sweat were accumulating only to realize his hand was damp and sweaty as well.

Ted looked over at Dora, hoping for an ally, but she sat, silent, her face unreadable to him. He struggled to process how Ben had turned things in this direction, but his body was throwing off so many physical responses—his leg now twitching as well—that it took all his energy to breathe and head off a full-blown, panic-driven breakdown. This was unreal, as if he were in a nightmare from which he would soon wake up. He wondered for a moment whether he should pinch himself and see if it would disappear into a fog.

"Ben, a good friend of my wife's works at Western PA," Ted answered, trying to keep his voice calm. "If you'd let me contact her, I'm sure we can resolve this. It's got to be a mistake . . . a clerical error of some sort."

"There's no mistake. It's all here." Ben patted the stack of paper. Ted was sure he saw a tiny smile as Ben looked down, gone just as quickly when he resumed his hard stare at Ted, his mouth in a firm, straight line. "We're going to have to let you go, and I've convinced Dora that we don't need to press charges since the money was returned by Western PA. However, we'll turn your name over to the banking regulators, and you'll never work in the finance industry again."

"I know why you're doing this, Ben!" Ted was on his feet now, yelling, all the emotions he'd tried to control exploding from every pore in his body. His heart was racing, adrenaline surging. He clenched his right fist, the other hand holding the laptop, to keep from lunging across the desk and hitting Ben. He turned to Dora. "I caught his plan to embezzle millions—he and Bob Thornton. He's setting me up."

Dora frowned as she looked quizzically at Ben. Ted knew the logs meant nothing to her. She couldn't read them and had to trust Ben's assessment of the data.

"Ted, Ben had Connor take a second look to make sure it's not a computer error," Dora said.

Ted felt himself folding, deflating. He was alone, and there was no possibility of enlisting Dora's support. She'd been briefed ahead of time, and she was here to escort him out the door. His rage simmered, turning from panic to a cold, hard, deep level of hatred for the man before him.

"Connor pulled the logs and reviewed them for me, then I took a look myself and called someone I know at Western PA Bank to confirm the account was opened and the amount missing was in there." Ben's tone was at an even keel, his face frozen into a calm, steady look, but Ted could see his eyes narrow with anger. "That's when we found out the account was in the name of Kelsey McCord, a minor."

"That's convenient, because Connor seems to be missing today and no one can find him to confirm your story," Ted snapped back. He wasn't going to hide his fury. Fear made bile rise up in his throat, but it also pushed him to realize Ben was seriously screwing him, and he decided he couldn't leave quietly.

"Connor's on vacation. I gave him some time off as I thought it would be uncomfortable for him when we fired you. We're letting you go, Ted. Leave your laptop and badge here on my desk."

Ted glanced at the picture of Ben and his wife smiling from a beach somewhere in the world. Soon, Ben would be gone with his embezzled money and living a life of luxury, leaving Ted ruined. He could hear his own heart thumping as if it were outside his chest. He took a deep breath to try to calm himself and pulled the lanyard with his security badge over his head. Laying it on his laptop, he handed both the laptop and badge to Dora in defiance of Ben's order, making eye contact with Ben. He hoped his look was hard, cold, and that when he spoke his voice would not shake. He wanted to give back to Ben some of the fear he was feeling, even if only for a moment.

"You're not going to get away with this," Ted said, keeping his voice even, his tone harsh. He heard Ben's phone ping and wondered if it was a text from his accomplices asking for confirmation that Ted had been taken care of and hung out to dry.

He looked at Dora. "You can walk me out and cut my last check, Dora, but it won't be long before millions are missing and Ben is nowhere to be found."

"Are you confessing to plans to embezzle even more, Ted?" Ben's face was red, his voice rising. Ted smiled. He realized he could be framed for a much larger scam if he wasn't careful, but it had worked. He'd gotten under Ben's skin just a little bit. He kept what he hoped was a smirky grin on his face, even though the feeling that his face was simply frozen in a clownish mask of sorts remained. Inwardly, his gut and his brain were churning at top speed. He needed to get out of here and talk to Leah. She worked at Western PA. She could check the records there, helping him prove his innocence.

"That's enough, Ben! That was uncalled for." Dora stood, holding Ted's badge and laptop. "We do need to let you go, Ted, based on the evidence Ben has presented. Let's avoid making a scene that requires me to call security. You'll come with me to sign a few papers and receive your final check, which we've prepared, then I'll walk you out of the building. I'll have one of your coworkers clean out your desk. We'll box up your things and send them to your home."

"I need to do a forensic review of that laptop, Dora." Ben looked worried for the first time. Ted guessed Ben had not closed all the loops in his setup. He resisted the urge to touch the USB drive he'd meant to hide in the apartment this morning but, instead, had dropped in his pocket while rushing to get out the door and on his way.

"I'm aware of the post-termination procedure, Ben," Dora said, her voice stern and cold. "You need to terminate Ted's access in the system and inform his team. I'll handle the rest."

Ted hoped his comments to Ben had sparked a question inside Dora as to who was telling the truth. "I didn't do this, Dora. I did not steal money. I demand an investigation before you fire me." His voice sounded thick, rough. He felt lightheaded.

"We can't do that, Ted. The logs show you did transfer company money into a personal account, and we have a verification from the bank that it happened." Dora maintained a business-like tone. He searched her face, her eyes, for sympathy, but she kept a closed countenance. Ted followed her, moving slowly, his knees awkward and rubbery. He turned around halfway through the open door, furious, searching for parting words, determined to fight his termination. Ben smiled at him and winked.

"You didn't actually think you'd get away with it, did you, Ted?" Ben's voice was so low he seemed to mouth the words. Ted knew Dora didn't hear Ben, and, if she had, she wouldn't have known what he really meant. Ted choked, unable to pull forth the words he longed to say but which he accepted, deep down, were meaningless now. He'd played poker with the devil and been beaten in the worst kind of way.

CHAPTER 6

"Want to join me today? I'm heading to The Abbey for coffee." Charlotte zipped up her backpack, hoping Grace would agree. For a moment, she felt the usual mild disappointment in herself that she always seemed to need someone else's help to sort things out.

It was close to three o'clock. She had an hour and a half before picking up Kelsey from day care, which was a couple blocks from The Abbey. A thought was formulating in her mind, but she wasn't sure yet what to do with it.

"Sure, I'll meet you there," Grace answered with a smile.

Twenty minutes later, Charlotte was placing her hands on unique door handles filled with coffee beans and opening the thick wooden doors of The Abbey on Butler Street. Grace had lived in Lawrenceville her whole life, long before it had become trendy with hip restaurants and coffee shops springing up everywhere. Ted rarely frequented this area, which meant, for Charlotte, it held a kind of private aura, a spot a bit separate from her marriage. Stepping inside, she paused for a second, out of habit, to read the "Eat, Drink, and be Abbey" sign over the inside door before scanning the coffee shop section of the restaurant and bar for Grace.

"Over here," Grace said, waving to her from a small table for two against the far wall, a few feet from a white marble fireplace, medieval crosses carved along the top edge and below the mantel. Ceiling fans, stilled from their constant summer rotation by the coming of fall, sat in massive, circular, overhead light fixtures suspended from the ceiling by chains. Charlotte dropped her tote in the empty chair across from Grace and sat down next to her.

"Let me order coffee for me and tea for you," Charlotte said.

Grace nodded and smiled. She was like a warm blanket, a safety zone for Charlotte.

The coffee bar melded into an alternate beer bar in a softened L-shape, its metal studded exterior reminiscent of a knight's armor flattened and rolled gracefully around a curve in a castle wall. Any somber church-like feeling that the ancient organ, sitting silently against the opposite wall, might have lent to the ambiance was countered with lyrics from the Beatles' *Abbey Road* album on a chalkboard above the cappuccino maker. Patrons inhaled modern meets medieval with the fantastic smells of coffee and blueberry lemon scones. Charlotte navigated around thick, brown leather chairs back to their table, carrying a French press espresso and an herbal tea for Grace. They sat in silence for a few seconds. Charlotte needlessly stirred her coffee as Grace waited calmly. She was a patient woman.

"Leah thinks I should go full-time at the museum," Charlotte blurted out, quickly taking a sip of her coffee, looking down. "She says I need to be independent and able to care for myself and Kelsey on my own if it's ever necessary."

"Did she have a reason for thinking you might ever find yourself in that situation?" Concern flashed across Grace's face. Charlotte had tried, once, to put her and her two friends together over coffee. It had only visibly reinforced to her the differences in the two women. Grace had been more wary than open and seemed hesitant later whenever Leah's name came up. After the one encounter, Charlotte had kept her friendships with Grace and Leah separate.

"I asked her for career advice. She's so successful, you know. I think she meant it as a precaution."

"Well, success is not always measured by the job title or the paycheck," Grace said, her tone even, noncommittal. "You're successful in ways that Leah is not."

"She grew up with parents who divorced. Her mother was an alcoholic and an itinerant artist," Charlotte said. "Life was uncertain and often out of control, so she gravitates to whatever puts her—and in her mind, me as well—in control of life."

"I won't lie, Charlotte. I really want you to take a full-time role and let me slide into partial retirement. And as long as you're making the switch because you like the work and the people around you, then I see the salary, benefits, and all the things that could give you independence if you needed it, as a bonus." Grace's smile and words projected the warmth and support Charlotte had been looking for.

"My sixth sense says there is something going on with Ted that has him very stressed. I want to ask him, but there's a difference between sixth sense and fear of knowing. We're so dependent on his salary, and I feel like, whatever it is, it centers around his job," Charlotte said, her ever-present concern always lurking, rarely suppressed despite her efforts to focus on herself.

"Do you think this is because of what you assume

happened or didn't happen between Ted and Missy in San Francisco?" Grace asked. She reached out and squeezed Charlotte's hand.

Charlotte sighed. "I've heard it from everyone that nothing happened between them, that they all got drunk and passed out in various places. It may have launched us into counseling, but that's now old news, and we're trying to work through how to balance his tendencies to be a workaholic with my wishy-washiness about where I want us to live and, I guess, what I want to be when I grow up. We're trying to get on solid footing."

"And are you . . . getting on solid footing, that is?" Grace asked.

Charlotte shrugged, unsure. Although she'd demanded they go for marriage counseling and try to fix what was wrong between them, she hadn't expected to have to face so much of herself in the process. It had been surprising and hurtful that Ted thought she was immature, a result of growing up easy and spoiled by wealth, and that he felt she had limited respect for his career. He'd told the therapist, his head down and avoiding eye contact with her, that he thought she was a great mother and wife but she needed to grow up. Even more astonishing to Charlotte, after every therapy session, they went home and had great sex, as if they were desperate, hungry, crawling back to each other after a grueling session that tore at the secrets and fabric of their marriage. Therapy demanded they step forward or lose what they had. Charlotte was pretty sure Ted hated it and, at this point, having crazy wild sex when they got home was what was keeping him going back each time a new session was scheduled.

"I think therapy is helping us . . . at least I thought it was," Charlotte said. "But Leah said he's been asking her strange questions about international money transfers and how they work. Stuff he doesn't mention to me. The old fears roll up and I wonder why he would go to Leah."

"Has Leah ever made a move for Ted? I can't see any similarity between the San Francisco trip, which involved drinking, and your husband connecting with Leah, your best friend, to ask what sounds like work-related questions." Grace was thinking like a mature adult. Charlotte paused before answering. She had a niggling gut feeling that something was wrong somewhere, whether it was Ted or Leah, but her head was telling her it was her own sad lack of confidence in her marriage and herself that was causing it.

"For the past month, I've noticed that Leah seems to know small, casual things about Ted before I do, and when I ask her about it, she says they're in the same line for coffee every morning before work and they talk for a few minutes. She acts as if it's nothing," Charlotte said. She hesitated, then continued. "It irritates me, but Leah can be irritating. Ted too."

"I agree with you . . . at least about Leah. I'm not a fan. But I firmly believe Ted loves you and he's not always smart about how he shows it."

"Well, we could argue about that, but you may be right," Charlotte said. "I was in the 61B Cafe on South Braddock a few months ago when I saw Leah and Ted leaving El Burro, the little Mexican restaurant across the street. It looked like an intense conversation, and all of a sudden I started feeling paranoid and insecure."

"What does all of this have to do with whether you'll take a full-time job?"

"I was embarrassed when Leah said their conversation was just about my upcoming birthday and I think, maybe, I do need to be more independent, mostly for my own lack of confidence, not because I want to leave Ted or anything like that."

Charlotte slowly ran her finger around the rim of the coffee mug, distracted. She could hear a little shake in her voice. Was she going to cry, right here in front of Grace, over something she wasn't even sure about?

"Why didn't you open the coffee shop door and wave to them?" Grace looked a little stern and perhaps disappointed, which hit Charlotte in the gut. She was angry with herself that her feelings were so disorganized and that, somehow, she couldn't evolve out of these basic fears. Her face flushed with shame.

"Would you like my honest opinion, specifically about Leah?" Grace leaned forward, hands wrapped around her mug, her eyes connecting with Charlotte in a firm, direct way.

Charlotte knew if Grace was being careful and asking first, her opinion probably wasn't good. She nodded. It couldn't be worse than what she'd heard from Ted and Shay.

"Leah's a piranha with men and maybe most people. It's the vibe she gives off, and from what I've seen and heard, it's a valid assessment," Grace said. "Who knows what her motives are for anything. But she appears to hold you, and Kelsey, separately. Her one sacred thing. Ted isn't included behind that partition in her head, but I doubt Leah would ever go after him or that she would be up to anything that might hurt you. What if she simply wants you to be in a more stable job situation, should anything happen to Ted, especially in light of her own childhood?"

Charlotte appreciated Grace's comments but couldn't see herself that way. She hadn't yet been able to separate herself from her role as a wife or as a mother, see herself as an individual, something she'd disliked about her own mother and swore would not be true of her when she began her adult life. She'd always envisioned herself as a very independent woman. And yet here she was, having gone from dependent on her parents to dependent on Ted, unsure of what to do with her education, unsure of who she was or if she could make it alone.

"Leah's independent nature and her ability to bring in a good salary are appealing to most men," Charlotte said.

Grace leaned in far enough to reach her arm around and pat Charlotte's shoulder. "Leah is . . . how shall I put it? More worldly. But you're finding your own power as an individual. Not for Ted, not because of another woman, just for yourself. That might eventually separate you and Leah, but it's a good thing for you." With a quick eye roll and shrug, she smiled. "Not a lot of men would be interested in someone like Leah. Someone who is that self-involved doesn't provide any balance in a relationship. Ted loves what you and Kelsey bring to his life."

"I know you're right, and if I'm honest, I'm pretty sure Leah has a new boyfriend." Charlotte shifted the conversation in an attempt to halt the whining, insecure path she felt she'd been rolling along since they'd arrived. "I think it's a married guy because she's being more covert and secretive this time."

"So what happened to Leah? How did she become the woman she is today, a woman you seem unsure about?" Grace sat back, arms crossed, waiting.

"I've known her since we were in grade school," Charlotte answered. "Leah was always outgoing, and I was quiet . . . a bookworm. Leah was always putting on an upbeat front to cover her inner sadness due to her home situation."

Charlotte closed her eyes and thought about how she'd

covered for Leah their senior year in high school when Leah rammed the fender of her car into a steel pole while driving drunk, switching places with her friend when the police officers arrived and stating it had been she, Charlotte, who had been driving and lost control. She'd passed all the sobriety tests given at the scene while Leah sat quietly in the car. She thought about sharing this with Grace, but it wasn't the answer to her question.

"You must see something there that keeps the friendship alive," Grace said.

"I see glimpses of the old Leah . . . when she's with Kelsey, who she adores, when she's casually leaving another failed relationship sure-footed and seemingly confident, but at other times I see something else in her eyes. A hardening toward people, closing doors inside herself and shutting down empathy." Softly, Charlotte added, "Leah doesn't have a lot of female friends. Women don't really like her. She needs me, in a way . . . I'm just not sure I feel the same way about her anymore or that I want to need her friendship in return. I have some guilt over that."

Grace nodded her head in quiet understanding. "So you've been Leah's family, so to speak, and she's been the outgoing friend who helps her quieter friend move forward?"

"Yes, I guess so, except . . ." Charlotte hesitated.

"Except?" Grace watched her intently.

"Over the years, as I went to college, got married, and had Kelsey, I moved in a different direction. Or at least I thought I did, until therapy and the recent realization I haven't gotten as far as I imagined," Charlotte said with a sigh.

"Quit worrying about what was said in therapy. Ted gave

his opinion, and, if you agree with it, then you work on it. If not, you tell him you're fine the way you are."

Charlotte nodded. "Anyway, I didn't need Leah the same way as we got older, but she needed me. She needed to unload about her revolving door of boyfriends but wouldn't take my advice. Her constant climbing over others at work brought out the worst in Ted when we were all together. They would drink too much, and then for weeks he'd be even more focused on his job as if they were in competition." Charlotte watched Grace, her face serious, wondering what she was thinking about all of this. "Leah was always looking for boys, then men, she thought would give her stability."

"She wasn't headed for a career?" Grace asked.

"I don't think so, not in the beginning," Charlotte answered. "She wanted a degree, and she had some scholarship money to help. But she craved a home, family, kids, stability. I think her mother's sober now, but that came much later. She met this guy in college. He was in law school, and his family had money. She went crazy for him. The few times I met him, I didn't think he was as into her as she was into him."

Charlotte paused. She stared down into her coffee, now cold, seeing that younger, softer Leah in her mind's eye.

"She got pregnant," Charlotte said. Even after so much time, her eyes watered with the deep sadness the memory brought. "Leah was ecstatic, sure they would marry. He told her to have an abortion, and she refused. There was a big fight, and he dumped her."

"That's when Leah started getting a bit crazy, talking about how she would have the baby and he would pay." Charlotte shook her head as if she were still standing in front of Leah, disagreeing. "I told her she was just a college student and she couldn't be a single mother too, not with so little family support. She was sure once she had the baby he would come around."

"What happened?" Grace asked.

"She miscarried. I was home for Christmas break, and we were out shopping when she ran to the restroom in the mall. She was cramping. I took her to the emergency room, then back to my house because my parents were out of town for a few days. She was never the same after that," Charlotte said, her eyes tearing up a bit at the memory. "And when she told the guy . . . well, he was an insensitive jerk anyway, so you can imagine how that went. At first, Leah simply ran wild, drinking, partying, then she turned all the anger and energy toward having a career. I'm probably the only person she trusts. And she loves Kelsey, but that . . . me having a baby . . . it shifted something between us as well."

Grace reached across the table and laid her hand on Charlotte's forearm. Charlotte reached up to wipe her eyes, then held her friend's hand on the table for a few minutes. "Many women go through what Leah experienced," Grace said. "It's terrible, and sad, and life-altering. But they find a way to heal. She's dependent on you to give her a feeling of normalcy, a small connection back to who she was, but I'm not surprised that she can't be friends with other women. In my limited interactions with her and what I've observed from working with you, Leah's world revolves around her wants and needs. I agree you would benefit by having more economic independence, for yourself and, in my opinion, personal independence from Leah. She triggers all of your insecurities. That makes it hard to move yourself forward."

"I can't just dump her. I'm not that kind of person." Charlotte traced the grooves in the distressed wood of the table.

"That's not what I meant." Grace hesitated, as if looking for the right words. "I meant back up from Leah, be busy, dive into a new full-time job. Take her advice, regardless of how she meant it when she offered it."

"Ahh, Grace. I wish you were my mother." Charlotte meant that more than she thought Grace could ever appreciate.

"You're like the daughter I never had. I don't think biology makes a bit of difference here," Grace said with a smile.

"Next time, let's meet at the bar instead of the coffee shop and have some wine."

"Sounds good to me." Grace stood and began putting her jacket on. "And Charlotte? You know my home is always open to you and Kelsey."

Charlotte stood and wrapped her friend in a hug, her quiet "Thank you" buried in the soft cashmere of Grace's scarf. "Well, hopefully it never comes to that."

She would email her acceptance of a full-time role tomorrow morning. Charlotte felt stronger just making the decision.

Halfway to the car, her phone rang. She pulled it out of her pocket, Leah's name appearing on the screen. She hesitated before answering, thinking of what she and Grace had just discussed.

"Hey, Lee. What's up?"

"Charlie, I have something difficult to tell you." A hesitation, a shakiness, was audible in Leah's voice. "Sometime happened at work today, and it involves Ted."

Five minutes later, Charlotte sat in stunned silence in her car, moving the words that had come from Leah's mouth around and around, her mind in disbelief but her gut telling her this was the missing piece. This was what Ted had been hiding from her. She exploded in anger, banging her fist on the steering wheel and yelling so loudly passersby stopped on the sidewalk and stared.

She hit Ted's name in her contacts list and waited, but it went to voicemail. "What. The. Fuck. Ted, how the hell could you do this? Call me back now."

CHAPTER 7

Ted walked into the lobby of Western PA Bank. He'd been here once before to chat with a loan officer about what level of home loan he might qualify for. That time he'd breathed in the beauty of the older building dating back to the early 1900s, its high ceilings and marble floors creating a hushed atmosphere as a dozen or so people, from tellers to customers, moved about. Today he barely looked around him as he focused on searching for Leah, his head swiveling right to left, scanning the room. Ted felt like an island of panic in a sea of normalcy. He began pacing, cracking his knuckles, until he noticed the security guard eye him with what felt like suspicion. He'd had enough trouble for one day. He was here filled with desperate hope that he could fix things and get his job back. With relief, he saw Leah stepping out of an elevator and walking toward him. She carried a small file folder.

"Hey, Leah, thanks for meeting me on such short notice." Ted shifted from one foot to another. "I really need your help."

"I shouldn't be doing this," Leah said. "And I'm not sure I can help you."

She seemed nervous to Ted as she looked around the lobby, then led him to a small grouping of chairs placed around a round table in a room too small to qualify as a conference room. She shut the door and handed him the folder. "Take a look, and then we can talk."

Ted laid the folder on the table and opened it. He could see Leah's foot tapping quickly on the floor as he looked down toward the documents and hear her fingernails clicking erratically on the tabletop. Minutes later, his stomach in a tight knot, his head throbbing, he gazed absently through the windows at the people in the lobby wrapped in their own troubles and triumphs, oblivious to Ted. His mind spun in a circle, shocked. The world he'd built was melting like a glacier, crashing in huge, resounding chunks and smaller fragments all around him. The stark overhead lights in the room illuminated the paperwork Leah had handed him. He could feel his hand shake a bit, and he struggled to stay focused, to prevent his mind from going completely numb with fear. The papers were marked as copies, but they were as clear as original documents. Ted could see it was all there, in black and white. A savings account in Kelsey's name, an electronic signature in his name as the person opening the account, deposits totaling three hundred thousand dollars made by wire transfers, then the money returned in lump sum to River City Trust two days ago and the account closed.

"I didn't do this." Ted slid the papers into his backpack rather than into Leah's open hand.

"You should give that back to me, Ted." Leah looked nervous.

"Why? It's a copy, for starters, and supposedly I opened

this account and I'm paying the price for that." Defiance overrode his earlier unsteady, frightened demeanor. This was his life, his job, on the line. To hell with rules and protocol.

"The bank regulators have contacted the Department of Justice, and they want to bring charges." *Tap-tap-tap.* Leah's manicured nails clicked on the arm of her chair.

"Ben said they would not press charges after they fired me." He clutched his backpack tightly, wishing Leah would stop fidgeting, tapping, and generally heightening the anxiety he was working desperately to channel into a firm stance. He'd thought she would shore up his fears and help him; instead, her nebulous response was concerning in a way he couldn't yet dissect.

"River City Trust isn't pressing charges, but Western PA Bank's a stickler for the law, and my boss is turning this over to the DoJ." She leaned forward, her hand out to indicate he should return the folder. He pretended not to notice.

"Then my lawyer will have a right to a copy of this information. Maybe the DoJ will end up figuring out how this was done to me," Ted answered.

He stood and opened the door, stepping out quickly and heading toward the lobby doors leading outside. He wanted out of there, away from Leah, away from the chaotic feelings churning within him. Everything seemed to be closing in. Ted wanted fresh air. He wanted to talk to Charlotte. This was a walking nightmare he couldn't shake off, run from, or deal with alone.

"You know I didn't do this, Leah." He was two steps ahead of her, but her heels were clicking behind him, following him. He was sure she was close enough to hear him.

"I want to think that, Ted, but you were asking me a lot

of questions about bank transfers over lunch not long ago."
She said this rather loudly, and Ted stopped, one hand on
the lobby door, then turned to look at her. He shook his
head in disgust even as she again whispered protests that he
not take the file. If he couldn't have a copy, why wasn't she
setting off an alarm or creating a scene? The panic inside of
him was matched only by his fury at having been so thoroughly duped by the very people he'd thought himself
smart enough to con. He'd played in too big a field with too
much at stake, and he'd been hoodwinked—bamboozled, as
his father would have said. He needed to talk to Charlotte,
but he not before he spoke to Shay.

He stepped out onto the sidewalk and began walking
quickly away from the bank, turning down the first alleyway
he saw, then making a couple more turns before he felt
hidden by the shadow of a large building. He leaned against
its cold brick surface, pulled out his phone, and saw text
messages from Shay and a missed call from Charlotte.

> Dude, where are you? What happened? ‼️

Ted hit reply.

> Can you meet me somewhere, asap?

Shay answered in seconds, and Ted provided a location.
He dropped his head to hide his face as tears ran down his
cheeks while he listened to the voicemail. He'd never cried
in public—his father had taught him that. But right now, his
anger, fear, and pain at hurting Charlotte were causing him
to cry in a way he felt unable to control. The only saving
grace was his location in a small alley, in the shadows, rather
than on a public sidewalk. He looked around, frantic for

someplace to hide and pull himself together. Was there a warrant out for his arrest? He wasn't sure how these things went, but crying in broad daylight, no matter how hidden he felt, wasn't a good idea. He wiped his eyes with the sleeve of his jacket, taking deep breaths and trying to quell his anger, to think beyond his pain and fear. Carefully circling back to where he'd parked his car, he ducked into a nearby Starbucks and headed for the bathroom. Once inside, he splashed water on his face several times, struggling to calm himself and find some inner level of control. His eyes were red and swollen, but after a few minutes he was composed enough that there were no tears. Stepping out into the coffee shop, Ted realized it was surprisingly empty. Grateful for the quiet environment, he ordered a coffee, then sat down at a counter seat near the window facing the street and called Charlotte. No answer again, only her voicemail.

"Hi. I'm guessing you heard from Leah. I lost my job today. Please . . . please, Charlotte, know they set me up. I didn't do this, and I want to talk to you . . . to explain. I love you and Kelsey, you have to know that."

She would know he was serious. A chronic serial texter, he rarely left a voicemail, let alone one so panic-driven, but he needed to know he hadn't lost her over this.

God, where should he begin to fight back, to unravel this house on fire he stood in the middle of, his life burning around him? He felt something poke his upper thigh and reached into his pocket, the smooth plastic of the flash drive in his hand. Where could he hide it as quickly and safely as possible?

Ted could see Leah from his window seat standing outside the bank, on her phone. Suddenly, a black BMW pulled up, and she got inside. As it pulled away, driving past him, Ted thought the driver looked a lot like Bob Thornton, the senior finance manager at River City Trust he knew was knee-deep in the embezzlement scheme with Ben, but he wasn't sure. That didn't make sense. Nothing made sense today. He was so tired, and he was convinced if he let go of his emotions for one minute, he'd lose control and break down again. He needed to turn the anger into fuel to propel him forward until he could figure out where to turn for help.

Thirty minutes later, Ted parked near the Guardian public storage facility on Centre Avenue in Shadyside where he and Shay had agreed to meet. Charlotte rented a small storage unit here for some art, family heirlooms, and other items they couldn't fit in their apartment and were saving to use when they bought a home. His footsteps echoed as he walked through the empty building.

Charlotte had never opened this storage locker in the three years since they loaded her extra stuff in it, which is why he'd hidden the box containing two copies of solid evidence in the locker six months earlier. A quick glance assured him that nothing had been moved—the printouts and hard drive backups as proof of what Ben and Bob were planning. He'd thought of it as protection for himself at the time. Too bad he hadn't been savvy enough to assume they might turn the tables on him, knowing he had so much damaging information. Now he needed a safe place to hide both copies. They had to stay out of Ben's hands, and a storage locker in his wife's name could very well be opened under warrant or perhaps broken into. There was no one he trusted more than Charlotte, but after today's events, he was determined to shield her wherever possible from his mistakes. Ted thought about Leah getting into the BMW. Could she be involved? Did she know about Charlotte's storage unit?

Shay also had a storage unit here. An only child, after his mother died earlier this year, he'd struggled to find a solution for the furniture and personal items he wanted to keep but couldn't fit in his small condo. Ted suggested putting it in storage. Shay now had a big unit on the other side of the facility. Ted didn't think he'd ever bothered to mention to Charlotte where Shay stored his mother's belongings, and she hadn't asked. Still, he couldn't be sure. Maybe he had dropped the information casually and then forgotten. Which meant he also didn't know whether something this insignificant would have been mentioned to Leah. He was looking for a hiding place neither Leah nor anyone associated with her could find, and Shay's storage locker was one of two options he thought would work. But while waiting for Shay, Ted began to have second thoughts. He shouldn't drag his friend into this, and, following what he'd seen with Leah, his instincts told him to trust as few people as possible with as little as possible. He pulled two thick manila envelopes out of the box, tucked them in his backpack—now nearly empty without his work laptop—and threw the box back in the storage unit, closing and locking the door. The second option was the only one he could fully count on to be a foolproof hiding place.

"Ted?" He heard Shay calling from the elevator area.

"Over here."

Shay rounded the corner, moving quickly toward Ted, his face tense, concerned. "What happened?"

"What did they tell you?"

"Just that you had been let go," Shay answered. "No explanation, and Ben told me I was temporarily to take over your responsibilities until they sorted everything out."

Ted looked down at his feet, then up to the ceiling before

looking Shay in the eye. "Does Bob Thornton drive a BMW?"

"What? Why are you asking that?"

"Does he?"

"Yes, why?"

Ted had an odd feeling as if everything should be obvious, yet somehow he was missing a piece in a dangerous puzzle. "Something's wrong, but I can't put my finger on it."

"You were fired. That would be what's wrong," Shay said. He grabbed Ted by the shoulders, and Ted was unsure whether Shay was about to hug him or shake him in frustration. Instead, he simply stood there for a moment, silent, brows furrowed with concern, then patted Ted's shoulder and let him go.

"They said I embezzled funds into an account at Western PA Bank set up in Kelsey's name," Ted explained. "I didn't do it! Since Leah works there, I went straight from the office to see her. It's all there in the file . . . but I didn't do it."

Shay leaned against the wall, arms crossed over his chest, and looked away from Ted as if needing to process this on his own. "Shit, dude . . . what do you think happened?"

"When I left the bank, I texted you, then ducked into a Starbucks nearby to call Charlotte and wait, out of sight, until coming here," Ted answered. "I saw Leah getting into a BMW, and I could have sworn Bob Thornton was driving it. But it couldn't be. That doesn't make sense."

"You got bigger things to worry about right now, buddy, than whose car Leah's riding in." Shay turned to face Ted once again. "Is River City going to press charges?"

"No, no. The money was returned, and I'm fired, career ruined. But someone at Western PA verified I opened the account, then Western PA turned me over to the Department of Justice. I swear I didn't do it." He was repeating himself. He felt dazed, his anger dissipating into confusion and a pounding headache.

"Did you tell Charlotte?"

"Leah must have told her. She left me an angry voicemail, and I tried to call her, but no answer." Ted crouched down, head between his hands, forehead on his knees. "I don't know what to do."

"Go home, Ted." Shay grabbed his arm and pulled him up. "I'm not sure how I can help you, but I'm still your friend, and I think the best thing you can do right now is go home."

"Do you believe me?" He wanted to clutch Shay's arm as if it were a lifeline. For a moment, he felt an odd desire to beg his friend to believe in him. But he was still Art McCord's son, and so he stood, arms straight, hands clenched, waiting stoically for an answer.

Shay stood silent for a few seconds. "Yes, I believe you. But I don't understand why . . . why would someone set you up out of the blue like that? It doesn't make sense."

Ted closed his eyes to avoid the disappointment and anger he felt sure he was about to see on Shay's face. "I did something I shouldn't have. Not this, but something else. I was . . . I was desperate, and now . . ."

"This is some sort of payback? Spit it out, Ted," Shay said, his tone incredulous, shock and concern evident on his face. "What did you do?"

"I'm not sure it matters now. Just know I didn't tell you or Charlotte, or really anyone, to keep you out of it."

"Bullshit. You knew we'd be angry at whatever you did. Well, I'm here, and I'm involved now. I mean, why ask me to meet you at a storage locker unless you needed to hide something?" Shay looked angry. Ted should have known that, of all people, Shay would be suspicious, would demand truth. He took a deep breath and faced his friend. In his mind's eye, he could still clearly see the information that had started everything, that brought him to this moment. The results of an investigation on his computer screen which might have been inscrutable to most but came together for him like puzzle pieces, quickly showing a clear picture with only a few gaps remaining.

"Back about seven or eight months ago, HR put in a request for an investigation of a guy in the Clarion branch office. I deployed the software package against his laptop's asset tag number like we normally do to monitor what he was sending out to his personal email account and whatever else he was doing."

Ted paused. "The request came in at the end of the day, and I was in a hurry. I needed to make it to a marriage counseling session. I made a typo when inputting the asset tag number and deployed the package to the wrong laptop."

"That happens sometimes," Shay said with a confused look. "I can't see how that would get you here."

Ted was silent. His next words might mean Shay would walk out and that would be it, the end of a friendship.

"So whose laptop did the package land on?" Shay looked unnaturally still, as if holding back a storm inside him, waiting for Ted's response.

"Ben's laptop." Ted let that sink in for a minute, then took the plunge. "What I saw is in the envelope and on this flash drive."

"Oh, man . . . oh, man . . . what did you do?" Shay's fists were clenched and he looked miserable. Ted could see he didn't want to hear the rest, but there was no way out now.

"I went to Ben with what I'd discovered and told him

that if he gave me the promotion to Carl's old job, I would keep quiet about it."

"You didn't report him?"

Ted shook his head. He looked away, anywhere but at the disgust in Shay's face as he processed what Ted was telling him.

"You blackmailed a VP to get a promotion because you couldn't get it on your own?" Shay smacked his open palm against the wall. "Ted, I don't know you. I don't know who you are, putting everything on the line."

"I knew it was wrong, but at the time I thought I had good reasons."

"What reasons? Not that I'm sure I'll believe you when you tell me."

"You do know me. I'm still the same person. I did it for Jesse, to cover the fact that I drained our house fund to bail out the ranch for him. I kept that from Charlotte. I needed the promotion—the salary increase—to rebuild it, fast."

"This gets worse by the minute. You lied to me, to Charlotte, and to Jesse. You blackmailed another person. And you expect what from me, from any of us, right now?"

"If I were you, right now I'd be thinking that I'm getting what I deserve," Ted said. "Maybe I am. One lie led to another, and here I am. But I did not steal money. They set me up."

Shay looked at him for what felt like much longer than a few seconds. Ted could see the struggle on his friend's face, and his gut told him Shay was thinking about whether to walk away or give him a chance.

"What did you find out that was so huge they would give you a promotion and then do this to you?" Shay asked. "Part of me, even as I ask that, is wondering if I really want to know."

"I'll tell you, but then it puts you in an even tougher position because if you try to turn them in, they'll lash back at you too." Ted watched Shay's face, so stern, and wondered if he was leaning more toward concern or disgust. Probably a combination of both.

"Is Connor involved?" Shay's green eyes flashed with his increasing level of anger.

"Yes. Connor's been helping Ben, Bob Thornton, and some external third person that I couldn't identify."

Shay closed his eyes and shook his head with a look of disapproval. "Connor . . . I knew he was up to no good. Okay, tell me."

"Ben, Bob, and this third person were planning to embezzle millions into a Cayman Islands account and leave the country. I'm pretty sure Connor was doing the work behind the scenes for them, but after I confronted Ben, he circled the wagons around Connor and cut off my visibility there," Ted said. "They were going to set Geri up to take the fall. Everything stopped once I called Ben out on their plans, told him what I knew, and got the promotion. I figured they would still do it, and then, once they did, I'd turn them in."

"A blackmailer who then turns hero and gets, what? Yet another promotion?" The bitterness in his friend's voice was clear. Ted felt the weight of what he'd risked and lost beyond the job sitting on him like a heavy mantle. They might salvage a friendship over time, but he wasn't sure the respect Shay had had for him would ever return.

"I know it's impossible to believe, but that's not what I was thinking at the time. I thought I would make up for not reporting them right away by eventually turning them in after I'd straightened out my personal funds. I've been terrified, sick, over what I've done and what it could cost me."

"What it has cost you, you mean."

"The ranch was in deep financial trouble. It's all Jesse has."

"Why didn't you tell Charlotte? Be up front, give Jesse some money or cosign at the bank with him. He owns the ranch. It's his responsibility," Shay shook his head in disbelief as if Ted's choices made no sense.

Ted sighed, the exhaustion of everything rolling over him in waves. "Actually, Jesse doesn't own the ranch. My father made sure of that. A couple more years, and I can sign it over to Jesse, which I'll do gladly. But the ranch goes under, and it's my credit rating that is destroyed."

"I still don't get it. Why not come clean with Charlotte about this?"

"I can't tell anyone why my father refused to leave the ranch to Jesse and locked me in four years of ownership. You may not believe me, but everything I'm doing is to protect Jesse from the hurt that that truth, that secret, would bring." Ted hesitated, tempted to finally unburden what he'd carried with him for so long. He'd lost so much today in things he should have placed more value on, things he now thought he had perhaps taken for granted, like the friend standing in front of him and a wife who, until today, he'd been sure would never leave him. "And if Charlotte found out I owned that ranch, she'd insist we move back. But the ranch is going to Jesse, no matter what my father's dying wish was."

"So Charlotte doesn't know whatever this big secret is either?"

"No, and it's better that way." Ted let go of the struggle. He couldn't bring himself to share this with his friend, and in that he accepted the flaws in their friendship, in his marriage, came more from him. Even in this moment of realization, he froze, tucking everything inside.

"You've built a house of lies, Ted. I'd say your decision-making on what is better probably won't cut it based on your current track record." Shay looked furious. He shook his head and shifted, his back now facing Ted. "I'm leaving."

"It depends on how you view the best route to the right thing," Ted answered. "I thought I could do this without hurting anyone I loved. I was wrong."

Shay faced him, hands clenched. "No offense, but these guys were too big, too far up the chain, for you to try to play games with them. And you may have protected Jesse, but you've definitely hurt your wife and daughter, and yourself, in the process."

Ted's knees felt weak. A chill ran through him in opposition to the moderate temperature in the building. He sat on the concrete floor, back against the wall, and put his head on the backpack in his lap. Tears trickled down his face, defying his best efforts to hold them back. "I know I hurt our friendship too." He heard a sob, like a hiccup, a strange sound coming from within him, and he closed his eyes.

"I don't understand, with all the money Ben makes, why he would want to steal money and leave the country. It doesn't make sense." Shay was still standing there, despite declaring he was leaving, waiting quietly for Ted's response.

Ted was silent, unable to find his voice. He wiped his eyes and struggled to regain some level of composure.

"You documented everything?" Shay asked.

"Yes. Ben thinks I gave him the original and no copies exist."

"Did you leave the proof at the office?"

"No, no . . . I've been an idiot, I admit that now, but I'm not that stupid." He pointed to the storage room door. "I just pulled two copies from there because it's in Charlotte's name. They won't find anything on my laptop."

"Okay, let's put them in my storage locker."

Ted took a deep breath. "I considered asking you to hide one for me, but it's too much of a risk for you. I know what I've done to our friendship. You don't have to stay involved with me, I just wanted to tell you myself, in person."

"What you did . . . I'm disgusted, furious. Part of me wants to punch your lights out and walk away. The other part knows . . . or I think I know . . . who you are underneath all of this. Heart in the right place, head and decisions all messed up."

Ted stood up and put out his hand to Shay. It was shaking slightly. "Besides Jesse, you're the best friend I've probably ever had. I'm sorry."

Shay shook his hand, arm around his shoulders in a half hug. "Let's go." He started walking toward the elevator. His storage unit was located one floor above.

"Are you sure?" Ted felt he was asking himself as much as he was Shay.

"Yes, I'm sure," Shay stopped and turned, eyeing Ted. "If you had doubts about trusting me, then know that I'm making this decision fully aware of what it could do to me if I'm not careful."

Ted nodded, then slipped his arms through the straps on his backpack and followed. He'd created a world where he was now begging for morsels from the few people left he could trust.

They stood quietly in front of Shay's locker as he entered the combination and unlocked the door. "Here you go," Ted said, handing an envelope to Shay. "One in your locker, one goes somewhere else. I'm keeping the file I took from Leah for a while to see what I can figure out."

"I'm investigating this too, to see if I can help," Shay said as he opened the drawer to an old desk and lifted a latch, revealing a false bottom with space below. He neatly slid in the envelope and dropped the latch over it. "Make a copy of that Western PA file for me."

Ted put his hand out to Shay, then surprised his friend and himself by giving the other man a quick hug. "I appreciate that, brother. But I don't want them doing to you what they did to me. Storing the evidence for me is enough."

"You and Charlotte have been my family since my mother died. I want to help," Shay said.

Ted hesitated, his mind struggling with the wish that he not endanger his friend and the desperate need to have someone on his side as he tried to unravel the predicament he found himself in.

"Okay. But be careful if you're going to investigate. Be very careful," Ted said.

"Go home. Talk to your wife and fix whatever she heard from Leah," Shay said.

Ted nodded in agreement. He had no words for the level of gratitude he felt.

"And stop carrying whatever that secret is around with you. It's corrosive, man. Let it out into the world and share the load with your wife."

Ted stood silent for moment. "You're right. What if I tell you, and then you tell me if I should lay that on her as well?" Ten minutes later, Ted finished, watching Shay's face as it went from disbelief to a softening of sorts.

"How long have you kept this to yourself?" Shay asked.

"Since I was eighteen years old." Ted shifted his backpack, shuffling his feet, waiting as his friend absorbed his words. "Do you see now?"

"I see, to a point," Shay conceded. "Yes, you should tell

Charlotte and Jesse both. And what you did was still very wrong, regardless of your intentions." He pulled the door down on his storage unit and locked it. "Go home, Ted. Find out what's left and fix what you can. We'll be in touch."

Ted had one more stop before he went home. It was the safest place he could think of to hide the second envelope, somewhere the people who set him up, and were probably hunting for any evidence he had, would never consider. Fifteen minutes later, he walked into Staples and stepped up to the UPS counter, their smallest shipping box in his hand.

"Do you have a piece of paper?" he asked the clerk.

As Ted walked through the parking lot to his car, receipt in hand, he knew even if his package was tracked to Jesse, they'd never find it. They were McCords. He'd simply written "Hide this" on a note taped to the envelope. Jesse would know, instantly, it was a secret needing to be kept. Ted could see him lifting the trap door in the barn, placing it in the iron box below, then rolling a large mat and equipment back over the top. No questions asked, no answers needed.

CHAPTER 8

Ted heard Charlotte's voicemail warning about the break-in just as he entered the building, before he reached their apartment. Even so, he was not prepared for what he saw. The apartment was ransacked—cushions off the couch, cabinet doors open in the kitchen, his personal laptop gone. Ted touched an app on his mobile phone and, with a few quick clicks, erased the laptop remotely and then reported it stolen, an automatic, reflexive action for any cybersecurity expert that a normal person might not think of until it was too late and the device had been hacked. It would be tough for the thief to figure out his login, then there was his two-factor authentication to work through. He'd know if they got that far because a text would come through on his phone. By the time the jerk managed to gain access—that is, if they got in—everything would be erased. He hadn't stored anything work-related there anyway. What they were looking for was safely hidden.

"Mr. McCord?" Ted turned to see two Pittsburgh police officers standing in his doorway. He'd been too stunned at the scene before him to remember to close the door.

"Yes?" Panic was rising inside Ted.

"Your wife called us when she got home and saw this. She left before we could arrive, but she came down to the station to file a report; said she didn't want to wait in the apartment, but needed to go somewhere she felt safe. She left the address of a Grace Winters with us."

"Yes, I know. She left me a voicemail." Ted was relieved that Charlotte and Kelsey were safe with Grace.

"Your wife seemed to feel you might know who did this?" The police officer gave Ted a fairly unfriendly stare.

"I lost my job today, but . . . hmmm . . . I don't think there's a connection," Ted said, his voice tapering off to a mumbled response.

"You feel this was work-related?" A guy in a dark-colored suit—unbuttoned and revealing a holstered gun as he moved—white shirt, and conservative matching tie came in and moved around the officers to address Ted.

"No, no, that's not what I said," Ted answered, eyes averted, hands shaking and tucked in his pockets. He hoped he seemed more certain than he felt. "I'm a little stunned right now. I can't think. I need to go, to find my wife and daughter and check on them."

"Well, I think I'm going to need to talk to you first." The man was obviously law enforcement of some type, but not Pittsburgh Police. He watched Ted with a steady gaze while the police officers, both a good deal bigger and more muscular, stood blocking the doorway.

"Then give me some space to give her a call." These guys were serious, and they weren't going to let Ted out of the apartment until he satisfied some of their questions. Distrust coursed through him at the sight of them watching him. His first priority was to speak to Charlotte and make sure she and Kelsey were all right.

"Sure, sure . . . mind if we look around while you do that?" This guy seemed a lot friendlier than the officers. Still, Ted wasn't going to trust anyone at face value.

"Could I see your badge?"

The man nodded, slipped his hand into his suit pocket, and held the badge in front of Ted's face. Startled to see the words "Federal Bureau of Investigation," Ted heard himself gasp, panic surging through his body. "What's the FBI doing looking into a simple burglary?"

"I can't answer that for you right now. Okay to check your place out?"

Ted nodded and moved to a corner of the kitchen that felt slightly private. He didn't really care who took a look around his home, he just needed to talk to Charlotte. His neighbor from downstairs stood in the hallway, peering into the apartment and at him.

"Could you shut the door?" Ted asked the police officer.

One officer went out into the hallway, shutting the door behind him and leaving his partner in the apartment. Ted could hear him asking if the neighbor had seen or heard anything as he tapped Charlotte's name in his phone directory and waited for her to pick up the call.

"Ted? What's going on?" The fear in Charlotte's voice was palpable. He felt a deep, penetrating rage at whoever had done this and disgust with himself for dragging his family into his dark and dirty work secrets.

Ted avoided the question. "How is Kelsey? She must be terrified. Are you both okay?" He needed, desperately, to know his family was all right and that the small pieces of his life he might still have—Shay, Charlotte, Kelsey—were not lost to him forever.

"She's confused, and she's been asking for you. I got her to lay down and take a nap, so for right now she's fine."

Ted shut out the mix of fury and fear he could hear in Charlotte's voice, and allowed a simple, deep sense of gratitude to wash over him at finally being able to speak to her.

"You didn't answer my question, Ted. It's bad enough you lost your job, and, if what Leah said you did is true, I don't know what else to say. But why was our apartment broken into the same day? Is there even more that you're not telling me?" Charlotte was pure anger now, and Ted knew he had to explain, but they needed to be alone.

"I'm not sure why our home was broken into. I am sure that River City Trust accused me of something I didn't do," Ted answered. "It's hard to talk right now. The police are here, and, strangely, some FBI guy is here too, looking around the place."

"I've convinced Kelsey we're having a sleepover at Grace's house. I haven't told my parents. I don't want them involved yet," Charlotte said.

Neither of them spoke as Ted struggled with the weight of the tension between them.

"Please, please, hold off telling your parents or believing what Leah has told you until I can explain to you. I can't do that right now." Ted was keeping his voice as low as possible, but the police officer had stepped back inside the apartment and the FBI agent was now standing only a few feet away, waiting. "Charlie, you're probably safer at Grace's for now," he said, raising his voice level and working to sound as normal as possible. "I'll have this cleaned up by the weekend so you can come home."

"Leah says you did this. She says she's seen the proof." There was an icy quality to Charlotte's voice. "Is that why our apartment was trashed?"

"I don't know." Ted wanted to tell her the full story in person, not with police and an FBI agent close enough to hear him. He struggled, trying to get her to let it go until they were alone. "Do you believe Leah?" The minute he said her name, the FBI agent turned his head, focused and obviously listening.

"I'm not sure I trust Leah any more than I do you at this point."

Ted felt a sliver of relief. He didn't know why, but for some reason Charlotte was not fully open to Leah's version of things."

"Seriously, Ted. What if Kelsey and I had been home when they broke in?" Charlotte sighed, then sniffled, as if she were crying. "I feel like there's a lot you're not telling me. It's not just the apartment or whether Leah—who, yes, I don't fully trust—is right. It's the lies, Ted. You had to have lied to me about something, maybe a lot of things."

"I'd rather we talk about this in person . . . alone." Ted could tell the FBI agent was pretending not to listen as he tapped his iPad. "There are too many people here right now. I need to see you."

"We've had our issues, Ted, but we had a nice life. We had love, our child . . . I have to think about her now, only her."

"Please, Charlie . . . don't say 'had' as if it's over. As soon as the police leave, I'm coming over to Grace's house and we'll talk."

"I'll let you know when I'm ready to talk. Right now, I don't want to see you. I don't know if I can do this anymore. Don't come over here."

There was a firmness in her voice, despite the emotion, that scared him. "I have to see you. We have to talk. I'm coming over there, and if I have to sit outside all night waiting, I will." Ted felt his voice rising. The officer was looking at him, concerned.

"Do not bring this drama to Grace's home, Ted. I'll agree to come by the apartment tomorrow—just me, not Kelsey—and we'll talk. I'll text you when I'm on my way."

Ted wanted to protest. He wanted to scream, beg, but she'd hung up the phone. He turned to the FBI agent, all the fury inside him clamoring to punch a wall or throw something across the room, and focused on the stranger standing in his living room.

"What's your name, and why is the FBI here over a burglary?"

The man's eyebrows rose at the hostility in his voice. Ted was barely under control. He felt as if he were holding tightly to a relief valve that was backing up and ready to blow.

Ted watched the agent say something to the police officer in a voice too low for him to hear. The officer nodded, took the agent's business card, and left, closing the door behind him.

"My name is Nate Morgan," Nate said, laying his badge on the kitchen table and motioning to Ted to pick it up and check for himself. "Did they take your personal laptop?"

Ted nodded as he fingered the badge tentatively, then dropped it back on the table in acknowledgement and looked at his phone. "I have a tracking app, but it doesn't appear to be showing where the laptop is right now."

"I'd like to ask you a few questions," Nate said, pocketing his badge. "First, let's put some of your furniture back together."

Nate walked into the living room and began setting cushions and furniture in order, continuing to talk to Ted. "The police will interview people in the neighborhood. I told them I needed to talk to you alone."

"I'm in a world of trouble, aren't I?" For the first time in many years, Ted wished he could pack up and go to Montana. Instead, he set the couch in its place, reinserting the cushions.

"Yes, you probably are in a good bit of trouble." Nate righted a lamp that had tipped over.

Ted made what sounded like a jumbled cry of despair covered by intentional coughing, his clenched fists an outward display of angry denial. "I'll get the rest later," he said, motioning to the hallway leading to the bedrooms. He returned to the kitchen table and sat down. "Okay, let's talk."

Ted wasn't ready to trust Nate. One thing he was sure of was that he would proceed carefully now. He wasn't going to incriminate himself any further. Ted had no intention of telling this guy what he'd found or how he used it to get a promotion until he'd sorted a few things out for himself. For all he knew, Nate was as dirty as all the rest of them.

"Anything on your laptop you think someone would want?" Nate asked calmly, seating himself at the table.

Ted considered whether mentioning he'd wiped the device clean would sound incriminating. "Our personal financial information, apps connecting to our medical records, stuff like that," he answered, pulling out a chair and sitting across from Nate. "In my profession, it's standard to immediately wipe a stolen laptop remotely, whether work or home. I think you know that."

"And you did that?"

"Yes, just before you arrived. I used an app on my phone."

Nate jotted a few notes. "Was it backed up to the cloud?"

"Yes, it's all there. Once I can get a new laptop, I'll download our personal files and apps."

"You realize that information may be requested at some

point?" Nate was watching him closely. Ted tried to breathe evenly, hoping he didn't look like what an FBI agent would classify as suspicious.

"If there is a court order to produce it, I'll be fine with that. Like I said, there is nothing to hide, but it is our personal information—bank accounts, identification numbers, things like that—so I would like to be careful and protect that from hacking or compromise of any type."

Nate nodded in what looked to be understanding or agreement. Ted could feel him shift gears. "Let's start with Leah Hanson. She's your wife's friend, right?"

Ted nodded in affirmation.

"She signed the verification for Western PA Bank that you'd set up an account in your daughter's name into which you embezzled funds, and yet she is the first person you went to see today. Why?" Nate was still staring at him with an intensity that made it hard for Ted to maintain even a minor outward appearance of calm.

"Leah signed off that I'd embezzled money?" Ted asked. Panic rose inside him at the knowledge that Leah would do this without so much as warning him or defending him; that she'd not even told him it was she who confirmed his supposed guilt when he sat right in front of her asking for her help. No wonder Dora believed he'd done something criminal. He'd not only been played, he had played right into their hands. "How do you know I went directly to see Leah? Were you following me? Or maybe you're working with them too."

Nate was quiet for a moment. Ted thought he might be trying to gauge Ted's reaction to his response. "We've been following a number of people, including Leah, as part of a larger investigation."

Ted stood and began pacing, running his hands through his hair. He wanted to scream, to throw a chair or hit the wall. Anything to expel the fear crawling over him like an army of ants, making his skin tingle and his nerve endings quiver. "Leah said Western PA was filing charges with the Department of Justice. Is that why you're here? To arrest me?"

"I can't give you the specifics regarding exactly why I'm here," Nate said. His voice was steady, but Ted sensed the wheels turning inside the FBI agent's head, deciding carefully how much to say. "I'm not here to arrest you. It's part of an ongoing investigation."

"You said that already," Ted snapped. "Yes, Leah is my wife's friend. Do you know something about her that I should know?"

"I'm pretty sure you know some things I need to know."

"Well, either it's an even exchange here, Nate, or I'm not talking to anyone today without a lawyer." Ted was nervous but determined. He'd been screwed over by just about everyone except Shay and Charlotte. His last stint with negotiating had backfired, landing him in this current pile of shit, so he wasn't confident in his abilities, but he couldn't just fold to this federal agent. His instincts told him he needed the guy's help.

"I can't make you talk or share confidential case notes," Nate answered, closing his iPad and standing up. "But know that I'm here to try to help you, and I'll be back. At some point, you'll have to talk to me."

"If you're not here to arrest me, then please leave," Ted said, his voice dropping to a whisper.

He knew, deep down, he should talk to Nate, open up, ask for help, but he was a McCord. He'd hoard his secrets a while longer, see how much he could figure out on his own. Turning his back on Nate, he walked down the hallway and began straightening up the bedrooms until he heard the front door open and close, a police officer calling to him to come back to the kitchen and give a statement.

CHAPTER 9

The process servers arrived in tandem at ten the next morning, just minutes after Ted had finished the last touches in putting the apartment back to as normal a state as possible, hoping to calm Charlotte's fears and convince her to return home with Kelsey. River City Trust was bringing a civil suit against him, contradicting Ben's assurance that no charges would be filed. Ted figured either HR had refused to go along with Ben's request or Geri was pushing through her own agenda. He was pretty sure Ben wanted the spotlight off of this until he could safely grab the money and run with Bob Thornton and their mysterious third partner. The Department of Justice was following up on Western PA Bank's complaint, but no decision had been made about whether to file charges, according to the attorney Ted had called yesterday and who he would meet with later today.

Ted slid the papers into a desk drawer. He didn't want Charlotte to see them. Another quick, hard rap sounded on the door, and he approached cautiously, looking through the peephole. Nate was standing there.

"Who is it?" Ted wanted to be sure.

"Nate Morgan. FBI."

Ted opened the door a crack with the chain lock in place and double-checked before he removed the chain and let the man inside.

"Looks a lot better in here." Nate sat down on an armchair with a good view of the door and pulled out his iPad.

"Listen, my wife will be here in about an hour," Ted said. He sat on the far end of the couch, away from Nate. "Could you please be gone by then? We need to talk privately."

"Sorry, Ted, but we need to interview your wife as well," Nate answered.

"My wife doesn't know anything. Leave her out of this."

"I want to help you. I think you know why what happened here occurred, and you aren't telling me everything." Nate tapped a stylus on the side of the iPad, casually crossing one leg over the other.

"Did you know you're not my first visitor this morning?" Ted leaned back, arms crossed over his chest. "A process server came with a notice that my former employer is suing me, and Western PA Bank has filed a complaint against me with the Department of Justice. My wife will be here later to tell me she's leaving me and taking our daughter with her unless I'm able to talk her into staying to navigate a lawsuit, unemployment, and potential bankruptcy from the legal fees. It's highly unlikely I'll convince her to stay. Where can you help me, Nate?"

"I already spoke with the DoJ lawyers, and the complaint will sit on hold, no arresting you, due to our ongoing investigation. So, you get a break . . . for now," Nate replied, rolling the stylus between his hands. "I can share some of my investigation with your attorney to help him build a defense. It's up to you."

"So it's 'you scratch my back and I'll scratch yours'?" Ted asked. He felt a palpable level of bitterness toward the world right now, and this FBI guy was going to take the brunt of it.

"Can we start by agreeing to what we both know is true? That this was not a simple burglary?" Nate watched him again with that intense gaze that seemed to align neatly to the close-cropped, military-style haircut, clean shave, and perfectly pressed shirt. Giving in and working with this guy might bring some relief. Ted was so tired of worrying, tired of being unable to trust, tired of carrying this ten-ton load of his own creation. And yet, this was a federal agent in front of him, and his mind pushed to override his emotions and insisted on caution.

"Okay, I concede it probably was not a simple burglary." Ted felt he could give him this much. Not necessarily meeting Nate halfway, but it was an olive branch of sorts.

"Yesterday, after a chat with my supervisor, I obtained a small level of clearance to share some information with you that may help you to trust me, or at least to feel willing to speak more openly with me," Nate said. "I get it. The last twenty-four hours have not put you in the state of mind to trust or cooperate."

Ted stood up. "I'll tell you what. You fill me in, ask questions, and I'll make coffee." He needed to keep busy, to move, and to turn away from Nate's direct gaze, giving him space to exhale and think.

"Good enough." Nate followed him into the kitchen. "We've been investigating specific activity at Western PA Bank for a while on a tip from a bank regulator. Your connection with Leah Hanson, not this burglary—although it's probably linked in some way—is why I'm here. First question . . . do you think you were set up to take a fall, or did you do what you're accused of doing?"

"Set up," Ted replied as he pulled the bag of ground coffee and two mugs out of the cabinet. "By Ben Keene and Bob Thornton."

"Were they trying to transfer money for themselves, or was this a separate move to roll you under the bus?" Nate asked.

"It's definitely a roll under the big wheels of the bus." Ted poured water into the coffee maker and dropped a filter in place. "They're planning a big embezzlement heist, although I'm not sure they'll go through with their plan now. Evidently, they wanted me out of the way."

"Why didn't you report them . . . turn them in?" Nate was typing on a small keyboard attached to his iPad now.

Ted sat down, silent, the popping, gurgling sounds of the coffee maker in action filling the room with a familiar morning smell.

"Did you blackmail them, Ted?"

Nate was nothing if not direct. And he was no fool. "I needed a promotion and the money it would bring," Ted said, arms crossed defensively over his chest. "For personal reasons. It wasn't that I didn't deserve a promotion, and Gerilyn Leslie, my nemesis at River City Trust, continued to do everything possible to make sure that didn't happen. I couldn't keep waiting because our family ranch, which my brother runs, has been in some trouble for a while. So, when I found out, by accident, what Ben and Bob were up to, I said I would stay quiet about what I saw if they promoted me. I told myself I was just making a deal."

Even as he spoke, Ted could feel the shallow nature of his words, his thoughts, the arrogance in any defense of his actions, no matter how seemingly mild.

"I know it was stupid, wrong, desperate. Pick any word that works for you." Ted met Nate's gaze directly, aware he needed to quell his ego, hoping he seemed as sincere as he felt.

"Right, and the deal backfired," Nate said. "Was this Gerilyn the ringleader?"

Ted could feel the temptation niggling at him. It would be so easy to say yes—he hated her that much—but lies were what had landed him here in his kitchen desperate for help from an FBI agent who might deep-six him instead. "Ben Keene, the VP who fired me, is the primary person leading this stuff. He's the one I confronted. I know he's been working with Bob Thornton in Finance on a scam. There could have been others."

He'd chosen not to say yes or no about Geri. Let her hang out there with the unnamed "others" for a while, even though he suspected there were plans in place to use her as a cover or deflector when they finally tried to pull off this heist.

"What about Connor?" Nate asked. He had been typing furiously, but now he paused.

"Connor?" Ted asked. He got up and poured two cups of coffee. He hadn't mentioned Connor. How did Nate know about him? "Cream or sugar?"

"Black is fine," Nate said, taking the mug from Ted.

Ted sat down and slowly sipped the hot liquid. It made him feel alert. "What do you know about Connor?"

"You first, Ted. Then I'll answer your question."

"Connor reports . . . sorry, reported, past tense . . . to me," Ted said. "He's what we call a pen tester and you might think of as a white hat hacker. He checks the company systems for vulnerabilities." Ted wanted to nail Connor and say his actual job was being a gopher for Ben, but he needed

Nate's help, although needing Nate and trusting him were still two separate things. "He's what I'd call more street smart than the average cyber geek. Most of his work centers on direct requests from Ben."

"Your neighbors described someone looking a lot like Connor as being here around the time your apartment was ransacked," Nate said.

Ted shook his head, fists clenched. Shay was right when he claimed the little shit wasn't out of town with family. While he was getting fired, losing his livelihood, his career, Connor was lurking in the wings, doing Ben's dirty work. Every new revelation added to the realization that he was at the bottom of a huge pile-on, fast becoming a total hack of his existence. Despite his churning stomach and the tension headache now starting to drum a steady beat at his right temple, Ted stayed silent, drinking his coffee and working to keep his face as composed as possible. Privately, he was thinking about how it would feel to squeeze Connor's neck until he choked, although he'd put down a bet that Connor was actually gone—skipped town with a nice fat wad of cash compliments of Ben—and wouldn't surface anytime soon, if ever.

"So, you've had your eyes on Connor too?" Ted could hear the angry tension in his own voice. He struggled to keep his usual ability to hide his thoughts and feelings intact.

"You said Connor is an experienced hacker? Could he have hacked Western PA and created the account you claim was used to set you up?" Nate took a drink of his coffee and waited, ignoring Ted's question.

"Connor knows how to hack River City's internal systems as part of normal checks to make sure the security controls in place are good, but he's not talented enough for something that complex," Ted answered. "His ego is bigger than his abilities. I don't think there's any way he could've slipped past the firewalls and proxy servers at Western PA to hack into the system, open an account, and transfer money."

Nate nodded. Setting his coffee mug down, he wrote in a few more notes. "The first thing you did after you were fired was go to see Leah Hanson. What was that conversation with Leah like? I assume it was about the allegations against you that resulted in the termination of your employment."

Ted shifted uncomfortably in his seat.. If he took too long to answer, Nate would suspect he was hiding things, leaving parts of the conversation out. But he wasn't ready to unload everything to the FBI. Nate would have to live with the shortest answers Ted could provide for now.

"I went to see Leah because the account in Kelsey's name was allegedly in the bank where Leah works. I thought she could help me prove it was a hoax or tell me who set up the account. She's the only person I know working at Western PA," Ted said. "I've trusted her in the past, due to her friend-ship with my wife."

"And did she help you?" Nate was no longer typing. Ted sensed it was a throw-away question, that Nate held the answer already.

"No, she showed me the file, and it looked like I'd done what they accused me of. The signature was digital, not written by me. Not that I think anyone checks that sort of thing anymore." A deep flash of anger, like a lightning bolt, ran from his stomach up to his lungs, causing his chest to tighten in fear and anxiety at what people who were against him could do in the future. "It was obvious she thought I did it. She didn't believe me."

"And then what?" Nate eyed him closely, making Ted tense all his muscles in an effort not to squirm.

"And then nothing. I took the file—it was a copy anyway —even though she asked me not to, and I left."

"Did she call security? Did she report you for taking the file?" Nate was too calm. Ted thought he looked like the cat that caught the canary, but he wasn't sure who that canary was . . . himself or Leah.

"No, she didn't. I thought that was weird."

"Uh-huh." Nate nodded in agreement, smiling as if he enjoyed what he was hearing. "Did Leah know Connor?"

"I don't know. Ask Connor." Ted shrugged, trying to look disinterested. He intended to hold back a few facts from Nate until he could investigate for himself, but he suspected Nate was pretty far ahead of him and wondered what the FBI's investigation had uncovered.

"I'd love to, but it seems Connor's disappeared. Cleaned out his apartment and moved on with no forwarding address. We're looking for him.," Nate said. "You said you'd trusted Leah in the past. What did you previously trust her with ?"

Nate kept shifting gears, from Leah to Connor and back again. Ted would have to be on his toes with this guy.

"After my promotion, I kept wondering how exactly Ben and Bob would pull off embezzling money. I knew I'd have to turn them in just before they did it or as soon as it happened." Ted traced the rim of his coffee mug slowly with his right forefinger, remembering Leah's agitation at his questions. "I asked Leah hypothetical questions about how international money transfers could be set up, how they worked in general, and asked her not to say anything to anyone. She said it was possible but unlikely that anyone could do it and get away with it. They'd need someone to open offshore accounts for them in another name."

"And did she? Tell anyone?"

"Not that I know of. At least she didn't tell Charlotte, Charlotte's parents, or any of our friends." Ted felt growing concern that Nate not only didn't seem surprised, but that he'd stopped taking notes and his demeanor had shifted from inquisitor to something more aligned with sympathy. "You stopped taking notes. This is something you already know enough about, and you think I shouldn't have trusted her. I get that much. Why?"

"How did Leah act when you asked these kinds of questions?" Nate deflected so smoothly that Ted was already answering while he realized what had happened.

"Stressed. Agitated. Wanted to know why I was asking." Ted shrugged as if it were not a surprising response. "I told her I was simply trying to understand this to be better at managing my new team members who test the company systems and run investigations if anything is suspicious."

Nate tapped his stylus on the table, the repetitive sound irritating Ted's frayed nerves. "You assumed she accepted that explanation and moved on?"

Ted nodded a silent "yes." Leah never brought his questions up again, and he'd had no more discussions with her. He'd assumed, until now, that it was nothing much, that she'd been stressed because he sounded like he was looking for information as part of planning some nefarious action.

"You pressured Ben, thinking he probably couldn't do what he was planning and get away with it?" Nate leaned forward, stylus silent, his gaze serious.

Ted was silent.

"Or you knew he would get away with it and then you'd be the hero for blowing the whistle and turning in the evidence."

Ted remained quiet, staring at Nate. He could feel his leg twitch, his foot tapping the floor. He'd been intent on carefully spooling out small bits of information, enough to make a connection with Nate that would result in the agent, in turn, helping to exonerate Ted. Now paranoia and distrust filled his senses, tightened his gut, and made him unsure.

"A little of both, I guess," Ted finally answered. "I didn't think Ben could do it now that I was on to him. And I didn't think he had anyone to set up the accounts offshore. But on the off chance he tried and succeeded, I would step in to investigate, and, sure, it would have helped my career."

"I think it's your former career now." There was a faint tone of disgust in Nate's voice that Ted took as condescension and resented, his nostrils flaring, his face flushing, heated with anger.

"I don't need you to remind me, Nate. I fucked up, big-time, all over the place. Whatever I thought then is wiped out along with everything I lost yesterday. My only hope is I didn't lose my wife," Ted snapped. His voice sounded loud even to himself as he realized how transparently the FBI agent could see what he'd done. Anger rolled through him, as it had often over the last twenty-four hours, like a wildfire in a California forest. Nate's blunt, flippant tone, as he laid bare Ted's failures, was more than he could endure on top of everything else. "Who knows? Maybe one day I'll be like Mandiant or the *Catch Me If You Can* guy."

"Doubtful," Nate replied, nearly scornful. "You got your promotion, you went off and did your job, and one day they called you in and fired you for allegedly embezzling money into an account in your daughter's name."

Ted hesitated for a minute. "Times up, Nate. Your turn. I've answered all your questions, so what is it you know about Leah that's taken us from supposedly talking about a break-in at my apartment to an intense focus on her?"

"I can tell you we're investigating her and, specifically,

whether she has a direct connection to either Ben Keene or Bob Thornton." Nate looked uncomfortable as he shifted in his chair. "Are you aware of any connection between Leah and either of those men?"

As he had numerous times since yesterday, Ted saw again in his mind the moment when Leah entered a car driven by a guy he now was more sure than ever was Bob Thornton. He felt his eyebrows go up and his eyes widen the moment it clicked for him, the thing Nate was avoiding telling him.

"You think she's the third person in the embezzlement scheme, don't you? The person who'll set up the offshore accounts. The pathway for Ben and Bob to pull this off." Ted leaned forward, energized and more than a little proud of himself that he'd figured it out so quickly.

"I'm simply asking what connections you've seen between Ben and Bob and Connor and Leah, or between Leah and Connor with anyone that you might think is worth telling me."

"We've now moved beyond what you have clearance to tell me, is that it?" Ted smiled for the first time that morning. He stood, walked to the coffeepot, and brought it back to refill their mugs. He was ready to hear what Nate had to say, if he could get him to give up even a little information.

"There's something else that you know, something you saw, that would help here. You know it, and I know it. I'm asking you to tell me what it is." Nate seemed hungry for the information. For a few seconds, Ted felt a subtle shift of power before Nate brought him crashing back into the reality his own situation had trapped him in. "You need my help, Ted. And I can't help you if the people who you believe set you up disappear without a trace."

Ted deflated like a balloon, giving in to the desperate

need for aid from a person with actual power who could turn at least some part of this hell around. "After meeting with Leah, I left the bank and ducked into the Starbucks nearby to call Charlotte. While sitting there, I saw Leah get in a BMW driven by a guy that looked, from a side-angle view, like Bob Thornton."

"On a scale of one to ten, how sure are you that it was Bob Thornton?" Nate asked, now writing on the iPad with his stylus.

"Seven, maybe eight," Ted answered.

"Have you asked Charlotte if Leah ever mentioned him?"

"No. Leah got to Charlotte first. My wife . . . she does say she doesn't fully trust Leah. I'm not sure why. But she doesn't necessarily believe me either, and she's pretty angry right now."

Nate was writing quickly, head down, intense. Ted felt a nervous rumbling in his stomach that had nothing to do with hunger.

"And your wife is in the dark about why these guys set you up? About what you did?" Nate asked.

"That's why she's coming here, today, to talk this through," Ted said. "I wanted to go by last night and set the record straight with her, reassure my daughter, but she said she would refuse to see me. I didn't think it was a great idea for my daughter to see her parents fighting. I'm not expecting forgiveness, just the chance to tell her the truth and see if there is any hope for us."

Ted's voice sounded strangled, as if he were choking, and his whole body was tense with the effort to hold in the tangle of emotions pounding inside, punching him in the gut, the head, the heart. Until yesterday, he hadn't broken down and cried since was a boy, after he'd been bullied by bigger boys and come home desperate for sympathy only to be told to "man up" by Art. The ensuing lessons from his father in boxing and fighting had served him—a skinny, lighter-weight kid—well, and the next time the problem arose, he'd earned respect with his abilities to take bigger boys down. He appreciated the silent wisdom shared via Art's terse comments and the punching bag hung in the barn, but he'd never forgotten the longing for a hug or a kind word that remained absent. All these years later, he felt that longing again. He'd been bullied by Ben and lost spectacularly, but neither brains nor brawn would serve him well this time. He needed someone more powerful to step in.

"I'm exhausted, Nate. I know you want to talk to Charlotte, but I doubt she'll agree when she gets here. Any chance you could leave? I'll ask her to call you."

Nate nodded calmly, closing up his iPad and pulling his coat on. "I'll be in touch, Ted. Get some rest."

The cloak of secrecy and fear that hung across his shoulders whenever he faced Nate diminished as the door closed behind the FBI agent. Ted exhaled deeply, folding his body into the nearest kitchen chair. He hadn't realized until he was alone how hard he'd been working to hold everything in—his breath, his rage, his pain. He laid his head on his arms on the kitchen table and sobbed for the loss of his wife, his daughter, his career, and for the deep, ratcheting fear that he had not yet hit rock bottom. Once he reached that point, he could only pray he would see a ladder leading out of this dark pit of lies.

CHAPTER 10

Nate had been gone about thirty minutes when Ted heard the front door open. Charlotte stood there, dark circles under her eyes, trailing a large suitcase that she lifted a bit too easily. It was empty, waiting to be filled. She closed the door behind her, and they stood, silent, unsure who would begin what was certain to be the worst conversation of their marriage.

"I'm sorry." Two words that couldn't begin to encompass everything he wanted to say or how it felt to see her after agonizing over whether she would ever speak to him again.

"I'm here to pick up a few of our things." Charlotte slid the suitcase forward, its wheels clicking lightly, and began walking toward the bedrooms.

"I thought you were here so we could talk, so I could try to explain." Ted began to follow her.

Charlotte half-turned, looking over her shoulder at him, mouth set in a grim line. "I'll pack, then we'll talk."

"Don't . . . please, Charlie. Don't pack, give me a chance to explain first." She was already in Kelsey's room. He could hear the drawers opening and closing.

Ted turned back and took a deep breath. He looked around the kitchen, restless, nervous, wondering what an appropriate peace offering would be. Coffee, tea, beer, or wine? Probably not the latter. He filled the tea kettle with water, put it on the stove to boil, and dropped tea bags in separate mugs. It gave him something to do—pulling out spoons, sugar, milk, honey—rather than sit and listen to the last vestiges of his wife's presence here, in their home, being zipped up into a container to transport away from the rubble of their marriage.

She returned a few minutes after the tea kettle whistled out its notice of readiness. Choosing one of the two steaming mugs on the table, she sat in the chair furthest from his, added honey, and stirred aimlessly, eyeing him.

"Talk, Ted. Explain this to me, all of it."

Ted searched her face for the wife he knew—soft, unsure at times, always working to fix things and make their family better. He missed her desperately in this moment when he felt he was staring at a tough, determined stranger. Not a shred of emotion beyond anger visible. She unzipped her coat but did not remove it. The suitcase sat at the door, patiently awaiting her. Nothing he said was going to make her stay, at least not today.

"First, I didn't open an account in our daughter's name at Western PA Bank and then embezzle money from my employer into that account," Ted said, trying to keep his voice firm but hearing the shaky quality that, since he'd been fired, crept in and out at will.

"There's no way they did this to you out of the blue . . . for no reason. Either you're guilty as charged, or you did something to cause this to happen. I'm not so naive, Ted, that I can't figure out it's unlikely you're totally innocent."

Ted wrapped his hands around the warm mug to steady the tremors in his fingers, moving up his arms. The moment he'd hoped would never come. The moment he'd worried about and dreaded, not only for what he had to admit, but for what he would still hide from her despite Shay's advice to come completely clean. One remaining secret that would require a lie to add to all the other lies, each one crushing the fragile remnants of hope he now clung too, in spite of the damage he'd done.

"About six or seven months ago, I was asked to drop a monitoring package on an employee's computer," he said. "HR suspected them of sending confidential information outside the company. The request came late in the day. We were supposed to meet for our first counseling session, and you told me not to be late."

"So this is my fault?" Charlotte's face flushed, her hand clenched in a fist on the table.

"No, no. That's not what I'm saying. Let me finish." Ted took a deep breath, then a sip of tea. "I hurried, and I made an error . . . a typo."

Ted paused, looking down and then around the room. Charlotte sat silent, waiting. She was not going to make this easy.

"I saw something by accident . . . a plan, a scheme really, to embezzle money from River City Trust and send it to three offshore accounts—one for Ben, one for Bob Thornton in finance, and I never figured out who the third person was. Someone from outside the bank who would help with the international money transfer."

He watched Charlotte absorb this, her face softening to curiosity. "Is this why you were asking Leah about international money transfers?"

"Ahh, so Leah told you." Ted sighed. "Yes, I was trying to identify the third person working with Ben and Bob."

"If it's true that they set you up, Ted, is it retaliation because you reported them? And wouldn't they be fired based on what you learned, or if there was doubt, wouldn't that at least be taken into consideration before firing you from your job?"

Ted saw her anger shifting from him to River City Trust, and he wished he could lie right then. Let her believe this. Put hope back on her face and into this situation. Instead he would have to drop a bomb that was probably going to shred any hope of her forgiving him.

"I didn't report them. I told Ben what I discovered and asked for the promotion."

Charlotte became still, so still he wondered if she'd heard what he said.

"Why?" she whispered.

One word. The word that was going to mean he had to deliver a half truth, half lie, to keep one more thing from her in order to protect Jesse. He felt a deep and abiding anger toward his parents that was as strong today as it had ever been for saddling him with their secret.

"The ranch has been doing poorly for two years. The bank was going to call in the loans, and Jesse would go under, lose the ranch he loves, lose everything. I gave him our savings, our house fund in my company credit union account, to bail him out. I needed the promotion to rebuild the account, and, since Gerilyn Leslie got in the way every time I'd tried to move ahead in the past, I took this opportunity. I made a mistake."

Ted put his hands over his face. His wife's stunned look made him want to hide, to drown in shame.

"So you chose to leverage them rather than report them,

Ted? Seriously? What the hell were you thinking?" Rather than yelling, which was what he'd expected, her voice was like ice—a quiet fury he'd never heard before coupled with shock and disgust. It was coming at him, crawling over him like the north wind. He feared it was the sound of the death knell to their relationship.

"I know it's hard to see that I was trying to do right for the people I love, now that it's so clear I made a bad decision, but I love Jesse and wanted to help him, and I love our family and wanted to do better for us—buy us a home." His plea was not softening his wife; her face, her body remained tense, rigid.

"Why didn't you just tell me about the ranch? I might not have agreed to drain our savings . . . savings we were going to use to buy a home. But we could have cosigned on a loan for Jesse. That's valuable property he owns, and with a cosigner, he could have found a way. Maybe your sister would have chipped in as well." Charlotte's righteous confusion was, strangely, softening her anger somewhat. Ted felt a level of melancholy slide across him knowing what he now had to tell her and how much personal hope for reconciliation this could wipe out. Yet another piece of the ongoing price he was still to pay for his many corresponding layers of deception.

"I own the ranch," Ted said. He could give her that much. "My father left it to me when he should have given it to Jesse. The will doesn't let me sell it, or sign it over to Jesse, for four years."

Charlotte shook her head, disbelief playing across her beautiful face. "And if the ranch failed, it would be your credit rating that tanked, ensuring we couldn't qualify for a home loan?"

"Pretty much." Ted's throat constricted around his words.

"Were you going to tell me this at some point? That we own McCord Ranch?" Anger flashed from her eyes to him, and her face flushed a dark pink now, one hand around the coffee mug, the other clenched in a fist.

"Technically, 'we' don't own McCord Ranch. I do. And I have no intention of keeping it . . . or of moving there."

"Meaning you weren't going to tell me because you didn't trust me to work through this with you. You thought I would selfishly push to move back to Montana, that I wouldn't even try to help or understand. Damn you, Ted!" Her eyes watered, her look of despair combining with a tight, angry jawline.

Ted nodded helplessly, unable to find the right words, devastated by the combination of pain and anger he'd caused.

"Why would your father allow Jesse to help him run that ranch and then leave it to you with a stipulation that you couldn't sell it for four years, knowing you don't want to run the ranch?" Charlotte looked askance at him, clearly disbelieving his story.

"I don't know, Charlie," Ted said. He felt the weight of the lie, the guilt he couldn't seem to put aside even as he convinced himself that at least he'd told her as much truth as he felt he could. "He was a stubborn old man. He wanted me to come home, follow in his footsteps."

"Does Jesse know what you did to bail him out?" Charlotte's eyes narrowed. He knew she was suspicious that he and his brother had concocted this scheme.

"No. All he knows is that I gave him our savings but I was promoted and able to replenish the money."

"You asked him not to tell me?"

"Yes. In his defense, he didn't like it, but I said it was between us."

"All the bad feelings between you and Art, the tension and ill will, had nothing to do with him choosing you over Jesse?"

"I had no idea what his dying wishes would be. I was as shocked as you are right now." He was trying desperately to stick to a place where he could be truthful, and this was the truth. If he had known about Art's will, they would have had an argument to beat all the many disagreements in their past.

"And now we have no marriage and no savings? And ending up back at the ranch you've been running from since you were eighteen may be the least of your worries. You may end up in prison."

Ted winced at her assumption they no longer had a marriage, the pain physical as well as emotional, and felt his body tremble at the thought of years in prison. "I've almost rebuilt our entire savings over the past six months."

"Except now you're going to need it to hire a lawyer, and pay for your own place if you're not living in a cell soon." She looked so angry, the truth doubly harsh coming from her.

He reached across the table, trying to take her hand—still clenched and resting on the table—but she pulled away, shoving both hands in the pockets of her coat, her shoulders hunched, defensive.

"I really want us to find a way to fix this, fix us," Ted said. "I don't want you and Kelsey to move out, or us to live apart. I love you. I'm sorry."

Again, he could hear the words as they must have sounded to her—lame, ridiculous. No one would take anyone back after doing what he'd done. If he gave her the whole of it, the real reason beneath it all, she would be even angrier at him for the secret he'd kept, not just from her, but from Jesse.

"Finally, you mention Kelsey." Charlotte stood and walked toward the suitcase. "We, her parents, are supposed to teach her right from wrong, not by doing something so horrifically wrong that she's ashamed for the rest of her life, but by setting a good example. You must be delusional, Ted, if you think she's living in the same house with you after this." She swept her arm in a half circle around the apartment, and, even though he'd straightened up most of the intruder's mess, he understood what she meant.

"Don't leave, please. We can tell her together, somehow. Although I'm not sure at her age what she'll understand."

Charlotte turned to face him, her hand gripping the suitcase handle tightly, rigid, furious. He wondered if she would spit on him or throw the suitcase at him because, by the look of her, she wanted to.

"We're not telling her what you did. She's seen us have enough arguments. She's only five years old. I'll tell her we had a very big fight and we're not going to live together anymore." Beyond her anger sat the pain on her face at the thought of having to try to explain this to their daughter.

Ted nodded, defeated. "Where are you planning to live? Please say I'll still be able to see you and Kelsey."

"Here. We're going to live here, once you move out. You don't have a job, so you can't pay the rent. We're on this lease for another nine months. I start full-time at the museum next month and can make the rent. And Kelsey needs the stability of the home she knows and the neighborhood and school she loves."

Pieces of him were sinking, splintering inside, resulting in a terrible headache matched only by the physical pain radiating from his heart to his lungs and back again. "Okay. I'll be out in a week," Ted said. He lowered his head into his hands, listening with his eyes closed.

"Where will you go, Ted? I need to know it's somewhere safe for Kelsey before we work out arrangements for you to see her." Charlotte's nails tapped an angry cadence against the suitcase handle.

"With Shay, if he'll let me, I guess. Just until I figure something out." Ted was not at all sure Shay would take him in, but it was the first and only solution that he could think of right now.

"Was Shay in on this with you? Did he know?" He could see the level of fury, her anger seething directly at him.

"No, he's as angry with me as you are. But he believes I'm innocent of embezzling. He's going to help me investigate and hopefully exonerate myself." Ted watched her, praying his face looked as hopeful as he felt. Would she believe his innocence knowing Shay was willing to stand by him?

Charlotte snorted in derision. "Good for him. In that case, he's not as angry as I am."

One hand on the suitcase handle, she reached for the doorknob. The desperation to keep her here, with him, ran deep.

"Charlie, an FBI agent named Nate Morgan wants to talk to you. They're not investigating me. It's something to do with a larger investigation going on . . . of Ben Keene, I think."

"That has nothing to do with me." She opened the door to leave.

"He asked a lot of questions about Leah. I'm not sure what the connection is there, but I'm pretty sure he wants to talk to you about her." Ted watched her carefully, curious what her reaction would be to this news.

Charlotte closed her eyes and shook her head as if to toss out all the confusion and disappointment, the mess he'd just dumped on her, and the addition of Leah to everything else she was shouldering. Then she turned and walked through the door without another word, closing it behind her.

CHAPTER 11

"Hello?" Charlotte answered on the second ring, glancing at Kelsey, who was glued to the television where *Frozen* was playing on DVD.

"Hey, how's my favorite sister-in-law?" Charlotte reflexively smiled at the sound of Jesse's voice—the rich, deep, easy tones deceptively hinting at a mellow demeanor—then frowned in the realization that he'd probably been in on all that Ted had kept from her, possibly more than she was aware of.

"Not so good. I'm guessing you heard."

"Yeah, I know a little bit." She could hear the hesitation and discomfort in Jesse's voice.

Charlotte walked into the kitchen. The television volume was loud enough that it was unlikely Kelsey could hear her conversation. "Are you calling to apologize?"

She and Jesse had developed a great friendship over the years. Charlotte had one brother who covered all the ambitions her parents had for both of their children. An international lawyer, he was firmly entrenched in London with a British wife, no children, and an upscale European lifestyle. She saw him about once a year, and each year they found they had less and less to talk about beyond a cursory catch-up, their commonalities firmly centered in the past rather than the present. She'd always considered herself closer to Ted's brother than she ever would be to her own, until Ted was fired and she realized there were limits to her relationship with her brother-in-law.

Jesse was quiet for what was probably no longer than a heartbeat but felt lengthy, heavy. "I'm sorry he didn't tell you I came to him for money, sorry I felt I couldn't go against my brother and share with you what was going on. I told him we shouldn't hide it from you."

"And the fact that you haven't actually owned the ranch for, what, a couple years, but you let me think it was yours? Were you okay with that too?" Charlotte was surprised that, so far, she'd been able to keep her voice even—shaken, but not displaying the fury she felt. "Not cool, Jess . . . you know that, right?"

"I know, I know . . . none of this was cool, or fair to you." Jesse's voice cracked a bit, and he attempted to cover it up with a cough. "If I say I didn't want to keep anything from you, that would be true, but it makes me sound like I'm a weakling putting all the blame on Ted. Truth is, I told myself you are his wife, and if he wanted to handle it his way, keeping secrets or whatever, I should keep my mouth shut. I asked him to be straight with you, and he said he would eventually tell you. But I wanted everything out in the open. I know, now, I should have insisted we hide nothing, maybe even refused the money unless he came clean with you. Hindsight is twenty-twenty, I guess."

"Is there anything else my husband is hiding? Something maybe it'd be good to tell me now?" She could hear the sarcasm in her tone, a jarring, uncomfortable harshness that resonated through her body.

"You know everything I know." Jesse sounded sad, his voice low and laced with concern. "I hope you can forgive me, Charlie,"

Her anger toward Jesse slowly dissipated. He was waiting for an answer, but she wasn't yet ready to pull the words forward. She heard what sounded like him shuffling papers, then he cleared his throat a few times.

"Is Ted there with you?" Jesse asked.

"No, it's just me and Kelsey. We're staying with my friend, Grace, temporarily until Ted moves out of the apartment." Charlotte felt a surge of lonely desperation each time she said this to anyone.

"Are you sure that's what you want? I mean, I know things are bad, but I hate for you to be managing everything alone."

Charlotte believed deep down Jesse meant well, but it grated on her nerves that he assumed she needed Ted. "Did Ted ask you to call me, Jesse?" The sharp edge in her voice was followed by a few seconds of tense silence.

"Yes, but I planned to call anyway," Jesse answered. "I'm not here advocating for Ted. I'm checking on you, and Kelsey."

"I can manage on my own." She sat down to stop from shaking at a level that was making her knees feel wobbly.

"I believe you, Charlie. But you're not alone. I may be a few thousand miles away, but I'm here for you." His voice cracked with emotion, a sincere plea that nearly moved her to tears.

"He lied, Jesse, blackmailing his boss to get a promotion

so that he could help you keep the ranch afloat." Charlotte saw, through the kitchen doorway into the living room, Kelsey turn to look at her, eyebrows scrunched with concern. She realized she'd been loud enough to rise above the television's volume. She smiled at her daughter and waved until Kelsey turned back to her movie. "I know you McCords are private, but I never saw any of you as deceitful. I'm trying to digest all of this. Right now, I feel pretty foolish and naive." Charlotte was whispering now, but the rage in her voice encapsulated everything she'd endured since Ted was fired. If Jesse were in front of her, she'd slap him.

"I swear to you, Charlotte, I had no idea that Ted did not get that promotion fair and square. The first I learned of all of this was when he called me to tell me he'd been fired." Jesse made a sound that might have been a sob, which was so out of character for him that she softened.

"Enough, Jesse." Charlotte sighed, then took a deep breath. "I forgive you. That offering doesn't extend to Ted though." She stood and leaned against the kitchen counter for support against the faint feeling of vertigo that the panic rising up within her was causing. "You know the FBI wants to talk to me? Have they called you? I'm terrified this whole thing is worse than I thought. That Ted's done even more than I know about."

"I haven't heard from anyone but Ted so far." Jesse's voice sounded tired now, as emotionally drained as she herself felt. "But Ted told me he didn't think the FBI was investigating him. It sounds like they're interested in what he knows about your friend Leah, which is probably why they want to talk to you."

A stillness sat between them that lasted a few seconds, yet felt longer. Charlotte was sure Jesse could hear her breathing as, eyes closed, she channeled her yoga instructor and took a few deep breaths in her nose and out of her mouth. Relief that Ted was not under FBI investigation mixed with dread of what Leah might have done. She didn't want to be involved.

"Charlie? Are you okay?" Jesse's concern emanated across the distance, flooding her.

"I'm not sure what feeling all right is anymore. I just know I don't want to take on any more than I'm already dealing with." Charlotte sat in the nearest chair and lay her free hand against her thigh, gripping the flesh through her jeans in an attempt to stop the shaking. "Kelsey's confused as to why her daddy isn't living with us, my parents want to hire a divorce lawyer for me, and I've just found out my husband's capable of deception I didn't think possible. The last thing I want to do right now is talk to the FBI and find out something equally painful about Leah."

"You feel like a bomb went off in your life." Jesse spoke with the certainty of someone who understood, and she wondered what life crisis had led him to empathize so firmly with her.

"That about sums it up," Charlotte answered. Her voice didn't sound much better than her clenched, white-knuckled hand felt.

"You and Kelsey are the priority right now."

Something in Jesse's voice—smooth, soft, filled with concern for her and for Kelsey—broke a dam within Charlotte, and she lost control, sobbing quietly, unable to either get words out or hit the button and hang up the phone.

"Charlie? Charlie . . . take a deep breath. It's going to be okay."

Charlotte opened her mouth and closed it, like a fish out

of water struggling valiantly to breathe, jerked violently into a situation where oxygen was plentiful but that wasn't what it needed to maintain control. She needed to go back. Back in time, back to safety and security, yet there appeared to be no way home.

"Charlie, I'm going to sit here on the line with you as long as it takes until you're okay."

"I . . . I . . ." Charlotte stammered, then tried again. "I can manage." Kelsey was standing next to her now, patting her shoulder, fear on her little face.

"Mommy, why are you crying?" Kelsey's voice trembled, and she pushed herself against Charlotte, wrapping her arm around her mother's neck.

"Hang on, Jesse," Charlotte said. She set the phone on the table and hugged Kelsey. "Mommy is just a little emotional this morning, but I'm fine. Uncle Jesse is talking to me, and when we're done, I'll come and watch the movie with you."

Charlotte rubbed Kelsey's back for a few moments, then walked her back to the couch and covered her with her favorite blanket, kissing the top of her head. "I'll be right back, baby."

Returning to the kitchen, she took a deep breath before sitting down again and picking up the phone. "I'm back."

"Can you call someone to come over right now?" Jesse asked. "I don't want to hang up and leave you like this."

Charlotte felt ashamed at the clinging sense of desperation running through her. She didn't want Jesse to hang up; this phone was her lifeline. When cut, it would shred the thin veneer of control she felt right now and send her into a tailspin.

"I know you have to go, and I need to sit with Kelsey,

make sure she's not upset, but I don't want you to hang up."
God, she sounded so pathetic.

"What about your friend Grace?"

"She'll be back soon, I think. Sorry, I sound so weak."
Charlotte heard a car door close outside. She could see the
front door from where she was sitting and, through the
glass, Grace coming up the steps, then turning the doorknob to let herself in. "Jesse? Grace is home. I see her
outside opening the door."

"Listen to me, Charlie." Jesse's voice was firm, strong.
"None of this is your fault. You're the victim here."

"I still think he's keeping a secret of some sort," Charlotte said as she heard Grace opening the front door.

"You think he's still hiding something from you?"

"Yes. I don't have proof, but I think so."

"I swear, Charlie, I think I'm going to have to beat the
crap out of him."

Charlotte laughed in spite of herself. "Somehow, the
redneck in you can always make me laugh. Thanks for that.
Well, Grace is back, and Kelsey needs me. I've got to go."

"Love you and Kelsey both."

Charlotte smiled as she hung up, surprisingly relieved
that she had sorted things out with Jesse, at least to the best
of her ability to sort anything out right now around her mix
of confusing, painful feelings.

Grace stood in the kitchen doorway, still wearing her
coat. She stepped into the room, placed her purse on the
table, and opened her arms. Charlotte fell into the offered
hug with a deep sense of gratitude. "Take your coat off and
go sit with Kelsey. I'll make tea," Charlotte said, stepping
back and giving her friend a smile.

As Grace pulled Kelsey onto her lap for a comforting
hug, Charlotte filled the kettle with water and began to heat

it. Tea with Grace and deciding how to get a semblance of normalcy and structure in her life for Kelsey's sake needed to take priority here. She watched Grace and realized that her gratitude for the love her friend was providing didn't erase the strong desire to take charge and move her life and Kelsey's in a new direction that she was sure would include as little of Ted as possible.

CHAPTER 12

Grace had been gone an hour. Kelsey was down for an afternoon nap. A light breeze, cold enough to make her shiver and yet somehow refreshing came in through an open window in the living room where Charlotte now stood, gazing out at the swatches of sky visible in the gap between several old, stately American elms, storm clouds the color of a day-old bruise hanging low, lying in wait. She turned slowly in a half circle to survey her home.

The couch had lost any semblance of firm support long ago, in tandem with the fading of its color from a warm brown to something bordering on tan. It had been all they could afford at the time, and it was squishy and soft, enveloping a person. The perfect spot for a nap, something she and Ted had done often on lazy Sunday afternoons before Kelsey was born. Charlotte's cheeks grew warm, remembering other, more intimate, moments on that couch, the flash of old desire haunting her even as her now ever-present sadness rolled across in waves. The extra-wide armchair donated by her parents sat next to crooked bookshelves crammed with their favorites and interspersed with

Kelsey's books. How many times had she stood in the kitchen and watched Ted sitting in that armchair, Kelsey in his lap, her head on his shoulder, reading to her and felt a warm glow of love and satisfaction?

This apartment was her first and only home with Ted, the stepping stone where they began their life journey dreaming of so much more. The home they returned to from the hospital with Kelsey as a newborn. Her heart felt like an immutable weight in her chest when she thought of her husband. She wanted to think any trace of love had now become a faint memory, cast onto the wind and gone, but if that were truly the case, why was the mere sight of these ordinary items bringing her such pain with the memories they offered up so easily, unbidden?

"I need to make this place feel like a home, for Kelsey's sake, but it's packed with memories that might just be too much for me," Charlotte had told Grace earlier, looking to her friend for some level of comfort as they sat across the kitchen table from one another. She and Kelsey had returned this morning once she was sure Ted had moved his things and himself out.

"The last thing you or Kelsey need right now is more disruption in your life," Grace said, reaching across the table to take her hand. "I think you should get a normal routine in place."

Charlotte nodded, awash with relief, knowing her friend was right. She felt calmer when Grace was there. Alone, her fears invaded, her memories and tangle of confused emotions clouding the path forward.

They had talked about Charlotte's new job, Kelsey's return to school, and, when Kelsey was watching a favorite show on television, about whether Ted would be arrested or find himself the subject of media coverage. All topics Charlotte would have agonized over alone, but which felt like frightening things that she could somehow handle well when working through her fears and potential problems with Grace.

"I'm done. With Ted," she'd told Grace as she was leaving.

"I don't blame you," Grace answered, wrapping Charlotte in a tight hug. "But sometimes forgiveness comes when we least expect it will."

Forgiveness seemed a distant concept, unreachable, sitting on the opposite side of a vast canyon with no bridge in sight. Yet she missed their life here, reluctantly missed Ted even as she felt something dark and almost hate-driven toward him. How could she love him and hate him at the same time? Her mother, ever helpful, had suggested she missed what she thought things could be, loved the man she'd hoped he was, but now she should mourn the truth about him like a death and move on. Logical words her mind understood, her anger applauded, but her heart pounded an insistent drumbeat against them, choosing first denial, then the ease of giving in to the pain of need and loneliness.

Charlotte walked back toward her bedroom, stopping first to look in on Kelsey, who was curled into a fetal position on her bed, wrapped around her favorite stuffed duck, then moving on to her room. She sat on the edge of her bed and checked her phone for messages. There was another voicemail from that FBI agent, Nate Morgan. She lay down and closed her eyes. The walls, the furniture, and the bed she now lay on—especially the bed—called their stories out to her, memories pushing until they became a much-too-loud cacophony in her brain. The temptation to scream until her mind was silent pressed against her diaphragm, making her breathless as she held back, knowing she would wake her daughter. Kelsey, so small and confused, so tired and scared, missing Ted. Running her hands slowly over her own body, Charlotte let herself remember the moments of passion in this bed that still ran like a deep river of desire through her, trying to embrace the memories and set them free. Trying to free herself of longing and sorrow so she could build a way forward.

Eyes closed, she thought of the meditation classes she'd taken the year before and tried to focus on something positive, to remove the negativity from her mind. Laying one hand on her belly and the other hand atop it, she played with her wedding band and tried to breathe in and out, slowing her heartbeat. She took herself away in her mind to the Crazy Mountains in Montana, imagining the heat and movement of a horse below her as she inhaled the endless blue sky, the mountain peaks still partially snow-capped and glowing a light pink as the sun began its descent behind them. It was late afternoon. She and Ted had gone riding. She could hear him close behind her, calling to her. She turned and saw him pointing to a small stream and indicating he wanted to stop. His mother had packed food and wine for them. She took a deep breath, part of her wanting to keep riding, alone, away from him despite the fact that she was in love with him; to ride the mountain trails and choose the paths on her own. Final college exams and graduation were looming, both exciting and terrifying for Charlotte, who did not know what she should or would do with herself in the adult world, one half of her wanting to lean on Ted and the other wanting to strike out on her own and find her own way. But, instead, she turned her horse and followed Ted. Their horses drank from the small stream and munched on sweetgrass as they sat on a blanket eating and drinking wine, the sun now creating an orange-red glow against the fading blue sky, white clouds, and majestic mountains. It was in that magical setting that Ted asked her to marry him. She'd absorbed the moment, the stillness, the beauty surrounding them and felt loved, wanted, at peace as the word "yes" rolled off her tongue as easily as the gentle movement of the stream in front of her, its current rolling ever forward. Forgotten in an instant, as the ring slid on her finger, was her desire to strike out on her own.

It wasn't working. The memory was not calming her. Instead, anger pulsed through, breaking any chance the meditation would work. She had tossed aside her instinct of chasing an independent life so easily for the comfort of being led by someone else. She sat up and hugged her knees to her chest, hands clasped tightly around them, regretting that she hadn't stuck with her meditation classes and longing for some way to quiet her mind. Everything she felt for Ted could not simply be swept out of her with a broom of hate or anger; it wasn't who she was. She would have to sit with the dead weight of her memories and power through the pain until she could see a way out, a light of some kind. She eyed her phone, then punched a few buttons and held it to her ear. The first step to moving on would be to do what was needed to move herself and Kelsey as far away from Ted's current situation as possible.

"Hello, Nate Morgan." The voice on the line was soft, a slight Southern accent combined with a faint raspy quality.

"Mr. Morgan? This is Charlotte McCord. I understand you want to speak with me." Charlotte knew he would keep calling her until she met with him. Better to answer his questions and then, perhaps, he'd move along to someone else.

"I would appreciate it if you could answer a few questions. Would you be able to meet with me at the Pittsburgh field office?"

She wasn't sure how she wanted to approach this, whether she wanted to meet him in person or just request that they speak over the phone. "I don't have a sitter for my daughter today, and managing that isn't always easy. I also work a number of jobs. Can we talk now, on the phone?" She heard him tapping something, probably a pen, and felt his hesitation.

"What do you say I ask you a few questions now, and then if we need to take it further, we'll set up a time to meet in person?"

His tone was so calm, so even-keeled, she felt a desire to trust him. He was probably trained to make people feel this way in order to extract the information he needed. "All right, let's give it a shot." Charlotte hoped she sounded calm and confident, two emotions she was decidedly not feeling at the moment.

"Will you agree to my recording of our conversation?" Nate asked, his tone now very formal.

"Yes," she said, suspecting he'd started recording before he asked her that question, probably to get her agreement on record.

After a few questions to confirm her name, places of employment, and that she was Ted's wife, Nate moved to the heart of what he sought from her.

"What is your relationship with Leah Hanson? How long have you known her, and when is the last time you saw or spoke with her?"

"Leah and I go back to our childhood." Charlotte sighed, realizing he wanted more than they could cover in one call if he wanted her history with Leah. "Nate, I think this is going to be a long conversation and one I would prefer my daughter, who is now asleep, doesn't hear. Maybe I should come to your office."

"Does tomorrow work for you?" Charlotte noticed he didn't designate a time. He was opening his whole day. Leah must be in some deep level of trouble.

"Yes, tomorrow works. Let's say 9:00 a.m. after I drop my daughter off at school. Text me the address." Charlotte ended the call, and seconds later, her phone pinged, announcing the text from Nate with his office address. She stood up, swayed a bit, and sat back down on the bed, trying to remember the last time she'd eaten a good meal. Charlotte stood again, steadying herself, and headed to the kitchen. She would cook something good for her and Kelsey, comfort food to bring some normalization back to their world, and make sure she walked into Nate Morgan's office tomorrow as strong and sure of herself as she was able to summon from within the tangled mess inside her.

CHAPTER 13

Cigarettes had killed her mother, and they would probably kill her one day, but not before Gerilyn Leslie got to the bottom of why Ted McCord had been fired. A nice, smooth hit of nicotine helped her think; helped her sort through things when she needed to solve a problem. She blew contemplative, perfectly round smoke rings, watching them float up and over the open garbage bin in the alley beside the River City Trust office building. Smokers were banished outside, like a near-extinct species, made to feel as if their habit was too dirty for the pristine lungs of their coworkers, in Geri's opinion. Most of her fellow smokers were contractors from third-world countries where everyone smoked and no one cared. Geri often thought if she retired and moved overseas, she could smoke as she liked, except she couldn't stand listening to the babble of strange languages. She didn't like foreigners. She didn't like Ted either, but something was out of place in the reasons Ben had given for firing Ted. The office rumor mill was buzzing about what may have actually happened—speculation, comments, but nothing solid.

For one thing, Ben wouldn't make eye contact when he told her Ted had embezzled money. Geri didn't trust anyone, man or woman, who couldn't look her in the eye. She had seen Ted as someone who defined success by titles and recognition. Promotions were more about validation that he was important than about money. She was sure he liked the money that came with it, but it had never been about that. It had been about his need to sit in a certain spot on the organization chart.

Geri dropped her cigarette to the ground, popping a wintergreen mint in her mouth while stomping out the dying embers. She'd come out to the alleyway midday. In early October, it was getting a good bit colder at this time of day, clouds and a cool wind dispelling any hope of warmth from the noon sun. A woman who insisted on wearing suits year-round, Geri still felt comfortable outside without a coat when she needed a cigarette break. She reached into her pocket and sprayed a little light perfume around her, then headed indoors.

"Shay, do you have a minute?" Geri asked, watching Shay sharply inhale as he kept his eyes on the rising number of elevator floors, shifting his body away from hers.

"I'm buried in work. Mine. Ted's overflow. Sorry, Geri," Shay answered as he bolted off the elevator at the fifth floor.

Geri hurried, doggedly following behind him, her breathing a bit erratic as he picked up the pace. "Two minutes. I want to talk about Ted and why he was fired."

He turned around so quickly she almost slammed into him. "I'm definitely not talking about Ted with you!" Shay said. His eyes were spitting fire, his mouth in a hard, straight line.

Geri looked around her. The cubes were empty. People were still at lunch. She grabbed Shay's arm tightly and pushed him into a small conference room, shutting the door.

"Why do you want to talk about this?" Shay asked.

His body language let her know she'd better get to the point. She wasn't sure if Shay was truly angry or just afraid his peers would see him in here with her. They all hated her, and, deep down, she knew that blaming Ted for that had been misguided. Her management style was as much a habit as her Marlboro Lights.

"I don't think Ted did it. Something is wrong here," Geri offered, keeping a friendly tone.

"Oh, sure. You think I'm going to believe that you're on Ted's side?" Shay said, snorting with derision.

"Hey, I'm not saying I liked Ted. Ted was all about attention, titles, prestige to beat his insecurities. But he wouldn't steal and risk his goals by getting caught."

"What makes you think he didn't change? Roll over? Go bad . . . bad like you?" Shay asked.

"Don't get nasty," Geri snapped back at him. "I'm still a manager here." She could see the utter lack of respect for her on his face, and she struggled against regaining control by demanding he do whatever work or investigation she requested.

"How do I know you didn't set Ted up to take the fall for something you and Ben are doing?" Shay asked with such seriousness that Geri thought she should tread lightly.

"You don't, but I want you to help me figure out what really happened. Even if Ted isn't guilty, they'll never take him back here."

"I'm not helping you do anything. You figure out whatever you're looking for on your own." Shay shook his head in disgust and moved toward the door.

"I thought Ted was your friend."

"He is. That's why I can never trust you."

They stood in silent suspicion of one another, neither budging an inch.

"If I tell senior leadership it wasn't Ted who was at fault, that he was set up, they'll believe me," Geri said.

"You bring me proof that you are not trying to hurt Ted more than he's been hurt, that your investigation has a positive for Ted, then I'll consider working with you . . . maybe," Shay said, his hand on the door handle. "Otherwise you're the same old Geri who's hated Ted, and probably me and every other young guy around here, since our first day on the job."

Geri watched Shay walk out of the room, stung by the truth in his words. She was alone, her past mean-spirited actions and naked ambition coming back to bite her. What she couldn't reveal to Shay or anyone was that she believed whatever Ben was up to, he was going to make her the next scapegoat. Ted was a casualty, a nuisance to move out of the way. She would be set up to take the fall. She needed to figure out Ben's scheme before he pulled it off and she was in the unemployment line. Instinct told her Shay had enough information to get her started, but he wasn't letting her past sins go that easily.

Geri had had a few hours, as she finished her afternoon meetings, to plan her next steps. She could see Shay watching her as she leaned against the wall of Missy's cubicle. "Missy, I have a project for you." Missy eyed her suspiciously. "Follow me into my office."

Geri was convinced Missy would run to Shay as soon as she left the office, but she couldn't decline an assignment like Shay could. She reported directly to Geri now that Ted was gone. Shay had initially taken over Ted's job, but then managed to obtain a transfer to the insider threat team, leaving Geri to run Ted's former team until they hired a replacement. It would be better to have Shay do the work, but maybe Missy would lean on him for help and he'd see Geri wasn't trying to make life worse for Ted.

"Is this about Ted?" Missy balanced herself on the edge of a chair as if ready to run.

"Not exactly. Have you been talking to Shay?" Geri asked. She waited for an answer, but Missy sat, silent, a worried frown creasing her forehead. "This project is confidential."

Missy remained silent. Her fingers were tapping her upper right thigh in nervous rhythm, the only outward display of her internal stress.

"I won't lie and tell you I liked Ted or that I want him back," Geri said, leaning back in her chair. "But I'm not entirely sure he was at fault, and neither is Dora in HR. I have permission to run a quiet investigation. Shay turned me down. He doesn't trust me."

Geri hoped Missy didn't follow up with Dora, who had no idea Geri was continuing to track Ted's termination long after his file had been closed.

"No one trusts you," Missy said, her soft voice trembling but her eyes flashing angrily.

"Well, I wanted Shay to do the work, and he won't. That means you'll do it," Geri snapped, handing Missy a jump drive. "Everything I've uncovered on my own is there. I'll elevate your permissions in the system without notifying Ben. I want you to run an investigation."

"And how do I know you won't take the results and push me out of my job?" Missy asked.

Geri sighed. "Despite popular opinion, I'm not dishonest or unfair. Tough, maybe, but I won't fire you."

"If you use whatever I find to make things worse for Ted, you won't have to fire me," Missy said. "I'll quit."

Geri was surprised. The normally vulnerable Missy, afraid of losing her job, had a spine.

"Good, you've got some spunk in you after all! I like that. Now go, be careful, and give me a report every Friday. I'll tell you when the project is over."

Geri looked at her watch as Missy left the office. Four in the afternoon. She could head home, make some dinner, and wait for the call. Her cousin, Joey, was the bartender at Roscoe's, a neighborhood bar near Missy's apartment and not far from where Shay owned a condo. Geri made it her business to know where these millennials she managed hung out after work. It amazed her that Joey had gotten a job there. He was a bum, as far as she was concerned, but evidently he made good drinks and was tough enough to handle the late-night crowd. She'd bet they never put him on the lunch shift with the business crowd. Her instructions to Joey were to watch for Missy and a guy named Shay, the request made on a hunch that Missy would grab Shay for drinks and beg for help. Geri had overheard talk that Ted was living with Shay, so she was sure Shay would show up.

"Why should I spy on the nice girl and her friend for you?" Joey had asked. Geri could easily imagine Joey, the phone tucked between his shoulder and chin as his muscular, tattooed arms put away bottles of bourbon on the shelf behind the bar.

"Because we're family, Joey."

"Nice try. I don't want to help you mess with a couple of nice, young kids."

"I'm not going to do anything to hurt them. I want to keep them from ending up like you."

Joey laughed. "I'd never work for your sorry ass."

"You can't work for my sorry ass, shithead. You have a criminal record." Geri chuckled, imagining Joey silently flipping his middle finger at the phone.

"A juvenile record that is sealed from the likes of you," Joey answered. "What's in it for me, Geri? Because every minute we talk, I like you less."

"A hundred bucks and I'll take your place at Aunt Mildred's Thanksgiving dinner next year," Geri said, hoping this would push him to agree.

"I'll take the Benjamin, but no one wanted you at Thanksgiving dinner this year, and they don't want you next year. You can forget that part."

Geri knew this was true. It was possible she was less popular with her family than she was at the office. They thought she looked down on them, and, in fact, she did, but she was also slightly afraid of them. They were a roguish, rough-and-tumble lot, with more than a few of them sporting less than savory jobs and prison records.

"Okay, once I hear from you, I'll drop off the money within twenty-four hours."

"Yes, you will, or I'll send Susie to beat it out of you." Joey's sister was known to have held her own in a few bar brawls.

"Lovely. We come from such a nice, refined family, Joey."

"A good salt-of-the-earth family that's always been too good for you."

"Yep, I'm way too good to rack up a police file or work for Uncle Sal running numbers."

"Screw you, Geri. You're an asshole."

The call disconnected before Geri could say another

word. Just talking to Joey made her nauseous. She'd been an only child, her cousins the closest thing to siblings. They'd grown up on the same block in Homestead, but her parents had held steady low-wage jobs without defaulting into the criminal side of the family business. They'd insisted she go to college, further separating her from her cousins. Now she had a nice condo on Mount Washington, and the rest of them used it as an example of how she looked down on them from her mountaintop. Moving up and out of the old neighborhood hadn't stopped her from missing the feeling of family she'd had in her youth. Resented for her tough demeanor by the work crowd and for her success by her family and her old neighborhood gang, she was truly alone. Her parents had died five years ago.

"Hey, George," Geri said to the voice whose number was always in her list of recent calls for easy dialing. She held the phone with one hand while she shoved her laptop into a backpack and zipped it up. "Busy later?"

George Flannery lived three blocks from her condo in an old row house that had been in his family for years. It sat next to the small tavern he owned and ran, where Geri often found herself grabbing a glass of wine and a meal after work. George understood her old world and had a gentle disinterest in her new world of high-priced managerial jobs and condos with a view.

"Nope. Wanna come on by?"

Geri envisioned his shaggy, white hair nearly touching the surface of the bar as, with one hand wiping its surface while the other held the phone, he smiled.

"Yes, it's been a long day. The bar or your place?" Geri asked. She felt the heat rising between her legs, and she wanted to be naked with him, to forget for an hour everything about her life.

"My place." George chuckled. "Hurry up, I'm horny."

Geri laughed as she hung up the phone. It was a perfect arrangement. They serviced each other's needs—no strings, no kiss and tell. She wasn't gorgeous or slim, but George didn't care. She liked it fast and hard, and sometimes a bit rough. He never seemed to tire of her, nor she of him. The stress relief would be great, and then she'd head home to drink a glass of wine and wait for Joey to call.

CHAPTER 14

Ted smiled, even as his heart clenched and he thought he would double over at any minute. The shade and huge trunk of the sixty-foot oak tree partially concealed him, its tender green leaves brushing against his face each time he shifted his feet, angling for a better view of Charlotte. She was seated on the old Apache-style blanket, sandwiches and snacks scattered nearby, arms wrapped around her knees as she watched Kelsey running back and forth with a little boy he'd never seen. It brought back memories of weekends at the ranch, he and Charlotte horseback riding in the Crazy Mountains, ending somewhere secluded. They'd spread out a blanket with food and wine, watch the sun set, and make love in the open, miles from any other human being. Carefree days when they seemed to have everything in common, when they couldn't get enough of each other, naked and in love.

Now, here he was, hidden like a stalker, wondering if he should approach her or watch from a distance. He was aching to join his family, to toss his miserable life with all its mistakes behind him and start anew. He rubbed his eyes as if that would somehow prevent tears, a common theme with him lately.

"Daddy!" Kelsey had spotted him. She was running full force in his direction. Charlotte stood, shading her eyes. He stepped forward just as thirty-five pounds of frantic little girl threw herself at him. He picked her up, gulping, sniffling into her hair as he hugged her.

Charlotte stood very still, making no movement in his direction. Holding Kelsey like a shield, Ted began walking toward his wife. Her face held no expression that he could discern, a relief because he'd expected instant anger.

"Ted." He watched her eyes as her mouth, set in a grim line, said his name while she crossed her arms over her chest, defensively.

"I was hiking and I saw you." His voice sounded shaky, and it must have had an effect on her. Her face softened slightly.

"Mommy, Daddy can have my sandwich." Kelsey shifted her sweaty little body in his arms, twisting to look at her mother. Ted couldn't see her face, but whatever Charlotte saw made her look as though she might cry. Ted stayed silent, his stomach churning.

"Sure, Daddy can join us." Charlotte looked at Kelsey, avoiding eye contact with him. "There's an extra sandwich."

Ted settled Kelsey on her feet, gently, but she clung to his hand as they walked to the blanket and he sat down. He'd actually been out for a hike—at least he wasn't lying to her about that. He was on the South Braddock Trail when, just before he reached the second set of man-made steps heading down into the ravine, he heard Kelsey laugh. Looking down, he saw them in the open grassy area, one of a number of people with children or dogs, sitting and enjoying the day. He headed down the steps instinctively but paused before going over the small pedestrian bridge. He had no idea what Charlotte's reaction would be if he joined them uninvited. She avoided conversation for the most part when he picked Kelsey up every other weekend. He waded into the shallow creek, then up the hill a little bit to linger behind a tree not far from a dirt pathway. The path gave him a bit of legitimacy if she saw him.

The park was cool and pleasant today, tiny brooks running parallel with the trails on their way to connect with Nine Mile Run, a beautiful creek with waterfalls and wildlife. The hushed peaceful rhythm of the six hundred some acres that made up Frick Park soothed him no matter what life stresses awaited him when he left, the trees in full photosynthesis now, their stunning array of October fall colors as breathtaking as they would be fleeting.

Ted tried to think of a way to break the uncomfortable silence between them. Part of him wished Kelsey would answer the little boy calling out to her to come back and play, but a bigger part wanted her to stay. He knew they would both try a little harder for her sake.

"Kelsey's new friend?" He pointed to the child and his parents, sitting fairly close to Tranquil Trail. A quick flash of remembrance took him back a year as he thought about teaching Kelsey to ride her new bike with training wheels here, outside the range of the cars and crooked sidewalks on their block. Tranquil Trail was flat and straight, with only a few walkers, joggers, and occasionally a bike or two.

"Nobody I know. He's just a friendly little kid who asked her to play."

Although she was too young to sense that her parents

needed to be alone, Ted silently felt both relief and fear as Kelsey stood and began running toward the little boy, looking over her shoulder to make sure Ted was still there.

"Stay right where I can see you," Charlotte called to her retreating back.

Ted twisted the cap on his water bottle, loosening and tightening, taking a sip, then nervously twisting the cap again. *Take it easy when you're around her, man. Don't push things. Let her come to you.* He could hear Shay's advice in his head. Easier said than done when he'd had so few chances to speak to his wife alone. He watched her reach into a tote bag and pull out a sandwich.

"Peanut butter and jelly okay?" Charlotte extended her hand, without moving toward him, from her corner of the blanket.

"I'm really not hungry." Ted smiled and waved away the sandwich he was too nervous to eat. "Seen Shay here today?"

It was a legitimate, if foolish, stalling question. Shay liked to come down here for a workout on Nine Mile Run, the favored runners pathway feeding off the far left end of the field, often doing the full length of the trail and back again. Ted remembered the few times they'd been here when Shay was dating Natalia, one of their coworkers. He always took her for a run, knowing Charlotte and Ted had a limit to how much time with Natalia they could manage before a friendly discussion turned argumentative.

"No, I haven't really seen much of Shay since you moved in with him." Ted could see the firm set of her mouth, her eyes avoiding him. Was this yet another thing she held him responsible for, that she and Kelsey no longer saw their shared friend like they had before? That he was somehow in the wrong by moving in with the guy when he had no money and nowhere else to go?

He wanted to see her happy the way they had once been when their dreams fit together; a giant jigsaw puzzle rather than divergent paths that caused friction and created walls between them instead of bridges. Somehow, he had to find the words to say this to her, to tell her that she meant everything to him.

"Can we talk?"

Her shoulders stiffened. "About what?" Charlotte finally looked at him fully, locking eyes, and he felt the fierce, powerful impact of her emotions on a physical level.

"About us . . . about what happened . . . about whatever you're thinking or feeling." Ted reached for her hand, closing his fingers around hers. In seconds, she both instinctively grasped his hand in return and just as suddenly yanked hers away.

"Let's start with why, Ted. Not why you did it. You told me that. But why you didn't trust me enough to tell me about the will, the ranch, all of it."

Ted coughed, looking down for a moment. The way he answered was important, but he couldn't find a good answer, an answer that would begin a healing process for both of them.

"I was wrong . . . I screwed up."

"You think? Well, that's not news. Tell me something I don't know." She pulled her long hair around and over one shoulder as if it were a scarf, a comfort, and began twisting the ends. He could feel her waiting, defensive tension exuding from every part of her.

"I should have trusted you, trusted us, to work things out together."

"But you didn't." There was a challenge in her voice that came from the pain of having been lied to, and he could see he had nothing more to lose and only a slim chance of gaining Charlotte or her trust back.

"I'm asking for a second chance. I know . . . it's probably impossible, but . . ." Ted picked at a stray thread on his cargo pants as if he were an eight-year-old boy, waiting for something, anything. Waiting for even a small morsel of forgiveness.

Charlotte was silent for a very long moment, then she stood and began packing up the items on the blanket. "I love Jesse too, you know that, right? You didn't trust me, but you want me to trust you, put all this behind us."

"Don't leave yet." Ted stood, frantic. It had taken months to have this bit of conversation. "We have to start somewhere."

Charlotte called for Kelsey, folding the blanket and slinging the backpack over her shoulders. "I don't have to start anything with you. Not until I'm ready. Maybe not ever. Definitely not now."

"I'm coming!" Kelsey hollered from the middle of the expanse of green grass as if she were atop a mountain in western Virginia. She reached them before he could beg, plead with Charlotte. She hugged his knees, and he lifted her up slowly, kissing her forehead and holding her close. "For her, Charlotte. We need to talk."

Charlotte nodded, the movement of her head almost imperceptible, a minuscule flicker of agreement. "Not now. I'm not ready."

"Daddy, come home with us." Kelsey was clinging to him now. Ted put her down gently, taking a step back.

"Kelsey, it's time to go, and Daddy's going to Uncle Shay's house. You'll see him on the weekend." Charlotte adjusted her backpack and tucked the rolled blanket under her arm, then put her hand out to her daughter.

Kelsey crossed her arms over her chest, her face defiant as she looked at her mother. Ted knew what was coming next. He squatted down and met his daughter at eye level, hoping to diffuse the situation.

"Kels, Daddy does have to go to Shay's house today, but next time I pick you up, we'll go to the zoo." He put his hand on her back, exerting light pressure to get her to move forward. She locked her legs, digging her shoes into the ground.

"No! I'm not going unless Daddy comes." Kelsey's face was flushed. A full-out meltdown was seconds away.

"It's okay, honey. Go with Mommy. Everything will be fine." He could feel her tension ease a bit. She was in the moment between reflex and decision, then her shoulders sagged and tears began to flow.

Ted turned her around and held her for a minute. He looked up at Charlotte, expecting a reflection of the sadness he felt, but all he saw was the fury of one trapped in a situation out of her control. His heart sank as he realized Charlotte was not only not ready to talk, but she might never be ready for much more than where they stood now—on either side of a broken, dismembered marriage with a small, vulnerable child possibly the only thread of hope left between them.

"Kelsey, now!" Charlotte's voice was tight with the rage Ted accepted was actually meant for him.

"I hate you, Mommy." Kelsey said the words so clearly Ted heard Charlotte gasp as if it were an echo of his own quick intake of breath. Charlotte's hand curled into a tight fist, her arm trembling slightly.

"Don't ever say that again, Kelsey," Ted said, looking his

daughter directly in the eyes. "Mommy loves you. So do I. We know this is hard for you, but these problems are Daddy's fault, not Mommy's."

Ted could have ripped his own heart out of his chest with less pain than he felt when Kelsey looked at him, her face so sad, and, giving a little wave, turned and began walking forward, past her mother, on her own.

"Ted . . ." Charlotte looked at him for a moment.

"Go. I shouldn't have dropped in on the two of you."

She nodded, then turned to follow Kelsey. Ted stood watching them both walk away until they disappeared around a bend in the trail and were gone. He could imagine, for a moment, the three of them heading home as they'd done so many times before. Just a year ago, it was Ted carrying Kelsey and a backpack while Charlotte and Shay shouldered a cooler, blanket, and tote with toys and the remains of lunch. The sun was often descending and a little blinding, so they would head up the Braddock Trail, trying to stay in the forest shade, quiet and pleasantly tired, stones and twigs crunching under their feet, watching squirrels dart across the path and up the stately old trees. Ted could hear the birds calling to one another today, as he had then, and when he closed his eyes, he felt the remembrance of Kelsey, a dead weight lying sound asleep in his arms, as he gently kissed her forehead. A deep sensation of love and contentment flooded his body. He'd let himself build a small fantasy, a little pool of hope that he dipped into each day and convinced him he was not only forgivable, but once Charlotte forgave him, they could begin their life together as a family again. That wishful scene was crashing down around him now, loudly banging in his ears, tapping him on the head, an inner voice telling him the damage he'd done was more permanent than he'd allowed himself to believe.

Walking back to the car, his feet felt like lead, his hands shaking, and he wished he could let out a primal scream, but instead he tucked himself behind the steering wheel, closed the door, and pulled out of the parking lot, holding his inner despair tightly inside. He was, after all was said and done, a McCord, his father's son.

CHAPTER 15

"I didn't date a lot of guys in college, Grace, and I've only been with one other guy, a one-night hookup, besides Ted," Charlotte confessed, her feet tucked up onto the couch and under a warm, homemade afghan, gazing at the trees now bare of leaves and moving softly with the cold late-October wind. She and Kelsey had stayed with Grace for a week after Ted was fired until he moved in with Shay and she moved back into their apartment. But it still felt safe and homey to come to Grace's place.

"And you want to see what's out there?" Grace asked. "Play the field a little? Or you want to give your marriage another try?"

"I don't want to see Ted or talk to him, possibly ever again." Charlotte found herself telling people this lately in a firm voice that belied whether there was an inner truth to the statement. She wondered, each time, who she was trying to convince, the person she was speaking to or herself. She didn't know what she felt or believed, frustrated that her head and her heart remained at war, each stubborn and, it seemed, entrenched, immovable.

"Of course you don't, but that's really not a choice now, is it?" Grace replied. Her honest, practical advice was, for once, annoying. "You have a child with him. Even if you're going to end the marriage, that means lawyers and meetings over custody, money, possessions."

"Gee, thanks, Grace." Charlotte sighed. "I'm tied to him for life, I get it. I feel like I hate him right now. As if I could never forgive him."

"Never is a long time," Grace answered. "But Kelsey loves him, and she misses him. She needs to see him more often, and you need to do something about that."

"I know. He's picking her up tomorrow. He's got a small job at a computer repair place now."

Charlotte felt a tangle of painful emotions when she heard Ted's voice or saw him. She wanted to bury herself in work. Kelsey needed stability, and Charlotte needed to navigate the waters of her marriage, Ted's legal issues, and this growing feeling of wanting to run away or run wild and simply shuck all responsibility for a while. But first she needed to straighten things out financially. Their savings would soon be depleted. She'd asked her father to find a lawyer for Ted to navigate the claim against him, and she'd given Ted half of their savings, but the legal fees and paying the everyday bills from her income only was draining what little they had. Charlotte's parents were only offering to pay for a divorce lawyer for her, a subject she'd avoided so far, although she wasn't sure why. She didn't feel ready yet and, angry as she was with Ted, didn't want to pile a divorce on top of the rest of his problems. She still had a wide range of feelings, all of them running hot and cold, to the point where she wasn't able to sort them into a correct answer to this mess.

Tomorrow, while Ted took Kelsey for a trip to the zoo

and then kept her with him overnight, Charlotte was going to take on the difficult and painful task of asking her parents for money. She'd stay at their house for the night, then head out the next morning to what was, now, a full-time job at the museum. She dreaded doing this, but she needed a nest egg until she had about six months of paychecks behind her. At least the decision to go full-time had provided medical insurance for her and Kelsey.

"Well, regardless of what decisions I make going forward, no more fun part-time jobs and being dependent on someone," Charlotte said. "One of us has to give Kelsey some stability."

"Sometimes you have to fall to find the strength to pick yourself up," Grace answered. "You'll look back on this as a wholly different woman one day."

"I hope so, I really do. If I thought I lacked confidence before, this is making me less sure of myself, not more."

Grace seemed hesitant. She crossed and uncrossed her legs, tapped her fingers on the arm of the chair, and looked off into the distance as if deep in thought. "I hate to bring this up with everything else you're dealing with, but you know you're going to get pulled into Ted's legal issues."

"No, I'm not. I didn't do anything wrong. The only connection is our finances, and he'll probably bankrupt us, but I've set up a separate checking account for myself as a start. To separate myself from him."

"Have you spoken to the FBI yet? I get that he did something wrong, but you lived with him, and there will be questions."

"Yes, I told them I knew nothing about what Ted's been accused of doing." Charlotte picked at a stray piece of yarn on the afghan, feeling the discomfort of her meeting with Nate Morgan all over again. "To be honest, the FBI was more interested in what I knew about Leah than Ted."

"Leah? Why?" Grace's brow was furrowed, her look both surprised and concerned. Charlotte hesitated, not sure how much to share.

"They asked more questions than they gave explanations, but it appears they think Leah is involved in something shady, and it's connected to Ted's discovery of an embezzlement scheme and his eventual termination by River City Trust," Charlotte said, taking a deep breath as she watched Grace take in this new twist to the story. "They wanted to know how long I'd known Leah, when did I last see her, had she said anything that might seem odd, and had I met the guy she's dating or know anything about him. I didn't have much to offer. Leah knows how to keep things private, even from me."

"Do you know who she's dating?" Grace asked. "And why that has any relevance?"

"I don't know for sure. I've suspected for a while he might be married simply because she's more covert this time, but now . . ." Charlotte's voice trailed as her mind went back to the sterile little interview room—white walls, bland beige rug, the whole room smelling of rug shampoo and cleaning supplies—where Nate Morgan had asked how she and Leah could be such close friends and yet she didn't know her current boyfriend.

"You've been close friends since childhood, and yet you don't know who she's dating? Never met him?" Nate's voice had gone from an even tone to something sharper, more cynical. Charlotte could tell he thought she was lying.

"Leah goes through men very quickly. I don't meet all of them. Sometimes they're married and she keeps details private. She's not the kind to settle down. I simply assumed, whoever he

*is, he's married and he'll be here and gone in a few months."
Charlotte's voice quavered, and her foot tapped on the floor, her
nerves on edge. She sounded like she was hiding something. She
tried again. "Look, I know how this sounds, but this is classic
Leah. I did feel like she was being more secretive this time, and
maybe something was different—or she seemed different. I poked
her a bit about him, but she got uptight and didn't want to talk
about it."*

Charlotte looked at Grace, patiently watching her,
waiting for a response, and said the words she had stuffed
down inside herself, the words she wanted to forget, to deny.
"I think she's been seeing someone who works at River City
Trust. Someone Ted believes was part of the plan to
embezzle and . . . she might have been part of setting Ted up
to be fired."

"Did you tell the FBI this?"

"No. It's a hunch, from something Ted said . . . but what
if I'm wrong?" Charlotte shook her head. "I'd have to be sure
to tell the FBI this, and I'm not."

"So you think Ted's innocent?" Grace leaned forward
and took her hand. She felt warm and comforting as Charlotte shivered despite the blanket covering her.

"Maybe . . . I don't know. I'm confused." Her love and
anger for Ted mixed with a desire to deny that he could do
something so terrible and a belief that he may have actually
done it. "I love him. I hate him. I miss him. I want him gone
forever. I want Kelsey and I as far away from the mess he's in
as possible."

Grace sighed. "Still, Charlotte, eventually this is going to
hit the media and you're going to be asked a lot of
questions."

Charlotte looked away. She felt defensive, stubborn; she
wanted freedom from what she thought of as Ted's problem.

She wanted to shake it all off like a heavy coat, tuck it in the closet, and head forward into spring.

"I'm trying, every day, to think of how to become stronger, how to make this a new beginning, and then Ted's stuff attaches itself to my ankle like a dead weight and slows everything down."

"At some point—if not for yourself, then for Kelsey—I think you have to decide if you think he's innocent and whether you're going to help him or walk away."

Charlotte started to shake her head again, willing herself to throw the truth of what her friend was saying aside, out of her pathway. But one look at Grace watching her so intently, her face sad, and Charlotte knew avoidance was no longer possible. This was her reality.

"I can't run or hide from it, can I?"

"Unfortunately, you can't. Like most things, it will follow you everywhere until you face it, stare it down, and make a decision."

Everyone wanted a decision from her. Ted wanted to know if she believed he was innocent of embezzlement, despite the blackmail he'd admitted to. He wanted to know where they stood, where their shaken marriage sat in the middle of his mess. Kelsey wanted to know why Daddy wasn't living with them and when he would come home. Her parents wanted to know why she wasn't filing for divorce. Helping Nate with his investigation seemed to mean betraying Leah. And Leah, well, she was the only one asking nothing. In fact, Charlotte felt a distance, as if Leah were avoiding her. She got a text here and there, checking in on her well-being, but any invite she sent to Leah to stop by or meet for drinks was met with an apology and explanation about how busy she was at work.

"There's this push and pull in me that's becoming

exhausting," Charlotte said. "The pull of the past, my marriage, needing to decide what to do about Ted's mess. The push to get on a new path of my own and leave Ted and his woes behind, find myself, which I've never really done before. I'm not sure which way to go."

Grace simply smiled and nodded. *But what could she say?* Charlotte thought. What could anyone say to wrap all this up in a neat package for her right now?

CHAPTER 16

Ted tried to keep Kelsey from bouncing into other people as she jumped up and down in the short line to the escalator. She loved the Pittsburgh Zoo.

"I'm a kangaroo!" she announced to the smiles of several adults.

Seconds later, he guided her onto the steep escalator, leaving the parking lot and ticket booths below and ascending upward and into the zoo. The ride took them past tall grass lining the hill where wildflowers, once abundant in the spring, had disappeared in the face of the October chill. He could feel Kelsey twitching with anticipation inside her warm, puffy jacket as he held her hand firmly.

"It's like we're going up to the tops of the trees," he told her. He watched her face—rapt, thrilled, her head in its knit cap turning this way and that—and wished they could fly up, hand in hand, above the trees, traveling to someplace beautiful, tropical, away from the muck and mire of his life. He wished with every fiber of his being he could put a look like that on her face every day.

Kelsey watched, wide-eyed, as the slow, long, rattling

escalator advanced, flanked by enormous trees on either side, taking them up the mountainside to emerge even with the treetops. Ted breathed in a sense of deep happiness, his first in a month or more, watching his daughter take in one of her favorite places and knowing he could do this little thing for her despite the situation he'd created and which his confused child had to navigate. Helping Kelsey step off the mile-high escalator, he promised himself he would shake everything negative off of his shoulders and be in the moment.

"Can we ride the horse?" Kelsey was pointing to the carousel.

"Maybe when we come back," Ted answered. "We're going to see the tiger first."

Kelsey squeezed his hand a little. "The tiger has big teeth, and he's scary."

"Yep," Ted said with a smile. "But remember, he's behind a huge fence, and he can't touch you, and you can't touch him. You'll just look at each other."

Kelsey nodded, her small brow furrowed, sniffing as they emerged from beneath an overpass and into the pungent animal kingdom.

"What's that smell?" Kelsey asked loudly, giggling a little bit.

"That's animal poop," Ted said. Kelsey's laughing was pulling out an emotion he hadn't felt in a long time, the feeling of joy so exquisite that his own laughter rolled up as naturally as an ocean wave. Their shared happiness carried him along, freeing him gracefully, separating him from his despair. He was simply a father with his daughter, experiencing wonder, awe, and fun.

"Did you think animals use a bathroom?"

"No, I know . . . I know they don't have underwear or

toilet paper." Kelsey smiled as if this explained the forest and the habits of all of its creatures.

"What's the difference between a tiger and a panther?" Ted asked. "Hurry, tell me before we see the tiger."

He watched Kelsey, her face thoughtful for a few seconds, knowing she was trolling through pictures she'd seen in her books at home. "A tiger is orange with black stripes, and a panther is all black," she announced.

"Good job, sweetheart!"

Seconds later, she gasped just as they rounded the corner and the Amur tiger came into view. The tiger was pacing along the rim of his confines, touching the metal fence at times. Kelsey was very still as he passed the plexi-glass at the viewing pavilion where she stood, her face a study in awe and amazement. Slowly, gingerly, she raised her hand and waved to the tiger. Each time he passed, she waved again, but he kept going. She turned to Ted, disappointment across her face.

"He didn't see me," Kelsey said.

"He saw you," Ted answered. "But tigers don't wave. And they're very dangerous, which is why there's a special wall between you and him. Did you see his big teeth?"

Kelsey nodded her head vigorously and grabbed Ted's hand. He knew she wanted to see the lion and then the giraffe. They walked for a while, looking at the Komodo dragons, the lynx, the lemurs—the sun offsetting the cooler air as they moved along. When they reached the lion, a big sign said the animal was not there, that the zoo was remodeling his habitat.

"Where is he?" Kelsey asked.

"Looks like he's gone somewhere else while they fix up his home a bit," Ted said.

"No," Kelsey answered, stomping her foot angrily. "The

lion is like you. It's not fair. I want him to come back in his home."

Ted sensed she was getting tired, maybe a bit hungry, and if he didn't want a full-blown meltdown, he'd have to adjust quickly. He remembered a food kiosk a little further along the path.

"Let's get some food and sit down for a little bit," Ted said, taking Kelsey's hand and walking forward.

Minutes later, they reached the little food hut, and he ordered them both a drink and some chicken nuggets and French fries. They sat on a nearby bench in the shade.

"Once we're done, we can take the tram to the giraffe so you don't have to walk as much," Ted said.

Kelsey nodded, munching away then sipping on her drink. "I want to see the lion."

"I understand, honey, but the lion isn't here."

"Maybe he's somewhere else in the zoo while they fix up his house." Kelsey's face was set in a stubborn look he knew well. She was not letting it go.

"He's not somewhere else at the zoo, he's gone away for vacation, maybe to another city's zoo, but he'll be back."

"How do you know that?"

"I saw it on the sign outside of his home." Ted was taking creative license with the actual message on the sign because Kelsey couldn't read very well yet. But if he didn't give her an answer, this conversation could go on for quite a while and result in a tantrum or Kelsey insisting he ask a zoo employee.

Kelsey pushed the rest of her food away. "I'm still mad," she said.

"Life doesn't always go as expected, Kelsey," Ted answered, distracted as he glanced around for a safe-looking mom or zoo employee, knowing Kelsey would soon need to use the bathroom. This was the tough part about being a single father and facing the million little places where he needed Charlotte to be there parenting with him. "Sometimes that makes us mad, but we just have to deal with it." He kissed her gently on the top of her head. "Let me know when you need to use the bathroom, and I'll find someone safe to go in there with you while I stand at the door."

"I can go myself," Kelsey said in the same stubbornly angry tone she'd used to inform him of her feelings regarding the missing lion.

"No, you know the rules," Ted said. "I'll wait outside the door and ask an employee or another mom who seems safe to go in with you."

"If you didn't leave, Mommy would be here to go with me," Kelsey said.

Ted thought he might double over as if he'd received an actual, physical punch in the gut, her hurt palpable, her accusation monumentally painful. He assessed her defiant look. She'd moved from disappointment at the missing lion and being tired to challenging him. He wasn't sure he was ready for this discussion, or that this was the best place for it to happen, but here they were. He took a deep breath, hoping it would not escalate to tears and a scene of some sort. Charlotte was much better at managing Kelsey in a meltdown. Ted fervently wished she was here to manage this with him, but he was on his own, and he had to pull it together, be the father Kelsey deserved.

"That must feel scary for you, I know," he said, reaching out to hold her hand.

"Mommy was mean, and she made you leave." Kelsey pulled away, tucking her hands in her jacket sleeves. "I got mad at her for that."

"Don't be mad at Mommy," Ted answered. "She's disappointed in me because I wasn't being a good husband and daddy. I was too busy at work and . . . well, some things happened that were bad. So Mommy and I are taking a break and thinking."

Ted wasn't sure that last part was true, but he needed to give her as much truth as she could handle at her age.

"You don't have your job now," Kelsey said. "A fire happened."

"Do you mean that I was fired?" Ted asked.

Kelsey nodded vigorously. She had her hands wrapped around her drink, but she wasn't moving the cup. She was watching him seriously now.

"Fired means that my boss asked me to leave and not to come back," Ted explained. "I wasn't being as good at the job as I should be, so they told me I couldn't have my job anymore."

"Now you have loads of time for me and Mommy," Kelsey said. "So why can't you come home?"

Ted's eyes watered. He rubbed them quickly, furiously, determined not to cry in front of his daughter, let alone in public. He coughed, clearing his throat, trying to find the right words when, more than anything in the world, he longed to grant her wish. Leaning right, he tipped his head, making the antelopes visible through openings between the foliage. They were beautiful, grazing amidst the backdrop of an enormous, elegant tree as if perfectly positioned in a painting. For a moment, he was back in Montana watching elk, bison, cattle, all grazing on the open plain, and he longed to go home in a way he had never felt before.

"It's complicated, Kelsey," Ted said. "I don't know how to explain. But I have a small job now, and I love spending time with you like today."

"That's what Mommy said," Kelsey answered with a sigh. "It's complicated."

"Can we just have a nice day today and agree that sometimes things don't always go as we want them to, but maybe it will all work out in a good way another time?" Ted asked.

Kelsey sat quietly, seriously, as if thinking about this for several minutes. Then she stood up and held out her hand.

"Can I go to the bathroom now, please? And then can we go see the giraffe?"

Ted gathered up their trash and dropped it in the can, taking her hand. One of the young girls working at the food kiosk had stepped out and was heading toward the bathroom. He quickly asked if Kelsey could walk in with her and if she'd keep an eye out and wait for her. The girl, probably about high school age, agreed with a smile, taking Kelsey's hand and walking her into the ladies' bathroom while Ted waited outside the door, checking the map for the giraffe location and watching for the tram. He wondered if he should let the conversation go or gently try again later, after Kelsey had had a nap back at his place.

Fifteen minutes later, Kelsey was nearly in a backbend trying to look up at the giraffe, which was craning its neck as close to the fence as possible, only the small man-made ravine preventing it from stepping forward. Ted was relieved that maybe, in the way children can often do, she had shrugged off her questions about why he wasn't living with them and shifted her attention back to the animals. It was such a gift for him to have this day with her, to have her spend the night if she would agree to do so later. She'd seemed excited for a sleepover the last time he'd scheduled one, and then she backed out, wanting Charlotte, and insisted he take her home.

"When we get to Shay's house, you can take a nap, and later we'll watch a movie and order pizza."

Kelsey nodded. She looked tired, and Ted suspected she would need the nap soon. "Want to ride on Daddy's back the rest of the way?"

Kelsey put her arms up as she had when she was a baby, and Ted picked her up, carrying her across his chest instead, even though she'd soon be dead weight and his arms would be killing him. He saw a tram stop and sat on the bench to wait. By the time the tram dropped them off at the escalator, Kelsey was fast asleep. Ted walked slowly, carrying her to the car, then strapping her in. She woke for a moment as he buckled the seat belt.

"Can Mommy come for pizza?" she asked sleepily.

"Sure, honey," Ted answered, knowing such a request would be futile. "We'll ask her and see if she can make it, but remember she might be busy."

Kelsey drifted back to sleep, the smile on her face in sharp contrast to the sorrow and concern on Ted's, something he was grateful she couldn't see. He'd begun to wonder if it would have been better for him and Charlotte to have stayed in Montana, or perhaps to have returned there when she'd continually asked him to consider it. Maybe he wouldn't have been as intent on climbing a corporate ladder filled with sharks and deceit that he arrogantly thought he was smart enough to conquer.

They were about ten minutes from Shay's home when Kelsey woke up. "I want to sleep in my own bed," she said, her voice slightly groggy.

"Mommy is having a sleepover with your grandma, honey. You have to stay with me until it's time to go to school tomorrow," Ted said.

"Please, can we go home, Daddy? And you can stay too?" Kelsey asked.

"That's not how it works, Kelsey, you know that." Ted glanced at her in the rearview mirror. "Mommy and Daddy are not living in the same house right now. I'm sorry, honey, but this is the way it has to be."

Kelsey was quiet the rest of the ride to Shay's, seemingly resigned to the fact that she could not have her own bed or her parents in the same place tonight. His daughter's face, her disappointment and hurt, lived with him permanently now. It broke his heart that she was paying for his mistakes this way. He was doing what he could, with a little help from Shay, to investigate, but it was tough. Ben might be watching Shay, and he didn't want his friend in the same boat he now found himself in. He'd been hired by a small computer repair place. It wasn't much—cleaning malware off of home computers and helping owners understand how to keep their laptop safe—but it paid for a day at the zoo. Shay turned down his offers to pay rent. Determined not to sponge off his best friend, he brought home food and picked utility bills where he could.

Ted thought again of the choices that might have prevented him from losing so much. He could have found a small job in Bozeman or in Missoula. He could have told his wife the truth. Trusted her to help him protect Jesse. Too late now. He feared his next home might well be a prison cell.

CHAPTER 17

I t had been a quick and easy ride over the Highland Park Bridge to Old Rt. 28 and on via the Fort Pitt Bridge to the Ohio River Boulevard, then into Sewickley. Traffic was light. As Charlotte entered the little town where local celebrities mixed with business elite in the quaint shops and eateries, she wondered why she'd vehemently eschewed living here. Its well-kept streets and parks, Victorian homes, and brick mansions made Ted love it. Kelsey was crazy about the Fun by the Pound shop across from Charlotte's favorite indie bookstore. Maybe it would have been healthier for them, as a family, to have moved out here like Ted wanted.

Her life these days was a litany of second-guessing herself, followed by anger and, sometimes, angry outbursts. She felt a loss of control at every turn, unsure of so much, on a path with no visible, sensible ending that would afford the best life possible for her daughter. As she parked in front of the three-car garage and gazed up at the lovely open portico above, and then on to the huge semi-wrapped porch beyond, she suspected it was unlikely her insecurities would be alleviated here in this home where the roots of many of her struggles still lay. Church bells in the distance were playing "Morning Has Broken," and she wondered what occasion warranted Sunday music on a cold Saturday morning as she slipped an overnight bag over her shoulder and headed up the flagstone pathway, past the impeccable white wicker porch furniture, now covered for the winter, and through the front door.

Charlotte removed her shoes and walked forward silently across the white marble tiles, past the curved mahogany staircase of the foyer, until she reached the thick hall runner stretching back to the kitchen. Her mother was back there, alone. Her father was golfing or at work, his usual Saturday morning routine. Charlotte had timed the visit to prevent her parents from double-teaming her. Divide and conquer had worked seven out of ten tries when she was a teenager.

"Mom?" Charlotte asked, watching Rosalyn Porter look up from her newspaper. "Are you busy or heading out soon?"

"Where would I be going at eight in the morning?" Rosalyn folded the newspaper and set it on the table. "Where's Kelsey?"

"Kelsey's spending the day with her father," Charlotte said as she draped her coat across the back of a chair. She walked to the coffee maker to pour herself a cup before sitting down across from her mother. "And I asked because you're nicely dressed with full makeup at this early hour, so I thought, perhaps, you had plans."

"Just because I don't work doesn't mean I sit around in a bathrobe looking a mess. You never know who will stop by."

Charlotte sighed. As usual, they were off on the wrong foot. "Of course, Mom. And you look lovely."

"You look exhausted. Dark circles under your eyes, and

you've lost weight. I don't understand why you need to continue living in that apartment rather than staying here with your family."

Charlotte felt her body tighten, her hands gripping the coffee mug. She needed her mother's help, but the age-old habit of snapping back in response sat on the tip of her tongue, ready to explode. It left a sour taste in her mouth. Taking a deep breath to steady herself, she exhaled slowly, feeling a level of calm descend, allowing her to let it go. Whatever the source of her mother's unhappiness was, she couldn't shoulder that with all of her other problems right now.

"I thought I'd stay here tonight. Kelsey is with Ted for the weekend." She leaned back and closed her eyes, imagining a hot bubble bath in one of the three large bathrooms upstairs followed by a solid, deep sleep in her old bedroom.

"Of course, you're always welcome," Rosalyn said with a casual shrug. "But why allow Kelsey to stay with Ted?"

Her mother loved her, but she was always so formal with Charlotte. As a grandmother, she was far more relaxed, treating Kelsey in the same way Charlotte remembered experiencing as a small child. She supposed her mother was simply better with very small children, before they grew older and disappointed her at every turn.

"He's her father. She misses him," Charlotte answered. "I thought maybe we could spend the day together, Mom. Have lunch or go shopping, or maybe some wine and a movie?"

"Soften me up before you ask me for money?" Rosalyn asked, her voice laced with light sarcasm. For the first time, Charlotte noticed hurt in her mother's eyes, pain that she'd put there. "I rarely see your brother unless we fly to London to accommodate him. I see you when you roll in here trailing all the anger and mess of your life because you need something." She stood up and walked to her purse, sitting on the kitchen counter, and pulled out a checkbook.

"No!" Charlotte raised her hand as if she were a school crossing guard. "Forget the money. I mean it, let's try, Mom. Let's just spend the day together and try No lecture about Ted, no requests from me for money."

"And how long will that last? Today? Tomorrow?" The checkbook slid back into the brown Gucci handbag.

"The problems between you and me run pretty deep," Charlotte acknowledged. "If you want to hash them out this morning, fine with me." She could feel herself tightening into a ball of rage, ready to explode out of what had been a living, breathing protective shell around her for months now.

"Your idea of hashing it out has always been criticizing who I am, then claiming I won't let you be yourself . . . that I want you locked in some mold of my making." Rosalyn's voice resonated with bitterness. For a brief moment, Charlotte saw herself judging Ted for not seeing her vision of ranch life in Montana as idyllic, labeling him work-obsessed while continuing to be dependent on the very financial support that his job had provided. She stubbornly shoved that thought down, focusing on her mother instead.

"Well, Mom, don't you? You don't like who I married, where I live, my choices of college and career." Even as the words left her mouth, she wondered what she would do if Kelsey turned her back on all the dreams Charlotte had for her, viewing them with disdain, rebelling against her at every turn. She chafed at the thought of it and at the realization that, for the first time ever, she was facing rather than running from a candid conversation with her mother.

"What a terrible mother I am to want you to live in a safe

neighborhood, to not be dependent on a man to get by as I am, and to enjoy having you live nearby!"

They were both in combat mode this morning. Charlotte knew she was regressing to her sixteen-year-old self again, and she struggled not to fall into the old habit of yelling back and walking out. A habit that had, she was coming to realize, made her fifty percent of the problem.

"It's all my fault then? Where we find ourselves? If I'd married a guy from the club, moved into a house down the street, and parlayed my local college degree into working at Dad's office; if I'd made my life a carbon copy of yours, then it would not be the mess it's become and you and I would be picture-perfect?" Instantly, Charlotte regretted lashing out; regretted letting things devolve to the state they had always been. Her mother sighed and closed her eyes. Charlotte sensed it was on her to build a bridge here, to let decades of stubborn resentment go and find a way to meet her mother halfway.

Rosalyn walked to the coffee maker, keeping her back to Charlotte, a slight tremor in her voice as she spoke. "Why don't you go upstairs and rest. You look like you need it. I can make us some brunch or lunch later."

Charlotte looked around the perfect kitchen, the symmetrically aligned bird feeders outside in the carefully landscaped yard. Everything sat poised as the backdrop for her stately, impeccably groomed mother, and she faced the fact that she'd run after her own desires without much consideration for the woman before her, the woman who bore her and raised her, who loved Kelsey as much as she did. Her rejection of this home and her upbringing had hurt her mother in a way that would kill her if Kelsey did the same.

"I'm sorry, Mom. It would truly hurt me if Kelsey felt

that way about me," Charlotte answered. "You deserve better than that from me."

Rosalyn was quiet, sliding into the role Charlotte had always seen her in. Yet now it looked more like a protective barrier than a cold steel wall. Charlotte rose and walked to her mother, gently leaning against her, wrapping her arms around her. "I love you, Mom. Can we start over?"

Her guilt mingled with a strange sense of relief, the heft of a decades-old weight lifting off her shoulders. She waited, their faces so close she could see the fine lines under her mother's carefully applied makeup, see the mascara smudging as a tear escaped. Charlotte felt a deep desire to be small again, to crawl into her mother's lap as Kelsey often did. Rosalyn patted her shoulder then hugged her quickly, as if unable to release any words.

Charlotte held on to her mother, not letting the hug feel perfunctory. "A rest before lunch sounds nice I think I'll take a bubble bath and lay down for a while, then we can fix a meal together." They had crossed a good line in their relationship, but her mother needed space to compose herself. Rosalyn Porter was not comfortable without at least a modicum of self-control in place, and Charlotte had thoroughly knocked her mother off of her normal game.

Charlotte stood up, slipping her bag over her shoulder. At the kitchen entranceway, she thought she heard her mother say something, so softly, that she half turned, unsure.

"Mom?"

"Stop." Rosalyn was facing her now, tears running small black rivulets of mascara down her cheeks.

"I'm sorry, truly. I didn't come here to fight with you. I've been losing my temper a lot lately," Charlotte said.

Rosalyn shook her head, putting up her hand as if to

halt Charlotte's incoming words, then wiped her eyes with a tissue and cleared her throat.

"I never wanted your life to be a carbon copy of mine. My mother taught me to keep up appearances, not to talk about certain things. It was all about image." Charlotte watched her mother struggling, as if choking the words out, and yet these were things she already knew. She remembered her pompous, uptight grandmother well. "You think your father is at the office or golfing this morning, don't you?"

"Well, that's been the routine for years, so yeah, I assumed he was one of those two places."

"He's not. He's been with his mistress of many years since last night. That's been his usual Friday night or Saturday morning routine for a long time. He only breaks it when Kelsey is here."

Charlotte's lungs constricted like the air had been knocked out of them. She opened her mouth and closed it, but no words would come. She breathed in and out, eyes closed.

"Dad's cheating on you?"

Rosalyn nodded, all formality gone from her face and voice. Charlotte saw a lonely, sad woman, and she fought the desire to run to the bathroom and throw up. If she was this sickened and hurt, how terrible had it been for her mother, day in and day out, for years? Indignation rose within her, tamping down the nausea and denial.

"Where is he? Right now?" She was furious at Ted, at her father, and she wanted to take that outrage and level it right at her father and his girlfriend.

"No . . . no . . . there is no point in this. Do you understand why I want you to have a career like Leah? Why I didn't want you to marry Ted?"

"The Leah part, yes, although we could have a longer conversation about her personal issues, but Ted had a good job. There was no reason to be against him except that he came from a less affluent family, Mom."

"I saw someone consumed with career and self," Rosalyn said. "Maybe I misjudged him in the beginning, maybe I saw your father in him a little too much, but I wasn't half-wrong, was I?"

"I'm not sure yet." Charlotte could feel herself deflating, the shock from her mother's revelation leaving her shaky but clearheaded. "He says he's innocent and that what he did to get that promotion was to save Jesse and the ranch. He's never cheated on me."

"I'm sorry to lay this on you, Charlotte, after so many years of silence. I can see I've added to your stress."

Charlotte walked forward and put her arms around her mother, feeling her mother grab her, tightly, in return. "I've been a child about things in many ways . . . in my marriage, my career . . . with you. Can we start over?"

She could feel her mother's heartbeat, that ancient rhythmic movement that sent comfort and love to her long before memory, that lay next to her after childhood nightmares, that faded away in the face of her teenage rebellions and the uncomfortable wall they built between them.

"Go, Charlotte. Go take a bath and a nap, and then we'll get something to eat. We'll start over."

Wiping tears from her cheeks, Charlotte picked up her bag and turned to go.

"I never liked Dad much," she said over her shoulder. Even as the words left her mouth, she felt the painful impact of truth in that statement. She loved him, but she hadn't liked him much over the years.

Fifteen minutes later, Charlotte slid into a hot bubble

bath, her overnight bag in her old room, and let herself connect with the memory of the mother of her childhood—who sang songs and read books to her—like a worn, smooth puzzle piece inserting into the fabric of the mother Charlotte had become. She saw herself as she'd been, locked in a kind of arrested development, struggling to build a marriage when she and Ted were both too young, too unworldly, perhaps too immature to have become parents together, let alone try to take on all that was happening now. Maybe all young couples eventually figure it out if they have enough love and honesty and determination. She tried to imagine healing the chasm between her and Ted the way she'd attempted to do with her mother just now. But what emerged inside her was more an old memory of love, lost among the cobwebs in a dark passageway created by her anger. Charlotte wanted to run in the opposite direction. She wanted to be free to explore. Being with Ted equaled being trapped with pain and failure, with a memory she couldn't absorb, that she couldn't make part of her present. Perhaps not ever. It painted a future in which she became what she now knew her mother's life to be. And yet that love they had once felt lingered on the fringes of her being like a willing shadow, and she couldn't quite bring herself to sever it completely.

A bath and a power nap gently pulled from her the toxicity created by her ongoing anger and sorrow. She sat up on the side of the bed, stretching her arms overhead, looking around her childhood room with a nostalgic fondness she hadn't allowed into her mind in ages. This feeling wouldn't last. Tomorrow morning, she'd head back into the city and into the hot mess that was her life, but for this sweet moment, she simply inhaled.

"Feeling better?" Her mother was leaning against the doorway.

"Much better! What do you say we go out for lunch?" Charlotte asked. Her mind was devising a plan to hold onto this feeling for as much of the day as possible.

"I'd like that," Rosalyn said. Charlotte knew what was coming next. "I'll call the club and reserve a table."

"No . . . no, Mom," Charlotte said, feeling a smile stretch across her face that sent soft, tingling vibrations throughout her body. "I'm taking you somewhere else. It will be a bit of a drive, but you'll love it."

"Where?" Apprehension crossed her mother's face.

"No pubs or taverns. Somewhere we haven't been in a long time." She winked at her mother. "Casual attire and walking shoes, Mom. Fifteen minutes, and then we leave."

TRAFFIC HADN'T BEEN BAD, Charlotte thought as she pulled into an open parking slot and shut off the car. She glanced at her mother's face, so happy once they'd turned onto Schenley Drive and she realized they were heading to the café at the Phipps Conservatory. They'd come here about once a month when Charlotte was young, before they could no longer be in the same room without arguing, and after lunch they'd walk through gardens that had provided an oasis of nature in the midst of a busy city for 125 years, her mother pointing out different flowers and herbs. None of it had stuck with Charlotte, who hadn't inherited her mother's green thumb, but she'd loved the feeling of togetherness. Perhaps in this place where they'd only made good memories, they could find a way to heal.

"Do you have your membership card, Mom?" She should have asked before they left.

"Always." Rosalyn said as she opened the car door and stepped outside.

An hour later, they were walking off kale Caesar salads and alternately talking about the intricacies of creating a Japanese garden, Kelsey, and Charlotte's new full-time role at the museum. Attendance was sparse today, and at times it felt like they had the whole conservatory to themselves. Charlotte had been treading very carefully in an effort not to mention her father, despite the strong pull to learn more about this mystery woman he'd been having an affair with, determined not to remove the joy from her mother's face.

"How did we lose this?" she asked, careful to keep her tone casual, lightly touching the giant palm fronds as they looped back through Palm Court to the Serpentine Room, her mother's personal favorite with its flowers gently curving in a snakelike pattern end to end. From the corner of her eye, she saw Rosalyn's face tighten, her body stiffening slightly, making Charlotte instantly sorry she'd gone in this direction.

"Lost or misplaced, Charlotte?" Rosalyn looked wistful, her face sad but not angry. Charlotte's sixth sense felt an opening here, a door she needed to walk through if she was ever to close the distance that had grown between them year over year.

"Misplaced, I hope." She felt like a child hungry for a hug, waiting for something, a sign perhaps. Her mother was never demonstrative in that way in public. She took her mother's hand. Baby steps.

Rosalyn squeezed her hand in return. "If two people want the same thing, then it can't be truly lost. But the longer it's misplaced or locked away, the harder it can be to repair."

Charlotte was intrigued at this new side to her mother. Despite her desire to feel like a child again with the woman before her, to seek comfort as if she were a little girl, she liked standing here, woman to woman, as equals on the threshold of something that could be a new beginning if she would grow into the moment rather than ruin it.

"Are you thinking about us right now? Or about you and Dad?"

Charlotte sensed a hesitancy in her mother. Rosalyn let go of her daughter's hand, sliding her own hands into the pockets of her perfectly pressed pants.

"Your father and I qualify as lost. He left the relationship a long time ago. What's left is for appearances' sake . . . and the avoidance of a messy and expensive divorce." Rosalyn leaned forward slightly, gazing at the lotus flowers floating in Monet-like splendor across the pond. "I was thinking of you and me, and of you and Ted."

Her mother turned toward her, and Charlotte met her gaze full-on, knowing what was coming. "And you and Ted? Are you lost?" Rosalyn's voice had gone from soft to steely, but Charlotte knew, as a mother herself, it was a result of controlling the desire to protect her, to tell her she should remove something painful, and perhaps even dangerous, from her life.

"I don't know." It was as truthful as she could be. "My head wants to tell you yes, but my heart still feels things that even disgust can't seem to fully shake."

Her mother nodded with an understanding Charlotte now knew emanated from her own experience. They began walking again, quiet for a few moments, drinking in the luxurious green of palm fronds, trees, and a cacophony of colors blooming all around them.

"Well, he'll either kill what's left, or he'll turn himself around and beg your forgiveness," Rosalyn said, stopping in front of exquisite lavender orchids looking as fragile as Charlotte felt in this moment. "To be honest, it will be easier for you if he is actually as selfish as I've always thought him to be. Then you can move on. Otherwise, you'll be faced with a tough decision."

"Which is why I need you, Mom." Charlotte's hands were trembling, her voice shaky even to her own ears. She needed this new version of her mother, perhaps a version that had always been there and she'd been too blind to see it. Or maybe someone who was evolving, just as she was, into a person she could have a better relationship with. "Not to judge me, no matter how I handle this or how everything lands in the end, but to listen, and to love me."

"I'll always love you, but with that comes my desire to shield you from pain." Rosalyn shifted back and forth a bit, then reached forward and pulled Charlotte into a hug. "You won't get out from under my opinions, but I have no place judging you from where I sit with your father."

Charlotte relaxed into her mother's arms. She could see, over her mother's shoulder, a group of college students looking at them curiously, and she smiled. If only she could tell them not to waste as much time as she had.

"Mom, don't move." She pulled away and walked toward the students, amused by the uncomfortable looks on their faces.

"Would you take a picture of my mother and I?" she asked, handing her phone, camera ready, to a young man who looked about the right height to take a decent shot.

Charlotte put her arm around her mother's waist and felt her mother respond in kind. "Smile, Mom. To a new beginning."

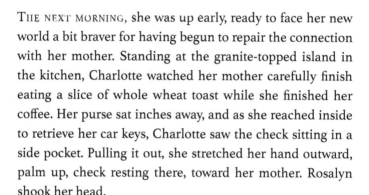

THE NEXT MORNING, she was up early, ready to face her new world a bit braver for having begun to repair the connection with her mother. Standing at the granite-topped island in the kitchen, Charlotte watched her mother carefully finish eating a slice of whole wheat toast while she finished her coffee. Her purse sat inches away, and as she reached inside to retrieve her car keys, Charlotte saw the check sitting in a side pocket. Pulling it out, she stretched her hand outward, palm up, check resting there, toward her mother. Rosalyn shook her head.

"I don't want our fresh start to be about money," Charlotte said. "I can manage on my own."

"No, I want to help." Rosalyn had a stubborn, determined look to the set of her jaw and mouth that Charlotte knew well.

"Mom, if this is at all about Dad . . . I'm not going to say anything to him. I'll respect your request, as much as I'd like to hit him . . . hard." Privately, she was thinking of ways she could catch her father with this woman on her own, absolving her mother of revealing his infidelities to her, and have it out with him, really tell him how she felt.

"It's not hush money, Charlotte. Or guilt money. Or trying to buy your love. It's simply me, your mother, helping you when you need a hand." Rosalyn stood, walked over to Charlotte, and wrapped her in a hug.

"I'll send you a copy of our picture soon. One for me and

one for you." Charlotte squeezed her mother close, kissing her cheek softly, then set out to tackle the turmoil that was her life these days, yet again.

CHAPTER 18

Charlotte found a parking spot off of Federal Street. Pulling her knit cap down over her ears and her scarf up over her mouth, she headed into the stiff, icy late-February wind, her eyes and nose running by the time she stepped inside 40 North, a little bistro tucked inside the City of Asylum, the world's largest sanctuary for writers in exile. Charlotte loved the all-in-one bookstore and restaurant on the first floor. It was an open space—no quiet corners like most of the local pubs offered. The restaurant area sat to the left of the front door and to a comfortable sitting area with welcoming couches set in a semicircle over a brightly colored rug, while the bookstore, which featured the works of writers granted asylum in the U.S., was located to the right of the front door and sitting area. Before Kelsey, she'd often curled up with a book in a sitting room chair to read after spending her money in the small but well-stocked store. It was a neighborhood familiar to her for its galleries and music events. It was a neighborhood Ted rarely frequented. Feeling tired and a little nervous about a meeting that seemed like a strange cross between a normal follow-up interview for a freelance article and an almost date, she needed this safe spot. Kelsey was with her grandmother this weekend, and Charlotte was using the time to pick up a little extra money freelancing.

"Hi, been waiting long?" Charlotte asked, slipping into the chair across from a muscular man with a boyish grin and thick, dark, wavy hair. The smell of soup and coffee mixed with the warmth inside began to shake off the chill. Even though it had been only a short walk from the car to the restaurant, she was shivering. Ever since her initial interview for a local magazine article assignment about the Pittsburgh River Rescue team, she'd been making excuses to continue accepting invites from rescue team leader Danny Manella for coffee, and now for beer and Saturday brunch, writing them off in her mind as follow-ups to the article she was drafting.

"No, just long enough to order a beer," Danny said as he gestured for the waitress to return. Charlotte ordered a Blue Moon on tap.

It had been almost five months since she'd moved back into the apartment and Ted moved out. The lease ran another six months, but her full-time job at the museum plus a little freelance work, along with some financial help from her mother, left her able to pay the rent and bills. She felt independent, almost free, her feelings for Ted locked in a separate space inside her mind and heart where, if she limited her engagement with him to dropping off and picking up Kelsey, she was able to ignore them—or at least keep her ongoing confusion about her estranged husband at bay. She'd put all the photos of their life together in a box at the bottom of her closet.

Leah had been sniffing around, trying to find excuses to have a drink or two, always prodding Charlotte with strange questions about Ted. Charlotte had had many conversations with Nate Morgan over the ensuing months since their first meeting, and she'd learned Ted's claim that Leah was part of the group who had framed him was grounded in a disturbing level of truth. Leah held firm that this was Ted's guilt talking, that she had no idea he'd opened an account or embezzled money until he showed up at the bank the day he was fired. But when Charlotte brought Leah's claims back to Nate, he obtained permission to show her a small part of what the FBI investigation had uncovered. It wasn't everything, she knew, but it was enough that her instinctive need to doubt the federal authorities regarding Leah disappeared. Nate needed Charlotte to get closer to Leah, but she preferred to avoid both Leah and the FBI as much as possible. When she did see Leah, she shifted their conversation to other subjects to stop any uncomfortable questions. So far, it appeared Leah was responding with a lessening of texts and lunch invites and generally connecting a bit less each passing month.

She blushed as her last conversation with Leah ran through her head, watching Danny give her a quizzical look.

"There's nothing going on, Leah. He's just cute."

"You need to have hot sex with a cute guy, Charlie."

"Still married, remember? That's not what I need right now."

"It's what you need. Trust me."

"What I need is some space, some freedom, and not to talk about Ted."

Danny had been her guide through the world of the River Rescue team and her primary source for the article. He told her he'd noticed she wasn't wearing a wedding ring, after he asked a couple of gentle questions over beers and barbecue at the River Rescue charity fundraiser. She'd told him she was separated. She wouldn't share much more, and there had been no press coverage about Ted or the investigations and legal issues he faced. Charlotte was pretty sure the FBI was keeping a tight lid on everything. But lately, she'd been lonely, opening up to Danny a little at a time, telling herself they were just friends and she wasn't dating.

"Sorry I'm late. Finding parking was challenging," Charlotte said.

They sat in silence for a few minutes. Her article was nearly completed. She hoped to submit the final draft in a few days. Then the connection between her and Danny would end, leaving them with little common footing.

"How's work? Anything new out there on the rivers?" Charlotte quizzed with a grin.

"Nothing new for me. How about you?"

"Trying to juggle the job, the freelance writing, and my daughter. Not much time for anything else these days."

"No time for dating?"

Charlotte hid her face behind the glass of beer, taking a long drink. She'd hoped he wouldn't go right for this topic, that maybe they'd have light conversation to take her mind off things. But she couldn't lead him on either.

"I'm married, Danny. I think you know that."

"No wedding ring," Danny said, reaching over and tapping her left hand.

Charlotte pulled her hand away, rubbing her ring finger as if the band was still there. "We're in limbo. I'm not sure what will happen with that. He wants to get back together, I don't know what I want."

"I'm sorry . . . really, I am," Danny said, looking worried. "That was insensitive."

"I'm not sure I should be here." Charlotte pulled her purse onto her lap like a barrier and wondered if she should stand and leave.

"I like you, Charlie. I feel a connection between us." Danny kept a steady gaze on her, making Charlotte blush at the brazen flirtation and begin to squirm at being put on the spot.

"No offense, but you've never been married. My life is in some sort of transition, but I'm not sure where I'll ultimately land. Can't we simply be friends for now?" She wanted to kick herself for the pleading tone in her voice. "I could really use friends that have nothing to do with my husband and our problems."

Charlotte watched him, the disappointment moving across his face like a shadow, and she knew he wanted to agree to be friends, to take it slow, but he might not be able to back up and give her that space. This was really her fault. She'd shown up with no wedding band, no mention of Ted, smiling and enjoying his company as she worked on the story. She'd known deep down she was sending the wrong message, letting the vibe between them roll in a direction she couldn't travel quite yet, but it had felt good to shrug off her marital woes for an hour here and there and inhale a sense of freedom. Danny made her wonder what it would be like to leave her old life for a new beginning.

"Friends it is," Danny answered, his unsmiling face in contrast to his words. "At least, I promise that I can try."

"Look, this is my fault. When I'm with you, I can shake off the pile of problems in my life right now," Charlotte said, the sincerity of her apology resonating as the tension in his face relaxed. "I was totally giving the wrong impression. I like you, but I can't even think about getting involved with anyone right now. It wouldn't be fair to you . . . or to my daughter."

"You should let me worry about Danny Manella," Danny answered. "But, all right, if we're going to be friends, then you need to tell me what is going on with you. Friends care about one another. They help one another."

Charlotte hesitated. She looked around the room, checking to make sure they were out of earshot of anyone else. They were at the tail end of the Saturday brunch crowd, and most of the tables were empty. "My husband, Ted, is a brilliant cyber security geek who had a bright future in a hot profession. But he went too far."

"Too far how?" Danny asked. "He cheated on you? He hacked into something he shouldn't have?"

"Worse . . . he claims he caught two managers planning to embezzle company funds, and instead of turning them in, he bartered with one for a promotion," Charlotte said. "Then, according to Ted, they set him up to look as though he'd embezzled money into an account in our daughter's name at a bank where my childhood best friend works, and he was fired."

Charlotte paused, watching Danny's face as he took all of this in. "He has legal claims against him from both banks and the DoJ with the FBI investigating," she added.

Danny let out a low whistle before he cleared his throat and leaned forward, his muscular forearms and elbows resting on the table. "Whoa, that's a lot of heavy stuff. Where is he now?"

Danny looked stunned despite his casual tone. Charlotte waited a moment, wondering if he was contemplating how to bolt and run, but he seemed intent on staying and hearing her out.

"He can't leave the area. He's staying with our friend, Shay, and working at a computer repair shop where he's vastly overqualified and underpaid but they don't care about his legal issues."

Charlotte saw the waitress approaching and picked up

the menu, relieved for the interruption. "I'm not super hungry, but let's order."

"Sure, then you need to finish your story," Danny said.

After they'd ordered omelets, Charlotte continued. "So far, I've been lucky that the papers haven't picked it up, but I don't know how long that will last. Ted does give me money when he can, and he spends most of his free time with Kelsey . . . if I let him."

She suddenly wondered why she felt the need to validate that Ted had a good side in the middle of an explanation that basically painted him as the worst kind of liar and possibly a criminal.

"Do you think he did it?" Danny asked.

"My gut says he would never bring our daughter into a dangerous situation," Charlotte said, her voice as firm as her conviction on this fact.

"No offense, but given the right situation, lots of people you think would never do something wrong or illegal might be tempted to do it."

"Ted's very close to his brother, Jesse, who runs their family ranch in Montana," Charlotte said, feeling the innate need to defend Ted even as she wished they could talk about anything else. "He says the mistakes he made were to save the ranch, which has been in money trouble for a while. He's always been determined he would earn his own way honestly. He may not have met that goal, but he didn't steal."

"You believe he's innocent?"

"I guess I do. It's the first time I've said it out loud. He's a lot of things but not a thief." Charlotte was not about to tell him that Ted had also lied to her about inheriting the ranch. She'd probably said too much already.

The waitress returned to check on their drinks. Danny

ordered another beer, but Charlotte moved her half-finished glass to the side and requested coffee. Keeping a clear head in what was evolving into more intense a conversation than she'd anticipated was probably best.

"I see why you need friends and why you're not ready to date," Danny said. "This is a lot to deal with on your own."

"I need real friends. Outside of Grace, I'm not sure who my friends are these days. Ted believes Leah, my best friend since high school, might have helped set him up. My family hates Ted. Shay is both Ted's friend and mine . . . I can't put him in the middle. It's nuts. All of it." Charlotte put her face in her hands, hoping she could keep from crying openly in the restaurant. "Please don't share this. I'm trying to hang on to what little privacy I still have."

"Your secrets are safe with me," Danny said, taking her hands in his, his touch reassuring. "But why hang out with me then? Why accept my invites?"

"Because you make me feel better. You're right, there's a connection between us. I just don't feel free to fully explore it. I have to think of Kelsey. This is all confusing and painful for her."

"Then let's start with that. I'll make you feel better. No strings attached."

Charlotte looked at Danny across the top of her coffee mug and, in the same way thousands of ill-fated people attracted to one another had done before her, silently acknowledged the truth that lay within her in the face of his offer, so intricately complex in the very simplicity of its utterance. She should leave. It was a lie that she could just maintain a friendship, and she might very well hurt this kind man who was refreshingly different from Ted. The attraction would tangle even their best intentions.

"No strings attached. It's a deal," she said with a smile,

pushing the tiny slivers of guilt down inside of her as deeply as they would go.

He gave her a little bit of time that was all hers, time she didn't have to share with anyone, time that was separate from the wreck of her marriage and the responsibilities of motherhood. A tiny getaway from her larger life.

"Would you like to bring Kelsey on Saturday for a ride on the River Rescue boat?"

Charlotte hesitated for a moment. Such an innocent question that assured this brunch would not end their meetings. Something to look forward to, and yet she wasn't sure she should bring Kelsey into whatever this was between them.

"Yes, that would be nice. She'd like that," Charlotte answered. "Providing you're ready for a ton of questions. She's only five years old and filled with them."

It was a safe step forward. Nothing more. A day out with her daughter and a new friend.

CHAPTER 19

"We were a family of whisperers," Ted called out softly from the Sixth Street Bridge in the cold, early-morning hours, listening as the March wind carried his words into the darkness.

He thought about the family he was part of before Charlotte and Kelsey as he watched the Allegheny River ripple in cadence with the brisk breeze that moved over him. He talked to God about the essence of where he'd come from and where he'd fallen, but his prayers were like rolling sorrows carried up beyond the clouds as if gone forever. Ted waited, but the wind brought him no response.

Ted would follow Charlotte to the ends of the earth if she'd let him, but he'd created a mess that he couldn't find any reasonable way to clean up. He couldn't envision a life without her or imagine how he could ever convince her to return to their marriage. She was the strongest person Ted had ever known. Walking in her shadow, he'd come to know just how weak he could be. Charlotte said she still loved him, but she couldn't go back in time. Too much, too late from Ted, and now she was moving forward without him.

Kelsey had been mentioning her mother's new friend who took her on the River Rescue boat. Shay had finally confirmed last night that he thought Charlotte might be hanging out with a guy, but Ted didn't have the guts to ask her if he was a friend, a flirtation, or something more serious. He didn't know if he could live with the response to that question.

Tucking his cold hands into the pockets of his hoodie, he leaned his body against the railing of the bridge—the river below, its movements peaceful and enticing, singing a false promise of escape. Water always had a soothing effect on him. Its lapping movement undulated like prairie grass in a subtle breeze. When sunlight spiked off its rippling surface on a clear day, it recreated memories of his Montana childhood along the outer edges of his conscious mind, asking to be acknowledged rather than ignored. The running lights of a River Rescue boat flickered softly to his right. For a brief moment, he wondered whether the guy Charlotte had written about in her article, and who seemed to have moved from an interview to a permanent fixture in her life, was just below him on that boat. What would she do if he actually moved past his uncertainty to end this pain?

"No, no . . . no," Ted muttered, shaking his head from side to side.

"You okay, dude?" Ted turned to see a young guy, dark curly hair poking around the edges of a ball cap, slim runner's torso on pause as he stopped his morning jog to eye Ted with concern.

"Yeah . . . yeah, I'm fine. No worries." Ted nodded to the man and turned away, pulling his hood up over the thatch of sandy-colored hair, long overdue for a cut, grateful for the concern but willing the man to resume his run and move on.

He could feel the jogger's hesitation seeping through him for several seconds, then heard footsteps moving away, the pace increasing to a run. For one weak moment, he wanted to call after the man, cry for help, but what good could a stranger do? No one could turn the clock back and undo his mistakes. His life with Charlotte and Kelsey, his job, his reputation, his money were all gone.

Ted had always been a better floater than swimmer. He didn't remember much water beyond the Gallatin River in his early life, Montana's grayish-green sagebrush moving rhythmically in the wind beside it, shaded by mountains. The locals called it "big" sagebrush, and it grew in every valley, basin, plain, plateau, and mountain slope around McLeod and Big Timber. Some nights, Ted still dreamed he was flying above the four-hundred-acre McCord Ranch, riding the wind and bent in obeisance to its power. As a child, there were angels flying with him in those dreams— hovering, gliding, whispering to him as they moved quietly above. He'd tried to tell his mother about it one morning.

"Ted McCord, you're a dreamer, and a dreamer gets nowhere in this world," Pearl Ann McCord whispered so his father wouldn't hear. "You've got to get some sense into that head of yours. The day you try to fly like an angel, you'll be dead, and that'll break your mama's heart."

Ted closed his eyes now. He could see them the day he left for college. Art McCord handed him fifty dollars and mumbled a quiet reminder to be on the ranch and back in the saddle during school breaks. Pearl Ann snuck him another twenty from her egg money, pulling it from the pocket of her worn blue jeans, her long blonde braid slipping across her shoulder as she leaned into Ted's truck to slide it under the home-baked cookies she'd set on the passenger seat.

"Don't go." Jesse's hushed, tearful voice had floated across from the passenger-side window where he hung off the running board, watching his brother pull his sunglasses from the glove compartment and set them on the top of his head.

Becky, his annoying teenage sister, stood on the porch, staring at Ted, arms crossed over her slim body, mouth slightly open as she chewed and smacked her gum in an offbeat but graceful way.

"Take me with you," she pleaded softly as Ted stepped around to the front of the truck, packed and ready to go.

"I'll be back, I promise," Ted said. Becky flipped her middle finger at him without her mother noticing.

"Liar," she mouthed silently.

Ted had gazed across the land toward the Absaroka Mountains, its peaks clear in the late-August sun that day, then started the truck and left.

All the misplaced ambitions, the running from his roots, were done now. He wrestled with whether he could change for the better. Maybe he was too weak to fight his demons, too flawed to repair the damage he'd done.

In spite of everything that had happened since he was fired, he hadn't told Charlotte why his father so adamantly wanted the ranch to go to Ted over Jesse. Like all McCords, it was his nature to keep a secret, to hoard it, to bury the words and only whisper about it with other McCords. This secret, however, remained between him and his parents.

"People change, Ted," Charlotte had argued when his parents were still alive. "And people make mistakes. Art is old and stubborn, but he loves you in his own quiet way."

"No matter how much I accomplish," Ted answered. "He'll only see me as a success if I take over his ranch."

"He doesn't see your job as a place where you have a

sense of pride and self-worth, but a place where you could never feel satisfied or successful until you get the next promotion," Charlotte had said, cutting into him with his father's own words. "Art wants you to feel what owning the land, working the ranch, makes him feel."

Ted had never found a way to explain that the draw of corporate life was as enticing to him as the draw of the land to his father. They were both stubborn and unable to communicate well with each other, sitting in their own corners seeped in anger and misunderstanding, unwilling to meet in the middle.

What was Art McCord thinking now, looking down on his son, mired in failure, standing on a bridge contemplating taking his own life? Ted could almost feel the letdown thrumming like a heartbeat from his father to him.

Ted went back to McLeod for the funeral, standing stiffly next to his siblings and the neighbors at the gravesite. Jesse stepped in to shoulder the responsibilities of a ranch he should own but did not. If only Art had moved beyond his stubborn pride. Not all secrets should see daylight. Most should be buried and forgotten, in Ted's opinion. In that final decision, Art left him with a burden beyond a struggling ranch. Ted kept his promise to Jesse to send money and shoulder his share of ranch expenses until he could sign the property over. In the beginning, it had only been a little money here and there, a tiny bit less dropped into his savings and handed to Jesse instead. But then there had been two tough years, and the McCord Ranch went into debt; debt that was coming due and would affect the credit rating of the ranch owner. Ted's credit rating. And so he stood here today.

He thought about Jesse now, bighearted and kind, a gentle giant at over six feet tall with thick, black curly hair and a solid, sturdy frame. Jesse was the only McCord who looked like he could be a linebacker. The rest were, like Art and Ted, wiry, lithe, with sandy-blond hair and well under six feet height. Only Ted knew Jesse was actually his half brother, the terrible secret whispered in anger by their father during a fight over Ted's rejection of the ranch. Fortunately, Jesse didn't witness the argument and, as far as Ted knew, he had no idea their mother had strayed or the father who raised him lacked a biological connection. Ted wanted to call Jesse so badly right now, but he wouldn't know where to start, what his brother could even do if he did ask for help. Last night, the thought had floated inside Ted's mind that if he were simply no longer there, then Jesse would own the ranch, Charlotte would go on to find a happy life, and Kelsey would grow up without the stigma of a father who sat in prison, disgraced, a stone around her neck that she had to explain away. Without Ted, everything could go back to normal for the people he loved.

Here, on this bridge, Ted was waiting for those angels of his childhood. Perhaps he'd always been headed for a moment when he could fly with the angels once and for all. But he didn't really want to jump from a spot this high. Actually, he really didn't want to jump at all.

Quick footsteps and the rattle of wheels on the pavement jolted him back to reality. Turning, he saw a young woman with a jogging stroller pass quickly behind him, a glimpse of a pink knit cap and tiny hands resting on a blanket before they were gone, continuing on their morning run. He'd had something similar that he strapped Kelsey in when she was small and they went for morning runs together. His heart ached with the memory, and in that moment, he accepted he could never leave his baby girl willingly.

"I don't think I can do it, God," Ted whispered as he rested his elbows on the railing and put his hands over his face. "They'd be better off without me, but I can't do it."

Still, the temptation was strong. He imagined floating along the Allegheny out to the Ohio River and beyond, until he fell asleep and quietly sank to the bottom, one with the sediment, one with the earth.

CHAPTER 20

The digital clock showed six in the morning. It was Saturday, and Charlotte sleepily wondered why the alarm was ringing. Sitting up, she realized it was her phone, the caller having now gone to voicemail. She tapped the phone icon and checked recent calls, then lay back on the pillows smiling. It was Danny.

The bed pillow next to her still smelled like his aftershave, the sheets of sex and sweat and satisfaction. Kelsey was with her grandparents for the weekend.

Danny had been here for the first time last night, but she'd spent the night with him twice at his house when Kelsey was with Ted or her parents. What Charlotte occasionally found lacking in their conversation over dinner or coffee was more than adequately made up for in bed where no conversation was required. She felt an insatiable need for the release that he offered her when she was naked and lost in the sheer intensity of connecting her body with his. It was unfair, she knew. Danny was more serious about their relationship while she simply savored living in the moments of escapism it provided.

"Couldn't get enough of me?" Charlotte asked, her voice husky and dry, when he answered the phone. He'd had to leave at three in the morning for his work shift.

"Didn't you listen to my voicemail?" Danny's voice was tense, clearly stressed.

"No, sorry. I just woke up."

"Charlie, this is serious. Early this morning, my team saw a guy looking like he was going to jump off the Sixth Street Bridge. They watched until he walked away and then looped back later to find him standing at the base of the bridge, talking to himself, talking to God. He was starting to walk into the river. They brought him back here." Danny hesitated for a moment. Charlotte could almost feel the tension rolling through the phone lines toward her. "It's Ted, Charlie. He hasn't broken any laws, but you need to get down here now."

Charlotte couldn't move. A wave of emotions assailed her—guilt, sorrow, panic.

"Are you there? Did you hear me?"

"Yes, I heard you. I'm on my way."

She hung up, panic-fueled adrenaline kicking in, and pulled on a pair of jeans, bra, and T-shirt in minutes. As she was splashing water on her face, she heard a knock. She ran for the front door, disoriented, hoping through her muddled feelings of shock and fear that it was Ted and they had the wrong guy. It was Shay.

"I don't have time, Shay. Something's happened to Ted."

"I was afraid of that," Shay said, holding up a large manila envelope and a jump drive in his hand.

"Why? Why were you afraid? He's been living with you. Did you know he was thinking about jumping off a bridge and killing himself?"

"Holy shit! No, Charlotte . . . what are you saying? Ted committed . . . Ted . . . is he . . ." She could see Shay's face register the shock. He took a step back, shaking his head in denial, arms crossed tightly over his chest as if to block what she might be about to say.

"He didn't do it. Danny's crew first saw him up on the bridge looking like he'd jump. Then they found him wandering into the river, as if he was still going to . . . going . . ." She couldn't finish the sentence. "He was talking to himself. That's all I know. Danny called me. I have to go down there."

She grabbed her purse and keys, pushing past Shay into the hallway. "Why are you here, and why did you think something had happened to Ted?" Charlotte snapped as she locked the apartment door, her guilt and fear turning to anger that maybe Shay had suspected and not warned her in some way.

"I'm going with you," Shay said. "Ted left me a note to give you this file and explain what's been going on. I'll fill you in on the way there."

Charlotte looked at him for a long, silent minute, deciding whether to be furious that, once again, things had been kept from her and this time Ted was the one having some sort of breakdown, or put that aside in the face of her need to get to Ted as quickly as possible. "Okay. Let's go."

As she headed down Braddock toward I-376 West, the fastest route into the city, Charlotte listened to Shay, her fingers tapping nervously on the steering wheel while they sat at a red light.

"Ted left me a note on the kitchen counter to grab the file he hid in my storage locker right after he was fired and give it to you," Shay explained. "I saw the note this morning.

Ted wasn't there and hadn't slept in his bed. I called his cell, but he didn't answer."

"You didn't suspect?"

"No, I thought he must be with you, that he was going to tell you about the investigating he's been doing on his own, so I picked it up and headed to your place."

"Why hasn't he given this proof to his lawyer?"

"He has, I think, given copies of some things. He's paranoid. He thinks everyone is in Ben's pocket."

She could see concern and something else on Shay's face. Something that looked like guilt. "What do you know about all of this, Shay?"

"Nothing about Ted considering jumping off a bridge, although he's been upset about you . . . and Danny. I've been helping him prove he was set up by Ben and others. I've seen the evidence he kept on Ben, and I begged him to let me turn it in to HR," Shay added. "But he said that would only make them come after me; that first he wanted to find evidence that they set up a fake account at Western PA and set him up, then we'd provide that information with the evidence he found when he should have turned those guys in for their original plans to steal from our company."

Charlotte was silent. The light turned green, and cars began moving forward. Traffic was slow. "Well, we both know Ted lost everything for a promotion that he might well have received anyway if he'd turned these guys in and done the right thing. He should have left the investigating to the FBI and to his lawyer."

Shay nodded his head, his face reflecting the misery he still felt.

"I don't think Ted would steal. I'm furious with him for a lot of things, but I can't see him doing that."

"I think Ben set Ted up," Shay answered. "But I'm sorry,

Charlotte, for not encouraging Ted to turn everything over and let the FBI handle it. I think I feel as paranoid about who can be trusted as he does at this point."

"None of this is your fault. I give you credit for forgiving Ted . . . for believing him, sticking by him after he lied to you," Charlotte said. She reached over and patted Shay's hand. He was their friend, a good guy who had been carrying guilt that solely belonged to Ted and no one else.

"Open the folder. Tell me what's in there."

"I already know what's in there. I looked at it the day after Ted told me to hide it. It's a download of all the information gathered when he dropped that package onto Ben's laptop, plus emails, notes on conversations he had with Ben, and proof that Bob Thornton and a third person were involved."

Thirty minutes later, Charlotte walked into the River Rescue office, deeply shaken by what Shay had told her and angrier than she'd been in a long time.

"Danny." She whispered his name softly as he wrapped her in a hug. "Where is he? Is he in there?" Charlotte glanced at a long, black body bag. Obviously someone had jumped.

"No, Charlotte, that's not Ted," Danny said, turning her gently away from the body bag as he opened the door to his office. "We think he was a homeless guy who fell." He eyed Shay suspiciously.

"This is Shay, Ted's best friend," Charlotte said, motioning to Shay to follow her.

She stood in stunned silence as Danny shut the door, leaving Shay and Charlotte alone with Ted. Ted was sitting on a bench near the wall, knees hugged into his chest, rocking back and forth, mumbling to himself. He ignored them as Charlotte knelt in front of him and touched his arm. Shay squatted down next to her and called out Ted's name, but Ted simply closed his eyes, leaned his head against the wall, and went silent.

"Call Jesse," Charlotte told Shay, her voice shaking. "Tell him he needs to come here and take Ted home."

CHAPTER 21

I t would be easy to curl up in a fetal position—head on his backpack, eyes closed—and ride the airport tram until its jostling motion numbed his mind and emotions, but Jesse was beside him, keeping him moving ever forward. Ted had felt both fear and relief when his brother showed up at the hospital in the early-morning hours, alone, with a suitcase and backpack packed with Ted's things, ready to go.

"Can I see Kelsey before we leave?" Ted had asked earlier as he emerged from the hospital bathroom where he'd shed the standard blue-and-white gown for jeans and a flannel shirt, belting them in so they fit, adding his old Adidas running shoes. He felt shaky. He couldn't run now if someone paid him to do it. He sat down in the only chair in the hospital room and clasped his hands together to stop the small tremors evident there.

"You look kind of rough, man," Jesse had answered. "It might be a lot for a little girl."

"Please?" Ted asked. Pain was gripping his insides like a vise.

"We'll FaceTime with her when we get home," Jesse said

with a look so sad Ted wondered if his own heartache might
be virulent enough to have spread across the room.

"I'm not really supposed to leave town, right? Won't this
get me in more legal trouble than I already have to deal
with?" Ted shifted his nervous energy to the plastic hospital
identity bracelet, moving it around and around his wrist.
"Maybe I should stay here, in the mental ward."

"Charlotte worked with your lawyer, that guy from the
FBI, and the doctors here to get permission for you to stay
with Jesse," Shay answered, appearing in the doorway, car
keys in hand. "Because you haven't been officially arrested,
the deal comes with a promise that you'll stay in counseling
and check in with your lawyer regularly. You're going to the
ranch while we figure out how to clear your name."

Ted saw the surprise on Jesse's face mirrored his own.

"I'm driving you both, Jesse," Shay said.

Ted stood, picking up the backpack and his jacket as
Shay grabbed the suitcase. "Don't worry, I won't run."

Fifteen minutes later, they were exiting William Penn
Hospital. Jesse sat in the front passenger seat, leaving Ted to
tuck himself into a cocoon in the back for the forty-five-
minute ride to the Pittsburgh airport. Ted lay across the seat
and pulled his Pirates ball cap down over his face. He felt
eternally tired. The shame he carried came in a kaleido-
scope of feelings that made him want to disappear.

"Hang in there, buddy." Shay pulled into the departure
area, a light stream of early-morning travelers making it
easy to park in front of one of the doors. He reached around
his seat to give Ted a smile and a quick pat on the shoulder.
"I'll be in touch soon."

"Be there for Charlotte and Kelsey?" Ted asked,
sitting up.

Shay nodded and grabbed Ted's hand, giving it a quick

squeeze before he turned back, eyes forward, hands on the wheel. Ted felt weighed down, too heavy to move. An immense wave of exhaustion rolled over him, making getting out of the car a struggle. Once on the sidewalk, his balance seemed uncertain until he felt Jesse's hand under his elbow.

"You okay?" Jesse asked, his face registering concern.

"Yeah, yeah . . . I'll be all right," Ted answered, not sure if there was truth in that statement.

Jesse hoisted his small carry-on bag onto Ted's suitcase. "Okay, let's get going."

"You guys good or you want me to come with you?" Shay chimed in from the car.

"No, we're fine," Jesse said. "We'll text you when we get to Bozeman."

Fifteen minutes later, Ted's bag checked in, they moved through a sparsely populated security checkpoint with only their backpacks, jackets, and Jesse's carry-on bag. Jesse showed both boarding passes and drivers licenses, and then they moved forward, one step at a time, slowly, steadily hiking the airport terrain of trams and escalators, food courts and high-end shopping until they arrived at gate A8 to wait for United Flight 1218 to Denver.

"Sit here, Ted." It was a relief to Ted to have Jesse giving him orders, firm and in charge, now pointing to a seat in the far corner, away from foot traffic and the ticket taker's desk but near the window. "You look really tired. I'm going to get us some decent coffee and a better breakfast than the one the hospital offered."

Ted nodded, putting his backpack on the seat next to him, then swinging his feet up and laying his head down on it. He didn't really care if they had coffee or food. He felt submerged by so much that he wanted to sleep endlessly, perhaps without ever waking up to his life as it stood today. But he knew Jesse was trying hard to take care of him.

"Thanks, brother," he mumbled, then closed his eyes.

Jesse must have let him doze for a while until a baby's cries made it impossible to block out his surroundings. Ted sat up, rubbing his neck, now stiff from the makeshift pillow. Wordlessly, Jesse handed him coffee and a blueberry muffin. He inhaled the smell of the coffee for a moment before taking a sip.

"No one in the mental ward could make a decent cup of coffee," Ted said.

"Don't call it that," Jesse admonished. "It was a hospital stay to make sure you were okay after . . ."

"After I tried to drown my sorrows and myself by walking into the Allegheny River?" Ted's stomach rumbled, and he was amazed that his body continued to signal its basic desires even as his heart felt no joy in its need.

They sat in silence as Ted ate the muffin and washed it down with the still-warm coffee, watching crews buzzing around their plane, now connected to the jetway, filling up the gas tank, loading the luggage, and running safety checks.

"You can rest at the ranch and get your second wind," Jesse said. "Find your way back to yourself."

"Maybe I can help. You can put me to work," Ted suggested, surprised that exhausting manual labor actually sounded appealing to him.

Jesse shook his head. "I'm not bringing you home with the idea of getting free labor."

"Why are you here?" Ted asked. "I'm not sure my good intentions have made me a very good brother to you. Actually, I haven't been a very good anything to anybody."

Jesse stood, his mouth set in a grim line. Leaning

forward, his mouth next to Ted's ear, he said, "Not now, okay? Not here."

Ted opened his mouth to apologize, but Jesse put up his hand as if to say "don't." Or perhaps he meant it as a gesture to ward off evil, Ted thought, watching his brother walk to the trash can to dump his empty coffee cup, then continue on to the restroom. People were beginning to line up according to the numerical designation on their boarding pass. He wondered how angry he'd made Jesse and what he could do to fix things before the flight left. Maybe he could sleep the whole way, making it easier for both of them.

"I'm gonna do the same," Ted said when Jessie returned, dropping his coffee cup in the trash on the way to the restroom.

When Ted returned, Jesse handed him his backpack and led the way to wait in line.

"We're boarding group three," Jesse said.

"Thanks. And sorry . . . I mean for earlier," Ted said. "I really appreciate you being here, even when I'm being an asshole about it."

"I'm here because we all love you," Jesse said. "Even though you can be a real asshole sometimes."

Ted's face fell into a natural grin for the first time that day. Jesse smiled back, and a small lift of energy invaded Ted's lethargy and depression. He wasn't sure he'd call it happiness—that was an emotion that he felt so far removed from he didn't know if he'd parted company with it for good. It was more like gratitude for Jesse and the love and caring his brother offered despite everything Ted had done. With Jesse, he was somehow safe from not only his problems, but safe from himself.

"It's still your ranch," Jesse said.

"No, it's never been my ranch because to own it, you should love it," Ted stated, his voice firm. "The way you do."

"Have faith, Ted. I think you'll get there and have a change of heart."

Their boarding number was called, and they moved forward quietly, Jesse in the lead, scanning both passes from his phone. Ted followed down the jetway, then down the aisle to the cheap seats in the back. He hoped the plane wasn't a packed flight.

"Art wanted you to have the ranch," Jesse said, his voice quiet but clear. "You know that."

Ted looked at his brother with surprise. He'd never heard Jesse refer to their father as anything but "Dad."

"A foolish notion on our father's part," Ted said. "When we get to Montana, let's talk to a lawyer and see if we can make you the sole owner, even if the timer he set in his will isn't up yet."

The rumble of the runway below increased as the plane picked up speed. Ted closed his eyes and absorbed the power of the lift as they became airborne. Through it all he sat, silent, staring out the window, contemplating how to respond to his brother. He closed his eyes for a moment and took a deep breath. Jesse had fished a Nevada Barr novel out of his sack and begun reading, probably giving up on conversation with his silent, morose brother.

"You still like reading westerns and mysteries, huh?" Ted asked.

"Yeah, I like her stuff," Jesse said with a smile. "Every mystery is set in a national park. I get to be a park ranger without doing the job. I could loan you a few of her books when we get home."

Silence settled over and around Ted like the white clouds now surrounding the plane. He thought about how his father had felt, deeply, the deficiencies of the McCords before him. A hard, lean man, Art had been determined to show he could earn the respect of the other ranchers. He spoke little about the less than illustrious members of the family tree to his children. His love was of a strict, tough variety coupled with a demand that they love the land and the ranch as he did; expecting their loyalty, expecting them to stay. Growing up under his expectations had been bad enough for Ted, but it must have been much worse for Jesse, who could never hope to meet Art's standards and who would have had no idea why his father was colder and less interested in him than in Ted.

"When did you find out?" Jesse asked, book closed, voice hushed in an attempt to find privacy in this public space.

"The night before I left for college," Ted said. "We got in a big fight out in the barn about me leaving, and it came out."

"That's why you were barely speaking to one another when you packed up to go?" Jesse asked. "I was so little, and sad you were going, but I remember the tension. He and Mama had arguments later, but they kept the door shut and their voices low. I couldn't make out what they were saying."

"How did you find out?" Ted asked. "I never wanted to tell you, to hurt you that way. It makes no difference to me. You're my brother, and that's that."

Jesse glanced at the passengers across the aisle before responding. "Let's leave it for now, Ted. Maybe later, when we get home." He picked up his book and settled into his seat, then began reading again.

Ted closed his eyes, reclining his seat a bit, and thought about that word: home. What would that mean for him now without Charlotte and Kelsey? In ways he'd not imagined a year ago, returning to the ranch sounded comforting. He wanted to lose himself in hard labor and open spaces until he collapsed, exhausted, praying he could somehow diminish the emotional pain inside. But home might soon be a prison cell, and the thought of this made his stomach clench. He crossed his arms and, leaning his head against the window frame, prayed for sleep to come.

CHAPTER 22

The smell of his own sweat mixed with the scent of Merlin below him, seeping into his bones as if it had always been part of his DNA, something he loved rather than ran from. It was unseasonably warm for early spring, but there was a breeze rippling eastward that dried Ted off as fast as he worked up a sweat again. He and Jesse had been checking their cattle, dispersed across the four hundred acres of McCord Ranch, happily grazing the new spring grass after a winter of man-made hay. A group of cattle were bunched up at the base of the mountain, nervously lowing. Merlin's ears were pinned back, letting Ted know something was wrong.

"Jesse?" He called for his brother on a two-way radio, the cell service this far out sketchy or nonexistent. He could see only one bar of reception on his phone and hoped Jesse was within the twenty-five-mile radius of the two-way.

"Yep?" Jesse's deep voice pinged into the quiet around him.

"Where are you? I'm at the base of the mountain, and we

might have a problem." Ted shifted in the saddle, still stiff and out of shape after his years in the city.

"On my way. Ten minutes tops."

Ted approached slowly, searching the terrain above the cattle for a predator. Wolves were the most likely, but a coyote or mountain lion wasn't out of the question. He didn't have a rifle with him, but Jesse did. His ankle monitor rubbed uncomfortably against his skin and the stirrups, reminding him with a quick twinge why he, like the cattle in front of him, couldn't roam far or carry a weapon. Like the animals, he had to rely on others for protection.

Merlin's ears were flattened now, and he was snorting. Ted could see a slight movement about twenty feet up the slope of the hill amidst the ponderosa pines and creeping juniper bushes, a flash of brown fur.

"Coyote. Are you almost here?" Ted spoke quietly into the radio. The coyote's ears were up—he must have smelled or heard Ted and Merlin. Ted began moving Merlin to a spot between the path he thought the coyote would take and the cattle.

The loud crack of a rifle shot rang out, and the coyote took off up the mountain. A second shot, and he was down, dead or would be. The cattle were running, dispersing quickly in the opposite direction, passing a smiling Jesse seated on his favorite mare, Ruby.

"Two shots to get him? You're getting old, brother!" Ted laughed as he turned Merlin in Jesse's direction.

"Let's see you take a try," Jesse called back as he flipped his middle finger at Ted.

"Against the rules. The law might come to get me." Ted wasn't sure whether he wanted to pick up a rifle again or not.

Jesse handed Ted the gun. "Nobody out here but us. And neither me nor the cattle are going to tell anyone."

Ted ran his hand over the stock, then dismounted from his horse, handing Jesse the reins. "You know Merlin spooks easy," he said. "I don't want to take a shot and land on my back, my horse galloping away."

He raised the gun to his shoulder, feeling the cold steel, and aimed at a pine tree. He could hear Art in his right ear as if his ghost were breathing on Ted's neck, instructing him. The feel, the rhythm of it, was coming back. Feet planted, he pulled the trigger and shouldered the kickback as if he'd never taken a nearly ten-year hiatus from the power of a rifle. Jesse handed him Merlin's reins and rode over to the tree.

"Not bad!" Jesse called. "Not a bullseye, but decent."

"I could hear Dad in my ear, instructing me. Kind of creepy. He always liked your ability to shoot better than mine."

"Maybe, but he liked you better than he did me overall." Jesse shrugged and looked toward the cattle now grazing and scattered widely. Ted felt the old twinge of guilt and sadness at Art's favoritism toward him.

"Want to let the horses graze and grab a couple sandwiches?" Ted pointed to a shady spot between a large rock and a cluster of trees as the afternoon sun moved westward.

"Sure. Then we'll start moving them back in toward the ranch for the night." Jesse dropped his six-foot frame to the ground, grabbed his rifle and saddlebag, and followed Ted.

As they sat quietly on a grassy patch, dusty and tired, Ted wondered if his brother still carried the weight and disappointment of Art's favoritism or if, unlike Ted, he was able as an adult to roll these things off his back and move on.

"You know, Dad was an ass. You worked twice as hard and did twice as well at everything that mattered to him, and he still left the ranch to me, knowing I didn't want it." Ted wasn't sure what he was doing right now, opening this conversation up. They'd been settling into a groove together these past months that wrapped Ted in comfort—his brother's patient, quiet support of his sessions with a therapist, his pain at missing his wife and daughter, and his fear of what that ankle monitoring bracelet meant for the future, helping him center and heal.

"I did work hard to earn Dad's attention and respect, but it never seemed to work." Jesse picked up a few small stones next to him and began throwing them one by one.

"He was a hard man. Hard to love too."

"As I got older, I noticed I looked different from the rest of the family," Jesse said, tipping the brim of his hat back and looking directly at Ted.

Ted leaned over to shift his court-ordered monitoring device and massage the area where it had been rubbing all day. He felt a lump in his throat, and he coughed softly, trying to ease his discomfort, to find his voice.

"I know growing up was hard for you. I don't want to make it harder right now, but if there's one thing I've learned this past year, it's that we McCords need to quit keeping secrets and get stuff out in the open." Ted put his hand on Jesse's back and met his gaze. He wanted him to know that they were and always would be brothers. Jesse watched him try to find the words, his face calm rather than curious.

"You thought I didn't know." It was a statement, not a question. Jesse was so matter-of-fact that Ted caught his breath, waiting. "I developed a huge crush on Kristi Connelly senior year of high school, and I asked her out."

"Kristi Connelly? I thought we were talking about Dad

and you." Ted could feel confusion rising in him. He'd been on the verge, the painful words he'd held in since he was eighteen years old and tucked away again on the plane about to tumble off his tongue, but Jesse appeared to shift gears, wanting to reminisce about an old high school crush. Maybe it was Jesse's way of deflecting a serious conversation he wanted no parts of.

"Mom found out we were dating from Kristi's father, and she sat me down, told me I couldn't date Kristi because she's actually my half sister and Trevor Connelly is my biological father." Jesse lay back on the grass and closed his eyes. "I was doubly crushed, and I gave Mom the cold shoulder for a good long while, like a typical teenager, until I noticed all the things about Art that were difficult for all of us probably drove her to that point."

Ted faced forward and squinted as the midafternoon sun reached eye level. "Why didn't you tell me?"

"I guess I could ask you the same." Jesse stood up, looking in the direction of their horses, grazing a few feet away. Ted stood as well, uncertain of what to say, and brushed dirt off his jeans, something Jesse barely noticed or bothered to do. "I didn't want things to change between us."

"I should have told you. At first you were too young, and then . . . well, there was never a good time." Ted walked toward his horse, guilt surging through him that his brother had gone through such pain alone and not come to him.

"After the lawyer read Art's will and I saw how furious you were, I figured you might know, but it didn't seem important anymore." Jesse hooked his foot in the stirrup and mounted his horse in one fluid motion.

Ted hoisted himself back onto Merlin, and they began a slow trot toward the cattle. "Did you ever talk to Trevor

Connelly about it . . . then or maybe later? Kristi's an only child, isn't she? You must be his only other child."

"I talked to Trevor about it a couple months after Mom told me," Jesse said. "She said he wanted to speak to me—explain, clear the air—but I was young and immature and I refused. I didn't know who to aim my anger and hurt toward. I was just angry at everyone for a while. Eventually, I tossed a saddle over Rosie . . . remember that old mare I loved? And I rode over to his ranch one morning. We went for a short ride, and he told me his door was open, but he'd leave it up to me if I wanted to walk through it and get to know him."

"Pretty brave of you," Ted said. He inhaled the familiar scents of sweetgrass and manure, wishing he could inhale the strength that came easily to his brother.

"He's so different from Art, and nothing like the fictitious slimy, evil guy who cheated with my mother that I'd worked up in my teenage mind," Jesse answered. "When Kristi headed off to college, I would stop by to see him. After Art and Mom died in the car accident, we got closer, and as he's gotten older, I help him with the ranch. Kristi's not interested in taking it over."

"Being part of the Connelly gene pool might be an advantage, Jesse," Ted said. "Trevor Connelly was always a decent guy."

"Trevor told me he was always in love with Mom," Jesse said. "They had a dumb fight when they were young, and she started seeing Art on the rebound, then married him."

"She should have left Dad for Trevor." All of Ted's old angers toward Art were rolling up, mixing with his ongoing disappointment in himself. Why couldn't he feel the same toward his mother, whose infidelity may have caused his father's already taciturn nature to deteriorate?

"Trevor wanted him and Mom to leave their spouses, but two months after I was born, Trevor's wife told him she was pregnant with Kristi. That was it. Star-crossed, as he put it." Jesse's quiet laughter mingled with the rustle of the herd as they began moving them back toward the ranch.

Ted felt a letting go, a level of relief that came with seeing his mother in a whole new light. He'd seen her as having had a fling because she was weak and unhappy, an action that made Art mean and caused the dysfunction they'd dealt with all their lives. When he thought about how he'd privately resented her for it, he imagined the depth of what Art must have felt toward her, maybe even struggling to quiet the feelings that he carried within about Jesse. Ted wondered what he would do if Charlotte did the same with another man. The knowledge that this might happen and, worse, that it would be less a betrayal than fallout from what he'd done made him nearly double over in the saddle.

"You okay?" Jesse had stopped, cattle milling around them, and was looking at Ted with concern.

"Yeah, just a headache. I'm tired." Ted sat up straight and rolled his head, loosening his neck muscles.

"You're back in the saddle but not back in shape yet." Jesse grinned, his infectious smile putting the sadness of their conversation behind them.

Ted could see the ranch now. The cattle at the front were moving slowly into the pen on their own, out of habit. "Next week, Jesse. Let's get the lawyer out here, and I'll sign this place over to you."

"Deal. But it will always be your home, Ted."

Ted nodded in agreement. Talking this much, especially about Art, made him tired. He wanted to say the right things for Jesse's sake, but he wished he could focus on some of the better memories of his father.

"When I ride in after a long day's work, the sun setting, ready to rub down Merlin and get a hot shower and a meal, I feel a sense of home, and I think good thoughts about Dad." Ted looked down at the small creek as they crossed, Merlin's hooves splashing through and out the other side, the opposite bank sloping slightly upward.

"See any fish?" Jesse asked. "Fishing was when Art was as good as he could get as a father."

"I'd like to take Kelsey one of these days. Maybe teach her a little fly fishing." Ted imagined taking her out to a small creek, spending the whole day just talking and trying to catch fish. A connection to the land he'd denied for so long was opening up within him, moving through him like a familiar groundswell; a surge of desire for the first time to pass it on to his child. In that moment, he understood what his own father had desperately wanted from him, to share something he loved so deeply it ran through his veins like blood and through his lungs like the air he breathed, but Ted had turned his back.

"Sure you don't want to keep the ranch?" Jesse looked comfortable rather than concerned as he tossed the question at Ted. "I'll inherit the Connelly ranch and tie the two together, or you can keep this one."

They were home now, each dismounting and beginning to walk the horses into the barn. As happy as Ted felt, home and safe, his instinctive, immediate response hadn't changed.

"No thanks. I still love the cyber security stuff." Ted gave his brother a smile. "But maybe you could let me live in the house, do some chores, take care of the place when you move on up to Connolly's."

"Deal!" Jesse slapped him on the back and began brushing down his horse, singing an old Beatles song loud and off-key until even the horse snorted its dislike and Ted begged him to stop. Jesse whistled a tune instead all the way back to the house. Ted felt lighter than he had in a long time. A dark tunnel filled with trouble still awaited him, but time with Jesse, with the animals—the hard work and sore muscles replacing the emotional pain and loss each day— was healing wounds Ted should have faced long before he sank his career and marriage into a pit.

After showers and a quick dinner of burgers on the grill, he sat in Art's favorite rocker on the porch, watching the sun set, listening to the crickets calling to one another across an otherwise still landscape.

"It's good to see you laugh again." Jesse eased his large frame onto a wide wicker chair favored by their mother, its faded blue cushions worn in a way that comfortably shifted to fit a person seated there.

Ted ran his hands over the arms of the rocker, thinking about a time when he sat in his father's lap on this very chair. It felt good to laugh again. He savored the memory until a wish slipped through him like a soft whisper. He wished that he could hold Kelsey in the same way, on this chair.

"For all his flaws, Art was a better father than I am." Placing his elbows on his knees, his head in his hands, Ted felt waves of sadness crushing him. If he had even an hour of strength left, he should do something, anything, that would wear him out, numb his pain, until he could sleep.

"You made a huge mistake. But Kelsey will always love you." The stiff wicker creaked as Jesse shifted his weight. "I'd love to have a couple kids one day."

Ted sat back, mentally shaking off his self-pity to really look at his brother. Despite growing up with a father who was decent to him but kept him at an emotional distance, then finding out he was the product of an affair and there was another, biological, father, Jesse was more centered and content than Ted had ever managed to be. He would make a great father. No striving for the next thing on a career ladder getting in the way of what was most important. Ted struggled with the ever-present shame inside him. He wished he could FaceTime Kelsey right now, but she was probably in bed, sound asleep. Charlotte had asked that he schedule those times with her, and he'd done everything he could to accommodate her requests, hoping, on a wing and a prayer, that she would take him back one day, providing he didn't end up in prison.

"You'll be a great father, Jess," Ted said, giving his brother a big smile. "But you can't get there on your own. How are things with Suzanne?"

Jesse shrugged, looking away for a moment, then answered. "Good. Not sure what we're ready for just yet, though."

They sat in brotherly silence, watching the sun drop behind the mountains. Jesse went inside and came back out a few minutes later with two cold beers, handing one to Ted.

"Maybe not a good subject, but what happened that night before you left for college . . . when you found out about me?" Jesse pointed a finger at the barn, and Ted eyed the old structure, repaired in places by Jesse but still in need of some work.

He could still close his eyes and see that moment clearly, smell the hay, the scent of the horses as he and Art fed them. He'd confronted his father as they worked side by side in the barn, feeling the weight of his family's checkered history tied to his back, to his name, to his future. He'd wanted to shed it like an ancient, crusty skin, dead and stifling the air he breathed, blinding his eyes to the beauty of the ranch around him. It seemed so silly now when he thought of it. Ted had been cocky, judging his father for selling mineral rights on McCord Ranch and then hiding it from the neighbors who were opposed to it. It was a hot-button political issue among ranchers at that time, and he'd asked his father to come clean and admit to his family and neighbors he'd simply needed money to keep the ranch going.

"What do you care? You're leavin' for that big fancy school," Art McCord answered angrily. "You best keep this to yourself. No sharing with your new college friends."

"I told him to come clean on what he'd done and that I was sick of McCord secrets," Ted answered now, turning to face Jesse. "He accused me of being okay with Mom's secrets but angry with him over every little thing. He said I was 'running away' from my responsibilities by going to college." Ted could still hear his eighteen-year-old self and see his father's face as Ted spit on the ground, as if heaving out the McCord legacy and leaving it in a ball of spittle on the barn floor would change things.

"I was young and brash. I told him I was going away to be my own man." Ted shook his head in wonder, even all these years later, at how he'd spoken to his father. What if, one day, Kelsey brought up everything that was happening now and judged him harshly, using the same tone? The thought hurt, making him catch his breath.

"I'll bet he didn't take that well," Jesse said.

"Nope. I don't know how I'd take it if Kelsey were that harsh, which could happen one day depending on how what's going on ends for me."

Ted set his beer down on the table next to him. It had gotten warm before he could finish it, and it hadn't really helped much. Sleep would be difficult tonight. The only solution he'd found to shut off his mind was working until he was too exhausted to do anything but sleep. Jesse was frowning at him. Knowing his brother, the look came from worry, regret that he'd brought up this subject. Ted didn't want Jesse tiptoeing around him as if he were a porcelain doll. The therapist had told Ted he needed to get to the root of whatever deep-seated problems had moved him in a direction where he was unable to be satisfied or confident and at peace with his life. "Figure out why you need to keep secrets from your wife, knowing they can cause damage," the therapist had instructed. If he couldn't talk openly about the past with Jesse, purge himself of those conversations he'd kept secret, how would he change for Charlotte?

Ted cleared his throat and did his best to mimic his father's voice. "He said, 'You mean be a 'better' man, don't you, Ted? Better than your daddy or your grandaddy?'" Ted could see Art as he said the words, his father's lean body flinging the hay into the horse stalls as if he were an Olympic competitor with a javelin. "I told him that all my life he'd tried to force me into the choice he made for me and he couldn't stand that I was making a different decision for myself."

Ted felt an odd, furious heat rising within him at the memories mixed with his present-day shame, flushing his face, making his heart beat faster and his stomach nauseous. He sensed the truth in his father's words coursing through him now in light of the turns his life had taken, although then he'd fought against it with every part of his being. He began moving the old rocking chair back and forth, inhaling and exhaling with the movement until he felt calmer.

"You don't have to tell me." Jesse was eyeing him with concern, his brows furrowed, his body angled forward as if ready to jump up and move toward Ted should the need arise.

"No, no . . . I'm okay."

"You looked a little rough there for minute." Jesse remained in position, but his body was tense, as if waiting.

"It's what came next . . . when I defended Mom, told him not to throw trash talk her way just because he was mad at me," Ted said, stilling his chair and his body, turning slightly sideways toward Jesse. "That's when he told me you had a different father, although he never mentioned who it was. He was trying to make me feel as angry with Mom as I did with him."

Ted looked at his brother, so protective of him and so willing to help clean up the mess of his life, with a mixture of grudging love and resentment that Jesse was the better man. Ted decided he would never tell Jesse what Art McCord's exact words were in the barn that night. He shifted back to face forward, the sun now gone and the fireflies lighting the night air. He stared at the barn, seeing Art —as if he were in the moment all those years ago—as he turned around and faced Ted, locking eyes with him in a hard stare that made Ted long to turn away. But he'd thrown down a gauntlet at his father, and he had to stand his ground, to defend his mother.

"Look at me and look at you, son," Art had said that night. Then and now, his words were like a slow-moving lava—searing, hurtful, crawling over and through Ted. "And look at your little brother Jesse. Does he look even a bit like you and me? Does he look and act like a McCord? Don't you go whitewashing your mother's secret while I've been feeding and clothing it for ten years."

Art had tossed the pitchfork aside, pulling off his work

gloves and turning away as Ted remained rooted to the barn floor, stunned, trying to process his father's loaded words.

"Well, Dad, maybe that's why Jesse is the best of us then," Ted had snapped back, knowing, even as he said it, that he'd gone too far.

Art was on him in seconds, livid, his eyes narrow, his calloused hands around Ted's neck. "You just wait, you little asshole . . . you just wait until you love a woman so much it hurts and even when she betrays you, you love her too much to leave." Then he'd pushed Ted back onto the pile of hay and marched out of the barn. "It's in your blood, boy. You're a McCord. You'll do something sooner or later that you'll want to hide rather than tell the truth."

Art's words rang in his ears as if it were a curse that reached beyond death to sit between him and Jesse. A prediction, Ted knew, he'd now fulfilled. He sensed Jesse waiting for the end of the story, for some kind of closure that Ted wanted to provide but knew he couldn't even provide for himself.

"I told him what I'll tell you now, Jesse. You're the best of all of us. Remember that." Ted stood, his ankle monitoring bracelet clicking against the inside of his boot. He limped slightly, muscles sore, patting his brother on the shoulder as he walked past and into the house, heading for his bed, hoping sleep would come.

CHAPTER 23

Charlotte watched as Gerilyn Leslie entered the art gallery like a prickly porcupine navigating outside its natural habitat, nearly sniffing at the artsy creatures milling about her. A short, stocky woman dressed in a poorly tailored power suit, she parked herself against an empty wall near the bar. Charlotte was there on freelance assignment for the newspaper, but it was a gallery she knew well. She was at home in this place and with this crowd, whereas Geri was off her game, obviously out of her element. Exactly where Charlotte wanted her to be.

Due to the small size of the gallery and the fire department's occupational rules, people signed up for the right to attend popular exhibits. Charlotte regularly checked both the guest invitations and the random, last-minute registrations, looking for any famous artist or wealthy patron who might provide a good quote and a little celebrity juice to her review.

"Why didn't you tell me she was poking around, investigating Ted's firing?" Charlotte had asked when she called Shay immediately after seeing Geri's name on the guest list and suspecting her attendance might not be a coincidence. He'd responded by filling her in on the encounters he and Missy had had with Geri at work.

"I didn't take it very seriously," Shay admitted.

"Ally or enemy?" Charlotte asked.

"Not sure yet. She's acting like an ally, but I'm not ready to end her long tenure in the enemy camp."

"She'll be on my turf at the gallery. Let's see what I can find out."

"Any updates for me otherwise?"

"Check in tomorrow . . . after I see what she wants."

Charlotte had decided to let Geri sweat for a few minutes as she observed her, watching to see if there was anyone else in the room Geri might be meeting with. Since Ted's desperate moment on the bridge and Shay's subsequent admission that he not only believed Ted was innocent but was helping Ted try to clear his name, Charlotte had become an entirely different type of journalist. Hiding under the guise of research for the art reviews and random freelance pieces she did in her spare time she was tapping into her rusty investigative abilities. At some point, she would pitch to one or two editors at the *Post-Gazette* or the *Tribune* what she saw as, ultimately, a feature story with the power to clear Ted's name. But not yet. There were missing puzzle pieces, and Gerilyn Leslie just might be holding onto a few.

Charlotte chatted to several patrons closer to the bar, inching her way in that direction, keeping Geri in her vision at all times.

"Hey, Hank. White wine, please," Charlotte said as she smiled at the young bartender, her eyes focused on him. He handed her a glass of chardonnay.

Turning toward Geri, Charlotte walked firmly forward,

coming around from behind and then stopping in front of the woman. "Geri, doesn't seem like your usual kind of place."

"How would you know my usual kind of place?" Geri snapped, obviously caught off guard and a little miffed.

"Just a guess, since most of the crowd here are regulars . . . you know, show up at every gallery opening. Unlike you." They stood in silence, fake smiles on their faces. Anyone watching might mistake them for two women having a polite conversation.

"I came to talk to you," Geri said, softening her tone.

"Really? Why not invite me for a coffee?"

"I didn't think you would accept."

"Good point."

"Well, I'm here now. Any chance we can find a place to sit and talk?" Geri tapped her wine glass nervously with a newly manicured nail.

"Come with me," Charlotte ordered crisply, then turned and walked over to a gentleman in a black tailored suit and mid-length graying ponytail, whispering in his ear. He nodded, pointing toward the back of the room. Charlotte moved in that direction, and Geri followed as Charlotte opened a lime-green painted door and they passed into a small sitting room, populated with overstuffed secondhand couches and a comfortable-looking chair. Charlotte placed her wine glass down on the scarred pine coffee table, taking the chair and leaving Geri to choose where to sit to best position herself as a person who easily exuded some level of trustworthiness. Charlotte felt sure her chances to make a connection here that would benefit Ted were limited at best.

Geri sat, shifting gingerly as she appeared to test the gold, crushed velvet sofa, its curved, studded wooden arms and tasseled underskirt speaking of another time. Directly across from her was a large oil painting that Charlotte loathed, having chosen to sit with her back to it, its style a mock Picassoesque cubism with none of the master's finesse. The nude portrait looked disjointed—a human cut in pieces and rearranged. A stark and disturbing analogy to her life at this point that she preferred to ignore. She didn't need the reminder that she was living the reality of trying to put her own human pieces together.

"I find that painting disturbing and beyond my comprehension, even as an art reviewer," Charlotte said, noting Geri's smile as she observed it. She picked up her glass and casually sipped her wine. Most people were turned off by the painting, hence its relegation to the back room for now. The woman in front of her must be one weird piece of work that she was enjoying it.

"It kind of works for me. Is that unusual?" Geri asked.

"Not at all." Charlotte lied with what she hoped was a comforting smile. "I can connect you with the artist if you like." She held back a laugh, knowing that the artist would be thrilled to make a sale, especially of this piece. He held the quintessential "struggling" label, in Charlotte's opinion.

A small, uncomfortable silence settled between them. Charlotte watched Geri shift on the couch, waiting for her to make the first move.

"I don't expect you to trust me," Geri said, once again tapping her manicured nails, this time on the arm of the couch.

"I don't, but I'm listening," Charlotte responded. She remained in what she hoped looked like a comfortable pose, softly molded into the armchair, legs crossed, hand holding her drink. She felt anything but comfortable with this woman who had never liked Ted but, if Charlotte was lucky, might be in a position to help clear his name. It was a stretch, but she was willing to open the door to the possibility.

"I'll be honest, I didn't like Ted, and he didn't like me."

"Ted may not be on my good list right now, but he's still the father of my daughter, so no negative comments, understood?" Charlotte wanted that rule up front and out on the table. "He'll always be Kelsey's father. That's all I'll say about Ted on a personal level."

"Okay, I understand. That's not why I'm here. I think we're working toward the same thing from different directions," Geri offered, leaning forward, her expression rather earnest.

"I'm working on an art show review for the newspaper," Charlotte said blandly, quietly holding her breath, waiting.

Geri gazed around the room for a minute or two before looking Charlotte in the eye and continuing. "We both want to clear Ted's name. Maybe for different reasons. But we both believe Ted was set up and fired to get him out of the way."

Geri's foot tapped an offbeat rhythm on the floor. She shifted her weight on the lumpy couch and appeared to be waiting for a response from Charlotte.

"I'll agree that we're on the same page. What do you want from me?" Charlotte asked. She felt herself a study in self-control, her body still, her face immobile. By the reflection back to her from Geri, she was succeeding—none of the tension and desire to jump out there and beg this woman to work from the inside of River City Trust on Ted's behalf was showing. Part instinct, part years of hearing Ted describe Geri, left Charlotte aware that under no circumstances could she let Geri feel as if she were in control.

"I want you to work with me to clear Ted's name," Geri stated. She seemed to be more comfortable speaking directly than dancing around things. "I think Shay picked up investigating where Ted left off, and you know that, but he doesn't trust me, which means we can't pool our knowledge."

"From what I hear, Geri, no one trusts you," Charlotte said. She let a silence fall between them. Her heart was beating so quickly she thought Geri could actually feel her thinking, deciding. "Assuming that your theory is correct and I'm trying to help clear Ted's name, what's in it for you? Ben's job? What's to say you aren't a double agent?"

"I'm pretty sure that I'm the next person Ben, and whoever his partners are in this planned heist, will be setting up shortly before they take off with the money," Geri said. "I may not be particularly likable to the staff, but I'm not dishonest, and I don't want to lose my job, my reputation, and my savings."

Charlotte felt herself reluctantly liking this woman's direct way of speaking. "If what you say is true, I don't see how you could assist Shay. Or me, saying I am actually involved in helping Shay."

"I'm a manager at River City Trust. I have higher privileged user access and the ability to authorize investigations that Shay may need, as well as just enough power to potentially cover his tracks or mine."

"Give me your business card with your personal contact information on the back," Charlotte instructed. "I'll be in touch in a few days."

"Please don't wait too long. I think the whole scheme they have planned is happening sooner rather than later," Geri said, her tone pleading as she scribbled her phone number and personal email on the back of a business card and handed it to Charlotte.

Charlotte nodded, acknowledging Geri's comment

without expression in the hope Geri would believe that Charlotte was way ahead of her already; that Charlotte might not even need Geri's help. If Geri was right, they would need to speed things up or Ted would never be exonerated.

"I can help, Charlotte. I need to help." Geri's voice had taken on a soft, whiny sound that spoke of a panic she struggled to quell.

"Like I said, I'll be in touch," Charlotte said. She stood, hoping she displayed no indication of the emotions rolling around inside of her as she looked down at Geri. "Now, I have an art exhibit to examine and a review to write by tomorrow morning."

"Late May, Charlotte. That's when they are going to do it ... run off with the money."

Charlotte froze, her eyes locked on Geri's. That was less than two months away. She saw nothing but candor and desperation in Geri's eyes. The woman was offering her an olive branch, a piece of information to prove her worth.

"Why are you so desperate to help, Geri? I suspect there is more to this than seeing justice served on a couple bad people who may or may not be coming for you." Charlotte wanted the woman's help. She'd pass this along to Nate Morgan the minute Geri was gone, but waves of panic were exuding from Geri, that were concerning and did not make sense to her.

Geri set her drink on the coffee table and put her head in her hands for a moment, rubbing her temples as if to soothe a particularly painful headache. When she looked up, the intensity was gone from her face, replaced by simple exhaustion and fear. "I'm almost certain when they move the funds offshore, they'll do it under my name as approver, leaving me to take the blame."

"So, it's not really about Ted's name." Charlotte crossed her arms almost defensively and felt grateful for having kept up a barrier between her and Geri.

"Don't get me wrong. I sincerely want to both prove Ted innocent and help bring these jerks down," Geri said, her tone pleading. "And if I don't succeed, they sail off to new lives built on stolen money while Ted and I may be dining on prison food."

Charlotte nodded her understanding. "Give me a couple days, and I'll be in touch."

CHAPTER 24

Charlotte had never been a smoker, but watching, from the window of the FBI's conference room, Nate's relaxed posture and attitude as he smoked outside, while inside she struggled with her own stress, had her momentarily considering the merits of adding a bit of nicotine to her life. She glanced at Shay. He was shifting restlessly in his seat, watching the door. He had the most at stake here. His level of nervousness must be far surpassing her own.

"What if she doesn't show?" Shay asked as he tapped his fingers on the tabletop. "What if she tips them off?"

A mild scent of nicotine wafted across the room as Nate appeared in the doorway and removed his coat before taking a seat. "She doesn't know enough to tip them off, and she won't dare consider it after this meeting."

Charlotte admired Nate's cool demeanor. She imagined years of working for the FBI had hardened him to people far worse than Geri. He was immune, and he was definitely in charge.

The three of them had hashed out the possibilities around accepting Geri's offer to help before deciding to set up a meeting, which Nate would lead. Charlotte told Geri that she and Shay would meet with her at Nate's office, providing the address, to discuss how they could work together. Geri had requested a pub that Shay said he and his coworkers often frequented, which he found odd, but Charlotte wanted her on unfamiliar turf and, more importantly, where random people could not overhear. She'd simply told Geri that they were working with Nate, and he'd been clear the meeting would take place at his office.

"I wouldn't go as far as to trust her, but I think she has skin in this game and needs the same outcome we do," Charlotte said.

"We'll keep her in a box where she helps Shay continue to monitor what Ben and Bob are doing, that's it," Nate answered.

Charlotte pushed up the sleeves of her oversized sweater and sipped a diet soda she'd purchased from the vending machine in the office break room. Despite her uncertainty about Geri, she was relieved they were having this meeting and that Nate would handle the discussion. Charlotte had the same set of conflicting feelings about dealing with Geri as she'd had when she called Jesse to tell him Ted had contemplated jumping off a bridge. A week later, an envelope, its contents not just identical to those Shay had shown her but containing an additional backup drive, appeared in her mailbox postmarked from the McCord Ranch.

"Ted sent it to me the day he was fired," Jesse had told Charlotte when she called him from the museum office to avoid Kelsey overhearing their discussion. "Told me to hide it, so I locked it in an old hiding place beneath the barn floor that Art used sometimes."

"Thanks, Jesse. I turned it over to the FBI agent I'm working with. I was trying to decide whether to let him know that Geri, Ted's old boss, wants to help us. Getting this information kicked me over the line, and I decided to share everything with the feds, including Geri's willingness to help, and hope for the best for Ted."

"You sure about her? Geri, I mean?" Jesse asked, sounding skeptical. "Ted only told me one thing about that woman. She hates him."

"Desperation breeds strange bedfellows, apparently," Charlotte had answered with a laugh. "She was candid that she thinks she'll be the scapegoat to take the blame. Helping Ted is helping herself."

"Well, if it benefits my brother, then good. But I'd watch her like a hawk."

"I believe that's exactly what the FBI will do for me, and do much better."

Jesse laughed. "I still won't mind if karma bites her in the butt."

Charlotte nodded in silent agreement as she rolled a pen back and forth on her desktop. "How is he?" She heard the slight hesitation in her voice.

"Ted? About the same. Quiet. Keeps telling me he didn't do it, so I thought I'd better send you that envelope."

"Did you look inside?"

Jesse was silent. Charlotte suspected he had seen the contents. "Yup," he answered after a few seconds. "I didn't understand all of it. Hopefully he learned a lesson, but he doesn't deserve taking this bad of a life hit."

"Is he going to counseling?"

"Yeah . . . I drive him there to make sure," Jesse said. "He misses you and Kelsey."

"If I have Kelsey on FaceTime with him more often, will that help?" Charlotte asked, knowing that was less than

Jesse hoped for, but it was all she felt reasonably sure she could offer.

"Yeah, that'll help," Jesse said. "I keep him busy doing chores around the ranch to get him out of his own head a little bit."

"Thanks, Jesse," Charlotte answered. "How are you and Suzanne?"

Charlotte hoped all of this disruption wasn't causing problems for Jesse and his girlfriend. They'd been together for a while now, and she was pretty sure it had been heading in a permanent direction before she'd sent Ted back to the ranch.

"We're fine," Jesse said. "Suzanne gets it, and she's staying here with us about half the week, getting to know Ted and, I think, helping him a little."

"Good. I don't want Ted's problems messing up your relationship."

"No worries about that. She and I . . . we're solid."

Charlotte heard the office door open and paused, silent as a coworker entered. She waved to the woman, then stood and stepped out into the museum corridor. "Jesse, do you have any idea why Art left the ranch to Ted? I wish he'd told me."

Jesse cleared his throat and made a noise that sounded like a deep sigh. "I know why, but I don't know whether you should hear that from Ted or me."

There it was again. The frustration of being outside trying to look in, searching for all the missing pieces as to why she and Ted were in such a mess. She would not take it out on Jesse this time.

"Enough, Jesse. All of you have been keeping things from me over and over again. I need to know, to understand what caused Art to leave his ranch to the son who never wanted it and why that caused Ted to lie, to hide all of this from me—and from you. My marriage is in shambles. Don't you think I deserve to know?"

"Okay, Charlie. You asked. I'm Ted's half brother. Art isn't my biological father. Something Ted learned and kept secret not to hurt me, and something I learned later and kept from Ted because I wanted us to stay the same brothers we'd always been." Jesse sounded tired, resigned, as if he'd hashed this out in his mind a dozen times. "Maybe if we hadn't been keeping secrets from each other, it would have all worked out in a different way."

Charlotte registered the admission in a brief, stunned silence, then spoke quietly, "I'm sorry, Jesse. Truly, I am. Are you all right?"

"I've known for a long time. I met my real father a number of years ago, and I help him with his ranch. We have a great relationship. Don't worry about me, worry about Ted."

Shaking her head as if to dislodge the memory of that conversation and reinsert herself into the present, Charlotte turned from the FBI conference room window and faced the long table in front of her. Shay closed his laptop and studied her for a moment.

"You looked lost in thought," he said.

"Just thinking about my conversation with Jesse after he sent me the envelope Ted left with him," Charlotte answered.

"You know you can tell me about it . . . if it's bothering you," Shay said.

"Maybe another time. Today, we stay focused on Geri and whether we can trust her to help clear Ted's name. For Kelsey's sake, I hope so!"

It had been disturbing, shocking even, to discover the

missing pieces and realize how naive, how utterly foolish, Ted had been to step into such a shark tank and make himself and his family vulnerable. Shay seemed less surprised, more resigned to feeling that the corporate beast had simply eaten Ted for breakfast and spit him out for lunch in a bad and permanently damaging way.

"Here she comes," Shay said, seconds before the conference room door opened and Geri, followed by Nate, stepped inside.

Geri blinked a few times, surveying the room before seating herself at the table, keeping a few chairs between her and Shay. Charlotte moved from the window to a chair next to Shay, watching Geri's eyebrows furrow in concern as she assessed Nate, who casually slid into a chair directly across from Geri, forcing her attention to focus on him rather than on Shay and Charlotte.

"Hi, Geri," Charlotte said, trying to eliminate the hesitancy she felt from her voice and sound welcoming. "Thanks for joining us."

Geri nodded a silent assent. She'd switched the power suit for a loose sweater hitting mid-thigh on a pair of well-worn jeans. Charlotte noticed that she was seated on the edge of her chair as if perched to run. They all remained quiet, watching Nate open a folder on the table in front of him and shuffle through a few papers. Next to the folder was a yellow legal pad and pen. Charlotte suspected the meeting was being recorded, either by video or audio or both, but Nate was giving Geri a different vibe by putting aside the iPad in favor of an old-school note-taking approach.

"For quite some time, the FBI has been investigating aspects of a situation we believe Ted had knowledge of, but was not involved in directly, which resulted in the events that led to his being fired." Nate spoke directly to Geri as if she were already working for him.

Geri gave Nate a long look. "I saw you about nine months ago at the annual meeting with the auditors. You were introduced as a financial audit consultant."

"You have a good eye and a good memory, Geri," Nate said. "That'll be helpful if you're still willing to assist after we've talked."

Charlotte watched Geri give Shay a hard stare, but he looked down at his laptop, refusing to make eye contact. She could see how the woman worked, picking the one person she had authority over and trying to intimidate him as a way to center herself and regain personal power in the face of Nate's quiet domination of the meeting. It was clear that Geri functioned from a deep center of insecurity. Bullying or micromanaging to compensate was probably her default mechanism. So be it. Charlotte was certain these were weaknesses that would make her no match for Nate.

"Well, seeing that the FBI is looking into Ben Keene lets me know I was right," Geri answered.

"Hey, Shay, would you mind getting Geri a glass of water from the dispenser in the break room?" Nate's polite request was less about providing Geri with a drink and more about showing her who Shay was answering to in this investigation. Charlotte glanced at Shay to gauge his response, wondering if he was insulted or upset, although Nate had not sounded in any way condescending, but Shay seemed perfectly at ease, leaving the room with a smile on his face. Charlotte suspected the two of them had agreed to this little maneuver prior to the meeting.

"Ahhh, you're a smart woman, Geri," Nate said. Charlotte could see he was going to play to her needs. "Do you think Ben's working alone? And what, exactly, do you think Ben is doing?"

"No, you first, Nate," Geri retorted. She was getting cocky. "Evidently the FBI needs my help. What are you investigating, and what do you know?"

Charlotte began to relax, knowing Geri was about to discover she was out of her league.

"Actually, Geri, I don't need you," Nate said calmly, crossing his arms over his chest and leaning back, comfortable. "You came to Charlotte looking to work with us, and, frankly, you could be getting in the way of a key investigation by running rogue. I'm willing to work with you, but make no mistake . . . you're not in charge. And if you're thinking about leaving here with anything we talk about and sharing it or working on your own, know that I'll make sure that works against you when this investigation ends."

Geri's face began to pale. She leaned forward to take a drink of water, dropping eye contact and trying to adjust to the shift on the playing field. Charlotte could almost feel her deciding what to do next.

"Where do you think I fit in here? I'm assuming you know my career could be at stake as well."

"Let's start by talking through a few things before we decide if or where you might be able to assist." Nate's voice softened a bit, and he nodded at Geri as if in approval. Geri's shoulders relaxed as she sat back in the chair and crossed her legs.

"Charlotte tells me you have a theory on Ben Keene and Bob Thornton. Have you seen anything to make you believe there is a third person involved in what these two might be planning?"

"No, I haven't seen anything that indicates a third person. And I don't know who it might be, if there is someone." Geri was sitting up straighter now, her head cocked, alert. Charlotte could see a level of concern on her face.

"If they're planning to embezzle money, as you believe, how do you think they'll pull it off?" Nate was calm, tapping his pen on the pad as if waiting to take notes.

"I think they've obtained specific finance codes from Bob, then Ben had Connor set up an intricate system of some sort to bypass systems controls, ensuring that, when the money is transferred, no internal security alarms go off." Geri crossed her arms and gave Nate a small smile that indicated she felt they were on equal footing now. "Connor works almost exclusively for Ben. I wouldn't call him a 'third person.'"

"That, Geri, is what we think too," Nate said.

He was throwing her a bone. Charlotte believed he'd figured out a lot more than this, leaving her unclear as to why he wanted Geri's involvement. Charlotte and Shay had been wary about how much to include Geri and whether it would be an unnecessary risk or a benefit.

"I don't know what Connor set up, and I need Shay's help to work that out," Geri said, cutting Shay another look. "But he refused to work with me."

This time, Shay glared back at Geri, his body tense with anger.

"Shay's under orders from me not to disclose what he's doing for the FBI to anyone, including you," Nate answered, his tone deep, his inflections more severe. "He may work for River City Trust on his regular duties, but he works for me on this, and so will you if I decide you can be trusted."

Geri's face flushed a deep red, her mouth in a straight line. The woman was smart enough to realize Nate had boxed her in, but not quick enough to work around him. Geri wanted to work with them, but from a point of control, as the top dog, and Nate had now made it clear to her that that was not an option.

"If you decide to trust me and I decide to work with you, what is it you want from me?" Geri asked, her voice a tight cross of anger and tension.

"I want you to protect Shay during his investigation— covering his back, opening up permissions he needs, helping him with any analysis if he requires that from you," Nate said, softening his tone. "And in return, I'll make sure none of the fallout hits you, that your leadership knows you cooperated in bringing these guys down."

Geri nodded, tapping her sturdy walking shoes against the floor. "What about the third person?"

"You don't need to worry about a third person, if there is one. I have that covered."

"Okay, Nate, we have a deal," Geri answered. She rifled through her purse and extracted a business card, which she handed to him. "I suppose we should shake on it?"

"Almost . . . just one more thing," Nate said as he held the business card but ignored her outstretched right hand. "You are not to use your management status to pressure Shay for information beyond what I tell him he can reveal. No micromanaging his work. No asking about a supposed third party. He'll share what I say he can share."

Geri pulled her hand back, her face again suffused in anger. They sat in silence, waiting.

Charlotte cleared her throat. "Geri, Nate has been working on this investigation for longer than any of us were aware there was an issue. I've been helping, trying to clear Ted's name for my daughter's sake. This isn't about you, or me, or Shay. It's about doing the right thing."

Geri's face softened a bit. Charlotte thought she was probably the only one at the table who believed there might be a person under the rigid, domineering exterior who was halfway decent—just insecure and stumbling through life like everyone else. Shay already had his negative opinions. Interactions with Geri helped Charlotte fully understand how a person could get to the same point as Shay, but she felt an instinctive level of empathy that would have Ted rolling his eyes at her if he knew. Nate was a professional, trained to hone in on Geri's weaknesses and then work her until she became an asset under his control. He wasn't interested in harboring any personal feelings, positive or negative, about her beyond what she could provide to assist in his investigation.

Charlotte swallowed hard, her mouth dry with tension from the thought of her own part in helping Nate. Unlike Geri, she knew the third person was Leah Hanson, and it sat solidly with her to undermine and expose her best friend. Was she a best friend anymore? Probably not, but Leah trusted her, and she was going to betray that trust. Each time she thought about it, she felt sick, and she had to flash an image of Kelsey in her mind's eye to stay centered. One day, she would explain to her daughter that, despite her anger with Ted, she'd done something terribly wrong to do something terribly right and make sure Kelsey grew up with a father who was free and part of her life.

She watched as Nate extended his hand to Geri, silent. No one moved. After a pause that was barely a few seconds but seemed to stretch uncomfortably long, Geri put out her hand and clasped Nate's in agreement. Charlotte was willing to bet Geri would try to bend the rules to work around him at least a few times. In the end, it was and would continue to be Nate's game, and Geri would have no choice but to follow along.

"You have the easiest role to play, Geri," Nate said, his

mouth smiling in a way his eyes did not. "It's Shay, digging in where he could be discovered, who's on the front lines."

Charlotte was grateful to Nate for leaving her role in this out of the discussion, relieved that Geri didn't think to ask her. Even Shay didn't yet know how difficult Charlotte's role would be, one that might require her to include her unsuspecting daughter to ensure Leah's trust was rock solid. It was Leah Nate had been investigating on a minor whistle-blowing report made against Western PA Bank that expanded into an investigation of River City Trust. Ted's firing had connected a few dots and changed what Nate had initially thought might be no more than a small FBI surveillance operation into a full-blown sting in the making. Shay was necessary. Geri was a nice-to-have added protection for Shay. Charlotte was crucial to Nate's ability to close in on Leah and ensure the right person, not Ted, would spend time behind bars. No matter how many times Nate reassured her that this was the right path, the key to what she needed to accomplish for both Ted and Kelsey, Charlotte felt sick in the pit of her stomach, sick and afraid that she couldn't pull it off. She had no idea how dangerous Leah might be or what she might do if Charlotte aroused her suspicions in some way.

CHAPTER 25

The walkway to the small, working-class house, its history dating back to the age of immigrant mill workers and household servants employed in wealthier neighborhoods, had the air of an aging beauty, her fading poise and softened corners in need of a gentle facelift. The abundance of flowers on either side of the short concrete path cascaded forward, connecting with an explosion of floral color from both sides and ending in front of a small set of steps leading up to the narrow porch and front door just beyond. Impatiens in every color spread outward like a carpet, and yellow and pink roses climbed a wooden trellis against the house, artfully covering spots in need of a new coat of paint. Morning glories and deep purple clematis wound around the porch pillars. Dotting the flower bed were spots of orange marigolds and red zinnias.

Charlotte hadn't seen such beautiful gardening surrounding such a modest home in a long time. The house was in decent shape, probably due to infusions of money from Leah and a little sweat and muscle by her brother, who lived nearby. Still, the porch sagged a bit on the left, some windows were older and in need of replacement, and an air-conditioning unit jutting out from an upstairs window announced the lack of basic infrastructure modernization.

"Charlotte?" The screen door squeaked as a small, white-haired woman in a floral bohemian sundress and comfortable cardigan opened the door and stepped out onto the porch. A warm, happy feeling enveloped Charlotte at the sight of this woman she'd once felt more comfortable with than her own mother. A pang of guilt followed quickly behind, shooting through her as nostalgia made way for the real reason she was here today, hoping to surreptitiously glean information about Leah. She wished she could simply be honest with Leah's mother, tell her what she suspected Leah had done and ask for her help in righting a wrong. But the mother in Charlotte knew that type of information would never be willingly given. She'd remain covert and suppress her feelings of guilt as best she could.

"Hi, Mrs. Hanson," Charlotte said with a smile, feeling all of fourteen again as they, two adult women, stood facing each other and she had no idea what to call Leah's mother besides "Mrs. Hanson."

"I haven't been Mrs. Hanson for a long time. How about you call me Elaine?" Leah's mother responded, wrapping Charlotte in a warm hug that smelled of rose petals and mint tea.

"Sure, Elaine," Charlotte answered, the name clunky and unfamiliar as it rolled over her tongue. "I just dropped Kelsey off at my parents' house and thought I'd stop by. I would have called, but I don't have your number, and you weren't listed."

"Oh, I dropped the name Hanson when I finished my last visit to rehab, honey," Elaine said. "I've been Elaine

McIlhenny for quite a few years now. Back to my maiden name."

Elaine held the door open, and Charlotte walked inside. Memories came flooding back. As a kid, she'd always found Leah's house to be more comfortable, so much homier than her own larger house with its manicured lawn that always seemed polished to a cold perfection. Leah, on the other hand, had seemed ashamed of her mother's home, wanting to spend her free time in Charlotte's house. Before her was the same living room furniture, now a bit worn. Charlotte could see down the hallway into the kitchen where an inexpensive but newer table held a beautiful bouquet of roses, brightening the room and overshadowing its scuffed linoleum floors and ancient countertops cluttered with sturdy but outdated appliances.

"Tea?"

Charlotte nodded in agreement, sitting at one of the kitchen chairs while Elaine put a kettle of water on the stove and rummaged around for tea bags, her movements slower, more deliberate, than Charlotte remembered.

"It's so good to see you again. It's been a while."

"It's good to see you too," Charlotte said as she reached into her purse and pulled out her phone. "Would you like to see some pictures of Kelsey? She's really getting big." Kelsey was born shortly before Elaine's last stint in rehab. She handed the phone over and watched Elaine smile as she scrolled through the pictures.

"Oh, she's adorable. She looks so much like you, Charlotte. I haven't seen a picture of her in a long time." Elaine smiled a bit wistfully as she swiped through a few more pictures on Charlotte's phone. "I'm not a grandma yet, but I continue to hope."

"I used to send a picture to Leah now and then, and she

took some of her own when she'd stop by my home." Charlotte pocketed her phone as she spoke. "She didn't show you a few?"

Elaine wore a quiet, troubled look, her mouth opening as if to say something when the kettle began whistling and she turned, her back to Charlotte, busying herself with turning off the stove and pouring the boiling water into two chipped mugs, the tea bag strings, wet from the steam, flowing down softly over the edge. Setting the mugs on the table, she rummaged through a cabinet, pulling out honey and then searching the refrigerator for a small container of half-and-half cream. Charlotte remained silent, swishing her tea bag in the water, adding a bit of honey, and waiting. She was both patient and prescient, anticipating something she was unable to define but intuited was coming.

"I don't see much of Leah," Elaine said.

She looked sad, or perhaps weary was a better word. Charlotte wasn't sure if this had to do with Leah or if the combination of a hard life and hard-fought sobriety had left her perpetually frozen in this state.

"She doesn't come by?" Charlotte asked, hoping she didn't sound like she was prying while feeling duplicitous as that was exactly what she'd come here to do. Elaine seemed so lonely that it made concealing her intentions all the more upsetting as she consciously proceeded to use the older woman. "It's been a while since I had lunch with Leah and she gave me an update on you, but I got the impression she kept up with how you were doing. I assumed she'd been to see you since then."

"Well, Leah's been here all right," Elaine said. "She doesn't think I know because she slides in while I'm out of the house, but this is my home . . . I know when someone's come through."

"That's weird. How do you know it's Leah?"

"Because I moved a few things around in her room, as a test," Elaine said. "You know how picky she is about her things. And they were moved back to their original spots, the way she likes them. Not that she ever uses that room or has any visible nostalgia for me or this house. I asked the neighbor across the way if anyone had come by," she added. "She's the kind of neighbor that's home all day and doesn't miss much. It was Leah."

Charlotte shook her head, confused, then sipped her tea, uncertain of what to say. "I can't imagine why she would need or want to come here other than to see you. It doesn't make sense."

"I don't know either," Elaine said. "I know our relationship isn't perfect. Her brother tells me she checks in with him to see when I'll be here, and he thought it was to come by and see me, but it turns out it's to avoid me."

Charlotte's radar was going up as she considered this new information against what she'd learned about Leah from Nate's investigation. "I'm glad Steve is supportive. Will either of you confront her . . . ask her why?"

"No, no, I can't do that," Elaine said as she pressed her lips together and shook her head. "We have such a difficult relationship as it is that I don't want to start a fight with her."

Elaine got up, putting distance between her and Charlotte as she turned her back and began to reheat the water left in the kettle. When she pulled a few shortbread cookies from a box and placed them on a plate in front of Charlotte, she averted her eyes, her hands shaking mildly.

"Leah told me about your health issues. I assumed she learned of them from keeping in touch with you."

"Ahh, well, I did leave her a voicemail when I got the diagnosis, and she called me back. But since then, I think she gets most of her updates from Steve. She's providing money for my treatment."

Charlotte didn't know what to say to make this better. She wanted to ask about Elaine's treatment, her prognosis, but this would drag the already sad conversation down even further. And how much worse would all of this be if they ended up sitting on opposite sides in a courtroom.

"I know a lot about difficult relationships and not wanting to talk about it. I guess you know my husband and I are separated. He's gotten himself into some trouble."

"How's he doing? Leah told Steve what had happened, and parts of it trickled out to me."

"He's unemployed, in legal trouble, and out in Montana with his brother, hopefully getting himself together." Charlotte shrugged as if it were the norm for her now, even though she could hear a quaver in her voice despite the number of times she'd said this to others. Telling Elaine made her wish for a hug, for comfort, but at the same time it was the last thing she deserved as she sat here deceiving this poor woman. She closed her eyes for a moment, and when she opened them, tears were ready to spill. Elaine had leaned forward, reaching for and then clasping her hand.

"One thing I've learned, through the many sessions I've had with therapists, is to let go of what you can't control. I miss Leah, and I forgive her treatment of me whether I understand it or not, but I can't make her do something she doesn't want to do." Elaine squeezed Charlotte's hand for a moment then began aimlessly dunking her tea bag up and down.

"What are you up to these days besides creating a beautiful garden outside?" Charlotte asked in an effort to move the conversation onto a more positive track. It was obvious Leah was not communicating with her mother. Charlotte shouldn't have come here with expectations that Elaine was the key to any of Leah's secrets.

They sat quietly, sipping tea and catching up on Elaine's volunteer work with AA, Charlotte's work at the museum, and what they'd heard about members of her and Leah's old high school crowd. Softer subjects, comfortable as the old, large reading chair Charlotte could see in the living room, a place she'd loved to curl up in with a good book as a teenager when she spent the night here.

"You still have my Harry Potter chair," Charlotte said with a smile, flipping her hand in the direction of the living room. She felt sad, the nostalgia and the good memories colliding with the knowledge of what Elaine would lose if Charlotte succeeded in sacrificing Leah to win freedom for Ted.

"I read all of your art gallery reviews in the *Post-Gazette*," Elaine said, her smile wistful. "You have a life that seems interesting and even exciting to me."

"I guess it's good for me to get out of my own head and hear that," Charlotte said with a laugh. She checked her watch, then stood. "This has been so nice, but I'd better get going. I need to run a few errands before I pick up Kelsey."

Elaine stood as well, stepping forward to fold Charlotte into a hug, then began clearing the table.

"Elaine, before I go . . ." Charlotte hesitated, not sure, even as the thought crossed her mind, that it was a safe move.

"Yes?" Elaine was now depositing the mugs into the kitchen sink. Charlotte noticed the kitchen still had no dishwasher.

"Could I go up and take a look at Leah's room? For old times' sake?" Charlotte asked. She felt a funny tingle of anticipation on the back of her neck, strange after all these years. "I promise not to move or touch anything."

"Of course, go on upstairs. You know the way," Elaine said with a wave of her hand.

Charlotte took the steps two at a time, feet landing quietly on the worn beige carpet, carefully skipping the creaky fifth step, a fact that had driven both her and Leah crazy when they tried to sneak in late, unnoticed, as young girls. She could still go this route blindfold in the dark as she turned left and opened the first door on the right.

Nothing had moved. A high school girl's room frozen in time. A bookshelf with a dusty lineup of Leah's favorites sat under the window to the right. Classics like *The Great Gatsby* nestled next to the *Dune* trilogy, a collection of science fiction and fantasy taking up the entire bottom shelf to announce her preference for the genre. A single bed sat against the left wall below posters of Maroon 5 and Brad Pitt, its floral bedspread mildly faded in spots from the morning sun that played across it each day, curtains wide open.

Eyes closed, Charlotte could summon those youthful voices of Leah, herself, and their friends—the laughter, the whispers. Opening her eyes, she snapped out of it. That wasn't what she was here for, what she had suddenly thought of downstairs. The water had stopped running in the kitchen, and she knew she only had a few minutes. Tucked just beyond the bed was a small door to a cubbyhole under the eaves of the house. A large old-fashioned steamer trunk sat squarely in front of it. The home had no attic, only these smaller storage areas. The trunk felt light, nearly empty, a few items rattling around inside as she lifted the left end and, as quietly as possible, moved it at an angle that allowed her to open the door that led to the small space under the eaves of the house. Her phone substituted for a flashlight, revealing the little pile of old diaries and scrapbooks Leah had always hidden there. In their wilder teen years, they had hidden cheap wine and beer, even a little hooch stolen from Leah's brother, in this spot. Behind the old journals was a tie binder, the type of folder she'd seen lawyers bring to court. It looked new, crisp, and it was slightly expanded, indicating something was inside. Charlotte put her hand on it and lifted. It wasn't heavy. She could feel items moving, possibly file folders, and something small slid across the bottom. Maybe a jump drive, the USB providing a small but easy document storage option.

"Charlotte?" Elaine called from the bottom of the stairs. She heard Elaine's measured steps ascending and, a minute later, the creak on the fifth step as she hastily returned the folder to its original spot, closed the door, and moved the trunk back into position. She was sitting on Leah's bed when Elaine arrived at the door. She smiled at Elaine, working to hide her burning curiosity over the contents of the folder and disappointment that she'd lost precious seconds immersed in nostalgia when she should have seen what was inside.

"Nothing's changed. You've kept it the same," Charlotte said.

"Nice walk down memory lane, huh?" Elaine patted Charlotte's shoulder. "I was hoping Leah was showing up for the same reason that has you sitting here and, eventually, she would stay to spend time with me. One never knows with Leah."

"That's true," Charlotte acknowledged.

Right now, she was thinking the very same thing. No one ever knew for sure with Leah. What was her old friend up to, driving all the way out here to hide a folder, secretively

dating someone she refused to talk about let alone intro-
duce to Charlotte, possibly allowing two men to use Kelsey,
the little girl she adored, as a vehicle to set up and bring
down Ted?

"The divorce, my drinking, moving here, her father
abandoning the kids for his new life," Elaine said, staring
down at her feet, "it messed Leah up in ways I still can't
totally understand. And she won't let me help her."

"It wasn't your fault, Elaine," Charlotte said, standing up
and sliding her cross-body purse over her head.

Elaine shifted her gaze to Charlotte, shrugged and
nodded, a look of resignation that said she'd accepted the
turns life had taken, the things she could never put on pause
or replay for a better outcome. She turned to head back
downstairs, Charlotte following. Once in her car, motor
humming, having left Elaine with the promise she would
visit again, Charlotte tapped Nate's name in her phone
contact list, and the car's Bluetooth connected and called
him. As he answered, she pulled away from the curb and
began to tell him what she'd discovered in Leah's childhood
room and what she thought it might be. She assumed he
would have to get a search warrant, something he might not
yet have enough evidence to request. Doing that would tip
off Leah. Charlotte hoped the documents would remain
hidden and in place until Nate could find a way to extract
them from Elaine's house.

"Are you saying you took a look in the folder, or are you
guessing as to what might be in there?"

"Guessing. I didn't have enough time. Her mother was
coming up the stairs."

"Just as well that you didn't touch anything inside. If I
can get my hands on it, I don't want her using the excuse
that you tampered with it and planted evidence."

"I know Leah. She always covers her back. Even if she is in love with this guy, which I still doubt, she doesn't really trust anyone. I think her backup is in that folder."

Charlotte felt queasy. She'd been so filled with anger for Leah that it was now, suddenly, occurring to her that her old friend might be dangerous. Leah would turn on anyone she suspected of trying to bring her carefully built scam down around her ears, including Charlotte.

CHAPTER 26

Geri slid onto a barstool at Redbeard's Bar & Grill, ordered an Iron City Lite on tap, and watched various local and state sports teams playing via multiple television screens behind the bar while periodically checking the door. Shay was supposed to meet her here soon. He was due to show her the results of the many privileged user permissions she'd carved out for him and, to a lesser extent, Missy to ferret out what Ben was up to. He'd better tell her when he was ready to start the wheels turning on his plan. Her instincts told her that Nate was keeping this operation close to the vest and no one person was privy to all aspects of it, but she was sure Shay was closest to Nate's inner circle of trust, a level of knowledge that didn't include her.

"Wanna menu, Geri?" the bartender asked as he placed a cold twelve-ounce beer glass in front of her.

"Not today, thanks," she answered.

Redbeard's was a block from her condo, and she was a regular here. It kept the feel of a local Pittsburgh bar in the face of growing tourist demands, its walls littered with sports memorabilia and murals to the history of the city's many top teams. Geri grabbed her beer and moved to a booth toward the back of the room behind the high-top tables, quiet and almost out of sight. Shay walked in, pausing in the doorway to scan the room. Geri stood up and motioned him to the booth, ignoring the raised eyebrows of the regulars lined up at the bar. She wasn't known for bringing or meeting friends there. She usually hung out alone or, occasionally, met George to watch a game and eat dinner.

"Hey," Shay said as he set his backpack in the booth and sat down across from her.

The waitress had followed him to his seat. "What can I get you?" she asked as she set down a cocktail napkin.

"Yuengling . . . draft."

"Put it on my tab," Geri said. Shay looked like he wanted to protest, then thought better of it.

Geri ran her fingers over the cold condensation on her sixteen-ounce glass, watching Shay. She leaned toward him, forearms and elbows crossed and resting on the tabletop. "So, what've you got?" she asked, getting right to the point.

"A lot."

Shay paused as a beer was placed on the napkin in front of him, then he pulled an Apple Mac out of his backpack, logged in, and popped a USB drive into the right side port.

"First, let me show you the flow chart I made of how I think they're moving the money. Then I'll show you the logs."

"Did you scan Ben's emails?" Geri asked.

"Yeah, but he must be texting from his personal cell a good bit. There wasn't much, although I did make some inroads there."

"Do you know who the third person is?"

"No," Shay answered. His eyes remained on the laptop screen, and Geri couldn't tell if he was lying or actually didn't know the answer. He turned the laptop on the table to provide Geri a full view. "See? Ben approved shutting off the logging feature for four hours the day that the money Ted supposedly embezzled was transferred to an account at Western PA in his daughter's name. The approval was labeled 'maintenance,' the shutdown and subsequent maintenance check done by Connor."

Shay ran his finger along the laptop screen, pointing to the lines in the logs that showed the steps taken. "At the same time, Bob Thornton approved a maintenance check on the wire transfer software, but they obviously don't have an insider like Connor in Finance, and the person logged the maintenance check and the fact that Thornton requested a "test" transfer of the exact amount Ted supposedly embezzled."

"Pretty easy to connect the dots," Geri said. "Why wasn't this noticed and taken to HR?"

"Ben removed access for myself and others in key locations, then Connor was supposed to wipe everything clean," Shay said with a smile. "But Ted had written some code that he planted in the background to run regular scans. The scan results were continuously downloaded to a specified folder that only Ted had access to."

"So, I don't get it . . . why didn't Ted turn them in?" Geri asked, puzzled. "This could have ended long before Ted considered jumping into the Allegheny River."

"When they fired Ted, he hadn't downloaded everything from the password-protected folder to a USB, and, because they walked him out, he couldn't access the folder. He gave me his login and passcode, along with his two-factor authentication, but I didn't have enough authority to get past a few permission roadblocks to get to the folder's contents."

"And that's where I came in. I provided the right user permissions to help you navigate to the folder." Geri's mind was now connecting the dots to the chart in front of her.

"Right, and I learned that not only did they have no idea the folder was there, but it had been collecting evidence all along," Shay answered. He was smiling broadly now. "Plus, typical Connor, he bolted before finishing the job of wiping everything clean."

"Took the money and ran, huh?" Geri laughed.

"Yep, he always was a lazy butt."

Shay appeared to be relaxing, and Geri felt an appreciation for how wrong she'd been about this guy. When it was all over, she would see what she could do to promote him.

"Still, why didn't Ted tell this to someone?" Geri asked. "He'd lost his job, but he could have avoided all the court charges."

"He didn't think anyone would believe him," Shay answered. "He was working with me, trying to talk me through how to access enough proof to clear his name, but his bills were piling up and Charlotte had left and would barely speak to him. He was in a really dark place."

Geri was silent, staring at the screen and the logs showing the activities Shay had discovered. She could see immediately where Ben had ordered what looked like regular maintenance checks, every fourth check requiring the disabling of the logging system to make it look perfectly normal.

"On which maintenance check is he going to transfer the money and run?" Geri asked.

"Not sure, but I think it has to be next weekend, or two weeks from now, before Memorial Day," Shay answered.

With a couple clicks of the mouse, he displayed an unfamiliar screenshot. "This is the schedule for Finance. Bob Thornton has two wire transfer testers set up—one for May 27 and one for four weeks after that."

"Oh my god . . . the approvals are both listed in my name." Geri gasped. A ripple of fear ran through her. "Can we fix that?"

"I think so, but if they see it, it will tip them off and they'll switch it back," Shay said. "I showed all of this stuff to Nate to see if the FBI can pinpoint which of the two dates is the embezzlement date and which is a test run. You'll have to keep my access clear to allow me to switch your name to Thornton's right before the transfer."

"Are they going to allow the transfer?"

"I don't know. That's up to Nate," Shay said with a shrug as he closed the laptop lid. "This morning, I attached a tracking device to Ted's folder. The FBI can monitor it in real time. Without Connor to check and clean up for Ben, he's running some risks here. He can't afford to try to roll over any of the other employees. He's going to have to set everything up himself."

"Ted was pretty dishonest himself." She shouldn't bring this up, especially after Shay appeared to pull back from her when she pushed for more information about the transfer, but Geri couldn't help herself.

"Ted was insecure and ambitious," Shay responded. "He was, and still is, a good guy. He believed he was helping his brother, that his bad actions were for a good reason. He's working all of that out in counseling."

"Where is Ted?"

Shay finished his beer and stood up, sliding the laptop into his backpack and zipping it up. "He's where he needs to be after everything he's been through. Thanks for the beer, Geri."

"You're leaving? Don't you think you should have run all this stuff by me before turning it over to Nate?" Geri asked. She hated the itchy, queasy feeling that came with lack of control.

"Nope. Nate is running this show, and I, for one, trust him and don't want any trouble with the FBI. You should probably make sure you think the same way," Shay said as he hoisted the backpack over his shoulders.

"Nothing more to tell me before you go?"

"Nothing. I'll let you know if I need any help changing the requests to Bob Thornton's name."

Geri's eyebrows furrowed as she sorted through the odds as to which date seemed most plausible for an effective embezzlement to occur unnoticed. "Tell Nate that, historically, we get a lot of external hacker attempts around Memorial Day when we have a skeleton crew because most employees are off and government offices are closed," she said, trying to move things to a positive note with Shay before he left. He was her only source of information. "Ben knows this, and, since that is one of the dates you pinpointed, he might think all eyes will be on investigating those phishing attempts while he slides his scheme right through the system and heads out the door."

"Good thinking," Shay answered. He paused, standing by the table. "Can we find out if Ben has vacation scheduled?"

"I'm not sure. Let me think about it, but I might be able to order a pen test on a small section of the HR system under the guise of checking for security vulnerabilities and catch a record of requested and approved time off."

Shay nodded and, with a wave, was gone through the

doors, turning right toward the Duquesne Incline and, she knew, back down into the heart of the city to head home.

Geri sat quietly, a sick feeling creeping through her middle and up into her throat. She fished out Nate's business card, flipping it over and looking at the private cell number scrawled on the back. She could run a little side investigation on her own, get a little revenge on Ben and Bob, but seeing how carefully things were being positioned to pin the scam on her had shaken her to the core. Geri needed Nate's help, and she thought she could help him too. Most of her pen testers were contractors. If she hired someone from the FBI as a contractor, that would get Nate inside the firewall. She hadn't offered that to Shay. She was sure he was keeping things from her, and she would do the same in return.

CHAPTER 27

Charlotte paused under the steel archway to Heinz Lofts, the former ketchup factory now trendy apartment rentals that were outside her price range and the only place Leah would consider leasing. Once inside the lobby, Charlotte knelt and removed her daughter's jacket, adjusting the tutu and tights Kelsey had insisted on wearing despite the fact that her first ballet class wasn't until next week. She felt a pang of motherly guilt at using Kelsey's desire to show off her outfit and little princess wand as a front to drop in on Leah unannounced. Her hands shook slightly. No matter what Leah had become, she loved Kelsey. Charlotte was banking on it. Still, as a mother, her instincts were to bring Leah here, into the lobby, to Kelsey rather than show up at her doorstep. There was no way to gauge whether Leah was alone or what her mood might be, and she wasn't willing to go that far despite Nate's push to get a look around Leah's apartment. They had finally, at Charlotte's insistence, agreed on FaceTime.

"I'm gonna show Leah my magic wand," Kelsey

announced, waving a plastic stick adorned with stars and glitter.

"Sounds good. Give Mommy one minute to FaceTime her," Charlotte said.

Nate had assured her there was an FBI agent somewhere nearby. She glanced around the empty lobby, hoping the man sitting at the table outside reading the newspaper was that agent.

"I can talk first?" Kelsey asked, looking hopeful.

"Yep, here you go." Charlotte squatted down as she handed the phone, now ringing, to Kelsey. "Hold it steady so she sees your face when she answers."

A moment later, Leah answered, her face not quite filling the screen. She looked flushed, her hair pinned up on her head, and was clad in a silk blouse.

"Hey, Kelsey . . . Charlie!" Leah seemed flustered, nervously looking over her shoulder and then back to the screen. Charlotte smiled, trying to give off a casual air as if she were looking at Leah while eyeing anything she could see behind her. Leah appeared to be moving toward her couch, and Charlotte thought she saw a man move quickly out of sight in the background.

"I'm a ballerina, Leah!" Kelsey yelled loud enough to be heard across the Ohio River. "And I have a magic wand!"

Leah frowned, then struggled to soften her face, sitting down and smiling at Kelsey. "Hey, Kelsey, look at you! I love your outfit."

"We're in the lobby, Leah. Can you come down for a few minutes?" Charlotte hoped she was keeping her face neutral. She was sure Leah had been trying to position herself where they couldn't see whoever was in the apartment, and the result was a full view of boxes stacked against walls stripped of photos and artwork. Two large suitcases sat less than a foot from the door. Wherever the man was, he was staying out of sight.

"Uh . . . I wasn't expecting you," Leah said with a frown, directing her comment to Charlotte. "As you can see, I'm packing." She waved her arm to indicate the boxes behind her.

"We thought we'd surprise you," Charlotte explained, keeping her arm around Kelsey's middle to steady herself. Her nerves had been on edge all day, and now, realizing Leah was about to leave town, panic surged. She needed to call Nate immediately, but she couldn't let Leah see anything but a calm and normal call from an old friend. "I've been too busy lately to come by. I feel bad that Kelsey and I haven't seen you in a while. I know it's kind of spur of the moment, but she wanted you to see her ballerina outfit. Do you want to come down for a minute, or should we come up there?"

There was an awkward silence until Kelsey broke the tension. "Where you going, Leah? You gonna go away like Daddy?" Charlotte realized Kelsey had seen the boxes and though something was wrong.

"No, no, Kels. I'm going on vacation, and when I get back, I'm going to move into a new apartment closer to you," Leah said.

A flash of genuine pain crossed Leah's face, her eyes seeming to tear up, although it was hard to tell for sure on the phone screen. Charlotte saw the friend of her childhood, the woman she'd believed Leah to be, until she witnessed for herself how smoothly, how easily, Leah had just lied.

"Cool, Lee. Where's your new place? Can we help you

pack and move?" Charlotte asked, watching Leah wipe her eyes and shut down, her mouth in a straight line, a hard set to her jaw.

"Give me one minute, and I'll come down to give you a hug, then I've got to get going." Leah's smile seemed forced, fake, and Charlotte felt a moment of fear as the phone screen went black. How dangerous would Leah be if Charlotte couldn't keep up an appearance of casual normality?

"Is Leah coming?" Kelsey asked, looking up at her mother, all smiles and wide eyes. She waved her wand, and Charlotte hoped it had some real magic as she watched the elevator door open and Leah appeared.

"I've only got a minute," Leah said, crouching down to hug Kelsey and avoiding eye contact with Charlotte. "I love the outfit!"

When Leah stood, her face was firm, serious, but Charlotte saw a struggle to maintain an easy, calm demeanor.

"Hey, Charlie, can we catch up when I get back? I can show you and Kelsey the new apartment, and maybe we can have a move-in party, but right now I've got a plane to catch. My Uber ride should be here soon." Leah's tone held a hint of anger, heightening Charlotte's fear. This had been a bad idea. She should have insisted the FBI simply watch Leah's home.

"Sure, sure . . . we'll see you when you get back. Kelsey, let's go. We're going to see Grace now and show her your magic wand," Charlotte said, suddenly anxious to get her daughter out of the building and back to the safety of her car.

Kelsey, happy to show off her outfit to anyone, smiled and complied. "Okay, Leya, I'm gonna touch you with the magic wand, and then we gotta go."

Leah bent over with a tender smile to let Kelsey tap her head with the wand.

Minutes later, after giving Leah a hug, Charlotte took Kelsey's hand and walked calmly from the lobby to her car. She saw the man at the table fold his newspaper and stand up, but she kept going, unsure whether Leah and whoever was with her could see her and Kelsey from the apartment window. Charlotte started the car and dialed Nate's number so they were speaking from the hands-free Bluetooth before pulling out. He'd made it clear that he'd be waiting to hear from her.

"Hey, Nate! Kelsey is here with me," Charlotte said, trying to keep her voice calm.

"Who's Nate?" Kelsey asked, her eyebrows furrowed.

"Hey, Kelsey. I work with your mommy at her job." *Good save*, Charlotte thought.

"Wanna see my ballet costume?" Kelsey chimed in, unaware that her mother was heading straight for Nate rather than to Grace's house.

"Sure, I'd love that. I'm at The Abbey in Lawrenceville. Can you stop by?"

"We were on our way to see Grace," Charlotte said, "but we can stop in to see you first. Kelsey might be hungry."

Kelsey nodded her head vigorously.

"Fifteen minutes, and we'll be there."

"I'll show you my magic wand too," Kelsey said, waving the wand around the back seat. "Leah liked it."

"Oh, cool!" Nate said. "Did you have fun at Leah's?" *Smart*, Charlotte thought.

"We saw her on FaceTime and in the lobby. She's going on vacation, and then she's gonna move near us later, so we couldn't stay. Lots of boxes."

"Well, I'm sure when she gets back, she'll want to see you again," Nate answered, his voice reassuring.

"Leah's heading to the airport soon. We left so she could get going," Charlotte said, stressing the word "soon."

"Got it!" Nate answered. "I'll see you when you get here. I can only stay long enough to see your costume, Kelsey, then I've got to get back to work!"

Charlotte ended the call, praying that Nate had all the information he needed to catch Leah and her cohorts red-handed and arrest them before they got on the flight. Ted's name would be cleared before Kelsey was old enough to hear otherwise about her father.

"Mommy, is Grace home?" Kelsey asked.

"No, honey, not yet." Charlotte hoped her voice sounded normal, reassuring, the opposite of what she was feeling inside. "We'll go have something to eat, and Grace will be home a little later."

"Can I have a cheeseburger and fries?"

"Absolutely! You've been a good girl today. Maybe we'll get ice cream too!"

Relief mixed with a deep level of sadness that carried no specific name. It extended outward from the pit of Charlotte's stomach—as if now that everything was coming to a head, she could begin to deal with the grief and loss it encompassed. Ted's name would be cleared, her gift to Kelsey. But when she'd hugged Leah, the response from her friend had been stiff. A painful longing to feel them wrap each other in a warm hug enveloped her. The tightness in her chest would not loosen despite the ongoing silent conversation she was having with herself to justify kicking her husband out, using her best friend's mother to then betray her best friend, and starting a relationship with another man without tying up loose strings that threatened to choke her if she didn't face her losses and come to terms with her life as it stood now. She'd used anger and fear to power herself forward, but the acute pain in her heart warned her there would be a reckoning soon, that avoidance would no longer work. For Kelsey's sake, she could not crash and bring what stability remained down with her.

CHAPTER 28

S he shouldn't be lurking around the Pittsburgh airport. If Ben spotted her, she could blow the entire FBI sting operation. Geri had worked hard to build a modicum of trust in her partnership with Nate. Even Shay had softened toward her, asking her to analyze a bit of what he was seeing. It was the perfect opening, and Geri had been careful to continue to foster that trust. If she were honest with herself, she would admit she'd come to like and respect Shay. In the future, perhaps she'd try a little harder to build better relationships with the staff.

The wire transfer would go through in one hour, as their plane was taking off for Bermuda. Geri had seen the insertion of the bank routing number and the mock simulated phishing attack they'd set up, mimicking a well-known hacker group. They were attempting to deflect their activities onto a Memorial Day–inspired email that pretended to ask for donations to help veterans in need, just as she'd suspected. It would have been weeks before the digital forensics team determined what had actually happened if

Shay hadn't been able to stay a step ahead and feed the information to the FBI.

Geri wanted to know who the third person was and why it was such a big secret. She'd had a thing for Bob Thornton once, but he'd spurned her advances in a pretty demeaning way at a company Christmas party. Since then, she'd hoped that some bad karma would come around and land right on Bob's head.

Pittsburgh was one of the few airports that allowed "terminal tourism." In 2017, they'd been featured in *Fortune* magazine for allowing a set number of non-travelers special passes to go through security and shop, dine, and otherwise enjoy the offerings in the terminal formerly restricted to ticketed travelers. People could enjoy the high-end shopping available, along with a nice martini bar and a few restaurants. It would serve Geri very well today if she was able to get to the airport in time to snag a pass. She brought ample identification and wore black jeans and a black Bar Symon T-shirt under her jacket to appear as though she were a restaurant employee out on a break once she was inside.

Luck was with her, and she obtained a tourist pass to go "shopping." Geri could see them as soon as she exited the top of the escalator—seated at a table near the round martini bar in the middle of the airport lobby, its blue neon lights casting a perennial glow on the triangular-shaped glasses in front of its customers. Geri pulled up the sides of her jacket collar and yanked down the rim on the baseball cap she'd added at the last minute before leaving.

Ben had his head lowered over his phone while a woman resembling the photo in his office sipped a pale pink martini. Geri assumed she was Ben's wife. Bob sat, his back to Ben, on the other side. When he laid a light kiss on the lips of an attractive woman who was stirring a skewer of olives around the inside edge of her glass, Geri was sure she had the third conspirator in her sights. Moving slowly inside the Collezione store until she could eye the bar from another angle, Geri pretended to shop, picking up one thing and then another at random, watching the group surreptitiously. The woman was vaguely familiar, but Geri couldn't place her.

"Can I help you?" asked a young woman with rings in her nose, eyebrow, and lips as she stood before Geri, blocking her view, her gaze suspicious.

"No, just on my break and looking a little," Geri answered.

She didn't want to buy something and leave any trace of herself there. The girl smiled, still planted firmly in Geri's line of vision. Geri was going to have to move to another store or the coffee shop in order to keep watch on the martini bar.

"Do you know the bartender at Bar Symon?" the girl asked, pointing to Geri's T-shirt. "The cute one with the green hair?"

"No, sorry, gotta go," Geri replied, pushing past her and out into the airport corridor at the same time two men with military haircuts and FBI jackets nearly ran into her.

She stepped back and huddled against a wall, watching. A woman and another man with the same jackets were moving in from the direction of the Armani store. Bob saw them first. He snapped his head from left to right, then grabbed the woman's hand. They grabbed their belongings —backpacks, totes, purses—and began moving at a fairly brisk walk. Ben threw some cash on the bar and pushed his wife in the same direction.

The FBI agents closed in, grabbing Ben, Bob, and the woman with Bob, while Ben's wife stood clasping her designer handbag to her chest, a look of terror on her face. The agents moved them back toward the martini bar. Ben yelled and pushed, starting a commotion, demanding they allow him to the gate because he had a plane to catch. His wife looked startled, frozen in place. Suddenly, Geri's view was blocked by Nate as he nudged Ben's wife toward a female agent, said a few words to his team, then tossed his head in the direction of the down escalators that led to the tram and, eventually, outside. Nate leaned into Ben, who was still protesting, and put his mouth against Ben's ear. Whatever was said, Ben went silent. The trio, escorted by FBI agents with Ben's wife trailing behind, stepped onto the downward escalator, and then they were gone. Geri began following them when suddenly she saw Nate had turned and was walking away from the escalator directly toward her. Her head swiveled frantically in several directions, and she moved toward the nearest shop, hoping to appear to be casually shopping.

"Not so fast, Geri!" Nate said, locking her elbow in a death grip. "You could have ruined this for us. Why are you here?"

One look at Nate's face and she knew she needed to deflect his anger if possible. Nate's hand clamped on her upper arm like a vise as he began walking, half pulling, half jerking her along until she cried out in pain and he slowed down.

"You can't force me along like a common criminal," Geri argued. Her arm felt only slightly less bruised than her ego.

"I suggest you drop the attitude," Nate replied. They were on the escalator now, heading to the tram. "I could easily arrest you for attempting to obstruct a federal operation, and, believe me, if they had spotted you first and taken off before we could grab them, I would."

For the first time, Geri shuddered, the realization dawning on her that if he'd made good on his threat, she would have a criminal record like so many in her family. She'd have lost everything just to satisfy her vengeful need to see Ben and Bob arrested, and to know the identity of the third conspirator—something she'd been sure all along Nate, Shay, and Charlotte were hiding from her. She sat on the plastic seats of the airport tram as it transported them to the exit, rubbing her arm while Nate stood over her, holding a pole. She could see the butt of his gun where his jacket sloped, unzipped and loose, across it. She'd let her defiance mix with jealousy, ego, and anger, ending in a mistake. Now if she could quickly make it home and put this behind her.

The tram doors slid open, and Nate held her opposite arm firmly but not as tightly. They were heading toward the arrival area outside sprinkled with taxis, rideshares, family members waiting patiently, and local news vans. Several camera crews were filming as reporters called to anyone with an FBI jacket for a statement. Nate stopped. He appeared to be thinking, then he turned to Geri.

"Go! Go home and stay home. This is an FBI operation. You have no business getting involved, do you hear me?" His voice, barely above a whisper, was fierce.

Geri considered complaining that this arrest was as much due to the help she'd provided as to Nate's work, but then thought better of it and bolted, heading for a door that was the furthest away from the cameras and crowd, intent on getting to her car. She blended in—just another airport worker leaving her shift for the day. Looking over her shoulder, she saw Nate walk directly into the TV crews and photographers to give a statement. All Geri could think of now was a hot bath, a stiff bourbon and water, and curling up on her couch to become one of about three hundred thousand people in the Pittsburgh area watching the FBI sting of her coworkers unfold across the evening news.

CHAPTER 29

Charlotte studied the small coffee stain on the pressed white cuff, an untidy blemish marring the potential for perfection on the Armani shirt. Its outline was shaded by gold cuff links, then disappeared under the fine weave of a Brooks Brothers suit. She wasn't about to speak to him, nor he to her, knowing as they did that they were on opposite sides of the courtroom lying behind the heavy oak doors across from the hallway benches where they sat.

The foot and a half of tension-filled space arose between them the minute Charlotte recognized Brad Harrington, one of Leah's ex-boyfriends and an attorney who now, it seemed, was back in her good graces when she needed him to bail her out of an impossible situation. The public, and even her friends, said there was no way Leah would escape doing some time in prison. They didn't know Leah. Charlotte would not be shocked if Leah wormed her way into community service, and in and out of Brad's life again as she had a couple years ago.

"You think something is funny?" Brad asked as he gave her an angry glance.

Charlotte realized she'd been smiling. She'd been remembering Ted in a carefully pressed white shirt from JCPenney, fretting about the minuscule spot of coffee on the shirt's cuff. Charlotte, using a soft cloth and seltzer water, scrubbed the spot while trying not to chuckle at the level of Ted's anger over something so inconsequential.

"What I was thinking has nothing to do with you," Charlotte replied.

She let out a deep breath, relieved that, for the first time in months, she was able to have a good memory of Ted, a memory that caused a smile to spread across her face and might even have made her laugh had Leah's attorney chosen to ignore her. As they waited, she thought about her mother sitting in a law firm's conference room, a few blocks away, across the table from her father, negotiating a divorce. She'd felt her mother's fear when she hugged her before they parted ways on the sidewalk, her slim frame trembling.

"I know how frightening it is to face being on your own," Charlotte whispered in her ear. "Kelsey and I are here for you."

"Sometimes it's lonelier in a relationship than it is on your own," Rosalyn had responded, taking a deep breath and straightening her back. "At least that's what I've heard, and I'm counting on it."

"I'm sorry I can't be there for you." Charlotte said, the turn her relationship with her mother had taken gently warming her from the inside out. They were two women on par with one another, mixing love with a new experience as friends.

"It's better you don't. Your father will see that as taking sides, something I don't want you or your brother to feel you need to do. I have a friend meeting me who will wait in the lobby and drive me home."

Charlotte kissed her mother on the cheek. "I've taken sides, though. I'm not sure when or how Dad and I will work things out, if we ever do."

Charlotte sent a silent prayer to her mother, hoping she remained strong through what would probably be a contentious meeting, complete with a private investigator's report on her father's affair. The courtroom doors swung open, and Brad stood, entering along with the journalists, prosecutors, and other defense lawyers to meet the defendants at the front of the courtroom. Charlotte remained seated. They would call her to testify today, now that they had heard from the FBI, the forensic accountants, Shay, Missy, and Geri. Nate had submitted everything, from Ted's original research to the work Shay had done to verify it and carry the investigation further with the FBI. All of it, along with the records found in Leah's mother's home documenting how she'd framed Ted at the request of Ben and Bob, had been accepted into evidence. All charges against Ted had been dropped. Charlotte, with Nate's help, petitioned the district attorney to take Ted's deposition via video from Montana, arguing he had been in therapy for months and wasn't ready to return to Pittsburgh. In some ways, that request was selfishly motivated, more for her than Ted as she struggled with whether she wanted to see him again. She really didn't want him to move back to Pittsburgh. Now that she'd cleared his name, it felt like closure, but also as if she were leading a new life here and hesitant to dip her big toe into the mess of her marriage. Kelsey was asking daily when she could see her father. Charlotte knew there would be no way out; she'd have to deal with her feelings at least for her daughter's sake.

"Hey there, want some company?" Grace asked, sitting down next to Charlotte with a smile. Charlotte leaned in for a quick hug. "I see a lot of reporters here. Are you writing an article, or are you agreeing to be interviewed?"

Charlotte grinned. When this trial ended, there would be an article in the paper fully clearing Ted's name.

"I'd hoped to write the story myself, but my editor shot that idea down. Said I'm not able to be impartial."

"Well, I agree with your editor. How do you feel about that?"

"I don't want to relive everything I've been through this past year, and writing the article would put me through exactly that. I'm actually relieved," Charlotte answered with a shrug. She genuinely meant what she said and hoped Grace could see that. "Let someone new and hungry for a byline take the assignment. My goal, through all of this, was to make sure Kelsey didn't grow up thinking her father was a criminal. I think that's been accomplished. Thanks for being there for me every step of the way, Grace."

Grace reached over and took her hand, giving it a squeeze. "Charlotte, are you feeling all right about going in there?" Grace asked. "I mean, facing Leah? You haven't talked to her since, well, you know . . . right?"

"She tried to get me to meet with her as soon as she was out on bail," Charlotte said. "I was appalled that she would even think . . . after what she did to Ted . . . to Kelsey and to me . . . but she was only thinking of herself, as usual. I had to ask my parents to stay away from her too, no matter how they feel about Ted."

"Still, it has to be hard," Grace said, her voice softening as she patted Charlotte's back. "You were close for so long. You know, Leah did a bad thing, but Ted did a lot of this to himself."

"She framed him using Kelsey," Charlotte snapped. "Sorry, but that's an open wound. Much more than how Ted was wronged. She could have set that fake account up in anyone's name but my daughter's."

"True," Grace said, nodding in agreement.

"Elaine, Leah's mother, is in there, supporting her daughter in spite of everything," Charlotte said. "The sadness I feel is for her. I hope Leah finally finds a way to appreciate her mother."

"And how is your mother doing? Today's the day, right?"

"When we parted ways this morning, she seemed nervous but determined. I know my father. He's fine with getting out of the marriage as long as it doesn't cost too much or affect his professional reputation," Charlotte said. "Both of which are about to happen when my mother's attorney slaps the PI's file and the settlement request in front of him." She gave Grace a mischievous grin.

"Now's probably not the time, but you know you have to decide what you want where your own marriage is concerned." Grace fidgeted, crossing her legs a few times. Charlotte knew her friend worried about bringing up this subject as much as she worried about Charlotte.

"I'm not ready to talk about that." Charlotte locked both Ted and the threads of her marriage in a little box in her mind, a problem to face later, and changed the subject. "Did you hear that Nate offered Shay a job as a digital forensic expert with the FBI?"

"That's some good news!" Grace didn't know Shay well, but the few times she'd met him, they'd seemed to hit it off. He'd told Charlotte she reminded him of his mother in some ways. "Will he move to D.C.?"

"Probably. I'll miss him a lot, but good for him. He's the hero in all of this, and he deserves it." Charlotte meant that. She'd told Shay he could only go if he promised to keep in touch, to stay a part of their lives and be a good role model for Kelsey.

The door opened, and the bailiff called Charlotte's name, motioning her to enter the courtroom.

"Don't say anything I wouldn't say," Grace said with a wink and a thumbs-up. She stood and followed Charlotte into the courtroom, taking a seat at the back.

Charlotte marched up the aisle toward the witness stand, confident, propelled by her anger and determination. Eyes on Leah as she raised her hand and was sworn in, she saw no sign of remorse, only defiance. She made eye contact with Elaine for a moment, and then the older woman bowed her head, eyes closing as if in prayer. Charlotte shifted her gaze to the back of the courtroom. There was Grace, her true friend, quietly supporting her. Charlotte smiled, hoping she conveyed the strength of purpose she felt.

CHAPTER 30
JACKSON, WYOMING

The icy, fast running waters of Upper Flat Creek in late June was an imperfect setting for serious fishing. The mountains were still melting, sending the runoff at a pace that meant actually catching anything today was unlikely. But the rhythmic cadence of the dance made by his arm and the rod, moving lightly as one to the music of the elements of nature, brought Ted a sense of peace.

Everything from the waders and heavy boots to the truck, rod and reel, and lures was borrowed.

"'Bout four hours to Jackson," Jesse had said, hands shoved into the pockets of his worn Levi's as he watched Ted load the fishing and camping gear onto his truck. "You staying the night?"

"Yep, I'll get a room at a small place halfway back if it ends up being too cold to camp outside."

"You're coming back . . . tomorrow." It was a simple statement fraught with concern.

"It won't happen again, Jess." Ted patted his brother's shoulder. "I'm trying to fix something. Or maybe find something again."

Jesse hugged him in the odd stiff way people did with Ted now, not knowing how or whether to touch him. "Go find whatever you need, brother. Then come home. I'll be here."

"If I don't have your truck back in forty-eight hours, you can call me in to the state police for theft," Ted said, flashing Jesse a quick grin.

"Oh, yeah . . . that'd be interesting," Jesse answered, finally cracking a smile. "Seriously, Ted. I doubt anyone in Wyoming knows about you or your story. It'll be you, the fish, and maybe a few elk."

"I'll just be another guy out there hoping to get away from things and catch a few fish." With a quick fist bump for his brother, he had climbed into the truck and headed east.

Now, as Ted listened to the seductive song of the creek, he carefully threaded the line through the rod, his stomach clutching at the memory of other waters—dark, murky, and smelling of ancient sediment—that were up to his thighs and would have closed over him had River Rescue not stopped him in time. Despite months of therapy, he still had moments when he wondered if being saved had been a good thing. Here, on the Jackson Elk Refuge, he thought he could quell those lingering, negative thoughts.

"Hello, God . . . hello, Dad . . ." Ted called out softly to the mountains above him.

It remained one of his favorite places on earth, taking him back to the few times when he'd come here as a boy with his father. Established in 1912 by various acts of Congress, executive orders, and other documents, the refuge provided a winter habitat for the Jackson elk herd. It was exactly that—a refuge, for him as well as about six thousand elk and the people who respected the need to keep this place safe and untouched by the more unscrupulous elements of humankind.

It's just me and my sins today, trying to find a way forward. Ted could see no elk as he'd turned from Refuge Road to Flat Creek Road in the early-morning hours. They would have left the lower elevations by now to follow the receding snow line back into the high country where they could feed on lush meadow plants and use forests for shelter. They wouldn't be back to the valley floor until winter, when the refuge was closed to all humans except park rangers. *I understand wanting to avoid humans, wanting open space and peace.* He'd driven slowly, searching for the perfect semi-secluded spot to fish and camp overnight, hitting the brakes as several tiny chislers, the Uinta ground squirrel of the Grant Tetons, zipped across the road. *I guess we're all inching our way out of hibernation today. Me, the chislers, hopefully not the bears . . . not yet.* The chislers chirped and scurried about.

Jesse had followed the pre-trial arraignments in Pittsburgh online with periodic updates from Charlotte or Shay. When Charlotte called to say Ted had been exonerated of all charges, she'd only spoken to Jesse. Ted saw her for a few seconds each week when she set up the FaceTime call with Kelsey, but then she left the room. Kelsey had learned how to hang up the call on her own, relieving Charlotte of the need for much more than perfunctory conversation with Ted. No matter how many calls or how many months went by, it hurt just as deeply each time. Ted would have to take a deep breath and put on his best face for his daughter, move aside the need—more a deep craving that blanketed his days and filled his nights with restless sleep—to speak to his wife, to know what she was thinking and if there was even the smallest glimmer of hope for them within her, waiting to emerge even as he waited for her. Shame colored his need every time, and he stopped himself from asking her for a call between the two of them. He didn't deserve her anymore. That knowledge mingled with the ongoing fear that hearing her answer would end things once and for all between them.

"I'm heading to Jackson to do some fly fishing . . . like when I was a kid," Ted had told his therapist when he canceled their next session. "I had some good times there with my father."

"Great idea! Reschedule with me when you get back. I want to hear all about it."

As soon as he'd entered Refuge Road, his mind began to settle, his heart running at a slower pace. Ted knew now that he'd first gotten off track after he left the ranch for college and began searching for a guide to a life destination he hadn't really figured out yet. He could look back and see how open and vulnerable he'd been when corporations came calling, offering a whole new way to define himself that he'd gobbled up like candy. He'd shoved his true priorities—his wife and his child—into a neat, manageable corner that didn't rock the boat where his ambitions were concerned. Charlotte thought Ted's fascination with ferreting out the secrets of others was the start of his downfall, but Ted saw the problem resting on the secrets he'd kept and the way his ego had pivoted him toward an inevitable crash. It had been all about him and his career.

"You've changed, Ted." He could hear Charlotte's voice calling from his past as he stepped into his waders and unloaded his gear on the banks of the river. "And not in a good way."

It was a warning bell he'd ignored, and now, although still legally married, he was, for all intents and purposes, alone.

A lot had changed in the time since he'd gone for the ill-fated promotion at work. He hadn't known himself well enough then to know what was true and what was not. What he'd felt then was safety in the structure of year-end reviews, titles, promotions, and corporate rewards. The institution could define, then dictate, success and failure to him. He didn't have to dig deep inside. Everything was laid out in front of him. All he had to do was log into the game and play it. He understood now how Charlotte came to feel disgusted with him. Here, far away from the source of his failings and stripped to the bare bones of his being, Ted searched for a way to move forward, to figure out who he could still be for his wife and child, given the chance.

"Lord, let me appreciate the land, the water, the fish, and my life." His father's fishing prayer came back to him unbidden, as automatic as breathing.

"Do you pray much?" his therapist had asked during their first visit as Ted eyed the serenity prayer hanging near a crucifix on the wall behind the desk.

"Nope," Ted answered. "Never saw much use in it."

"Do you know that prayer . . . on the wall?"

"My father had a few quick prayers he liked. I said them as a child. We didn't get along much as I grew older."

Ted attached the lure, rubbing a little fly goop on it—a solution that keeps dry flies floating on the surface of the water—like his father had taught him. He let his past in all its innocence and foolish egoism fade away with the splash of his boot entering the water as he shifted on the rocky creek bed, making sure he had a firm hold. He eyed the shadows around a fallen log, the hiding places in the reeds near the opposite embankment. He felt the need to hunt something again. A fish, any fish—idling in the spots where water pooled and mild obscurity protected them—would do, replacing the longing he felt to go after the cyber criminals he once chased through log files and laptop forensics, seeking a way to beat them and win a sense of self that was, ultimately, false. He raised his arm into position, and, with a perfect flick of his wrist, the line began the soft dance of his youth across the water. He'd come here hoping to shake off the months since he was fired. What he hadn't expected was to hear, in the stilled hush of the leaves and amid the birdcalls and rippling water, the voice of his father.

CHAPTER 31

Kelsey held her body so still, Charlotte was afraid she'd handled this the wrong way. Her tiny eyebrows were furrowed, and she focused on the muscled, angular body still about ten yards away, dismounting from a horse, the summer sun beginning to set behind him.

"Uncle Jesse?" She looked up at her mother, and Charlotte shook her head.

"Uncle Jesse is a really big guy, remember?"

Kelsey shaded her eyes to block the sun. Her small shoulders shuddered, and then she began running, her torso slightly ahead of her pumping, sturdy legs, heading straight for the man walking toward her. He dropped to one knee, arms outstretched, as she yelled "Daddy!" in both an exhalation of sorrow and an inhalation of joy.

Even after so much time had passed, with only limited FaceTime and no visits, Kelsey could forgive easily—something Charlotte was still working through. She'd told Ted he had to have his life back on track before she'd bring Kelsey to the ranch. Kelsey believed her father had been on a long trip, and when he came home, they'd see him. Because

Charlotte hadn't been sure what they would face coming to Montana, she'd said they were visiting Uncle Jesse.

Ted walked toward Charlotte, their daughter glued to his chest, arms and legs wrapped as far around him as they would go.

"Charlotte . . . good to see you again," he said. She could hear the hope in his voice around the awkwardness between them.

"How are you, Ted?" Charlotte asked. Kelsey's small suitcase and backpack sat in solitary alignment on the porch.

"Better. Working again. Healing." He closed his eyes and kissed the top of Kelsey's head, which lay on his shoulder. "Are you staying?"

Charlotte knew she couldn't. She wasn't ready. All her energy had gone into clearing his name for Kelsey's sake, and yet, as he stood in front of her—shaded by the porch roof just inches above his head, tan, fit, framed by the idyllic beauty of the open range behind him—she felt a pull toward him. It was an old feeling, buried somewhere deep below the anger that had been a constant within her since she'd left him. Anger at Ted, anger at Leah, anger at all the lies. It had all been too much.

"I'm leaving Kelsey with you for a few days, maybe a week, and getting away," Charlotte answered. "I'll do some hiking at Hyalite Creek and a few days in Bozeman, then in Livingston on my way back."

"Can we talk? Before you go?"

"We can talk when I'm done thinking. I'm not sure when that will be."

Ted gently placed Kelsey on a rocking chair. "Stay put, sugar. Daddy's gonna walk Mommy to the car." Kelsey looked at Charlotte and whimpered. Charlotte's stomach clenched. A wave of nausea rose inside her seeing them together, watching her daughter's raw, naked need for her father. Ted seemed the same and yet different, somehow at peace in the one place he'd said he could never live, and yet also lost, lonely perhaps. A pang of guilt stabbed her in the gut over that realization, an emotion she'd thought she could no longer feel where Ted was concerned.

"Kels, we talked about this. Mommy is going to take a little Mommy vacation, and you'll stay here," Charlotte said as she squatted down in front of the chair, hands on the little girl's knees. "Mommy will be back. I'll always come back. And I'll call you every day. You're gonna have fun with Daddy and Uncle Jesse."

Kelsey hugged her, then wiggled back into the chair to wait. Charlotte began moving toward the rental car, Ted following behind.

"Do you have a hotel booked?" Ted asked.

"Yes, I set everything up," Charlotte answered. "I'm even going to meet our old college buddy, Sam, for lunch in Livingston."

Ted was silent. She could see his struggle not to show the disappointment on his face.

"Sam still single?"

"Yep . . . and still gay," Charlotte said with a wink and a smile, watching Ted blush. A rush of pleasure at his jealousy whisked through her, making her tingle inside before she quickly tamped it down. At least he wasn't asking about Danny, if he was even aware of the relationship. She'd tried to keep things as quiet as possible where her private life was concerned. Kelsey thought of Danny as her mother's "friend," but Shay had told her it left him caught between her and Ted, and she thought, if asked, he'd feel he had to tell Ted the truth. Not that she was sure what the truth might actually be about her and Danny. Another struggle to work out, she hoped, by getting some alone time on this trip.

"Oh, right," Ted said. He shoved his hands in his pockets and looked down. "We need to talk. When you get back, I mean."

"I guess." Charlotte glanced at Kelsey sitting quietly, watching them. "For her, we need to talk."

"I won't lie. I want to know if there is any chance for us .. . you know . . . to be a family again."

He stood so close to her that she could smell the mix of sweat and sweetgrass on him. She closed her eyes and thought of Danny. It steadied her enough to maintain self-control.

"I don't know about that, Ted. That might be a little more than I can sort through in a week on my own," Charlotte answered. "But whatever I decide, I won't deny you our daughter."

She opened the car door and slid behind the wheel. Ted leaned into the driver's side window. "Take very good care of her, Ted. I'll call every day."

THE NEXT DAY, Charlotte grudgingly accepted that, despite fairly regular attendance at the yoga studio and hiking much of the expanse of Frick Park in her neighborhood back home, she could only go a certain distance on a hike before the elevation and exertion got the best of her. The escapism was what she loved. She'd come here with Kelsey as a baby gurgling in tune with the running stream then sleeping against her back as she hiked. In spite of being out of shape today, it was a couple miles of peace. She loved Montana. She'd hiked a lot of these trails in college and remembered them well. She had changed, but the nature she loved had not.

As she stepped around a fallen branch, Charlotte wondered if it had been wise to leave Kelsey with Ted. The child would be ecstatic thinking she was going to have her father back in her life full-time. Charlotte questioned whether she should have waited, held off the reunion until she had a firm plan for how she and Ted would ultimately work this out for their little girl. Instead, she'd dropped her daughter off with a father she hadn't spent time with in months and taken off for Bozeman, intent on riding through Yellowstone, hiking Hyalite, and maybe hanging out in a wine bar or coffee shop at night. Whatever would bring her to a moment of decision.

"I'll call you every day," Danny told her before she left. It had sounded like a great, comforting idea, but after two days of speaking with Ted and Kelsey followed by a call from Danny, she felt differently.

"I need some space to sort myself out," Charlotte told Danny the third night he called. She was sitting in a wine bar, trying to remove her mind from everything in her life except the warm liquid cascading down her throat and the soft cadence of guitar music drifting from a solo musician on the corner stage. "I have to figure out what's best for my daughter, and to do that, I need some space to think. Can you give me that?"

"Do I have a choice?" Danny asked, sounding sad, resigned. She wished he would be angry with her. Anger was easier to manage right now.

When she called Jesse to tell him that Ted was exonerated, Charlotte had expected that Ted would start packing, planning his move to Pittsburgh and his launch back into another corporation and another shallow climb to the top.

She'd been ready to tell him she and Kelsey wouldn't be joining him, and then have divorce papers drawn up. Instead, minutes after Jesse hung up and relayed the message, Ted had emailed her to thank her for helping him find his way back home. He wanted to stay in Montana. He liked the little tech start-up he'd joined in Bozeman. Charlotte thought about how often she'd suggested they return and slow down into a simpler life. Now here he was, a day late and a dollar short as her mother used to say, waiting for her to make a decision about whether she'd join him or sentence her daughter to a life of long-distance flights.

"Marry me," Danny had said before she left. She knew he was concerned about more than the trip to Montana. She'd been spending less time with him after Leah's arraignment and Ted's decision to stay in Montana. She wasn't sure why, but she suspected that without the old need to escape, he was a guy she really cared about no more, no less.

"I'm still married to Ted. I know we're more than friends, but I'm not ready for a step like that." Charlotte was uncomfortable, shouldering more than a little shame that she couldn't articulate what it was that refused to die between her and Ted. She was confident her feelings were not as strong as what Ted felt for her, not what led her to marry him all those years ago, but there was something between them that was more than sex.

"Then let's take it to any next step you're ready for, Charlie. I love you."

She'd panicked, feeling closed in by two men, each wanting a decision from her, an answer she couldn't give them because she still didn't have an answer for herself. It amazed her that, lately, even thinking about Danny or Ted left her with a new emotion she could only define as resentment. This was her life, her future, and it wasn't her responsibility to make a decision that met their needs and wants. Only Kelsey came first. After that, it was about what she needed, how to keep her own independence inside and outside a relationship with a man. She wasn't yet confident she could do that, and she wasn't willing to risk going back. She owned her life now, the tangled mess that it still was.

Charlotte stopped, sitting on a fallen log, its wood bleached white from sun and water. She was about eleven thousand feet up and a bit dizzy, but the pain in her chest was less from hiking and more from the memory of Danny's face filled with concern when she told him she needed to see Ted, to talk to him, to make some decisions about their family. Danny was clear that he wanted her to choose closure with Ted on this trip and return to Pittsburgh and to him. Charlotte pulled out her water bottle and took a drink. Closing her eyes, she inhaled long, slow breaths as she imagined her hikes at home across much flatter terrain. She could see the squirrels darting across her path, hear birds singing in concert with the stones and twigs crunching under her feet, all so familiar to her; her personal meditation as she took on a tiny corner of Frick Park's six hundred and fifty acres. Here she could hear the smaller falls cascading behind her. Opening her eyes, she saw a glimpse of the twin falls high up on the mountain peak above her. The stillness of the trees, the song of the water, settled on her like a prayer. Her mother's voice spoke in her head, "We often look for God in the big moments in our lives, but he's also in the stillness, in the quiet place within us."

Bozeman stretched at the base of the Bridger Mountains, a part of the Rockies running in a north-south direction between Bozeman and Livingston, separated from the Gallatin Range to the south by Bozeman Pass. The city was spread out in a mismatched kind of way. Perfect, brand-new homes, clumped together in cookie-cutter format. They butted up on Old Bozeman, its homes made of wood softened by the elements, paint chipping a bit, holding fast to the remnants of originality that spoke of the Old West people once knew. Trendy shops, restaurants, and tech start-ups competed for attention in a two-mile stretch of Main Street that gave both color and heartbeat, as well as frightening big-city encroachment, to the Montana cadence of the place. Hikers and fishermen, weathered older ranchers, and college kids mingled with overdressed corporate types trying on Montana like a pair of slippers, seeing if it could provide some type of semi-permanent escape they weren't innately geared to embrace. They instinctively knew they would go back, mounting a scenic picture in their cubicle or home office to tide them over, sliding back into the stress and structure of big-city life.

By the fourth day in Bozeman, Charlotte felt herself slipping into long, late-night conversations with Ted after he put Kelsey to bed. They were becoming friends again, and yet, when she slept, she dreamed of Danny boating on the Monongahela River, imagined giving in to his caresses and making love. Charlotte woke up confused, unsure what to do. Could she feel that way about Ted again? Could she forgive herself if she chose Danny and forced Kelsey to shuffle between two homes and two different states, seeing her father a few times a year? If she stayed, she needed her independence. A job, a sense of self, a separateness from Ted if they were to heal at all.

There were tourists everywhere along Main Street in Livingston, spilling out of The Murray Hotel, gobbling up parking slots, creating the chaos of the big cities they claimed to flee. You could spot them in designer shirts and Prada bags that, like their leather sandals and slip-on shoes, were not available in the local Walmart. They drove Range Rovers and BMWs instead of pickup trucks and Jeeps like the locals. They didn't let their hair go gray or their features age naturally, and they hadn't been relaxed and peaceful in at least a decade—no matter where their escapist vacation ideals landed them.

Charlotte squinted through the bug graveyard that was now her windshield. She grabbed a parking spot right in front of the Elk River bookstore. Moving at a quick jog, she turned onto Main and ducked into Montana Cup. A wave came from the far end of the coffee shop, and she smiled as Sam Sweeney, the editor of a suite of Montana publications and an old college buddy, stood and headed in her direction, his long legs covering the short distance easily. He'd taken over Sweeney Publications from his father last year.

"Charlie! Looking gorgeous as ever," Sam said as he wrapped her in a big hug. "Welcome home."

"Ha ... well, home is in Pittsburgh now. But it feels good to be back."

"You must be thinking of making a switch, though, huh?" Sam winked.

"Let me get a coffee, and then we can catch up," Charlotte called over her shoulder as she bolted for the coffee bar. Sam was Montana born and raised, but, as a social media and cable news junkie, he was always connected to what was going on in the world. She was sure he'd followed everything printed regarding Ted, Leah, and any legal proceedings.

As the barista made her coffee, Charlotte eyed the blueberry muffins. She decided to add one to her order, then walked back to the table slowly, both hands full and trying not to spill anything. "Thanks for reaching out," she said as she gently set her mug of café Americano on the small table, then the plate with a big, fresh blueberry muffin next to it, before she sat down. "I know you and I were always closer friends than you and Ted, but he's trying to heal, to start over. Jesse said you helped him get a job."

"I connected him with someone we both hung out with in college, and it worked out."

"You're making it sound so simple, but we both know that Ted's resume is easily tagged to his online notoriety, even if it's only out there on local outlets in Pittsburgh," Charlotte said. "It couldn't have been that easy."

"Well, there was some hesitation, but Ted has big skills, and he was willing to come in at half the price." Sam shrugged as if it were no big deal. Charlotte was sure it must have taken a good bit of negotiation.

"Is he on probation? On the job, I mean . . . until they see if he works out?" For Charlotte, part of deciding what was right for Kelsey required thinking with her head, not her emotions, to determine what choice created stability for her daughter. Ted's ability to earn a living was a huge issue.

"No, I think he's passed whatever markers they needed to see," Sam said. "I hear he's quiet, humble, and grateful. Imagine that! Not quite the old Ted I knew."

Charlotte looked down at her coffee mug. "You think he's changed?"

"Do you?" She looked up to see Sam eyeing her, smirking, a twinkle in his eye. She could feel herself blushing. "I'm not ever going to give in and say he's changed enough to make me a Ted fan . . . but the few times I've been around him, I'd say the last year has had a positive effect. He seems sad, quiet, but less cocky, less self-centered. He helps Jesse a ton around the ranch in addition to his job in Bozeman."

Breaking off a piece of the muffin, Charlotte shifted the

conversation before taking a bite. "So, you're living around here now?"

"Yeah, Bozeman has gotten too hipster . . . a bit too millennial for me. I like Livingston, but it's too touristy in the summer," Sam said. "I bought a place in Big Timber, down the road, for a little more peace and seclusion."

"Seriously? Since when do you like seclusion?" Charlotte chuckled. "Weren't you the guy who randomly slept in extra beds or on the floor at least once in every dorm room on our floor, then we'd have to sneak you out in the morning when the RA wasn't looking?"

"Gay man, safety man, when it came to the girls dorm," Sam said with a laugh. "But true, I wasn't exactly the guy who wanted to hide out in the library reading a book, huh?"

With a shrug, Sam pinched a piece of Charlotte's muffin, popping it into his mouth. "Well, I don't live alone anymore. But that is a conversation for another time."

Sam had been Charlotte's first friend in college. He'd taught her to love Montana in a deep, abiding way that Ted had never tapped into back then. She'd taught him that he could be accepted as he was and helped him come out of the closet as a gay man to the people who mattered most to him. They sat in companionable silence for a few minutes until Sam began shifting in his seat, grasping and twisting his hands as if trying to crack his knuckles. "Charlie, about the trial . . ."

"Just pretrial arraignment hearings so far. The trial is down the road, but Ted's off the hook now as far as legal actions pending against him."

"Must have been really tough for you." Sam smiled sympathetically at her.

"Yeah, lots of stress these past nine months or so," Charlotte said, hoping her tone discouraged more questions about Ted's legal issues.

Sam was now happily motoring his way through one half of her muffin. "How was it seeing old Teddy again?" he asked.

"He seems better."

"Are you sick of people asking you about him?" Sam leaned back, licking his fingers and any stray crumbs remaining.

"Yes . . . sort of. I mean, I get the curiosity, but I'm generally tired of everything being about Ted." Charlotte smiled as if it didn't bother her as much as it probably sounded to others like it did. "But let's get all the Ted questions out now so we don't have to talk about it again, okay?"

"Saw him one day a couple months back at a rodeo with Jesse."

"Ahh, the good old rodeo," Charlotte said. She sipped her coffee. "Well, shockingly, he seems to have rediscovered his roots. Says he's staying here in Montana."

"Hmmm . . . you believe him?"

"Not sure. Maybe."

Sam leaned back and crossed his arms over his chest, giving her a firm, direct look. "Personally, I think you've met the 'for better or worse' quotient in your marriage by now."

"Suppose I move back here too . . . and I'm not saying I will," Charlotte said, deciding to ignore his comment. "I need my own gig, you know? Something separate that's mine until I see if this works."

"You can do better than him. I told you that a long time ago, Charlie," Sam said, his face stern.

"Well, there's Kelsey . . . " Charlotte ran her finger along the rim of the mug. Kelsey running into Ted's arms flashed through her mind. "I'm not only making decisions for my own life. My choices will profoundly affect her."

"I don't have kids. I'm not going to pretend to understand what you're up against," Sam acknowledged. "All my decisions have been whatever works for me."

"He really seems to like his job in Bozeman, and he seems content to stay with Jesse on the ranch."

"Question is, would you be content living on the ranch, or living with Ted for that matter?"

Charlotte watched Sam, feeling like he was angling toward something, eyeballing her the way the old Sam did years ago when he was thinking about how to get what he wanted. "I don't know," she said. "I spent a week asking myself all these questions without much progress. I don't think I could live with Ted out here, at least not right away."

"I might have an idea or two." Sam was grinning at her.

"Why do I feel as if we're back in college and you want me to, oh, I don't know, pretend to be your girlfriend when your parents are in town? Or help you finish a paper because you have a hangover after partying all night instead of doing homework?" Charlotte laughed.

"Come on, Charlie! Hear me out. I had a couple college students writing for me, but they eventually quit to go see if they could make it in the big city," Sam said, his tone shifting. "I need a steady writer, and I'd like to start a new quarterly *Montana Arts* publication. See if I can take that, along with all the publications, to an upgraded digital platform too."

Charlotte closed her eyes. She imagined writing about things she loved, offering Kelsey a childhood filled with wide-open spaces, fresh air, and safety. No one in this part of the country felt a need to so much as lock their doors.

"There's this other guy," Charlotte blurted out. She

suddenly needed to talk about Danny, but wondered if she should have launched the topic here, and to someone who wasn't a particularly big fan of Ted.

"Oh, thank God, Charlie! Is he hot? Can you bring him out here and forget Ted?"

"He couldn't move out here," Charlotte answered with a laugh. "Pittsburgh's home for him. But, I admit, he's hot, and he would really like to make me forget Ted."

"Perfect. I like him already." Sam winked at her.

"Sam, if you'd seen Kelsey's face when she saw Ted." Charlotte's eyes teared up. She rummaged around quickly in her tote bag for a tissue, trying to blow her nose quietly as Sam waited. Her heart hurt thinking about how one wrong, selfish move could damage her child for life. And yet, if Ted hadn't changed, if this new Ted was temporary and only on display for her, would she want the old Ted to raise Kelsey with her full-time?

Sam reached across the table to hold her hand. Charlotte's heart burst with gratitude for him in this moment when she needed Grace to comfort her, she was trying to tamp down her physical attraction to Danny, and she remained emotionally and legally bound to Ted. Pulling back, Sam tapped the table with his fingers, forehead creased, thinking. Charlotte watched him, listening as the tapping moved from his fingers to his foot. The self-centered exterior was a camouflage. She knew, underneath, he was trying very hard to understand what she was feeling and noodling how he could help her.

"No one can make these tough decisions for you, Charlie. I know you know that," Sam said, his foot still twitching and tapping.

"I don't expect anyone to shoulder how to wade out of this mess but me," Charlotte said. "But, Sam, she's a little girl. She loves her daddy. Don't get me wrong, she really likes Danny, but she thinks he's our friend, nothing more. I could damage her for life, or I could raise her away from Ted's influence, just in case he eventually rolls back to the guy who did a lot of pretty unforgivable things."

"Look, the job is yours whether you get back with Ted or not. Writer for the current publications, editor of the new *Montana Arts* magazine, whenever I get it off the ground. I'll pay you ten percent more than whatever you're making at that museum." Sam grabbed both of her hands, steadily holding her gaze, his entire body sending the message that he was sincere.

Charlotte nodded, squeezing his hands. "Two to three weeks. I fly back to Pittsburgh in two days with Kelsey, and I'll have an answer for you in two to three weeks." She stood, and Sam stood with her, coming around the table to give her a hug.

"No rush getting me an answer."

"Thanks, but I don't want yet another decision hanging over my head month after month. I need to decide about everything in my life and then move forward, whatever that will mean for me and Kelsey."

"How does it feel being back here?" Sam whispered in her ear as she lay her head on his shoulder and he closed his arms around her.

"Like coming home," she said without hesitation. She meant Montana, not Ted. Ted was another thing altogether.

CHAPTER 32

The full moon sat above the mountains like a lightly shrouded beacon, its glow softened but not muted by mild cloud cover. Ted tipped the long-neck beer bottle against his lips, the fluid still cool. He'd kissed his wife slowly, steadily, until she pulled away and walked down the hall to the bedroom she was sharing with Kelsey. They would leave the ranch tomorrow, and he wondered if they'd ever return. He'd been as nervous as a shy thirteen-year-old, afraid she'd slap him or push him away. Instead, she'd responded, just for an instant, then she was gone.

Shay had told him, reluctantly, when he called after the arraignments of Ben, Bob, and Leah, and Ted's subsequent exoneration, that Charlotte was seeing another guy. The River Rescue guy. Probably the same guy who had called his wife after they fished him out of the river. Shay referred to things as "possibly getting serious" between them.

"Why didn't you tell me before?" Ted asked.

"I didn't want to mess you up again when you seemed like you were getting better."

"She hasn't said anything about divorce . . . actually, she barely talks to me."

"I'm gonna stop here, dude, and stay out of it," Shay said. "I'm your friend, but this is between you and Charlotte."

"Right. I get it," Ted said, conflicted about how much he actually wanted to know. "Thanks for everything you did to clear my name. You need to come out here and I'll take you fly fishing."

"Hey, I'd love that!" Shay said. "It might be a while before I can get some time off, though. I've got some big news! I accepted a job with the FBI, and as soon as the background check and clearances are in place, I'm selling my condo and moving to D.C. New beginnings for both of us."

"Congratulations! No more Geri."

They both laughed, then Shay stopped, his tone serious. "You know, we'll never be big fans of Geri, but she did do a lot to help us."

Ted shrugged as if acknowledging the truth in Shay's words, but was still unable to say it aloud. He felt a twinge of envy at Shay's new opportunity, the reality of his own situation weighing on him for a moment before he shook the feeling off. That was the old Ted with different priorities, not who he was now.

"Charlotte, too. She did a lot of the work to prove your innocence," Shay added.

"Yeah, but she did it for Kelsey. Geri did it for Geri. You did it for me."

Ted had read Charlotte's stories about the River Rescue team while he was still in Pittsburgh, had seen the pictures in the paper. He'd suspected as much, especially when Kelsey mentioned Danny often, bringing it up to Shay who, at that time, appeared to know very little. It was a small part of what had driven him to the bridge that night. Shay meant well, telling him the truth now before he got his hopes up or assumed something that might never happen between him and Charlotte. But Shay was right to not identify the guy and validate Ted's original suspicions. Knowing exactly who he was would have been too much information. Shay was a good friend to know how much to offer and when to draw the line. Charlotte probably kissed Ted back out of habit tonight. He didn't want to think about the person she might be kissing out of desire.

Stepping off the porch, he walked toward the barn. There was little hope he would sleep tonight, but maybe setting up breakfast for the horses or cleaning the stalls would tire him out enough that he could crash in the straw and catch some shut-eye. At times, since coming back to the ranch, he would break his insomnia by sleeping in the barn with the horses. Jesse had a "whatever works" attitude about the whole thing. He found it ironic that the very smells of horseflesh, hay, and manure that he'd tried to shake off and pretend weren't embedded in his DNA now comforted him, rocking him to sleep.

"I suppose irony would be the word, wouldn't it?" Ted said to Lady, the roan mare Charlotte had ridden that morning. Lady cast a long, brown-eyed gaze in his direction, methodically chewing hay as if to say his human musings were boring but she would accommodate him by appearing to listen.

After twenty minutes of talking to himself and the horse about the vagaries of his life, Ted threw an old blanket over the prickly pile of hay. He kicked off his boots and his shirt, then pulled off his belt, tossed everything to the side, and lay down. Sleep didn't come immediately. His body was tired, but his mind refused to shut down. He closed his eyes, willing a sense of relaxation that he hoped would end in much-needed sleep. He didn't see or hear her enter the barn until she was straddling him, naked except for an oversized T-shirt, her mouth on his mouth. His hands moved over her body once familiar and now a memory hungrily revisited. It had been a long time.

"Are you sure?" Ted asked as he felt her pulling his jeans down, her movements demanding, almost frantic.

"Quiet," Charlotte whispered.

He stripped them both of their clothes and made love to her on the old blanket with the candescent moonlight coming in through the open door, covering them, the horses snorting at being woken by two humans and their carnal needs. Ted memorized every inch of her body with his lips, with his hands, not knowing if she'd come to him in forgiveness or farewell. When he woke, both she and Kelsey were gone.

CHAPTER 33

"I don't know what to do." Charlotte rested her elbows on the high-top table and put her head in her hands, covering her eyes.

"I think you do," Grace said as she reached over to touch the top of her head. "I think you know."

They'd taken a table across from the bar at The Abbey, right under the stenciled lyrics stretching the length of the wall from bar to bistro. The irony that she'd landed right below 'Caught in a landslide, no escape from reality' was not lost on Charlotte. Kelsey was at Grace's house, the graduate student next door babysitting to allow them time to talk.

"I was sure when I returned from hiking in Bozeman that I couldn't leave my life here . . . you, Danny, my job," Charlotte said with a sigh. "Even after Sam rolled that wonderful job opportunity in front of me. Even after I started feeling at home out there, I thought it was simply nostalgia."

"You can't go back to him out of guilt about Kelsey, you know," Grace said.

Charlotte looked at Grace with surprise. A devout Catholic, Grace didn't believe in divorce. She'd stayed in a difficult marriage, her husband an alcoholic, until he passed away. Charlotte always saw her friend as a great listener, but with a solid, maybe even rigid, sense of duty.

"Don't look so startled," Grace said, letting out a light chuckle. "Maybe I've had time to think since my husband died and, well . . . maybe it would have been better not to stay."

"The pope might be listening," Charlotte admonished with a grin.

"Let him listen, then. I wasn't born yesterday. Tell me the rest, Charlotte."

Charlotte traced her finger around the rim of her favorite drink, the Old Greg's Shakeroo, a combo of coffee, Baileys, and Kahlúa with a kick of Jameson. "Something was different about Ted from the moment I saw him. He's changed. At night, I'd dream about finally giving in and being with Danny, and during the day, all I could think about was how Ted seemed changed."

"And . . ."

"And what?" Charlotte asked. If she closed her eyes, she'd probably smell the hay and feel the rough floor of the barn beneath her in an instant. "In three hours, I see Danny. I have to decide."

Grace took a sip of her white wine. "You don't have to decide anything until you're ready. Danny can wait. What happened to cause all this angst?"

"Ted kissed me, and it was as if we moved back in time to who we were before the trial, before our problems, even before Kelsey."

"So you slept with your husband, which is legal by the way, and now you're torn because you still care for Danny,"

Grace stated, lining Charlotte's internal struggle up in a neat row of facts.

"I fully trust Danny. I'm not sure I can put all this behind me and feel that way about Ted. What if we start building a life and he does something again to destroy it?"

The sun filtered in through the windows, highlighting Grace's snowy hair and the tiny lines at the corners of her eyes and around her mouth that disappeared when she smiled and crinkled when she pursed her lips, deep in thought, as she appeared to be doing now. Going back to Ted would mean losing these moments with Grace.

"Is this about honoring your commitment to Ted?" Grace asked.

"Maybe I could just live with you and date both of them to avoid this question," Charlotte said with a nervous laugh.

"No, as much as I love you and Kelsey, you need to move your life in one direction or another." Grace reached out to hold Charlotte's hand. "You can't sit in limbo."

"It's not about commitment in the traditional sense. I'm not staying in a marriage if it's loveless for Kelsey's sake," Charlotte answered. She picked up their empty glasses and walked to the rustic red bar for a refill, trying to focus on the row of beers on tap as she waited.

"You may not need another, but I do," she said to Grace when she returned, setting down the drinks.

"So, Danny is lust and safety with a sprinkling of guilt each time you think of Ted?" Grace asked.

"This all seems to sound familiar to you, Grace. Are we talking about me or you?"

Grace blushed and smiled, turning her gaze toward the lead-paned windows behind the bar, leaving Charlotte to feel as if she'd been left behind as Grace moved to another place in time. "I had a Danny once. My guilt was in staying, rather than leaving my husband to be with him. Catholic guilt, I call it."

Charlotte processed this slowly. Her kind, proper friend had had something, an affair perhaps, that she still regretted leaving behind. It seemed the secrets of youth one carries on into old age never lose their ability to spring forward on the wings of regret. She could see, for a brief moment, how those old secrets recreated the heat of that long-ago overwhelming desire. An intimate, lusty drive beckoning the start of a new existence, a turning of the page, for her friend.

"At first, I thought that even considering going back to Ted was a sacrifice for Kelsey," Charlotte said. "And, of course, my mother, in the middle of her own divorce and unable to forgive either Ted or my father, encourages me to leave him."

"What about Ted's brother?" Grace asked.

"Oh, Jesse . . . he forgives Ted everything," Charlotte said. "He doesn't push, but he wants us out there with him, and with Ted."

A quiet settled between the two women, like a worn, time-softened quilt they could both curl up under, a warm space that needed no words. All the words had been said and heard, turned and examined thoroughly. Feelings had been probed and memories shared as markers to be considered along the complicated pathway to decision-making. Now it all sat with Charlotte to turn a corner in her life that she could not only abide but also embrace.

CHAPTER 34

The headquarters for Cyber Scope sat in a small, partially renovated house slightly off Main Street in Bozeman. If the tiny start-up grew beyond its five employees, parking might become an issue, but, for now, they could all crowd into the driveway and juggle cars, or find available street parking. In the beginning, Ted drove in two days a week to collaborate with the team, working remotely from the ranch the rest of the week. He told his colleagues this arrangement allowed him to manage his job while helping Jesse keep up with all the chores a busy ranch created. But while he was grateful for the chance to work again in his chosen field, he still struggled against the pull to feel important in a bigger environment with a more powerful position. Working from the ranch kept him anchored and earthbound.

When he'd told Charlotte he was past all of that, it had been a half truth of sorts. Ted could sit at McCord Ranch running a pen test or conducting a digital forensics investigation for a client and feel fine, the past nearly behind him except for the empty space left by the separation from Charlotte and Kelsey. But in the Bozeman office, he often felt confined, small, insignificant. He didn't know what the other guys thought about him. They were on Google News off and on during the day, and he'd seen the stories following the arrests in Pittsburgh on more than a few screens. Cyber Scope was owned by his old college buddy, Russ Atkins, and he didn't care where Ted had been or what he'd done; he wanted Ted's skills to keep the start-up growing.

It was Russ who suggested quietly, privately, that Ted continue to see a counselor after discovering he'd discontinued the sessions Charlotte set up for him once the charges against him were dropped.

"I'm okay now. Not gonna jump from anywhere," Ted had said.

"Buddy, I think it goes beyond that," Russ answered. "Thinking about jumping was the result. It's like one of our investigations here . . . you gotta keep at it until you find the source of the problem."

"Well, I'm not crazy about the counselor," Ted grumbled, turning away to hunch over his laptop.

Russ gave him the name of the counselor he'd seen during his divorce, a combative and miserable affair that lodged his two young children in the middle of a marital war zone. Ted followed the advice, skeptical but knowing he might need someone for not only his past issues but perhaps to see him through a divorce from Charlotte. He'd shown up regularly now for several months, and he could feel progress. Only occasionally did he think about the impressive high-rise building in Pittsburgh where he felt important swiping his badge and giving orders to his team. When he called Shay, he didn't feel a pang of discontent anymore and was even talking with excitement about his job. Cyber Scope's little office began to feel like home away from home, Ted showing up with donuts or bagels some mornings for the guys, trying to be a part of things. Since Charlotte headed back to Pittsburgh, Ted had changed his schedule, coming into Bozeman nearly every day. He felt her missing presence most when he was at the ranch, a shadow between the empty pockets of sound and light and meaning where Kelsey had been when she sat in his lap on the porch or kissed him good night. Going to the office dulled the warm but painful memory of Charlotte, naked in his arms, that he felt every time he walked into the barn.

He was heading over to the counselor today as soon as he finished a project. He felt shaky, off his game, since Charlotte left without so much as a goodbye. They'd talked and texted since, mostly about Kelsey. Charlotte let Kelsey Face-Time with him regularly, but when he tried to open a discussion about their future, she backed off, begging for time, saying she wasn't ready. Ted didn't have the courage to ask about the other guy, but he needed to know, soon, if this was it, if this was how his life would be permanently going forward.

"Give her some time," Jesse had said after overhearing Ted make an appointment with his counselor. "I think she'll be back."

"Do you know something I don't know?" Ted asked.

"Well, you haven't been served with divorce papers. And I know she's been talking to Sam Sweeney about working for him."

Ted struggled to bottle the hope inside him into a manageable place. Jesse had run into Sam at a local music festival and picked up the news, but Charlotte had yet to tell Ted anything about what she was thinking, planning, or, even if she returned to Montana to work for Sam, whether that meant she wanted a life with Ted.

"Hey guys, I'm heading out," Ted said as he powered down his laptop and unhooked it from the docking station. "Got an appointment, then back to the ranch."

"Cool," Bryan, the young beatnik musician turned cyber geek, said, giving him a thumbs-up. "See you tomorrow?"

"Maybe . . . we'll see," Ted answered. With a smile and a wave, he headed out the door.

He'd almost reached the used, four-wheel-drive Xterra he'd purchased on a loan from Jesse when he heard the clear, bell-like sound indicating an incoming text message. Sliding behind the wheel, he dug his phone out of the front pocket of his backpack. It was from Charlotte.

> See you Saturday. We're on our way back.

What did that mean? Happiness tangled with anxiety as he wondered if it was just another visit, perhaps to discuss divorce and visitation rights. Ted sat quietly for several minutes, wondering how to respond.

> Can't wait to see you and Kelsey. Miss you.

He started the car, then hesitated before putting it into gear. Picking up his phone, he added a second text: *Love you both*. Dropping it into the backpack, he pulled away from the curb and headed toward the counselor's office, the silence from the phone escalating his deepest fears.

CHAPTER 35

The sun had begun its descent over the Crazy Mountains—pale streaks of tangerine, yellow, and orange replacing the fading blue, reflecting off scattered clouds white as a first snowfall. Charlotte lightly pulled Shadow's reins and turned the horse in the direction of the ranch. The beauty and openness of the land never ceased to take her breath away. She'd taken to riding on Saturday after a long week of writing and editing for the new magazine, letting loose to the sheer freedom of the space, the movement, the wind in her hair. It was late September, and soon the weather would be too cold to make this a habit.

As they moved through the back field, Shadow trotted more quickly, ready for home, food, and a good brush-down in his stall. A peace settled over Charlotte like a soft spring rain, relaxing her muscles, softening her eyelids, filling her with wonder that she'd finally reached this moment. It had not been an easy road. Saying goodbye to Danny with a determined mind and a confused heart still pained her, although less than it had during her first months here and more because she'd hurt him so much he couldn't bring himself yet to agree to a friendship with her. Missing Grace, who agreed to visit once or twice a year, had increased her loneliness. It was an empty space that phone calls and video chats couldn't fill. Charlotte had yet to find any women friends here that she could connect with in the same way. She'd never imagined it would be her mother who partially filled that gap, flying out several times since she'd moved to stay with her and Kelsey. They went to Pittsburgh a couple times in return. Rosalyn had begun to love Montana, wanting to explore and meet people, even softening toward Ted during her most recent visits. Charlotte hoped that one day, as her mother grew older, she would be able to convince her to relocate permanently.

And then there was, still, the fear and anxiety as she and Ted slowly worked on their marriage. She had no idea how that journey would end, whether it would work out or not between them. She could feel the old love, and she wanted him physically, but it seemed at times that it would be impossible to fully forgive him, to find a way to heal completely. That love now was a patchwork of scars—cauterized, semi-healed, amid a flat rolling plain of uncharted land. A horizon to move forward to, together, sat within her view, but there were minefields inside herself and between them to be navigated carefully. She was no longer young and naive, seeking purpose in life. She was a woman within her own right, battle-scarred and triumphant, filled with infinitely complex depths and the owner of her life and soul.

Jesse had been more than willing to make room for them in the ranch house, but Charlotte declined.

"One step at a time, Jesse," she'd said. "We're back in Montana, but I'm not ready to live with him yet."

She was renting a cozy, partially furnished house in Livingston, her office in walking distance. Kelsey stayed with her during the week for school and with Ted on the weekends, although sometimes they both stayed at the ranch or Ted would spend a few nights in her house. So far, she'd drawn the line each time after two nights, willing to go on dates, to get closer to him, but not yet willing to make it official. Jesse and Suzanne would be moving in with Trevor Connelly, who was aging and alone. Trevor and Jesse had been working to connect the two ranches. Jesse was even considering changing his last name, a fact that Ted supported and Charlotte didn't understand the need for but, as long as they remained a close family, she could accept. Jesse was planning to propose to Suzanne soon, and Charlotte was happy for them. It would take time, but Suzanne might become a friend as well as a sister-in-law one day. Ted would be alone in the ranch house, and he'd made it clear he wanted her and Kelsey to move in with him.

The house appeared before her. She could see Ted on the porch swing, Kelsey in his lap, their heads bent over a book. Shadow whinnied, tossing his head happily, and they looked up and waved. Charlotte inhaled the moment, her family before her, the pain of her difficult decisions sliding into the past, filling herself with the gentle newness of inner strength and resolve. Ted appeared to want only this, their life together; his old lust to climb a corporate power ladder no more than a miserable memory. She placed her hand on her abdomen. Sometime next spring, there would be another McCord born into this world, to this beautiful Montana life, solidifying the new beginning that was rising out of the ashes. Peace came not from whether they lived together under one roof, but from the freedom, her freedom, to choose to be complete apart from Ted, apart from

her child. As the sun set behind her, Charlotte rode toward
this life of her choosing, knowing she, alone, held the power
to create good for herself.

ACKNOWLEDGMENTS

As a child growing up in Erie, Pennsylvania, my prize possession was my Erie County Public Library card. The library was a huge, historic building with all the lovely smells of wood polish, dust, and floor wax, mixed with the crinkle of paper and books with plastic protective jackets. I loved opening the big doors with my father and brother on a Saturday morning, hearing our footsteps echo as we walked up marble steps below the highest ceilings I'd ever seen and entering a world of books. My card had tiny metal teeth on it, came tucked in a little paper jacket, and allowed a maximum of six books. I always came determined to get books big enough to last me all week. I firmly believed that to be a real writer meant your book must be on a library shelf.

With characters and ideas constantly swimming around in my head, at eight years old I tried poetry and small stories. I've been challenging myself to improve ever since. What I've learned along the way is that although the task of writing is a solitary and at times lonely endeavor, like many things in life it's impossible to accomplish successfully without the generous people along the way who willingly and graciously offer their time, expertise, feedback, and human kindness. Those amazing people ensure that the writer's fledgling creation crosses the finish line and into the hands of readers.

I'm grateful for the chance to thank all of those amazing

people who answered my questions, pointed out a better developmental path for the book, corrected my grammar, taught me the ins and outs of book publishing, and handed me empathy, friendship, and encouragement during the five years it took me to complete this book while managing a demanding full-time job.

Thank you Ashton Smith for the great cover design, and Lauren Blue for a superb copy edit.

Completing this book would not have been possible without tips and corrections from the best cybersecurity team in the business. They shared both their expertise and friendship, answering my sometimes crazy technical questions over lunch, happy hours, and, yes, as I interrupted their workday now and then. Thank you to Austin Rappeport, Matilda McVann, Justin Wright, Greg Hetrick, Aaron Gross, and Brian Gehrke. And yes, Austin, if there are ever action figures, I'll stand by our agreement!

Special thanks to my friend of many years, Angela Smith, who told me to stop complaining about people obsessed with having an important title and write about it. This book evolved into something very different from that little nudge, but I owe her for the first push. Thank you to my friend and talented writer Remo Hammid, who read my first draft when it was worse than a huge mess and gave me great insight and guidance, and to my friends Maureen Atkinson and Meagan Tudge, who were my earliest beta readers. Thank you to the second wave of beta readers—Michelle Anderson, Lisa DeGross, Sonee Singh, and Laura Dupier—for providing invaluable input. Special thanks to Ben Mackall, talented photographer, Montana resident, and all around good human being, who took me hiking in Bozeman, Montana. I know I was out of shape and didn't make it too far, but the beauty and peace of that hike resulted in a nice scene for Charlotte's character.

Ted's fly fishing scene would never have been possible if Wes Roberts, one of my two wonderful nephews, hadn't taken me for my first fly fishing lesson in Jackson Hole. It was magical. I loved it despite the borrowed, oversized clothing, and I've kept my one-day fishing license as a memento! Wes taught me the beauty of the sport, the magic of Wyoming, and, in doing so, made my favorite scene in this book possible.

I'm forever grateful to the Women's Fiction Writers Association (WFWA) for opening doors to a community of supportive writers. Special shout-out of deep gratitude to Orly Koenig for the invaluable developmental edit and the ongoing advice and support without which I might never have finished the book. I'm grateful each month to my WFWA critique group of excellent writers—Deb Atwood, Pamela Stockwell, and Ann Menke. You came along after this book was completed, but not before I needed help with the finishing touches. Your support and input are forever valuable!

Last but never least, my family. My mother, Shirley Roberts, and Jim, Kathy, Doug, Wes, Tessa, Dave, and Dao Roberts for ongoing support and thumbs-up emojis. Thank you for always being there for me!

Photo courtesy of Mariah Treiber Photography

Janet Roberts is a former global leader in cybersecurity education. A member of Women's Fiction Writers Association, Pennwriters, and Sisters in Crime, she lives in Pittsburgh and loves spending time on her porch swing. Learn more at www.booksbyjanetroberts.com